REDEMPTION

OF THE

Heart

MONI BOYCE

LOVE
SNACKS
PUBLISHING

REDEMPTION

OF THE

Heart

For all those looking for a little redemption.

1

Gemma knew there had to be the terrible noise of screeching tires and squealing brakes as she desperately attempted to avoid the inevitable collision. She knew she was screaming, but somehow sound no longer penetrated her brain. Bracing for the impact, her hands went up protectively in front of her face, hoping to block the glass that was seconds away from breaking into shards. The cars slammed into each other, and she felt her body tossed like there was no gravity while the car flipped end over end before her head struck the steering wheel and she was knocked unconscious.

Rapidly, she blinked her eyes. Police sirens sounded in the distance. She was dazed and disoriented. Something sticky trickled down her forehead. In the air, the smell of the dampness from the rain mingled with the scent of leaking brake fluid, gas and oil, filling her nostrils, along with the metallic scent of blood.

Why does my body feel so heavy? She tried to move. Suddenly the memories rushed back to her; the lingering alcohol in her system had caused her to fall asleep at the wheel. She'd hurt someone. Sharp pain knifed through her side, and she realized something wasn't right. Tears welled up in her eyes.

Is the other person okay? Oh God! Did I kill someone? She attempted to yell, to speak, but nothing. The sirens were getting closer, and then finally she heard car doors being thrown open and shoes pounding the asphalt as they ran to her car. Another set of footfalls could be heard running to the other vehicle. A bright light shone on her face, and she tried to blink, but the tears and the blood obstructed her sight. The cop's voice was barely audible, yet she heard him reassuring her that she would be okay. Her eyes fluttered once more before she succumbed to the pain pulling her under.

Alex ran his hand through his brown hair as he checked his watch for the fifth time in the last half an hour. It was unlike Sam to be tardy. His wife was never anything but punctual—always adopting the phrase that if you were on time, you were late. While he knew things had been strained between them lately, he was hoping to make things right tonight. She was upset at all the late nights he put in at the restaurant, but she would see, things would slow down once they'd been up and running a year. Pregnancy had been on her mind, but he kept insisting to her that he wasn't ready yet to be a father.

He toyed with his wedding band as he grew restless. His blue eyes glanced at the clock on the mantel and back down to his watch. Maybe he could appease her by setting a timeline on when they could begin trying for a baby. That would make her happy. He smiled to himself as he nervously checked the clock on the mantel once more.

The doorbell rang before he could look at his watch a seventh time. *Why is she ringing the bell? Doesn't she have her key?* He walked toward the door, expecting to find her rifling through her purse. He opened the door, ready to tease her, but came face-to-face with a cop instead. For a minute, there was only puzzlement as he eyed the face of the young cop who stood on his doorstep. When the realization of why the cop was at his door finally hit him, he got a sinking feeling in his stomach. The officer refused to meet his eyes as he began to speak. Alex held onto the door for support while the cop delivered the news that his wife was dead, killed in a car accident. He shook his head from side to side, willing it not to be so.

"No … no …" His lips moved with the words, but he almost wasn't aware of his voice. They were going to have a baby. They were going to be happy. They were going to be a family. The wetness rolled down his cheeks before it registered in his brain that he was crying.

The cop reached out to him trying to console him as he crumpled to the ground.

Three days later

Flashbacks of swimming in and out of consciousness during her rescue from the mangled vehicle, riding in the back of an ambulance to the hospital, and surgeons operating on her surfaced as she felt herself coming up through the layers of sleep and pain meds. Everything felt numb except the thoughts and memories swirling around in her head. All she had wanted to do was get away from the beatings and his verbal abuse. She figured now she'd get it sitting in a jail cell rotting away. How ironic that after years of hoping she'd see him behind bars, she would be the one doing time. She'd only been drinking that night because he kept forcing it on her. Usually, she never touched the stuff. Hot tears stung her eyes before spilling down her cheeks, and she realized she was crying.

Her senses were finally starting to adjust as her brain shook off the effects of the meds. The disinfectant smell of the hospital made her head hurt. Unfortunately for her someone had opened the blinds in her room, letting in the sunlight. Despite the number of hospital visits she had since being married to Jason, she never warmed to the atmosphere or felt safe. The sickening smell of the cleaning products, which tried to mask the stench of illness and death, always unsettled her stomach. The small beeping noises of the monitors and machines only intensified her headache.

Why does the room have to be so bright? Even though the medicine was keeping her brain from registering the acute pain, she still felt the heaviness in her limbs.

Someone entered the room, disrupting her thoughts. She lifted her head and saw an older woman dressed in nurse's scrubs approaching her bed. The woman gave her a warm smile.

"Honey, we are so glad to see you're awake. We had to sedate you for a while to allow you to heal without having to experience the pain while you're awake."

Staring at the woman, she licked her lips.

"Oh, sweetie, let me get you some water. Your throat must be parched." Reaching over to the side table, the nurse retrieved a cup that sat next to a pitcher of water. After she poured water and stuck a straw into the cup, she raised it to Gemma's lips and held it as she drank. Once she moved the cup, Gemma finally attempted to speak.

"The other person … the car … are they dead?"

A sad expression flitted across her face, and the nurse patted her shoulder. "Why don't I get the doctor?"

Swallowing, Gemma nodded her head. As the nurse exited the room, Gemma went to move her arm, and that's when she saw her wrist handcuffed to the bed. At that moment, the doctor entered the room with a cop on his heels.

Silent tears streamed down her face as the cop began to read Gemma her rights, and then told her she was being charged with involuntary vehicular manslaughter because she had a blood alcohol level over the legal limit. She nodded her head in acknowledgement when the cop asked if she understood.

Finally, the doctor got the officer to leave the room so he could tend to his patient. He gave her a sympathetic look. She averted her gaze as he began to explain all the damage her body endured from the accident, and then he cleared his throat to get her attention again. Gemma looked at the doctor.

"We noticed as we worked on you that you had older bruises and bones which had previously been reset and healed …" He seemed a little uncomfortable.

"Usually, that kind of thing is indicative of abuse. A man who claimed to be your husband–" He saw Gemma's eyes grow wide with fear, and she attempted to try and lift herself from the bed.

Materializing from nowhere, the nurse from earlier helped the doctor restrain her.

"Miss, please lay back down, you'll tear stitches and re-injure yourself. You don't need to be frightened. We didn't let him in to see you. He got too aggressive with some of our staff after we refused him entrance to your room. However, considering the old scars and evidence of what I suspected I figured it was for the best."

Once she settled down again, the doctor continued speaking. "Umm, we also found fresh vaginal tears, which would suggest that you were … raped."

Gemma refused to look at him. Now she knew why the nurse had been so sympathetic to … a murderer. They both felt sorry for her.

The doctor realized that she was not going to speak. "We're going to leave you to get some rest."

Before they could leave the room, Gemma requested, "Wait. Please shut the blinds." She swallowed when the doctor nodded his head at the nurse, giving permission for the blinds to be shut. The nurse crossed the room, blocking out the light. Breathing a sigh of relief at finally being in the darkened room, Gemma gave herself over to grief, self-pity, and despair as her mind drifted back to the night of the accident:

Jason came home all puffed up over something that happened on the job. She feigned happiness at his news as she continued with her housework. Gemma tuned him out, giving him the obligatory exclamations of surprise and congratulations. Then, before she knew it, he was taking the vacuum out of her hands and shutting it off, shoving her upstairs to change so they could go out and celebrate. After changing her outfit four times, and finally finding one that met Jason's approval, they left the house. Never-ending cocktails were shoved into her hands all night. He said she was more fun when she had a few in her. Luckily, she'd managed to spill some of the drinks to avoid drinking everything he forced on her. They went from bar to bar partying all night.

Her head was pounding, and her body ached by the time they arrived home. He wanted to "fuck" and all she wanted to do was sleep. When she resisted, he'd knocked her around and took what he wanted regardless. Now she lay there underneath him. His snores sounded in her ear. She tasted blood on her lip from where he'd struck her earlier. He was still inside of her, having fallen asleep immediately after he came. Once she pushed him out of her and off her body, she was able to get up and clean herself up despite the aches and pains her body suffered. She knew from experience that Jason would be asleep until the morning from all the alcohol he'd imbibed. Well, she wasn't going to be here. This time, Gemma didn't care what it took she was finally going to get free of him.

Ransacking her panty drawer, she located the scuffed pocket watch—her one meaningful possession—and stuffed it down her bra. Then she grabbed the car keys and left. Having been a ward of the state for as long as she could remember, Gemma had no family. She planned to drive until the gas ran out; stay in whatever town she stopped in and start fresh. Yes, she was a little drunk, but she didn't think she was that impaired ... until the headlights from the other car alerted her that she'd driven into oncoming traffic too late.

Fresh tears started as she thought about her decision to finally escape from him. Well, she was getting what she wanted. She was getting away to an eight by ten cell for who knew how long.

The light drizzle, which started twenty minutes ago, had begun to pick up. Soon it would turn into a downpour, but he didn't care. People had surrounded him all day long and he was glad to finally be left alone. He grew tired of being polite and showing his thanks for all the so-called, heartfelt condolences. By anyone's standards, it had been a nice ceremony. *Funerals could be considered nice, right?* A low, grim chuckle rumbled within his chest. *Nice funeral? Who cared if the fucking funeral was nice? I want my wife back.* His laughter tapered off.

Having no umbrella, Alex pulled his collar up on his coat. He stood by his wife's fresh grave alone. His family left long ago. They tried to coax him to come back to the house where everyone was waiting, but he didn't want to hear everyone tell him how sorry they were for his loss and have strangers tell him what a wonderful person his wife was. He didn't need to hear any of that. He just wanted her here in his arms, in his bed, saying his name, laughing up at him for doing something funny. Hell, he'd even be satisfied to hear her berating him right now. He wanted her here, doing anything, so long as she was here, not a cold, stiff corpse in the ground.

It was chilly out, but he welcomed it. The cold and damp helped numb his body. He wanted it to numb his mind, numb his soul. He missed her terribly.

Shutting his eyes for a moment, he hoped to dispel her presence, but it only made her come full-blown in his mind. His eyes shot open. They felt dry and puffy; probably from lack of sleep and weeping. He stared hard at the fresh mound, which now served as her final resting place. It didn't seem real that he would go to bed tonight alone … and wake up alone for the rest of his life. Clenching his fists, he dug his fingernails into his flesh, and welcomed the pain. It began to rain in earnest. He stood soaked to the skin as the raindrops mixed with the tears streaming down his face.

Hours had passed since they lowered her into the ground and the light began to fade from the sky. He finally walked to his car and sat for a while in the driver's seat. The rain beat the roof of his car with a ferocity that made it seem as if it mourned his wife's passing as well. His body vibrated with the pent-up emotion that was coursing through him.

Why did Sam have to die? Why couldn't it have been the other careless driver? He knew his family didn't understand why he chose not to attend the sentencing hearing for his wife's murderer. The woman pled guilty. What else would his presence do other than fuel the hate already growing in his heart?

Right now the only emotion he had time for was his grief. Nothing would supersede his mourning for his wife, not even the anger and hatred, which lay festering in his heart, lying in wait like a thief in the night, for the person who ripped her away from him. Finally, he let the dam loose. He allowed the rage, pain, and loss he felt to come pouring out as he howled and beat the steering wheel.

Why is life so fucking unfair?

Three years later

She had given a blind plea to the charges against her. Knowing she killed someone nearly made her hollow inside and she was determined to accept the punishment and her fate despite the public defender trying to talk her out of it. The judge sentenced her the same day. None of the family members attended the hearing.

Abigail Samantha Woodson. That was her name. The victim, her victim; the woman she killed inadvertently in her escape. She would never draw another breath, never kiss and hold her loved ones, whoever they were. Abigail Samantha Woodson would never do anything again. She, Gemma, was responsible for that.

Despite her heinous and negligent crime, the kind doctor who put her back together after the accident had sympathy for her. The doctor fit the pieces together after dealing with her husband when he showed up at the hospital. He told the authorities about her abuse after pulling her records, and despite Gemma's unwillingness to talk at that time; he figured she had been running away when the accident occurred. Thanks to the doctor for speaking to the court on her behalf, the judge had given her leniency.

Her time in prison started off rough. Many of the other women who viewed her as fresh meat and an easy target were soon disabused of that notion. Growing up in foster care, she learned to defend herself against not only unwanted advances from foster brothers and overly friendly foster fathers, but the other girls who often found her abundance of black curls and "pretty face" a threat. To what she never understood. She'd been thrown out like they had. Couldn't they see she was just like them? Unfortunately, what she knew in terms of defending herself, had been no match for Jason.

Eventually, the other prisoners left her alone when they saw she wasn't a pushover and wouldn't be made anyone's bitch or coerced into joining up with any gang. She was able to remain one of the few loners. One of the good things that came from this was Jason divorced her, not wanting the connection to her to taint his name since she was a murderer. She bitterly laughed when she heard that. The attorney that brought the divorce papers for her to sign must have thought she was crazy. Happiness filled her at the thought of being free of him. She wanted nothing from him; all she wanted to do was go back to her birth name—Gemma Peyton. No longer Gemma Johnson, she was finally, completely, a hundred percent rid of him.

The day of her release arrived; she served her time as a model prisoner. Twenty-six years old, with no college education and now a convicted felon, what was she going to do? She rode the bus that would carry her to the halfway house. Her meager belongings sat on the seat next to her; the pocket watch she'd saved that night in her pocket. It was the only thing she cared to get back. She was headed for Hartford, Connecticut, a place she had never been. Albany, New York was where she spent her youth being passed from foster home to foster home and where she survived a hellish existence with her ex-husband. The York Correctional Institution had been her home for the last three years because the night of the accident she had already crossed state lines, which resulted in her receiving her sentence in Connecticut. She could have fought to be tried in her home state, but what was there for her to go back to? No one wanted her. Plus, she hadn't cared where she served her time.

As she got off the bus at the home, she saw a blonde woman standing out front with an older Hispanic woman. Immediately, the blonde woman called her name, "Gemma Peyton?"

She nodded her head.

"I'm Shelby Mitchell, your parole officer, and this amazing woman is Ms. Ramirez. She runs the house here where you'll be staying for now." Ms. Ramirez walked over and gave her a hug, which Gemma was unprepared to receive. The woman then took her by the hand and smiled at her. "Let's get you inside."

As they walked up the steps into the house, Shelby continued to explain to her how things would work. "Once you get settled in, I will take you over to the restaurant where I've secured a job for you. You have to have a job to stay here …"

Shelby noticed Gemma's lack of conversation, or even some semblance of emotion.

"I try to make sure all the women don't have a hard time transitioning back into society. Despite how the media wants to paint us, we're not all crooked and corrupt. Some of us do care about the people we're tasked to look after. You made a mistake. It doesn't make you a bad person."

Shelby stared pointedly at Gemma's face and then smiled warmly.

"That's okay, Gemma. I know trust isn't given; it's earned. Hopefully, I'll earn yours … I'll let you settle in, and we'll head over in thirty, okay?"

Once Shelby left, Gemma sat on the bed, running her hand across the comforter while inspecting the room. In the past, people had let her down and disappointed her so much she wasn't sure how to feel about Ms. Ramirez or Shelby.

Are they really what they seem, or will they eventually morph into some nightmare? All she knew was this was her fresh start; she was finally getting it. She knew that her prison stay could have been much longer. Despite her crime, she had been given a gift. Tears welled up in her eyes. She stashed the few things she had in a drawer, along with the pocket watch.

After she came downstairs, she and Shelby got into her car. Shelby chattered on and on, but Gemma didn't mind. *It's nice to just listen.*

When they arrived at the restaurant Gemma gazed up at the building. The sign read 'Umbria Ristorante'.

"I hope you like Italian," Shelby remarked as they walked to the door and she knocked.

Gemma stared at the ground, nervous about what to expect. *How will they treat me?*

Suddenly, she heard a deep baritone voice yell that he was coming, followed by a crash and curses. Seconds later, the door opened swiftly, and she was staring into mesmerizing blue eyes. She felt like her breath stopped. He was very attractive; his brown hair was matted to his forehead, and the scruff, which graced his cheeks made him even more rugged and handsome. And his mischievous smile made her heart melt. His T-shirt clung to his sweaty body, showing his defined abs. She could see that he was no stranger to manual labor.

Instantly she became conscious of what she must look like, and mentally chastised herself for even thinking this man would be interested in her. Was it being in prison for so long without the physical contact of a man that was making her all googly-eyed?

When he reached his hand out to her she blinked herself out of her stupor and hesitantly shook his hand.

"Hi, I'm Alex Chambers. And your name?"

2

Her hand was soft in his, as he gazed down into the doe eyes of an attractive, black woman. Since she found a sudden interest in the ground when he attempted to make eye contact with her, he assumed she was shy. Taking in her ponytail, Alex found himself wondering what her hair looked like falling loosely around her shoulders. To many she would have seemed nondescript after just one glance, but he immediately saw the natural beauty she possessed. When she did turn her gaze on him, she stared at him for what seemed like forever without speaking. It had been a while since a woman had any effect on him.

Finally, she answered, "My name is Gemma, Gemma Peyton."

He noticed her lick her lips, and couldn't help but follow the trail her tongue made. Something stirred deep within that had been dormant for a long time. He chalked it up to lust. After all, she was a beautiful woman.

Letting go of her hand, he opened the door wider to permit them access. Shelby and Gemma walked past him into the restaurant. He ushered them to a table. Gemma didn't look like a hardened criminal. As they sat, he couldn't help but wonder what this woman had done to land in jail. She wasn't the first ex-convict the restaurant employed. He believed in rehabilitation, and that everyone deserved a second chance. Although he hadn't always held that belief, he embraced it now because he knew it's what his dead wife would have wanted.

"It's great to have you with us, Gemma. We're currently down a waitress so it will be good to take the pressure off the wait staff."

He continued going over the rules of the restaurant, letting her know the expectations of her as a waitress, but his head was a jumbled mess. There was something about her that had him enthralled. He wasn't sure what he expected from someone who'd just gotten out of prison, but it wasn't this meek woman that sat across from him. The sadness he read in her eyes seemed deeper than expected—like they always carried around pain. Not that Gemma would hold his gaze that long. She never seemed to look him directly in the eyes.

He finished up his spiel and went to get her an apron and a shirt since she would start by working tonight's dinner service. As he handed her the garments, it didn't go unnoticed that she glanced at his wedding band. He still wore it, but it was the first time he ever wished he'd removed it. He barely knew this woman. Why did he care if she believed he was married or not?

Watching her drive away with Shelby, he shook his head, thinking somehow he would be able to dislodge her from his thoughts. He needed to shower before the staff arrived. Thankfully, when he was building the restaurant he'd had the forethought to have a full bathroom with a shower installed in his office.

After his shower, he resumed getting the restaurant ready to open by taking the chairs off the tables. These moments alone were what he enjoyed. Alex's life was the restaurant. He practically lived here: always the first one in the door every morning, and usually the last to leave at night. Ever since his wife died, he had thrown himself into making the restaurant amazing. He loved his staff, but it had almost been too much the way they had rallied around him after Sam's death. It felt like he was suffocating the way the staff and his family smothered him every waking minute, checking on him, always making sure he was okay. Eventually, he had stern words with the lot of them.

As time passed, they all came to see him as some asexual being since he still hadn't seriously dated these past few years and never really seemed to notice the opposite sex. He wasn't dead. He was a man. It's just no one piqued his interest enough to warrant more than a quick glance.

Alex became accustomed to solitude, which he knew would be interrupted at any minute as everyone arrived to get ready for tonight. As if on cue, he heard knocking on the window. Instead of his staff, he turned to find his older sister and twelve-year-old niece at the entry door. A grin broke out across his face at the welcomed intrusion.

His niece, Chloe jumped into his arms. After he sat her feet back on the ground, he kissed and hugged his sister. If there was anyone that understood him completely, it was her.

"What are two of the most beautiful women I know doing here this afternoon?"

"Mom was hoping to get you to make us some lunch since we'd been out shopping," Chloe giggled.

Her mother playfully punched her in the arm. "Thanks for throwing me under the bus. I thought we were going to ease him into it, make him believe that it was his idea." His sister, Rachel, laughed and turned pleading puppy dog eyes on him. "Please, Alex? We're starving after roaming from shop to shop. Will you feed us?"

Chloe joined in with giving him puppy dog eyes and he laughed at their antics.

"Okay, okay … let's see what we have." They both jumped on him, giving him kisses as they all headed to the kitchen.

After they finished their meal, some of the staff started arriving. They greeted him, Rachel, and Chloe. His sous chef,

Brandon—who had been with him since the launch of the restaurant—was the first to bring up the new hire.

"So a little birdie told me we have a new waitress starting. Is she hot?"

Rachel laughed, dropping her fork onto her plate.

"And you think that Alex would have noticed?" Her comment got a laugh out of everyone. Alex looked at Rachel with an amused expression on his face as he playfully smacked her with a towel.

"I notice women ..." Alex seemed a bit sheepish.

"Gemma is attractive." Alex tried to appear casual when he said it. Unfortunately, he didn't do a good enough job of keeping a neutral expression, because he caught Rachel giving him a look. *Whatever she was starting to cook up, she better forget about it.*

His sister had been the one to start the joke about his asexual status as a way to get everyone to stop feeling sorry for him. He hated their constant pity. He knew his sister missed his sense of humor and did her best to try and help it return. Rachel watched him mourn the loss of his wife, but as time marched on she would remind him that life was for the living. The look he'd just seen on her face told him that she wasn't going to let his comment about Gemma go.

After leaving the restaurant, Shelby took Gemma to pick up a few items from Target. Shelby insisted on paying for her purchases, despite the fact she had some money from her work while incarcerated. Gemma knew that wasn't the norm, but she thanked Shelby and didn't protest—more money to put toward saving for a place of her own.

Time passed quickly, and before she knew it, it was time for her to head over to the restaurant. *Why do I feel anxious?* She wasn't going to lie to herself. It had a lot to do with Alex Chambers. *Why am I thinking about him?* He was a married man. She happened to notice the wedding band when he passed her the uniform. It was fine, her focus needed to be on more important things. She needed to do well on this job so she could get her life together and eventually move on to something better. She wanted more out of her life than to just be what people expected from an uneducated, jailbird orphan. It was important she make something of herself.

Yes, she let herself get sidetracked by the illusion of Jason making her feel special and loved. At the age of eighteen, her head was easily turned by his declarations of love, especially because no one had ever shown her that kind of attention before. Then it got bad, with the beatings and the abuse both physical and verbal. She was in so deep with Jason, it got harder to leave until he wouldn't let her go. Well that was then, and this was now. She was free, and she made a promise to herself she would not be easily duped again by a handsome smile.

When Gemma arrived at the restaurant people were already bustling about carrying plates to tables, taking orders, and refilling glasses. The cacophony of noise from the kitchen invaded the dining area of the restaurant because of the open floor plan. The guests could see the chaotic activity of dinners being prepared. It smelled heavenly. Glancing over into the kitchen, she saw Alex wiping sweat from his brow, and issuing orders to the other cooks. He looked up, and their eyes met. She couldn't look away, and neither did he. Someone stepped in her line of sight and broke the spell.

She looked up and saw the hostess trying to get her attention. The girl was a tall brunette with a perky manner.

"You must be Gemma; Alex said you were starting today. I'm Amanda."

At first, Gemma appeared confused. *How does this girl know who I am?*

Seeming to catch on to Gemma's puzzled expression, Amanda said with a chuckle, "You're wearing the Umbria shirt; it's how I knew who you were."

Gemma looked embarrassed and gave Amanda a shy smile. "Of course." She shook her hand and allowed Amanda to lead her around the restaurant.

It took Alex a moment to get back to barking orders at the line cooks. Brandon appeared at his side.

"Is that the new waitress? Jessica? Dude, she's smokin' hot."

Alex tried not to appear agitated.

"Gemma."

"What?"

"Her name is Gemma, not Jessica."

"It's cool, dude. I won't need to know her name 'cause she's gonna be too busy calling mine … if you know what I mean." Brandon nudged him in the side before he walked away, laughing at his own joke.

Alex liked Brandon, and usually, couldn't care less about hearing his crass, raunchy jokes about the opposite sex, but he didn't want him getting his hands on Gemma.

Why do I feel so protective of her? He glanced up and watched her for a second as Amanda showed her the ropes.

He made it a point not to tell the other staff when one of them was an ex-con. It wasn't everyone's business, and he didn't like to have someone start off on the wrong foot. Let everyone form their own opinions. As protective as he felt of her, somehow he knew Gemma could hold her own, especially with the likes of Brandon's pompous ass, who thought he was God's gift to women.

He went back to preparing meals, and before he knew it, the last customer was walking out the door. Saturday nights were always the busiest. As he began to clean up, he noticed Brandon already chatting up Gemma. The guy moved quickly. He shook his head. He knew what he was about to do many would view as cockblocking, but he didn't care.

"Brandon, this kitchen isn't going to clean itself."

The look Gemma sent him seemed to be one of gratefulness. He silently nodded his head at her in acknowledgement when he turned away. As he did so he couldn't help but let the smallest hint of a smile show. A knock sounded at the front door, and he looked up and saw Rachel. He looked perplexed for a moment while Amanda opened the door.

He called out to her, "What are you doing here?"

She held up pizzas. "I thought you guys might be hungry after a long shift."

Everyone cheered and forgot about their cleaning as they left the kitchen to go enjoy the pizza. Alex knew she was up to something. Rachel rarely came by at the end of the night. Alex was the last person to leave the kitchen. Everyone was diving into the pizzas and animatedly talking as Alex grabbed a slice and kissed his sister on the cheek.

"So where's the new girl?"

Alex looked around and saw Gemma trying to eat as Brandon regaled her with some story.

"Over there," he said around a mouthful of pepperoni. "Let's rescue her before Brandon does something stupid." He took another bite. Rachel laughed and followed him to the table. Before they could get over there, Gemma looked up at their arrival.

"Don't you have some other waitress you can use your lame pickup lines on, Brandon?" Rachel asked, embarrassing Brandon to get him to leave.

Smirking, he flipped Rachel the middle finger as he left his seat and headed to another table. Rachel sat in the vacated chair, as Alex remained standing.

"Gemma, this is my crazy sister, Rachel."

Rachel put her hand out and smiled warmly at her. "How do you like working in the nut house?"

Gemma laughed softly and looked down at the table, smoothing a loose strand of hair from her ponytail behind her ear.

Rachel grinned. "It's okay; you can speak your mind. Just because your boss is here you don't have to be afraid of retribution. I have influence."

Alex threw his head back and laughed.

Gemma was unaware that Rachel's eyes never left her face, as she stared at the corded muscles on Alex's throat while he laughed.

Gemma caught her gaze and quickly lowered her eyes to the tabletop again, ashamed that Rachel found her openly admiring her married brother's good looks.

As she stared at the table, too embarrassed to make eye contact, she heard Rachel send him away. She took a bite of her pizza, needing something to do to quell her nervousness.

"Go away, Alex. We want to have some girl talk."

Alex reluctantly walked away, but not before reaching down and tickling his sister. She giggled and pushed him away. Once Alex was out of earshot, Rachel looked at Gemma. "I think you have the hots for my brother."

Gemma choked on her pizza. *Is this chick going to be a problem? Am I already in trouble?* She knew she should have kept her head down. *What was I thinking?*

"I … umm, he-he's married. I would never …"

Rachel saw Gemma's flustered state and rushed to calm her down.

"Whoa! Sorry, I was just saying it to tease you." She loudly laughed as Alex had just done and Gemma could see the similarities between brother and sister. They obviously came from good genes, because Alex was attractive and Rachel was beautiful. Her dark brown hair fell in waves around her shoulders and she had a healthy glow to her skin. It made her wonder what she must look like to his sister. She touched her hair self-consciously.

"Feel free to ogle the goodies, girlfriend." Rachel's laughter subsided. "By the way, he's not married, just so—"

Gemma interjected, looking confused, "But he's wearing a wedding ring."

"I know, but he's not." Rachel glanced down at the table, wiping at something invisible, and her demeanor changed. "He's not, and the rest is his story to tell … I just wanted to make sure you know he is available."

His sister smirked at her, returning to her carefree manner. Gemma looked a little caught off guard.

"Okay."

"What are you up to tomorrow? The restaurant isn't open on Sundays. You should hang out with me."

"Why?" Gemma became apologetic at her rudeness. "I meant why do you want to hang out with me?"

Rachel didn't seem fazed. "You're the new girl, what other reason do I need? Plus, you're new to town, right? I can show you around."

Gemma didn't understand why Rachel was being so nice to her. First Shelby and now Rachel.

"Write your address down." Rachel commanded as she produced a small notepad and pen from her purse and slid it across the table to Gemma.

Gemma reluctantly wrote her address down as instructed before returning the pen and paper to Rachel.

"I'll pick you up tomorrow at noon. I have to run." Rachel said as she scooted out of the booth.

She gave Gemma a quick hug, kissed her brother good-bye, and as quickly as she had arrived, Rachel left. Gemma didn't understand why everyone was so sweet, but she liked Rachel's directness. She never really had friends before, but maybe things would be different. The thought made her smile to herself.

She looked up and saw everyone getting back to work and got up to help. As she worked, she didn't know why she felt relief as she thought back to Rachel telling her that Alex wasn't married. *Why am I happy about that?* Oh yeah, because she had been drooling over him all night and now she didn't have to feel awful about it anymore. *What am I going to do?* Nothing is going to come of this infatuation that is developing. She shook her head and continued wiping down tables.

Alex finished locking the doors. He was headed to his car when he saw a lone figure waiting at the bus stop a little farther down the street. He got in his car and drove over. Once he was closer, he realized it was Gemma sitting alone. *Did she not realize how late it was to be catching the bus?* He pulled up in front of her.

"You know it's not safe for you to be out here by yourself."

"I'll be okay … I have pepper spray." She held it up as she gave him a small smile while admiring his classic car.

"I don't mind giving you a ride home. It would help me sleep better tonight knowing you weren't mugged waiting on a park bench for a bus that may or may not show up."

He smirked at her. *Am I flirting? No, I'm just being concerned*, he told himself.

She stood up and came toward the car, leaning into the open window. "You've been my knight twice already tonight."

He stared at her, transfixed for a moment. Despite the sadness he saw there, her eyes seemed to twinkle for a moment. He didn't think she was aware of how beautiful she was. His tongue felt stuck to the roof of his mouth as he tried to respond.

"I'm not sure I know what you mean."

Smiling, she lowered her eyes. "Brandon." She looked back up at him.

"Ah yes …" He smiled back at her and laughed. "He thinks he's the Casanova of the restaurant."

They held each other's gaze for a moment, but Alex broke the silence.

"So, I won't take no for an answer," he stated, getting out of the car. Gemma backed away looking confused, as he came around to the passenger side and opened the door.

"I insist you let me get you home safely."

He could tell Gemma seemed uncertain. She bit her lip and eyed him cautiously. He stood there, willing her with his mind to say yes. For some reason, he wanted her company.

"I promise I won't bite." He smirked at her again.

She smiled at his joke.

His comment must have helped, because Gemma relented and got in the car. After shutting the door, he walked back around to the driver's side and got in the car.

The front seat was one long bench without any kind of divider. He realized for lovers it was ideal for cuddling and staying close. The thought made him swallow and he looked away from her as he pulled away from the curb.

They drove in silence for a while, and after a few minutes Gemma spoke. "I owe you another thank you as well."

Alex glanced over. Gone was the woman who had flirted with him moments before. In her place was this shy, unsure girl who sat fidgeting with her hands, not looking at him.

"We've known each other less than twenty-four hours. How much more gratitude do I possibly deserve?" he teased, trying to make things light again.

"For treating me normal."

"What? You are normal," he replied, puzzled.

"I mean for not treating me like an ex-con. Most people would have told everyone and treated me like I was going to rob the place. I appreciate you giving me a chance." Her voice was so small he practically had to lean in to her to hear what she said.

When Alex stopped at the red light, he turned toward Gemma. "Look at me."

He held so much authority in his voice when he said those words that even though Gemma hesitated she finally looked up into his eyes. He hoped he conveyed kindness. Before he could speak again, her eyes quickly returned to her lap.

"Listen to me," he said softly, "I'm not sure what cards life dealt you and what landed you in jail in the first place, but it's your past. Everyone deserves a second chance despite previous choices or mistakes. You seem like a very sweet woman, a woman who's trying to get her life back together. Who am I to judge you, Gemma?"

Whatever Gemma was thinking or feeling he wasn't sure, because she kept her eyes glued to her lap. Alex forged on.

"Don't let anyone make you feel small or like you don't matter, because you do.

" Gripping her chin, he turned her face up to him. Unshed tears glistened in her eyes.

"You're worthy of so much …" They stared at each other for a moment. He wasn't sure why he was saying all this to this woman, a woman he just met. Alex's gaze traveled to her lips before slowly making their way back up to her eyes. He leaned in like he was going to kiss her. Gemma's eyes fluttered closed. The car behind them honked before he could kiss her, bringing them out of their reverie. He let go of her face and moved back into his seat.

"I should get you home."

Gemma let out a breath and nodded her head. They drove the rest of the way in silence.

Once they pulled up in front of the house, neither said a word as she exited the car. He watched her walk to the door, and saw that she glanced back before going inside.

Alex drove home contemplating what had gotten into him tonight. They'd just met, and he'd almost kissed her. *What am I doing?* He was no better than Brandon. She was vulnerable, and he'd preyed on her. She was trying to get her life back together, and she didn't need him complicating things. The voice in the back of his head said that was a load of crap. It was he who was afraid to get close, to let her in. For the first time in a long time, he felt the weight of his wedding band. He held up his hand, looking at it. He wasn't ready. Gemma was stirring something inside of him that he wasn't sure he was ready to acknowledge. He was going to need to keep his distance.

3

Gemma lay in bed that night enjoying the silence. Even though the room was small and sparsely furnished, she didn't have to share it with anyone. There was never a time growing up in foster care, being married, or even in prison when she hadn't been engulfed by someone's presence, having to share the same space, breathe the same air. She inhaled deeply at that thought and exhaled on a sigh.

The pale yellow paint—although chipped in places—gave her a sense of peace and calm that she hadn't known in a while. Yet right now her thoughts were in turmoil.

Still stunned that Alex almost kissed her and that she would have let him, she rolled over to stare at the ceiling. She wasn't quite sure how she felt.

How could I let him be so familiar with me when I don't know him? Things started out the same way with Jason and look where that had gotten her. As much as Gemma felt drawn to Alex she wasn't sure if it was because of this need she had to be loved or if what she felt for him was more than that. She needed to pull back. Things shouldn't be progressing at this rate. She wasn't going to repeat past mistakes. It was decided, she would steer clear of Alex for the time being. After overthinking the situation a little more, she succumbed to sleep, only to have her dreams filled with Alex.

The next day, Rachel picked her up as promised, noon on the dot. Rachel's car was fascinating. Gemma eyed the car, as she drew closer, and Rachel noticed.

"You like it?" Rachel ran her hand down the side of her car. "It's a 1974, VW Type 181 Thing. I picked out the classic fire engine red color. I'm a bit of a car enthusiast."

"It's unique," Gemma said, noting the pride in Rachel's voice. Rachel held many surprises. She looked prissy upon first meeting her and come to find out the woman's a grease monkey.

They got into the car, and Rachel began talking. It seemed the topic of cars turned Rachel into a chatterbox, which was fine with Gemma. The less the conversation was focused on her, the better.

"I grew up working on cars with my father. I think he hoped when he finally had a son that he'd get to work on cars with him ..."

She chuckled at some old memory, and Gemma looked at her. She couldn't help but see Alex in his sister's mannerisms. They both seemed to have an easy way about them. She admired them for how they always seemed so relaxed.

"Much to our father's disappointment, Alex had no interest in cars. Just wasn't his thing. Oh, don't get me wrong, he could fix one if he had to, but what excited him was cooking. I can't cook to save my life."

Rachel let out a snort of laughter, which caused Gemma to giggle. Rachel turned to her. "I really can't. It's laughable how bad I am. That's why I always get Alex to feed me." She smiled at Gemma as she pulled into the parking lot of the mall. "I'm talking too much as usual. Tell me something about you."

Gemma nervously averted her gaze to her lap as she fidgeted with her hands. For some reason, she remembered Alex's words from last night and took a deep breath and lifted her head to meet Rachel's gaze.

"Not really much to tell."

Rachel seemed to accept what she said despite the questions Gemma saw in her eyes. From the little bit of time she'd spent in Rachel's presence she knew the woman wasn't easily put off. Rachel smiled at her warmly before speaking again.

"How about we go shop, then later we can grab lunch and swap funny stories over some margaritas?"

Gemma couldn't help but smile at Rachel's infectious, friendly nature. She was grateful and thankful to her for not pushing for more information.

"That sounds like fun."

They spent the rest of the afternoon trying on clothes. Rachel did most of the talking but didn't seem to mind. Despite her stint in prison where you had no privacy, Gemma was still modest, and Rachel was the exact opposite. Rachel barged into the dressing room where Gemma was trying on an outfit. She began complimenting her on her figure and saying how she should wear clothes that flattered her figure, poking and touching various parts of her body to emphasize her point. Gemma was taken aback when Rachel told her she should get a push-up bra to go with the blouse she was currently modeling so she could accentuate the "girls". Never having shopped with girlfriends before, Gemma was uncomfortable at first. She relaxed a bit more as the afternoon wore on.

Rachel continued to prattle on and even started sharing a dressing room with her as they continued shopping. She grew to like Rachel the more time she spent with her. There were no airs about her, and she didn't seem to give a damn. It was refreshing. She appreciated the compliments Rachel gave her although it made her feel a bit vain for liking it. In the past, her looks were what got her into trouble, with either sex, so she hid herself away, wore baggy clothing and made herself as plain and invisible as she possibly could. Jason only let her dress up when he wanted her on display, as a trophy on his arm to show off to other men.

When they finished trying on clothes, Gemma put all but one item back, and Rachel noticed.

"Are you crazy?" she joked, grabbing the items back off the rack. "Did you see how great you looked in these? You have to buy them. The men will be dropping at your feet." She giggled as she tried to put the clothing back in Gemma's hands.

"I can't." Gemma hung it on the rack again. While it was fun pretending and playing make-believe in the dressing room, Rachel just didn't know. Those clothes would bring attention. *Is that what I want?* Plus, she didn't have money. Gemma was at war with her emotions.

Rachel took the clothes off the rack again. "I saw the way you looked at yourself when you had them on. You liked it, and you seemed happy, Gemma."

Gemma tried to suppress the tears that were threatening to spill. "I don't have the money for all that, Rachel. I can barely afford to buy the one thing I was going to get." Gemma refused to go into all the baggage behind her dowdy appearance and allowed Rachel to believe it was purely about the money. She looked away, not wanting Rachel's pity.

Rachel rubbed her arm. "Hey, I'm sorry. I can be a bit obtuse sometimes. It's just you looked lovely in everything.

I wish I had your body …" Rachel teased, trying to make her feel better.

"Would you let me make a gift of some of the items? I just can't fathom you walking out of here without them … Consider it a welcome gift." She saw Gemma about to say no and put on her pouty face. "You'll hurt my feelings if you say no." Rachel pleaded as she gave her puppy dog eyes.

Rachel was right. When Gemma looked at herself in the mirror while trying on the clothes she felt different. Her appearance in the fashionable clothes made her smile and feel good about herself. She didn't want to keep hearing Jason's voice in her head or the voices of those girls who tried to hurt her, make her feel bad. Again, for some reason, Alex's words from the night before came back to her. It was all the past. Gemma smiled at Rachel.

"Okay … but only this one time. The puppy dog eyes won't work on me again."

Rachel grinned and grabbed the clothes. They walked toward the register.

Once they finished and were heading to the restaurant, Rachel said, "I hope you don't mind I invited Alex to join us."

Rachel cut her eyes at Gemma and saw the woman's anxious reaction to her remark.

"Why didn't you tell me that? Why do I feel like you're up to something?"

Gemma looked around frantically, wondering if Alex was already here. She was apprehensive about seeing him after last night, and she couldn't help but feel agitated with Rachel.

"I didn't think it was a big deal. It's only lunch. Why are you so spastic all of a sudden? It's only Alex." Rachel said innocently as she sported a Cheshire cat grin.

They got a table and ordered appetizers as they awaited Alex's arrival. Gemma was very nervous; her hands were restless in her lap as they waited.

Alex arrived five minutes later, very casual in jeans and a T-shirt. He was surprised to see Gemma as he slid into the booth next to Rachel.

"I didn't know you'd be here," he said, licking dry lips as he looked directly at Gemma with a tense gleam in his eyes.

"Rachel didn't tell me she'd invited you to lunch either," Gemma said, looking pointedly at Rachel.

Rachel sipped her water and read the menu, avoiding eye contact. They sat in silence for a moment before Rachel's cell phone went off. She answered it, and as the conversation from the other end progressed, she got this stricken expression on her face. Both Alex and Gemma appeared concerned. Rachel quickly hung up and started pushing Alex out of the booth so she could get up.

"What's wrong?" Alex asked. His question was laced with worry and anxiety over his niece.

"I have to go. Chloe got injured at soccer practice."

"What?" Alex jumped up from his seat.

"Is she okay? I'm coming with you."

Rachel quickly turned around and threw up her hands. "No!"

Alex stumbled back for a second.

"I mean, I'm sure it's nothing serious … just stay here and finish lunch."

Rachel quickly grabbed her purse and left the restaurant. Alex remained standing, looking after her perplexed. Eventually he turned around to Gemma and sat back in the booth.

"Chloe's your niece, right? I hope she's okay."

"Thanks," Alex said distractedly.

Gemma started to gather her purse and her shopping bag.

"I'll just catch the bus home." She went to get up from the booth, and Alex grabbed her arm to stop her. Gemma pulled back from him violently, and Alex quickly released her and held up his hands.

"Whoa!" He looked bewildered. "I'm sorry … I shouldn't have touched you like that … I just didn't want you to go." Slowly, he put his hands down.

Gemma realized she overreacted, but when he grabbed her arm memories of Jason grabbing her that way flooded her mind. She recalled the gesture usually being followed by him beating her. She exhaled a long breath. This line of thinking needed to stop. Every man wasn't Jason; every man didn't hit.

"You ... you startled me," she said in a soft voice as she looked at the table.

Alex stared at her bowed head. *What just happened? Why did she react that way? Who hurt her?*

As he took in her downcast face, for the millionth time, he thought how beautiful and unassuming she was, and she didn't even know it. Clenching his fists, he wondered who made her so guarded and afraid. He wanted to find them and break every bone in their body. He didn't want to think about what her life must have been like that resulted in her going to prison. The need arose within him to reassure her that she could trust him. At least now, he understood a little bit of the pain in her eyes.

"I'm sorry ... I should apologize for last night," Alex stated softly as he rubbed the back of his neck, feeling a bit awkward.

"You don't have to ..." Gemma faltered when she lifted her eyes.

"Yes, I do. You were vulnerable last night, and I took advantage." He dropped his gaze to the table. "I'm not that kind of guy, Gemma."

"I know you're not." She continued to gather her things, planning to make her getaway.

"Please stay. Don't go. We can still have lunch." He saw her uncertainty. "I'd like to have you as a friend, Gemma. Let's start fresh, okay? Let's forget last night."

He got up from the table and walked away, then walked back over and sat down like he was meeting Gemma for the first time.

"Hi. My name is Alex Chambers." He held out his hand with a warm smile on his face.

She looked down at his hand and back up into his eyes before giving him a small smile and placing her hand in his. "Gemma Peyton."

"Well, it's great to meet you, Gemma Peyton. I heard the food is pretty good here. Will you join me for lunch?" He wore a hopeful expression on his face.

Gemma's face broke out into a genuine smile as she responded, "I'd like that."

They ate their lunch falling in and out of conversation easily. Gemma seemed to relax a little more. She asked questions about the restaurant and his childhood. When Alex attempted to ask Gemma a question about growing up he was met with a pained expression. He was able to segue the conversation into a story about him and Rachel growing up that kept the mood from turning sour. Gemma gave him a grateful look as he launched into the story.

As they were leaving the mall, Alex felt a bit embarrassed. "I would offer to give you a ride, but I walked over from the restaurant." His sheepish grin colored his cheeks red.

"Umm, it's such a nice day … I could walk you home?" He suggested.

She gave him a small smile.

"I'd like that."

They walked for a while in silence. Even though Gemma's head was bowed as they walked he stole glances at her. He watched her chew her bottom lip pensively while her forehead crinkled, like she was mulling something over. He was about to ask if anything was wrong when she halted on the sidewalk and turned to him.

"You know … back there you asked me about my childhood." She said nervously.

Alex nodded. "Yeah. But, Gemma, if you don't want to talk about your past you don't have to."

"It's okay." She bit her lip before continuing. "I was a ward of the state much of my life. In and out of different foster homes. I didn't know my real parents. Just that mom was a junkie, and dad was in and out of jail." She shrugged. "Not exactly something that's worth sharing."

Alex jammed his hands into his pockets. Although she was looking at him, she still fidgeted with her hands.

As he watched her, he realized this was a nervous habit. He resisted the urge to take her hand. Then the wind whipped her hair across her face and again he found himself suppressing the urge to tuck it behind her ear. He was so thankful his hands were in his pockets.

Just friends. That was all he could handle right now. *Just friends*, he reminded himself.

Gemma tucked her hair behind her ear. "I mostly don't talk about it because I don't want pity. I don't want anyone thinking I'm a charity case."

"I wouldn't think that of you, Gemma."

A shiver ran through her and he wondered if she was cold. Neither said a word for a minute as they stood staring at each other. She cleared her throat and looked away first. She resumed walking, and he fell in step with her.

"I enjoyed your stories and hearing about your life; you and Rachel growing up as kids," she chuckled as she switched back to talking about him.

He felt lightness at hearing her laugh and cast her a sidelong glance, checking out her profile. It was cute how she covered her mouth with her hand when she laughed. Before she could look back up at him, he quickly averted his gaze. He wanted to avoid being caught checking her out.

"Will you tell me more?"

He nodded his head and proceeded to make her laugh with more stories about the crazy adventures Rachel used to talk him into, which usually resulted in him somehow getting punished and not her. The more she laughed, the more animated he became, gesturing wildly with his hands and making faces as he told her tales. Her laugh was like music to him. Before he knew it, they were at the halfway house. Gemma wiped a mirthful tear from her eye as they came to a stop. He enjoyed seeing her like this.

She turned to him with a beautiful smile. "Thank you for lunch and for walking me home, Alex."

"No problem. I enjoyed it."

They both stood staring and smiling like idiots. He wanted to hug her badly and inhale her scent. He didn't want the walk to end. Being in her company had been so relaxing and effortless. Being friends would be great if he didn't find himself so damn attracted to her. Alex finally thrust his hand forward, resisting the impulse to hug her. Gemma glanced down at his outstretched hand and shook it. He relished the feel of her hand in his. She pulled away first with a smile and walked into the house, leaving him on the sidewalk.

He stood staring at the house for a second before he sighed and walked away. As he walked away, he found himself glancing at his wedding ring. He'd almost forgotten. He could have smacked himself thinking about last night.

What must she think of me? She thought he was married. *Well, what did it matter now, right? We're just friends. Who am I kidding?* If he was being honest with himself, he wanted more than that with her, but knew they both had baggage. He needed to deal with his shit before trying to go down that road with Gemma. She most certainly didn't need him to complicate things for her any further.

As he walked, he absently twisted the ring on his finger. He would tell her so she wouldn't think he was some philandering bastard. He looked down at his ring again. There was still a small part of him that felt like he was cheating; although he knew Sam was dead, he still loved her. Part of him always would.

He remembered when the accident happened; everyone thought he would be out for blood. Don't get it wrong. He was mad, mad as hell that her life had been snuffed out like that, by some careless jackass too drunk to know better than to get behind the wheel of a car. At the time, he just didn't care to put that much time into hating them. His grief was already too much to handle so he chose not to know the identity of the murderer. He was afraid that once he opted to turn to his anger, he would have hunted them down and ended up sitting in a jail cell himself. Whoever they were, life would eventually deal them a bad hand. They'd get what was coming to them.

After walking aimlessly with no direction, he found himself at Rachel's. Well, at least, he could check on Chloe. Hopefully, his niece was okay. He knew how much she loved playing soccer and how disappointed she would be if she had to sit the season out.

He walked into the house without knocking and called out, "Rachel! Chloe!"

As he turned toward the living room, he saw Rachel trying to rush toward the door. That's when he saw Chloe in the living room jumping around, dancing to some video game. He turned accusing eyes on his penitent sister.

"Before you say anything …"

He looked past his sister and addressed his niece. "Chloe, how was soccer practice?"

"Hey, Uncle Alex! I didn't have practice today." Chloe waved to him and continued with the game.

"Someone has some explaining to do," Alex said as he stalked off to the kitchen with Rachel trailing him.

"I can explain." Rachel sputtered.

"Yeah? Well, I'm waiting. You went tearing out of the restaurant like Chloe had been severely hurt. I was worried. Then I come here to find her jumping around and perfectly fine …" Alex's eyes narrowed as they perused his sister's face. He knew what was going through her head. She was always getting into his business. *Damn her!* Where he and Gemma were concerned, he didn't need or want Rachel in the mix mucking things up because she thought she knew better.

"Don't meddle, Rachel! I don't need my big sister playing matchmaker for me!" He moved around to the other side of the kitchen away from his sister. She could tell he was seething with anger.

"Look, Alex, I know you like her … and I think she likes you. I was just trying to give you both a little nudge." She pleaded as she wrung her hands.

"I'm not ready, and neither is she." He said furiously.

Rachel looked at him curiously before slowly responding, "Why would you say that unless you were interested?"

"Rachel … just, please … there are things you don't know." He hesitated before saying, "She just got out of prison."

"So?"

He held up the hand that contained his wedding ring.

"A man who is still sporting a wedding band should not be trying to date someone." Alex said exasperated.

"Then take it off." Rachel exclaimed.

The glint of the burnished metal drew his eye. "I can't … it's not that easy."

"Those just sound like a bunch of excuses to me, Alex."

"I don't want to hurt her." Alex said softly as he looked at his sister.

Rachel looked at him pointedly before she quietly responded, "Are you sure it's just her you're worried will get hurt?"

Alex glared at her. Rachel glared back, her stare unwavering. He finally looked away first.

"I have to go."

Despite her protests, Alex left.

4

Two months passed, and Alex and Gemma were able to keep their distance, managing only the pleasantries that transpired between boss and employee. They were able to time their interactions to always coincide with another person being present. Alex knew Rachel was keeping company with Gemma, but he refused to ask his sister anything about her, lest Rachel tried to play matchmaker again.

Even though he chose to keep his distance, it didn't mean he wasn't completely aware of Gemma's presence. The woman would have to be on another planet for him not to be aware of her. Continually, he was drawn to her and many times watched her with hooded eyes. He liked that she wasn't showy or flashy. She seemed completely unaware of her sex appeal. Compliments made her uncomfortable and embarrassed, causing a flush to creep across her cheeks, and she would avert her gaze, avoiding the person's eyes as she bit her lip. Many times he even saw these symptoms of her shyness accompanied by the nervous fidgeting of her hands. He found it cute. The male cooks and busboys ogled her and always offered her help. Their behavior toward her bought out a jealous streak within him he wasn't aware of. Some of them even worked up the nerve to ask her out, but she always politely turned them down.

Over time, despite wearing a uniform to the restaurant, Gemma started to take more care in her appearance when getting ready for her shifts. She tried to tell herself it wasn't because of him, but deep down she knew better. She made sure her curls fell loosely, framing her face, and she'd started applying some mascara and lip-gloss. He probably never noticed. *Why would he notice me?*

He hadn't spoken to her at length for two months. She'd watched him, though, and heard little bits and pieces here and there from the other staff. Everyone liked him as a boss and as a friend. Rachel tried to ease him into conversations, but she had all the subtlety of a sledgehammer. Gemma listened to her speak of him, but never asked any questions. She didn't want to seem too eager. From what she gathered, he hadn't dated since whatever happened with his wife, which was a few years ago.

Today she ended up arriving early because of a change in the bus schedule. When she arrived, she tapped on the glass and waited, hoping against hope that Brandon or one of the other cooks would open the door for her and not Alex. A minute later, Alex appeared at the door and let her in. Upon seeing him, she knew it was just the two of them in the restaurant.

"Hi," she said with a nervous smile as she walked past him, taking off her jacket.

"Hey ... you're early."

She continued to avoid looking at him. "The bus schedule changed. I'm still getting used to the new times. I didn't want to be late."

"Uh, well since you're here, there is something I need to tell you. I meant to speak to you about it a while ago," Alex said, pulling out a chair for her to sit down.

Gemma saw the concern on his face as she turned to face him, before taking the seat he offered. They hadn't talked since lunch a couple of months ago. *What could he have to say to me?* Alex took the seat across from her, and she noticed his gaze fall to his wedding band.

"Is everything okay?"

She didn't try to hide the concern in her voice as Alex looked up at her before speaking.

"Gemma, I'm not married. I mean ... I was, but I'm not anymore." She saw the pain flash across his face. "That night when I drove you home and what happened between us in the car ... I didn't want you to get the wrong idea."

She bit her lip before responding, "I know you're not married, Alex."

By his expression, his confusion was apparent.

"Rachel told me."

Snorting, Alex mumbled something under his breath, then looked at her questioningly. "What else did she tell you?"

"That's it. She said the rest of the story was yours to tell when you're ready."

He said nothing as he glanced back down at the table. They sat in silence for a while. Alex seemed lost in his thoughts. After a few more minutes, Gemma stood up abruptly, wanting to end the awkward silence.

"Well, since I'm here early I can go ahead and get to work if you like?"

Alex gave her a grateful smile as he stood up.

"I'll help you."

They worked around the restaurant in silence, each taking down chairs and wiping down tables, silently ruminating over the other. Now and then when the other wasn't looking they stole glances at one another. Gemma stopped peeking at him and wondered yet again what happened to his wife. *Was it a bad divorce? Was she dead?* Whatever it was, it was obviously painful for him.

Alex may have been deep in thought about things of the past, but he was very aware of Gemma's change in appearance. The funny thing was, he thought she was just as beautiful without any of it.

"Can you help me with these?" Alex pointed to the stack of tablecloths.

"Sure."

Alex knew he could have done it by himself, but he wanted her closer so he could look at her without having to sneak. They each held opposite ends of one of the tablecloths. Even though they stood across the table facing each other, he could tell Gemma was purposely avoiding eye contact. Alex smirked as a mischievous thought occurred to him. He tugged hard on his end of the tablecloth, sending Gemma sprawling across the table. Her shocked expression had him doubled over in laughter. She stood up, trying to look angry instead of embarrassed, but she felt the laughter bubbling up inside her. Pretty soon they were both laughing hysterically. After a few minutes, their laughter subsided.

Gemma still chuckled a bit as she spoke, "I owe you for that."

"I'm sorry. I didn't mean to tug that hard. I should ask if you're okay." He sported a big grin as he laughed some more. "Are you hurt?"

"Only my pride."

This made Alex guffaw loudly. She laughed again as well, covering her mouth. His laughter quickly died away as he stared at her.

"You know you shouldn't cover up like that."

"What?" Gemma looked at him, puzzled.

"When you laugh, you put your hand over your mouth."

"Oh." Her laughter ended quickly after his comment, and she dropped her hand to her side.

They both stood staring at each other, neither of them able to look away. After what felt like an eternity, but was mere seconds, someone beating on the door broke them out of the spell they were under. Gemma looked at the floor, her hands fidgeting nervously. She could feel Alex staring at her for a couple of seconds before heading to the door and letting in Brandon and some of the other staff.

"Hey, new chick!" Brandon exclaimed.

Amanda elbowed him. "Her name is Gemma, Brandon. You'd think you'd know that after all the time you've spent hitting on her since she started."

Everyone erupted in loud jeers. Gemma squirmed and shuffled her feet, nervously joining in the laughter, before going back to putting on the tablecloth. Alex saw her struggling with the fabric and took up the other end, catching her eye for a moment as Amanda and Brandon playfully argued while the rest of the staff egged them on. She briefly looked into his eyes and then broke their gaze. Gemma tried to rejoin the merriment of her co-workers, but it all sounded like noise. *What just happened between Alex and I?*

Brandon and Amanda pulled Alex into their jokes. While he was engrossed in their banter, she took the opportunity to assess him. She loved the way his eyes twinkled when he was up to some mischief, like a minute ago when he made her fall on the table. She noticed his sinewy forearms as he continued doing work and making his staff roar with glee over some line about Brandon that she didn't catch. His hair looked so silky she wanted to run her fingers through it and over the scruff that covered his face and gave him a predatory look. Her eyes were drawn down to the cords of his throat that stood out as he threw his head back laughing. Moisture began to pool between her legs the longer she stared at him. She dropped her gaze to the table and realized she'd been wiping the same spot for a while. To keep herself busy, she started refilling salt and pepper shakers, laughing when appropriate with the group although she wasn't paying attention.

Alex continued his involvement in the group's pranks and jokes so he wouldn't keep thinking about her. When he thought no one was looking, he watched her. He loved the way her hair fell around her face in soft waves. The thought of what it would be like to run his hands through it as he kissed her kept running through his head. Those lips! It was hard not to stare at them. Her mouth became pouty, like now, when she was deep in thought. Her brow furrowed a bit, and he wondered what she was thinking. He wished he could see her eyes. They were this beautiful shade of brown that he just wanted to gaze into forever. She accidentally dropped the dishrag she'd been cleaning the tables with and bent over to pick it up which gave him a glorious view of her breasts. He had to readjust himself as he felt his dick twitch at the sight. Quickly, he looked away.

"Okay everyone, let's get ready for tonight." He said over the den of voices.

He sent everyone off to their stations, so they could finish prepping for tonight, but mostly so he could stop fantasizing about her.

Dinner service was busy and would have passed without any thoughts of Gemma, if he didn't have to listen to Brandon telling the whole kitchen his plans to finally get her in bed. He was tired of him running his mouth, and was this close to knocking Brandon on his ass. His anger got the better of him.

"The only thing your hand will be stroking tonight is your limp dick, Brandon, so put a sock in it."

There were some uneasy laughs. Alex sighed. He knew it wasn't what he'd said that was the problem; the tone had been harsher than he'd intended. He was sorry and knew Brandon's feelings were hurt when he saw his sous chef's face drop. They all cracked jokes on each other in good fun, but he knew he'd somehow crossed the line. He just wanted him to stop saying things about Gemma. The kitchen quieted down, leaving only the clinking of pots and pans and the sounds of foods being chopped and cut. Usually, he always tried to keep things lighthearted. He cared about his team and wanted them to enjoy their work. Unfortunately, he'd just soured the morale. No one spoke for the rest of dinner service. The change in mood was his fault; he would need to make it up to them.

Feeling contrite about what happened in the kitchen during dinner rush, he sent the crew home halfway through clean up to make amends, while he finished up alone.

He hadn't glanced in her direction all night, and now he was allowing them all to go home early. She almost offered to stay but knew that would look questionable. Maybe he wanted to be alone. *Why am I getting hurt feelings?* Just because they spent some time together earlier didn't mean anything changed. Plus, they barely knew each other. She grabbed her coat and purse and left with the group.

Everyone walked out and got into their cars. One of her co-workers offered her a ride, but she declined. She didn't want them asking questions about where she lived. She waved and said her good-byes as she walked toward the bus stop.

Gemma wrapped her jacket a little tighter around her body as the wind picked up. The streetlight overhead cast a dim light over her as she tried to walk with a confidence she didn't feel. Something about tonight made her anxious. Nearly to the bus stop, a car rolled to a stop near her. An uneasy feeling settled over her, but she kept walking and didn't acknowledge the vehicle. She gripped the pepper spray tighter in her hand. The car went into reverse, and then two guys jumped out, leaving the driver inside. One thug stood in front of her and the other guy behind her.

Biting her lip, she peered over her shoulder at the guy standing behind her. She turned back around to the assailant facing her and tried to appear unafraid. His gaze ran over her body in a suggestive manner.

"What are you doing out here so late, sweetheart? Don't you know only whores are out this time a night?" He stepped closer and ran his hand down her cheek. "That must make you a whore."

At that point she lost no time reacting; she sprayed the thug with the pepper spray and kneed him in the crotch. The goon started screaming and telling his buddy to go after her as she attempted to make her getaway. She could feel the fear and panic gripping her insides. In her haste to flee, she ended up dropping her purse. Unfortunately, there was no one around to help her. The restaurant was in a business district. All of the other businesses had locked up and gone home ages ago. *Damn!*

Her lungs were burning with the effort to stay ahead of her muggers. She turned down a side street hoping to get away, only to realize too late that it was a dead end. She looked around wildly for a weapon or another exit and eventually ended up backed into a corner. *What am I going to do now?* She could hear the footsteps of her attackers gaining on her. The screeching tires could be heard as the car entered the street as well. Desperately, she screamed for help; even despite knowing her pleas were going to go unheard. The thug she injured stumbled forward.

"Scream all you want, bitch! We're going to teach you a lesson." He brandished a switchblade as they advanced toward her.

She looked around again, unsuccessfully searching for some form of weapon, but finding none. Before she knew it, she found her back against the wall. The evil sneer of the one she kneed in the groin unsettled her as he reached for her.

"You're going to regret that you cunt."

He punched her hard in the gut, causing her to double over as the wind was knocked from her. Tears sprang up in her eyes as she fought for air, gasping, trying to take in a lungful of precious oxygen. Adrenaline kicked in as her assailant pulled her up by her jacket. Determined that he wouldn't take what he wanted from her easily, she clawed his face. Upon seeing this, his friends rushed over to help restrain her.

The clock showed midnight as he walked out the door flipping off the lights. He didn't have that much to finish up once he sent everyone home. As he fumbled with his keys on the way to his car, he thought of Gemma. He turned toward the bus stop. The few streetlights were either out or flickering, giving the street an ominous look. Not the environment where a lone woman should be waiting to catch the bus in the dead of night. *Did she already get picked up?* He glanced at his watch. Sometimes the bus came and sometimes it didn't. He was sure she'd mentioned a change in schedule earlier.

What if she'd come out of work and found the bus wasn't running that late anymore? Hopefully, she didn't end up walking home. He felt like a bastard. He'd been so caught up in his thoughts about what happened earlier to remember to make sure she got home safely. Even though they'd barely spoken these past couple months, he was always able to make sure she made it home safely. He would just go to the halfway house and make sure she was there.

As he was about to drive past the bus stop, he noticed something lying in the street and stopped to see what it was. After exiting the car, he bent down to retrieve the object, and realized it was a purse. He looked around before opening it to search for an ID. Someone must be worried. He'd make sure they got it back. Moving closer to the headlights, he was able to get a better look at the photo on the ID. Once he recognized Gemma's face staring back at him, he felt his blood run cold. Frantically, he looked around.

"Gemma! Gemma!"

No response, but the whipping of the wind. He hurried back to his car and drove with the windows rolled down. He could barely breathe. His heart was in his mouth. A minute later he noticed a car sitting near another street with the engine running. He cut his lights and coasted to a stop. Leaving the car, he hurried down the street staying in the shadows close to the building. As he drew closer to the empty car, he heard a scuffle and a commotion.

"Hold her steady, fuckwit. You can have your turn in a minute."

Gemma's cries reached his ears, and his anger and adrenaline ratcheted up a notch. He glanced around for a weapon. Spotting a two by four, he picked it up and stealthily moved down the street toward the group.

There was a light hanging halfway down the street. He could see two guys on either side of Gemma holding her to the ground, as the third man that knelt between her thighs, backhanded her. Her distressed whimpers reached his ears. At that, he took a running start and cracked the guy over the head. Alex proceeded to rain blows upon the other two who were completely caught off guard.

After a minute or so the thugs lay in a heap. The first guy he hit was slumped over Gemma, unconscious. Alex dropped the piece of wood and pushed him off of her. He clenched his fists as he took in Gemma's appearance. She had put up a fight. Unfortunately, three against one she hadn't stood a chance.

Gemma's wounds consisted of a busted lip, black eye, scratches along her face and chest, along with faint bruising around her throat from her attacker trying to choke her. Her blouse was torn open, and they'd cut her bra for easier access. Her pants lay discarded in a shredded heap next to her. Alex curled his fists in anger, wondering just how far those jackasses had come to violating her.

She wouldn't meet his eyes as tears silently streamed down her face. Slowly, he squatted down next to her and closed her blouse over her nakedness. He removed his jacket and laid it over her. Rage was eating away at him as he looked at her battered face. Pulling out his phone, he dialed 911, telling them what happened and where they were. Once he finished, he put his phone away. He wanted to hold her, comfort her, make her feel better, but he was at a loss.

"Gemma," he murmured.

After a few seconds, she turned her head to look at him. That all too familiar pain he'd seen swimming in her eyes before tonight was now raw and naked for anyone to see. It made his heart stop to witness her like this. Her tears had him in agony. A desperate need to hug her to his body and reassure her that she was safe gripped him. He was fighting his emotions when he felt her hand on his arm.

That tiny action opened the floodgates as she broke down sobbing even harder. Her crying was so broken and wounded it tore at his heart. He pulled her up into his arms and cradled her. He knew her distress was not just for what happened tonight, but also for so much more. All he wanted at that moment was to protect her. The sobs wracked her body, and he rubbed her back, trying to soothe her. Overwhelming guilt assailed him at not being there to make sure she got home safely.

"I'm sorry," she half whispered in between sobs. He stared down at her incredulously. *Is she apologizing for being attacked?*

"You didn't do anything, Gemma! Please don't blame yourself … I'm the one who's sorry. I'm sorry I wasn't here. I'm so sorry." He pressed her tighter to his body as he listened to her cry her heart out while they awaited the police.

Once the police arrived on the scene, Alex pointed to the thugs while he continued to hold Gemma in his arms. Medics came over to take Gemma from his grasp, and she clutched his hand.

"I'm here. I'm right here, Gemma. I'm not going anywhere."

The cop asked to take his statement. Squeezing her hand, he let her know that he would stay in her line of sight as he spoke with the cops while the medics tended to her. When he finished, he asked the officer if he could bring her by tomorrow to give a statement, instead of her speaking with them tonight. The cop reluctantly agreed, and Alex walked back over to the ambulance.

"Ma'am, you really should let us take you to the hospital."

"I don't want to go to a hospital, I just want to go home," she pleaded as Alex walked up. "Alex, please tell them to let me go home," she implored him.

"Umm, I can just take her back to my place and watch her, make sure she's okay." He turned to her to make sure this was all right with her, and she nodded. The medic looked at him and acquiesced. Alex knew Gemma needed to cling to something familiar, which was why she latched onto him following her traumatic night. He intended to make sure she felt safe and would do whatever she wanted to ensure her safety, well-being, and peace of mind.

They helped her out of the ambulance and Alex put his arm around her to walk her to his car, then assisted her as she slipped into the passenger seat. Alex noticed her wincing and wondered if he made the right decision by not insisting she go to the emergency room. He tucked the blanket around her they'd wrapped her in before he got in the driver's seat. He looked at her before starting the car. Gemma's eyes were closed as she reclined against the seat. Her hand tenderly touched her throat. He didn't know what to say. *'Are you okay?'* would be an absurd question. She was far from all right. He started the car and headed to his house.

As he drove them to his house, he glanced at her occasionally. She'd fallen asleep. She appeared so small and fragile. He turned back to the road and continued driving home.

After pulling into his driveway, he chose not to wake her. He unlocked the front door before going back and gently lifting her from the seat. Quietly, he shut the car door and headed into the house. She was light in his arms. He walked into the guest bedroom and lay her down on the bed. Her hair sprawled across the pillow. Alex sat on the edge of the bed and went to remove her shoes, forgetting she was no longer wearing any. The revelation rekindled his anger. His face softened and his fury dissipated as he gazed at her sleeping face. He covered her with the blanket again. Afterward, he stood looking at her for a second. He wasn't sure what he would have done if he'd gotten there any later, probably would have killed the three men. Giving her one last glance, he left the room and closed the door without making a sound.

In the shower, he couldn't help but think of the night he got the news of his wife's death, and how helpless he felt. The helplessness nearly did him in earlier tonight. He hated that feeling. His head was a mess of thoughts as he let the water cascade down his body. The water did nothing to calm his wrath. After a few minutes, he shut off the shower and got out, wrapping a towel around his waist. He was angry he hadn't been there. Gemma's attack would never have happened if he'd been thinking clearly tonight. This feeling of helplessness had him enraged. He couldn't save his wife, and seeing Gemma beaten and nearly losing her was overpowering. He gripped the counter and hung his head. Suddenly, his anger exploded.

"Fuck!" Alex yelled and punched the mirror.

Pieces of glass went flying into the sink. Alex stared at his fist, not feeling the pain. A few shards stuck out of his knuckles. Picking them out, he dropped them into the sink, and slumped onto the commode breathing heavily, trying to shake some of his aggression. After getting control of himself, he got up to bandage his hand. He'd clean up the mess tomorrow.

As he came into his bedroom, he found Gemma asleep on his bed. Confusion set in. He knew he'd put her in the guest bedroom. He paused in the doorway watching her, as he pondered why she chose to come to his bedroom.

Minutes ticked by as he watched her. He considered going to the guest bedroom himself, but realized Gemma came to his room because she didn't want to be alone. If he was honest, he didn't want to be alone either, especially if it meant being alone with only his thoughts for company.

Usually, he slept naked, but obviously, he'd have to dress. The last thing she needed was to wake up disoriented and frightened next to a naked man. He stepped into his closet and put on some basketball shorts and a T-shirt. Unsure whether he should sleep in the bed with Gemma, he sat on the edge of the bed contemplating. He looked at her back. Decided, he lay down next to her and put his hands behind his head. He glanced at her once more before staring back at the ceiling. It took a little while, but sleep eventually claimed him.

Gemma's head hurt and her throat was a little raw. As her eyes adjusted to the light, she looked down to see an arm draped across her waist. Before she could scream and lash out, memories of last night came flooding back to her, and she remembered how caring and gentle Alex had been with her. She recalled coming into his room last night because she didn't want to be by herself after what happened last night.

Alex was curled around her body, his warm chest pressed against her back. For a minute it felt strange and her body stiffened at being held so, but gradually the tension eased from her limbs. His nearness was comforting.

Alex woke up, but before he could open his eyes and stretch he felt a body pressed against him. He slowly opened his eyes and saw Gemma's hair. That's right, she'd come to his bed last night.

Oh my God! He needed to remove his body from around her before she woke up and had a fit. He hadn't meant to; it had just been a long time since he'd shared his bed with anyone. It was out of habit he'd curled his body around hers … she felt good spooning against him.

Oh no! At that moment, his body chose to react as it did every morning. He was aghast as his morning wood continued to grow against her. He needed to release her. He didn't want to wake her, though. Maybe he could gently extricate himself and go cook breakfast so things wouldn't get awkward.

They lay together not knowing the other had woken up, trying to figure out how to leave the bed without causing a disturbance.

5

A lex uttered a curse under his breath as he tried to gently remove his body from around hers. As he was trying to maneuver his body she rolled onto her back. Now he was leaning over her since he was lying on his side, resting on his elbow.

"Oh, you're awake," Alex exhaled softly and looked away, embarrassed.

"I'm sorry … about …"

Gemma's eyes were downcast as she fidgeted with her hands. She smiled slightly, but ended up wincing in discomfort. "It's okay."

They lay in silence for a moment not looking at each other. After a few more minutes of getting over the embarrassment he fixed his gaze on her. Her eye was now a dark purple. In the light of day, her injuries didn't seem so bad.

"Does it hurt?"

"Only when I blink."

They both shared a nervous laugh.

"I'm sorry. That was a stupid question."

More silence. Then Gemma looked up at him with a serious expression.

"Thank you, Alex." Her lip trembled a bit as tears threatened to roll down her cheeks. "I don't know what would have happened if you hadn't showed up." She bit her lip, trying to staunch the tears.

"I don't want to think about that either, Gemma."

Some of the tears she'd been trying to suppress spilled from her eyes as she swallowed before speaking again.

"Why do some men look at me and think they can take whatever they want? What is it about me they see that makes me an easy target?" She wouldn't meet his gaze when she asked the question. Unfortunately, there was no response he could give that would make her feel better, but part of him wondered if she meant to voice the thought aloud. He wanted badly to stroke her cheek, hug her to his body, and help her forget the brutality of last night.

"Promise me that you'll let me or someone take you home from now on? In a perfect world you could walk home any time of night without fear, but unfortunately, the world can be a dangerous place."

"It's not the world that's dangerous, Alex. It's the people in it," she said, finally looking into his eyes. At that moment, he wasn't sure what he was doing, but he hesitantly reached out and caressed her face where the slight bruise had formed. He lightly stroked the back of his fingers up and down her injured cheek. Gemma's eyes fell closed, releasing a single tear. Slowly, Alex leaned down and kissed Gemma softly on the forehead. When he pulled away, her eyes fluttered open and she met his gaze.

For once, the silence they shared wasn't awkward. He didn't know what came over him, but he wanted to show her some tenderness after what she'd been through last night. Before he could stop himself, he sunk his fingers into her hair, which he'd been longing to touch. His fingers worked their way over her scalp, slowly massaging. Gemma's eyes closed again, and another tear slid down her cheek. A small sigh escaped her lips. He wanted to make her feel better, and he didn't seem to be able to communicate with words what he felt right now, but he was trying to show her. Show her that whatever she suffered at the hands of those men last night and whoever the men were in her past that mistreated her, she deserved better, and was entitled to better. He wanted to show her those men were her past and now she was safe.

After a minute, Gemma curled her body toward him. Alex's fingers didn't let up; they kept stroking her scalp. Neither said a word. He could feel her tears soak his shirt. Once he felt her body shaking with the force of her sobs, he removed his hand from her hair and wrapped his arms around her body tightly. He rested his head on top of hers and just let her weep. After a while, they both fell asleep.

Alex felt someone tapping him on the shoulder. He was in such a deep sleep it took him a minute to come out of it. When some of the grogginess wore off and he was able to open his eyes, he looked down at Gemma, she was still sleeping soundly in his arms. He was confused for a moment and would have fallen back to sleep, until he heard someone harshly whisper his name.

"Alex!"

Startled, he turned to find Rachel standing next to the bed. *Damn!* Alex loved his sister, but she knew how to get under his skin. He forgot he'd given her a key. Maybe he would get that back from her while she was here. He gave her a serious stare down before putting his hand to his lips, motioning for her to keep quiet, then pointed to his bedroom door and shooed her out with his hands. She hesitantly walked to the door, but gave a quick glance back and made a motion for him to meet her out in the living room. Alex gave her a curt nod. After Rachel finally left the room, he regarded Gemma's face once more. He hadn't slept this well in a long time. Alex gently removed his arm from underneath her and eased himself from the bed.

He found Rachel pacing the living room floor.

"What's going on?"

"Shhhhh … you'll wake her!" he roughly whispered as he grabbed his sister's arm, dragging her into the kitchen.

"What are you doing here?"

"I asked you a question first," Rachel stated, folding her arms across her chest and staring him down.

Crossing his arms over his chest, Alex glowered at her. He quickly realized this was a contest he wouldn't win. Rachel could be relentless.

"Fine! If I tell you will you leave then?"

Rachel nodded her head, but Alex was no fool. He knew she would figure out some way to hang around even after he told her what happened. He huffed before beginning the story as Rachel took a seat on one of the stools, all the while smiling like the cat that ate the canary.

"Gemma was attacked last night …"

"*What?*" Rachel jumped up looking angry.

"Keep your voice down!" Alex glanced behind him, toward the bedrooms, before turning back to Rachel. He moved into the kitchen, hoping their voices wouldn't wake Gemma.

"She left work last night, I guess, headed for the bus stop and never made it. Some thugs chased her down and nearly raped her." His jaw ticked as he said the words. Just the thought rekindled his anger.

For once, Rachel was speechless. Her hand covered her mouth for a brief second before dropping to the countertop.

"Oh, Alex! Poor Gemma! How did she get away?"

She wiped a tear from her eye. Alex focused on the counter as he continued the story.

"I was headed to the halfway house to check and make sure she got home safely when I found a purse in the road. When I checked the ID, I saw it was hers. They had her penned in on a dead end street. I got there before they could do any further damage, but not early enough in my opinion." He glanced up to see Rachel crying some more, but her eyes were shining, and she had a big, goofy grin on her face.

"My brother the hero! You saved her!"

His face flushed a deep red, at his sister's praise. "If I'd been there like I was supposed to none of it would have ever happened."

Rachel came around the counter and enveloped Alex in an unwanted hug. "Don't beat yourself up, Alex. You did save her. She's all right because of you. I hope you beat those guys within an inch of their lives." As she pulled away, she noticed his hand.

"Did you injure your hand last night when you attacked those guys?" Rachel asked, grabbing his hand.

"No, I broke a mirror." Alex didn't even need to look up to know that Rachel was about to ask him about it. "Don't ask." He moved about the kitchen, grabbing pans and ingredients to start breakfast.

"Now that you know everything I'd like you to go. I don't want you here when she wakes up."

Rachel was about to respond with a sarcastic retort when they heard a noise in the living room and turned to see Gemma. Rachel rushed toward her.

"Oh my goodness, Gemma, I'm so glad to hear you're okay. Alex told me what happened."

Alex rolled his eyes at his sister's back. *So much for getting rid of her now.*

Rachel pulled Gemma into a tight hug. She peered over Rachel's shoulder at Alex. They smiled at one another. Gemma winced a little from the action. He gave her a questioning look, trying to make sure she wasn't hurting, and she gave him a brief nod to indicate she was okay.

"I'm sorry if we woke you. I kept trying to quiet my loudmouthed sister."

Rachel released her as she began to apologize. "Oh dear, yes, it's all my fault. I'm very sorry. I was so concerned after Alex told me what happened. I tend to get loud when I'm emotional."

Alex turned on the burner, as he said, "Isn't that all the time?"

Rachel flipped him the finger. "I heard you."

"I wasn't trying to keep it quiet."

Rachel whirled around to berate him. "Stop! Before Gemma thinks we're uncivilized."

She turned back to Gemma and took her by the shoulders, scrutinizing her face. "It's not bad. Nothing make-up can't fix."

Rachel gave Gemma a warm smile and Gemma half smiled back. Alex had to admit that Rachel was good at making the mood a bit lighter; even though he was annoyed she was here.

"Stop smothering her, Rachel."

"I'm not!" Rachel made a face at him as she and Gemma entered the kitchen. As they prepared to sit on the barstools he noticed that Gemma sported one of his t-shirts. It hung to her knees, which was good, since she had no pants. Gemma caught him eyeing the t-shirt and went to explain.

"I hope it's okay. I didn't ..." She stammered as she pulled on the hem of the shirt.

Before she could say anything else, Alex interrupted her.

"Of course it's fine." He said in a soothing tone.

"What do you like in your omelet, Gemma?" Alex asked as he gestured to the ingredients that littered the counter.

"Can you surprise me?" She asked as she sat on one of the barstools.

He smiled at her and nodded before facing the stove.

"Aren't you going to ask me what I want in my omelet?" Rachel asked.

Alex didn't even turn around when he addressed her, "I didn't invite you to stay."

Gemma tried to suppress a giggle, enjoying the witty banter between brother and sister. As they argued she took the opportunity to look around Alex's home. The living room was tastefully furnished in deep brown. A large flat screen TV was mounted over the mantel. She smiled to herself, wondering if he was a sports kind of guy or what type of movies he enjoyed watching. The floors lacked any carpets, the polished wood shone from every corner. The place had a homey feel to it. The kitchen was the real marvel though. It could rival the one at the restaurant with its stainless steel appliances and huge Viking stove. She could tell this was the room he spent the most time in. His love of cooking was evident in the design and use of the space. Her mind picked back up on their conversation after she finished her perusal.

"That's a fine way to treat your sister. What's Gemma going to think?" She smiled and winked at Gemma waiting for Alex's witty comeback.

Alex turned back around from the stove and addressed her instead of answering his sister. "Would you like to take a shower, Gemma?"

"Umm, yes. That would be great."

"You can use my bathroom. There are clean towels in there and soap under the sink …" He appeared a little sheepish as he continued. "I'm sorry it's not something more feminine."

He glanced up from the eggs he was mixing when she answered, "It's okay."

As she was walking toward his bedroom, Alex called out to her, "You should say good-bye to Rachel because she won't be here when you get back."

Gemma turned back at his words.

Rachel was incredulous as she whipped her head around to look at Alex. They grinned at each other.

"Bye Gemma." Rachel hopped off the stool to give Gemma a hug. "It sounds like we're going to have to catch up later."

Gemma nodded to avoid having to quirk her mouth into a smile. "Thanks so much for your concern, Rachel. I appreciate it."

Gemma disappeared into the bathroom as Rachel and Alex walked toward the front door.

"Kicking me out, huh, baby brother?" she chided him.

"Don't call me that," he said, slightly irritated, but then he grinned at her. "You can come back later … you cockblocker."

They both laughed, as Rachel put her finger in his chest. "Aha!"

Alex chuckled, but then sobered.

"It's not like that. She was attacked last night for crying out loud, Rachel. I wouldn't put the moves on her after something like that."

"Not what it looked like when I walked in," Rachel smirked.

"It was harmless. I was comforting her …"

Rachel didn't seem convinced.

"Fine, you want the truth? I like her, okay? I like her a lot. It felt good to be there for her, and I don't need you here in the way messing things up. The situation between Gemma and I isn't some grade school crush … I'm trying to get to know her. She's already shy as hell and you being here won't help. There! Have I spelled it out for you?"

Rachel sported a triumphant expression. "All you had to do was say so."

Alex sneered at his sister. "Is that so, pest?"

He started tickling her and Rachel squealed and tried to smack his hands away. They both erupted into peals of laughter.

"Okay … okay … I'm gonna leave … just stop," she said between giggles. Alex finally stopped tickling her. They stood staring at each other for a minute as Rachel caught her breath.

"I want you to be happy, Alex. I'm sorry for meddling, but I could tell something was going on between the two of you. I'll stay out of it. My job here is done."

They hugged each other. Alex opened the door for her, and Rachel gave him a smile before heading out.

Gemma found the towels in the cabinet like Alex said she would. She didn't know how she missed it before, but part of the mirror was smashed in. That would explain Alex's hand. *Was he upset about last night?* She didn't want him to feel guilty. Had it not been for him, who knew how far things would have gone last night?

She ran her hands through her hair, filled with thoughts of the gentle way he touched and held her. There wasn't anything sexual in it, just him comforting her, and it felt wonderful. She was basking in the reminder of those warm thoughts. No one ever held her so tenderly ... *And that forehead kiss?* That was her undoing. She wanted more of it. She wanted to feel the way he made her feel, always. He was slowly turning last night's nightmare into a distant memory. He'd helped erase some of the pain and the hurt, and he'd asked nothing in return. She couldn't be more grateful.

Gemma glanced down at the shards of the mirror lying in the sink. Finding the garbage can, she put the bigger pieces in there. Then she cleaned up the rest. She went to the shower and turned it on.

As she undressed, she came face-to-face with her appearance in the part of the mirror that hadn't been destroyed. She approached the mirror and lightly ran her fingers over her face, touching her black eye; then her hand ghosted over her split lip and rubbed her bruised cheek. Her trembling hand drifted down to her throat to finger the faint bruise there. After pulling his shirt over her head, she ran her fingers down her side where another bruise had formed. She'd experienced worse. She swallowed as the painful memories tried to creep in. Shaking it off, she finished the perusal of her injuries. Outside scars and bruises healed, so maybe, just maybe, the inside ones would start to heal, too.

Alex was trying to put the finishing touches on breakfast when the doorbell rang.

"I swear, Rachel, if this is you, I'm going to kill you," Alex said to himself.

When he opened the door, he found Shelby standing in his doorway.

"Hey, Alex, I came by because Ms. Ramirez said Gemma never came home last night, and then I got a call from the cops that she was attacked. The medic reported that she came home with you."

"Yeah, she didn't want to be alone."

Shelby noticed his bandaged hand.

"Can I come in?"

Alex shook himself. "Where are my manners? Of course ... Umm, Gemma's just taking a shower. Did you want anything to drink?"

"No, I'm okay." Shelby followed him into the kitchen.

As Alex began clean up he glanced at Shelby and saw she seemed unsure about what she was going to say next.

"You seem like you have something on your mind."

Shelby sighed as she leaned against the door jamb.

"Listen, Alex, I know it's none of my business, but things seem to be getting close between you and Gemma. I know when something like this happens it can push two people together rather quickly ..."

Alex was about to interrupt her, but Shelby put up her hand.

"Just let me finish. It's my job to look out for the people assigned to me, and I take that job very seriously. I don't want to see Gemma get hurt. The girl's been through enough."

Alex took a beat before responding.

"First of all, you're right. It's none of your business. Gemma's a grown woman, Shelby. Plus, I wouldn't do anything to hurt her. I appreciate your concern. Gemma needs more people like you in her corner ... That's the only reason I didn't read you the riot act." Alex tried not to be agitated, knowing Shelby was only doing her job.

They both stood staring at each other, trying to size the other one up. The two of them had dealt with each other periodically regarding other ex-cons Alex had taken on, but none ever garnered this type of conversation. Alex appreciated that Shelby took her job seriously, but was a bit unnerved by her thinking he would do anything untoward concerning Gemma. He tried to break the awkward moment by offering up a bit of a joke.

"You know, you're the second woman to come here this morning and question my motives. I'm beginning to wonder if I have Big Bad Wolf written across my back."

They smirked at each other.

"Oh yeah? Who else?"

"My sister," Alex replied as he poured himself a cup of coffee.

"On second thought, could you pour me a cup as well?" Shelby moved toward the counter, and Alex grabbed another mug, pouring her some coffee. At that moment, Gemma came out wearing Alex's shirt she'd sported earlier and a pair of sweats that were too big for her. Shelby threw Alex a look, and he had the decency to blush. Of course, to Shelby, it looked like something was going on between the two of them.

"Hi, Shelby," Gemma said upon seeing her parole officer. She was unaware of how things appeared.

"How are you, Gemma? I heard about what happened last night."

Gemma touched her face. "I know it looks bad, but it doesn't hurt as much ... I have Alex to thank for saving my life." She looked to him then.

Without looking at Shelby, he could feel her steely gaze, but she kept whatever she was thinking to herself.

"I'm just glad you're okay. The cops say you still need to come down and make a statement."

Alex interjected before Gemma could answer. "I was going to take her down once she had a chance to shower and eat breakfast." He gazed at Gemma then. "If that was okay?"

Gemma nodded and they both turned to Shelby in response.

"Well okay then, I'll just get out of your hair. I'll let Ms. Ramirez know that you're okay." Shelby swallowed the rest of her coffee and headed toward the door. "I'll show myself out, but please make sure to get down to the station as soon as you can."

Once they heard the door close they both eyed each other. Then Alex grinned, "Maybe we can manage to finish breakfast without any more interruptions."

She lifted the uninjured side of her mouth into a lopsided grin and took a seat as Alex placed her omelet in front of her.

"I hope you like it."

"I'm sure it will be delicious." Gemma looked up at him as she took a forkful.

"Mmmmm, it's yummy." She continued eating. "What's in this?" Gemma asked between mouthfuls.

Pleased, Alex smirked at her. He leaned on his elbows, content to watch her eat.

"A chef never reveals his secrets. Plus, if I told you then I'd have to kill you," he said, raising his eyebrow at her with a mischievous grin.

It took a second as her fork hung in the air and then Gemma let out the heartiest laugh he'd ever heard from her. He was so happy to hear that sound, he joined in chuckling, too. He finally grabbed his omelet and began to eat as well.

"By the way, I cleaned up your sink …"

Puzzled, he cocked his head to the side.

"Your mirror."

"Oh yeah." He looked down as he shoveled some of his eggs into his mouth.

"Thank you."

"No problem … it's the least I can do."

There was something implied in her tone that made him look up at Gemma's face. Now she was the one avoiding eye contact. She stopped eating, and her fork rested on her plate. He saw her hands fidgeting. He frowned knowingly and walked around the kitchen island to stand in front of her. Placing one hand gently over her two hands in her lap to still them, he then lifted her chin up, so she was looking him in the eyes.

"Gemma, you don't owe me anything. Do you understand? It was my duty last night to protect you … my duty as a human being." He stared into her eyes, searching for her understanding, her recognition that there was nothing she needed to do to repay him. He knew she was used to people taking and not giving; trading favors for the simplest acts of human kindness and decency, things that should be given freely without the expectation of something in return.

After a moment she nodded her head, and he pulled her into a hug. She wrapped her arms around him, too. They stayed locked in the embrace for a while. Alex realized it wasn't just Gemma that was benefitting from these vulnerable, intimate moments, he could feel something beginning to thaw inside himself.

6

After their moment in the kitchen, he got dressed and took her to the halfway house so she could change into some clean clothes of her own. The minute she hit the door, Ms. Ramirez grabbed her in a tight bear hug then began fussing and checking her over as he watched from the car. Despite Gemma being the one that was injured last night he watched her comfort and reassure the woman that she was okay as Ms. Ramirez softly cried before they disappeared into the house.

While Alex waited in the car for Gemma to come back, he called Brandon. He knew he was asking a lot considering he had yet to apologize for last night, but he needed him to head in early and get things set up at the restaurant. He didn't want to apologize over the phone—that would be too impersonal. He could tell Brandon was still a little sore about last night, but he was going to make it up to him. When Brandon agreed to head in early, Alex thanked him and hung up. Fifteen minutes later, Gemma got back into the car. As they headed over to the police station, they both stole glances at the other.

Upon arrival, the officer who was at the scene of the crime last night came to take Gemma's statement. Alex squeezed her hand, letting her that he was right there. As she began to answer the officer's questions, Alex noticed her hands moving restlessly on the tabletop. He wished he could take her hand and reassure her that she didn't have to be nervous. Alex watched her the whole time, making sure this wasn't too much for her. He admired Gemma. She was resilient given all that she'd endured.

After she finished providing her statement she was led back to another room to ID her attackers in a line-up. Alex felt bad that he couldn't accompany her. She looked so tense and anxious as she followed the cop out of sight.

They finished at the police station, and he drove her back home. She tried to tell him she would be there for dinner service, and he looked at her like she was crazy. After protesting for a while, she finally accepted that he would not allow her to work tonight, no matter how okay she said she felt. He let her know he would stop by after dinner to check on her and watched as she went inside before driving to the restaurant.

The staff's arrival to the restaurant was strained: many were still apprehensive after the incident during last night's dinner service. Once all the crew arrived, Alex pulled everyone off their stations and assembled them in the dining room.

"Before we start getting ready for dinner service tonight, I have to let you all know that Gemma was attacked last night …"

Everyone immediately showed concern as they started asking about her. Alex held up his hands for silence.

"She is doing okay, but I just want to make sure that everyone stays safe when they leave here at night. Use the buddy system, especially the ladies. Better to be safe than sorry."

Everyone stood around looking worried and a little shaken.

"I promise Gemma is okay. She may return tomorrow. It just depends on how she feels."

They were all about to head off to finish preparing when he stopped them again,

"Hold up everyone …"

The staff gave him their undivided attention.

"I owe the kitchen staff an apology for last night's dinner service, especially Brandon. I can admit when I've been an ass, guys, and last night I was a giant ass."

Everyone started laughing and relaxed a bit.

"Can you guys forgive me?"

The staff laughed and made smart remarks; some threw their towels at him. Alex moved over to Brandon and gave him a pat on the back. They shook hands, and Brandon walked off to the kitchen. Alex was happy that the morale was back to normal and not awkward.

As they were prepping for tonight, he couldn't help but think of Gemma. He wanted to know her, but it'd been ages since he dated or attempted to get to know a woman. He needed some help. He wasn't sure how to begin to get to know Gemma. Looking up, his eyes landed on Brandon and some of the other cooks conversing. As much crap as they gave Brandon, he did date a lot. He saw the trail of women that frequented the restaurant and always asked for him. The guy must be doing something right. Maybe he should ask him.

"Brandon, could you come here for a minute?"

"Sure, boss." Brandon stepped away from the other cooks. "What's up?"

Alex looked over Brandon's shoulder at the others to make sure no one would overhear him.

"So you seem pretty successful when it comes to women … what do you do? How do you get them to talk to you?"

Brandon wore a huge grin on his face. "Alex, you mean to tell me that you're into women?"

"What are you saying? Of course I'm into women!" Alex realized his voice had risen and called attention to their conversation. Grabbing Brandon, he pulled him away to a less populated area of the kitchen.

"There is a woman that I'm interested in, and I thought … maybe … you know … you could give me some tips or something."

Brandon cackled.

"If you're gonna laugh and not take this seriously then never mind." Alex went to walk off.

Brandon stopped him, still chuckling a bit.

"No, man, wait. I didn't mean anything by it …" He sobered. "It's just you've never been interested in anyone before so you have to admit it's a bit weird."

Alex gave him a scathing look.

Brandon put up his hands. "Okay, okay … step into my office."

Brandon and Alex huddled together while Brandon started to tell him what he should do.

Brandon agreed to stay and supervise clean up after dinner service so Alex could see the woman that held his interest. Alex hadn't volunteered the information on who the woman was because he didn't want to disappoint Brandon, since he knew he liked Gemma.

As Alex pulled up in front of the halfway house, he nervously stared at the place before grabbing the bag of food. Earlier, he called and told her he was coming by to check on her so she would be expecting him.

Gemma opened the door before Alex could knock. He was surprised she'd been watching for him.

"Hi."

"Hey, I brought you some dinner." Alex held up the bag.

"You didn't have to do that."

"I know … but I wanted to." He smiled at her.

Gemma avoided eye contact, but smiled as she held onto the door. Her face was hurting less than earlier.

"You know, I could have come into work today … I know I may look a little worse for wear, but I'm okay."

"I just thought you could use the time to recuperate. I mean, what kind of slave driver would I be if I had you working the day after your attack?"

"You have a point …" She smirked at him. "Come in. I think everyone is asleep." She opened the door wider to give him access.

Alex walked in, and they headed to the kitchen.

"What did you bring me?" she asked, retrieving plates from the cabinet.

He took containers out of the bag and began to talk in a bad Italian accent.

"Pinzimonio, some salumi, artichokes and pecorino, pappardelle alla lepre and for dessert Ciaramicola. Maginifico!" He kissed his fingers, sending Gemma into peals of laughter.

"Okay, Chef Boyardee, now will you give me the English translation?"

Alex chuckled as he started putting food on the plates. "Wait a minute, my food is way better than Chef Boyardee. He ain't got nothing on me."

Gemma continued giggling. "True. Your omelet was quite good, so I'm sure this food will be fantastic, too. Now tell me what it is." Smiling shyly, Gemma bit her lip.

Alex was beginning to find all of her little nervous habits endearing and a little sexy. He grinned at her.

"Okay … Pinzimonio is grilled vegetables in olive oil seasoned with salt, pepper, and some herbs—"

Gemma interrupted him, "Is that asparagus?" She wrinkled her nose. "I'm not a big fan."

"Oh, you're gonna like my asparagus." He waggled his eyebrows at her. The sexual innuendo there was not lost on either of them, but Gemma chose not to acknowledge it, wanting to keep things light, fun, and friendly, the way it had been earlier today. Alex's behavior was making her nervous, more nervous than usual. *Is he flirting with me? What's with him?* He wasn't acting like himself.

"Smooth, Alex, real smooth," Gemma giggled.

Alex chuckled. "Okay, that line was a little lame and corny I'll admit," he rubbed his hands together, "but I got better material." He smirked at her.

"Well while you work on your material, please finish explaining what the meal is." She laughed lightly, shaking her head. He kept trying to stare into her eyes, and she would look away, her face becoming flushed each time.

"I'm waiting." She said hoping to get his focus back on the food and off her.

She bit her lip as she looked over the food.

Alex moved closer and pointed out more food.

"There you have artichokes, a food known to be an aphrodisiac."

She cleared her throat.

"What's this?" She pointed to some other foods choosing to ignore his statement.

"That is salami and cheese; the cheese is similar to Parmesan ... pappardelle alla lepre is a rabbit ragu, it's got bacon, cloves, and lots of other tasty spices in a tomato based sauce."

"Mmmmm, it smells good. I've never had rabbit before."

"Well, you are in for a treat." He smiled at her. "And for the piece de resistance ... Ciaramicola for dessert."

"What does Charmacola mean?"

He gave a bark of laughter at her pronunciation. "It's pronounced Ciaramicola ... and its translation is sweetheart cake. It's a cake meant for lovers ..."

Alex looked pointedly at her when he said it, and the color rushed to her cheeks. She could only guess that he picked out this dessert on purpose.

She glanced away from him, biting her lip, and her eyes darted around like she was trying to decide what she wanted to try first.

"Here, let me fix your plate. You should try a little bit of everything, and we'll both save room for dessert."

Gemma swallowed hard. "Okay."

The topic of conversation needed to change and quickly. Food never sounded this erotic before. She decided to steer the conversation to something safer.

"How do you know all of this stuff? Did you go to school for cooking?"

He handed her a plate crammed with food and started preparing his own as she sat down at the table.

"After high school, much to my father's dismay, I went to Europe instead of going to college. I meant to just travel around getting high, being young and stupid, but then two weeks in I got to Italy and I met some girl ..." He chuckled softly.

"Thought I was in love. More like lust. That flame flickered out in like two weeks, but what I had fallen in love with was

Italian food. I already had a love for cooking, but I realized I wanted to master Italian cooking, so I began traveling around Italy getting some of the notable chefs to teach me."

"You just went knocking on their doors?"

"I know, stupid, right?"

"No, I think it's rather brave actually. You chased after your dream, what you wanted." Embarrassed by her response, she averted her gaze. "That sounded pretty cheesy didn't it?" She chuckled, tucking her hair behind her ear as she looked at him out of the corner of her eye.

He stared directly at her as he responded in a serious tone, "No, I thought it was very sweet of you to say."

Gemma stuffed food into her mouth, quickly trying to change the conversation.

"This is delicious," she murmured with a mouthful of food.

Alex started laughing. Gemma realized how silly she must look, talking with her mouth full. She swallowed the food and laughed along with him. She put her hand over her lips. Leaning over, he gently pulled her hand away from her mouth.

"I thought I told you about doing that," he said playfully. "You shouldn't hide your face when you laugh, Gemma. You're beautiful when you laugh."

Gemma couldn't hide her blush, but she tried to deflect his compliment. "I see you've found some of your missing pickup lines." She discovered something interesting on her plate after making the comment.

"A line would be me saying, 'I fancy you.'"

Gemma could feel the heat rising up the back of her neck.

"Isn't that a British saying?" She quirked a grin as she stared at her food, dragging her fork around her plate. *Why does it feel like it got twenty degrees hotter in here?*

Alex snickered. "What do you know about British terms?" he teased her.

Without looking at him, she giggled, "I've seen *Notting Hill* and *Love Actually*." Even before she said it, she knew it sounded ridiculous.

He roared at her comment. "So are you an expert now?"

She bit her lip, trying to stifle her laughter. "No."

"Well, I happen to like the term …" Alex raised his hands skyward. "Thank you, my British brothers, for coming up with such an awesome phrase."

Gemma couldn't contain her giggles as she smacked his arm. "Stop!"

She was laughing full out now as she cackled a full belly laugh. She was unaware that he watched her the whole time.

"I fancy you." Alex spoke softly.

Gemma wiped at her eyes, her laughter subsiding. "You said that already."

"I know, but I needed to say it again so you'd hear me."

She sobered immediately. They sat staring at one another. Gemma broke eye contact first.

"The food is going to get cold." She resumed eating.

Alex left his plate untouched for minutes.

"I think we should skip to dessert." He got up and searched the drawers for a knife. After finding one, he came back to the table. He cut the cake and put a slice on a plate. The fork sliced through the cake like butter. He held it up to her lips. She peered into his eyes as he waited for her to try the cake.

"You'll like it. Open up."

She hesitated only a moment and then she parted her lips, inviting him to feed her. Alex put the cake into her mouth. Gemma slowly chewed and swallowed as Alex watched. A smidge of frosting clung to the side of her lip.

"Wait, you have something ..." Alex reached out with his thumb and gently wiped away the frosting, never taking his eyes from hers. Then he licked his thumb slowly and sensually. "That's very good."

Gemma swallowed hard and reached for some water. The way he was staring at her was causing her panties to get soaked. Suddenly, they heard a noise in the hallway and Ms. Ramirez appeared in the doorway. They both sat up straighter. Ms. Ramirez had a disapproving look on her face.

"I heard noises ..." Ms. Ramirez glanced between the two of them. "Gemma, men are not allowed to be inside the house. You have to ask your guest to leave."

"I'm sorry … I'll show him out, right away."

Ms. Ramirez turned and left, but not before looking back over her shoulder, continuing to watch them as she headed back upstairs out of sight.

Gemma stood up. "I'm sorry, Alex."

He stood as well. "No, I'm sorry. I hope you won't be in trouble because of me."

"It's fine, but you better go. Thank you again for dinner."

Alex started cleaning up the table, but Gemma stopped him, "It's okay. I'll clean up."

He was still trying to clear the remnants of their meal. "Are you sure?"

She nodded her head. Alex reluctantly stopped and grabbed his jacket, heading to the door with Gemma trailing him.

He turned before heading out. "I'll see you tomorrow."

"Okay."

It was clear, as he lingered that he was debating whether to hug her or kiss her. She wasn't sure, but she wasn't going to wait to find out.

"Good night, Alex."

"Okay then. Good night." Disappointment wound itself around his words.

Gemma quickly shut the door behind him and leaned against it. Thank God for Ms. Ramirez. Who knew what would have happened if she hadn't come downstairs.

What had gotten into Alex? She touched the side of her lip where he'd swiped his thumb to remove the icing, and her mouth twitched upward in a faint smile.

She went back into clean up the kitchen. As she wrapped up the food, her thoughts wandered to Alex again. *What does he see in me?* She didn't feel she had anything to offer him; it would be a one-sided deal. However, when they were together, it just felt so right. Yeah, he'd been a little weird tonight, but she felt comfortable around him.

Even when she first met Jason it hadn't been the way it was with Alex. She sat down at the table for a minute. She admitted that tonight had fun moments, and it was nice to flirt with him. Yet it hadn't felt like him, like he was completely himself. She knew she wanted him, but if they were going to head down that road they had to take it slow, get to know each other and then see where things went romantically. Her thoughts of him continued as she resumed cleaning the kitchen before heading to bed.

As he walked off the porch, he knew he blew it. *What was I thinking?* Sure he scared her away, he sat in his car for a minute before driving away. That wasn't him. *Who was I*

*trying to be just now in there with her? What the hell was I
thinking taking advice from Brandon?*

He rested his head against the back of the seat. The feelings
he was having for Gemma were consuming him. He'd only
known her a few months, but he wanted to know more. He
hadn't felt this way about a woman … well, since Sam. As
scary as it was for him, he felt he owed it to himself to see
where it would go. He looked down at his wedding band,
rubbing his finger over the burnished gold.

Tears sprang to his eyes. He knew that life was for the
living. He'd heard that mantra time and time again when he
first tried out the grief self-help books and tapes about how to
move on. He'd tried them all in the first six months after losing
Sam, but he clung to her for dear life, not ready to let her go—
keeping her things, even spraying her perfume on the other
pillow sometimes at night to help keep him in remembrance
of her. It was only eight months ago that he finally packed up
all of her stuff and exorcised himself of her. The only item he
held onto was his wedding band. Of course, he still missed
her, but since Gemma came along his heart didn't ache as
much. Surely, that was a sign it was okay for him to move on.
This small knot of guilt will eventually go away, right?

"Sam, I'll always love you," he whispered, and a tear fell.
Quickly wiping it away, he glanced back toward the house. He
knew he couldn't keep living in the past. He was aware that

somehow Gemma Peyton was his future. Tomorrow, he would come by and get her to go for a walk so they could talk.

He started the car and drove home.

Gemma was making herself some coffee the next morning when the doorbell rang. The other three women who resided in the house with her and Ms. Ramirez were at work already. She went to the door and opened it, surprised to find Alex standing on the threshold.

He studied her nervously. "Can I talk to you?"

She stood gawking at him for a minute, unable to respond.

"Wanna go for a walk?"

She saw how upset he seemed.

"Yes, let me just get my jacket." After grabbing her coat, she headed out the door with him. They walked side-by-side in silence for a while. She didn't want to rush him. She knew he would speak what was on his mind as soon as he was ready.

"I'm sorry if I came on a bit strong yesterday ..." he began, his hands dug deep into his pockets.

Gemma nodded her head but didn't say anything.

"Can I be frank?"

Gemma nodded again.

"I wanted to impress you last night. I'm completely out of practice and like a fool I asked Brandon for help," he snickered, shaking his head.

"I don't know what I was thinking ... I haven't done this in a long time, Gemma ... but I like you." He stopped walking and faced her.

"I hope last night didn't scare you away."

Gemma started laughing.

"I'm sorry." She was trying to get her laughing under control as she saw the hurt and confused look on Alex's face. "I can't believe you would take advice from Brandon." She explained.

He saw the irony in the situation, and laughed along with her. After a minute, it tapered off. Her expression turned serious. Gemma stared into Alex's eyes for a moment before responding.

"I like you, too, Alex. I'm just ... I'm scared. Don't you think it's too soon? I mean, I don't know if I'm ready."

He grabbed her hand. "I don't know if I'm ready either, Gemma, but every day my feelings for you grow stronger. I know we both have things that we're dealing with ... I'm not saying we have to move fast, but I don't want to deny how I feel about you any longer." He searched her face. "I don't want to play games with you ... I'm too old for that," he chuckled softly resting his forehead against hers.

"The first step is admitting there is a problem … Gemma Peyton, I like you, and I want to get to know you better." He smiled warmly at her, and she couldn't help, but feel that warmth flow into her and it wasn't because their foreheads were touching. She grinned back at him.

"Just promise me moving forward that you'll just be yourself and not take any more advice from Brandon." She smirked.

Alex smiled at her. "I can promise that."

They shared nervous excitement as they leaned against each other. Both felt terrified, but exhilarated.

7

They were both in agreement that they wanted to keep the status of their relationship quiet for the time being. Hopefully, they would be able to do that. Alex was elated Gemma returned his feelings.

Gemma wasn't working today, and Alex couldn't wait to spend time with her, so he was taking his first day off … ever. He'd never taken a day off from the restaurant, but he was determined to do things differently in this relationship than what he did in his marriage.

Alex wiped the condensation from the damaged mirror. He needed to replace it soon. He was debating whether to shave or not when he heard his front door open and close. He hung his head and huffed as he heard Rachel and Chloe calling his name.

"Alex! Alex! Are you home?"

"Uncle Alex!"

He sighed. Then finally called out to them, "I'll be out in a minute!"

He ran his fingers through his hair as he stared at his reflection. *So much for shaving!* He grabbed some jeans and a black V-neck sweater from his closet. Quickly, he dressed and collected his shoes on the way out the door, before his sister could burst into his bedroom. As he came into the living room he dropped his shoes just as his niece jumped into his arms.

"How's my favorite niece?" Alex asked as he tickled her sides.

She giggled, "I'm your only niece, Uncle Alex."

He stopped tickling her and ruffled her hair, then glanced up at Rachel.

"What brings you here?" He sat down on the sofa to put on his shoes.

Without looking at her, he could feel Rachel's piercing, calculated gaze staring a hole in his head hoping he would divulge his secrets.

"So, a little birdie told me that you were taking the day off." She waited for a response, but he evaded her hard stare as he tied his shoes. Alex knew his sister was here fishing for information.

"Why are you really here, Rachel? I thought you said you weren't going to meddle?" Rising from the sofa, he approached his sister.

"I'm not meddling. I just came to see what you were doing on your day off, especially since you've never taken a day off before. So, I'm trying to figure out what … or should I say who you would break your perfect attendance record for." Rachel tried to look innocent.

"That sounds like meddling to me."

"I can't be curious?"

Alex picked up his keys and wallet from the table. "It's none of your business. And if you don't mind, I have to be going." Alex herded them out as he grabbed his jacket and headed toward the door.

Rachel smirked. "I hope you take her some place nice, Alex."

Chloe turned around quickly with wide eyes. "You have a girlfriend, Uncle Alex? When can I meet her?"

Alex gave Rachel a dirty look and then smiled at Chloe. "Your mother doesn't know what she's talking about, sweetheart."

"I didn't hear you denying it," Rachel scoffed, crossing her arms over her chest and staring at him.

Alex huffed. "Rachel, why do you always have to be so difficult?"

They glared at each other. Chloe looked between the two of them and then grabbed her mother's arm, making her the first one to break their staring match.

"Let's go, Mom. Uncle Alex obviously has somewhere to be, and we're making him late."

Rachel huffed this time. "The kid saved your ass, Alex." Rachel headed out the door first.

Once her back was turned, Chloe looked up at Alex and winked. He smiled at her and mouthed, "Thanks."

They headed out the door. Before he could make it to his car, Rachel shouted, "By the way, Dad says he hasn't seen you for a while. You should stop by and see him."

He glanced over at his sister as she got in her car and saw her smirk. She got along better with the old man than he did. He pushed thoughts of his father to the back of his mind and grinned as he thought of Gemma.

It was going to be their first official get-to-know-each-other date. She didn't know what he had planned, but she wanted to look her best. She finished her hair and cut the tags off the blouse and the new jeans Rachel bought her on their long-ago shopping trip. The temptation was there to call Rachel to help her get ready, but since they were trying to keep their relationship a secret she decided against it. Her nerves were getting the better of her. Things were different now since they both expressed how they felt about each other.

She finished dressing and peered at herself in the mirror. Thankfully, the bruise around her eye had begun to yellow so she didn't require any concealer to hide it. The new clothes weren't baggy, ill-fitting, or unflattering. The skinny jeans defined her shapely legs, and the blouse accentuated her breasts without being slutty. She stared into the mirror a bit longer. After so many years of trying to be inconspicuous, it had been a long time since she appraised her body. Hopefully, Alex would like her new look. She wanted him to find her desirable. Peeking out the window, she saw his car pull up. After slipping on her flats, she rushed out of her room, hoping to avoid another confrontation with Ms. Ramirez. Gemma threw open the front door just as Alex was about to knock.

"Wow! Someone's eager," Alex chuckled teasingly as his eyes roamed over her body not so subtlely.

"You look beautiful."

Gemma blushed as she shut the front door behind her. "Thank you, Alex."

They smiled at one another.

"Shall we?"

She nodded her head, and he placed his hand at the small of her back while they walked down the stairs to his car. Heat bloomed in her cheeks at his closeness as he ushered her to the car. He opened the door for her, and she slid inside. Once they were on their way they sat in comfortable silence as Alex drove. It felt nice just to be with him, not needing to talk.

Gemma's curiosity finally got the better of her.

"So, where are you taking me?"

Alex glanced at her and smirked before turning back to the road. "It's a surprise."

"You're not even going to give me a hint?" Gemma pouted.

"No," he laughed, and focused on the road. "Did I tell you how beautiful you look?"

Her happiness in his compliment beat out her shy nervousness and she beamed. His praise was giving her a confidence boost and making her feel bold. "Oh no, I know what you're trying to do. Attempting to flatter me by changing the subject."

Alex laughed. "Is it working?"

Giggling, she glanced at him out of the corner of her eye. "Maybe."

They both laughed softly and then grew quiet. After a couple of minutes, she noticed they were pulling up to the zoo.

Gemma turned to him with wide, expressive eyes. "Really?" She stared at the entrance of the zoo, excited.

Alex smiled even brighter, as he pulled the car into a parking space and put his arm over the back of her seat.

"I'm glad you're excited … I was afraid you'd think it was cheesy," he said nervously, not meeting her gaze, as he rubbed the back of his neck.

He finally looked up at her and saw the flush creeping across her cheeks. "Why do you look embarrassed?"

She bit her lip and looked out the passenger window before turning back to him. "I've never been to the zoo before." She dropped her eyes to her lap. Her cheeks were burning with embarrassment. Most kids visited the zoo a dozen times or more in their childhood, but Gemma had never been. None of her foster parents ever cared enough to do anything with her. They were usually dealing with a lot of kids; just in it for the government money they got each month. The few school trips where she might have visited the zoo saw her enjoying a hospital stay courtesy of a foster parent or sibling.

When Alex said nothing Gemma turned to him. She found him gazing at her with a small smile on his face.

"Why are you staring at me like that?"

"It makes me happy to get to share this first with you." Alex got out of the car, leaving Gemma sitting in the passenger seat looking at the spot he just vacated. The corner of her mouth lifted into a small smile. A short second later Alex was opening her door. She stepped out of the car, and they headed toward the entrance of the zoo.

Since it was a weekday, the zoo was not crowded. They slowly walked side-by-side checking out the animals, alternating between moments of conversation and companionable silence. After a lull in the previous conversation, Gemma looked over at Alex's profile. His eyes were downcast as he walked next to her with his hands stuffed deep in his pockets. She noticed that was a habit of his. As she studied his profile some more, she thought yet again, *No man has a right to be that handsome.* The curls on the back of his neck had her itching to thread her fingers through them. After admiring him for a minute longer, she asked, "Do you come to the zoo often?"

They stopped in front of the penguin habitat, and it was a moment before Alex answered her. He didn't look at her as he watched the penguins swim and play on the ice. Finally, he turned to her.

"I started coming here shortly after my wife died … I liked the company …"

Gemma looked at him with a confused expression.

"Animals can't talk back," he explained.

They shared a laugh, but she saw a faint sadness in his eyes. As he resumed his story, she saw his gaze drop to the floor.

"I was lonely … I had this house, and it was only me rattling around in these empty rooms … when I did bother to come home from the restaurant."

He paused in his story as he peeped at her. She was unable to hide the concern and sorrow in her eyes. Alex cleared his throat and looked away before continuing on.

"Everyone kept telling me to get a dog, but I was barely taking care of myself. Since I wasn't ready for a pet, I decided to come to the zoo. It was comforting. The animals just let me be."

She continued staring at him long after he stopped talking, as he looked through the glass at the penguins. All this time, she'd assumed that it was an ugly divorce, that his wife had cheated and broken his heart. She was right about the broken heart. Which explained why he was so reluctant to speak of her before, why everyone else only talked about her in hushed whispers. She wouldn't ask for details on how. It had already been painful for him to share she could tell. She couldn't imagine how much he must have hurt after his wife died, how much he may still hurt. She didn't want to pry, but somehow she wanted to comfort him like he did for her a couple of nights ago, so she moved closer to him. Her shoulder brushed his. They stood together staring at the frolicking penguins.

Alex looked at her with hooded eyes. He was thankful to her for just listening and not asking a bunch of questions. What a difference this woman was from his sister who could never seem to keep her mouth shut. Rachel could learn a thing or two from her. Sometimes people just wanted someone to listen. He slowly removed his hand from his pocket and let it fall to his side. His hand slightly brushed against hers. *Was that a spark?* He swallowed hard and then carefully grasped her hand in his. Her fingers curled around his. Their hands together felt so right wrapped around each other. His heartbeat quickened. He exhaled the breath he didn't realize he was holding.

They both smiled to themselves as they continued to watch the penguins. Alex stroked his thumb tenderly across the back of Gemma's hand. He didn't want to let her go.

After minutes of standing in silence and watching the penguins through the double-paned glass, they walked off still holding hands. Eventually, they resumed conversation as they continued to tour the exhibits. Alex pointed out his favorite animals as he alternated between stroking the back of her hand and using his finger to rub circles into her palm as they walked the zoo hands clasped.

Once they finished at the zoo, Alex had another surprise for her as he swung by a quaint café and bakery to pick up a picnic lunch. He drove them to the park and spread out a blanket. They ate and talked.

After a while of Alex once again talking about himself he wanted to know about her. Gemma was still laughing at something funny he'd said as he finished his story. He watched her with intensity as she held her hand to her stomach, laughing a full, throaty laugh. She wiped tears of mirth from her eyes as her laughter subsided. Alex stood up, brushing any remaining crumbs from his lap, then reached down and offered her his hands.

"Come with me."

She silently took his hands as he helped her to her feet. He guided them over to a swing set. She smiled at him when he motioned for her to sit on the swing, as he took the one next to her. They sat quietly together. Alex hadn't let her hand go, and the sight of their joined hands made him smile.

Finally, Alex spoke. "Tell me about you, Gemma." He looked into her face, seeing the trepidation there, and tried to reassure her.

"I want to know you, all of you. I know it's scary sharing the unpleasant parts of yourself, but I'm asking … as a man who is in serious like with you." He smiled warmly at her and squeezed her hand gently.

"Okay." She said shakily and looked away from him.

They swayed on the swings as Gemma recounted parts of her childhood to Alex as he listened intently. He could tell this was hard for her. Often, he would squeeze her hand in encouragement when she faltered or fell silent. He knew there were things she omitted or chose not to share. Hearing about some of the foster homes she endured made him livid. Despite hat, he couldn't help but be engrossed as she continued her story.

At the age of eight, an older boy named Ryan, one of the few foster siblings she grew close to, told her she reminded him of his younger sister he was separated from a few years ago. He became protective of her and would fend off their foster father for her as well as anyone else that tried to abuse her or attack her. Eventually he taught her how to fight so she could protect herself, since he knew it was inevitable that one day they would be separated.

When she got moved from the home, it came in handy since home after home she continued to fend off advances from either a foster father or foster brother, or had to defend herself against girls that wanted to disfigure her "pretty face" as they put it. She got labeled a problem child by the social workers because they had to move her so much, especially when the foster parents realized she wouldn't silently endure their abuse. Eventually, she learned how to go unnoticed, be nondescript. When she got booted from the system and had to survive on her own, she met Jason, her ex-husband.

"He said all the right things ... I was a young eighteen-year-old girl starving for love. I was going to try and go to community college. I had decent grades, but then he told me he wanted to take care of me." She looked at him with tears shining in her eyes. "No one had ever told me that before."

Alex saw not only the sorrow and regret swimming in her eyes but her raw vulnerability. He stroked his thumb over the back of her hand. Gemma looked away.

"I know it was stupid to believe that, but I didn't know any better. I thought I'd finally found someone who was going to love me forever. We got married at the courthouse, and as they say, the rest was history ... the honeymoon ended about a month later ..." She struggled with continuing on. She swallowed and wiped tears from her eyes.

Alex thought that maybe he'd pushed for too much too soon. He wasn't going to make her talk about her ex-husband. He rubbed her back.

"You don't have to talk anymore."

She nodded her head.

He looked at her with reverence. ,"I don't think you realize how strong you are."

Stunned, she lifted her eyes to meet his. Clearly, she hadn't expected to hear that come out of his mouth.

"You're resilient, Gemma. I've never met anyone like you."

"You mean a black, uneducated ex-con?" Gemma snorted.

He scooted closer to her. He had a serious expression on his face as he addressed her, rubbing her arm.

"Hey, don't do that. Don't demean yourself. Those things may be a part of what happened to you, but they don't make up who you are, they don't define you. You've been through a lot, and you're still standing." His eyes danced across her face, taking in her delicate features. Her rough life wasn't etched into the features of her face; she wore it in her eyes.

"You know what I see when I look at you?"

She shook her head.

Their eyes locked on each other. Alex raised his hand to her face and caressed her cheek. Gemma's eyes fluttered closed for a brief second as she felt his fingers lightly running over the contours of her face. Her skin felt flushed from his touch. When she opened her eyes again he was still staring at her.

"I see this strong but vulnerable woman who has been beaten up by life, yet refuses to let it break her spirit … I don't want to be just some guy, another jerk that uses and discards you. I want to know everything about you, Gemma Peyton, and I want to take my time … No matter how much you try to hide away, I see you …" His eyes roamed her face again. "And you're beautiful."

Without taking his eyes from hers, Alex stood from his swing and stepped closer to Gemma, pulling her up. Wrapping his arms around her, he drew her closer to his body for a deep, slow kiss. Gemma put her arms around his neck. He could feel her fingers stroking the curls at the nape of his neck as she passionately returned his kiss.

His arms wrapped around her waist tighter until there was no space left between their bodies. Slowly, he mastered her tongue and felt her moan softly into his mouth. He could drown in her mouth. Her lips tasted sweet, like honey. He didn't think he would ever have enough of her. His tongue trailed along her luscious bottom lip before he sucked it into his mouth and he felt her body tremble underneath his touch.

Gemma pulled away, breathless. Alex only allowed a fraction of space between them. He enjoyed the feel of her body pressed against his too much to let her go too far. "I've wanted to do that all day," he said, breathing heavily.

She chuckled softly and looked down briefly before meeting his gaze as she bit her lip. "Me too."

Alex leaned his forehead against hers. "I want to do that," he whispered in a husky voice.

"Do what?" Gemma asked breathily.

"Bite your lip," he said right before taking her bottom lip between his teeth and giving it a playful nip, before kissing her soundly on the mouth. Afterward, he pulled back to gaze at her.

He relaxed his hold on her but didn't let her go. Placing her hands on his shoulders, she leaned back slightly to gaze up at him. Gemma bit her lip again as her eyes perused his face.

"Stop biting your lip or I'll have to kiss you again."

Even though the light was fading from the sky, he knew he'd made her blush with that comment because she looked away from him with an embarrassed smile. He laughed softly.

"What's so funny?"

He paused in his laughter.

"You are! You're so cute and adorable with all your little nervous habits. I find it endearing." His fingers played with the ends of her hair.

"You do?" she asked disbelievingly before unconsciously biting her lip again.

Alex let out a bark of laughter and kissed her on the lips. He hugged her tightly against him, inhaling the intoxicating scent of coconut that lingered in her hair. Her arms encircled his waist a bit tighter, and he smiled. Gemma snuggled into Alex's embrace and pressed her face against his chest. They stood holding each other, just enjoying the moment.

Alex wished he could take away all the bad that happened in her life. He wanted to protect her and nurture her and show her that all people weren't bad. He wanted to give her what she lacked all her life, but knew that he needed to put to rest the skeletons plaguing him. As he held her in his arms, he felt the full weight of the wedding band he still wore. This relationship was going to get very crowded if he didn't put the other woman who resided in his heart to rest. He knew he needed to make his peace and move on so he could give himself fully to this, to her. Gemma deserved his all, not just a piece of him.

8

It was still twilight and dusk had yet to settle in. Subtle hues of pinks and oranges colored the sky. Alex had already dropped Gemma off at the halfway house. Their first official date would be something he'd never forget. He enjoyed their time together immensely; he felt relaxed and comfortable around her.

Now that he was alone, his thoughts drifted to Sam. Remembering the things he told himself while he was holding Gemma in his arms, he knew there was some place he needed to go.

He pulled into the cemetery and parked. It had been a while since he'd made the visit, but he needed to talk to her. He trudged to his wife's grave, his legs heavy with the weight of what he was about to do. Once he arrived at her gravesite, he stood looking at the weathered tombstone bearing his wife's epitaph. This was all that was left of her—the dates of her beginning and her end. He wiped dust and debris from the top of the tombstone.

Flopping down in front of the grave, he thought to himself, *I have to move on. Life is for the living.*

"Hey, Sam. I know what you're thinking … no flowers, that bastard." He gave a mirthless chuckle as he toyed with the unkempt grass. "Sorry, I hadn't planned to come here. I won't forget next time."

Tears gathered in his eyes, threatening to spill over. He knew the humor was for his benefit as the gravity of what he was about to say weighed on him. His voice broke as he spoke.

"I don't know how to do this, Sam. I don't know how to say good-bye …" His hands swiped at his face, trying to get rid of the tears.

"I met this woman. I think you'd like her. If you …" He could feel himself getting choked up. "If you were still alive … I think you would have befriended her." He tugged at more of the weeds that had cropped up.

"I don't want to feel like I'm betraying you, so I came here to tell you …" His voice cracked and broke. "I came here to tell you … I'm letting you go …" More tears slid down his cheeks. He wiped at them hurriedly.

"I want to see where things go with her. I think this could be something good, that her and I … that we … my feelings are strong for her, Sam." He stared at the tombstone with blurry eyes.

"I haven't felt like this since … since I first met you." He dropped his gaze to the patch of earth he'd been toying with and mumbled, "If that helps you understand." He gulped, swallowing the knot that formed in his throat, and swiped at his face, removing the tears again.

"I'm always gonna love you … but I've got to move on. I wanted to come by and tell you that … I just want you to be okay with this." He kissed his fingers and placed them gently on the tombstone. Sitting back, he stared at the grave a moment before finally standing up and heading back to his car, wiping his face as he went.

After leaving the cemetery, he decided to visit his father. Things had always been complicated between him and his father. Man of few words. After his mother passed of cancer when he was twelve, his father became more withdrawn. In his old age, he became a crotchety old man.

When he pulled up to the house, his father was tinkering with a car in the garage. As he saw the headlights he looked up from what he was doing. Alex made eye contact with him through the windshield before cutting the lights and shutting off the ignition. His father went back to what he was doing, and Alex let out a breath. Things were always awkward with his father. Pushing the car door open, he got out.

"Hey, old man." Alex approached his father.

"Hey, yourself ... Rachel must've told you I talked to her."

Alex didn't respond. Neither of them said anything for a while as his father continued working. Alex watched his father work the wrench under the hood of the older model car.

After minutes, his father glanced up at him again. "How are things at the restaurant?"

His father always asked this question.

"Things are good ... really good."

They stared at each other for a second before his father resumed toiling away on the car.

"Can you hand me that socket wrench over there?"

Bending down, he searched through the toolbox for the appropriate item and then handed it to him. His father went back to working on the vehicle without saying anything. Alex jammed his hands into his pockets and continued watching his dad. This silent indifference was why he didn't visit his father. It was always like this—an awkwardness that neither of them knew how to fill. It wasn't that Thomas Chambers was a bad father; he just didn't know how to be affectionate, especially after Mrs. Chambers passed away. It was like she took all of his warmth with her the day she died. Her slow death was hard on them all, but none more so than Thomas, whose light went out after watching his wife waste away from a long, arduous battle with breast cancer.

Alex understood how the old man felt. Being a man, who knew the loss of a wife, helped him understand his dad's behavior. He understood that self-preservation of wanting to revert inward and avoid any more pain of loving someone else who could so easily be lost. He looked at his father with knowing eyes. His father never knew it, but when he was a teenager, he had once caught him crying. His father never shed a tear at the funeral, but one night a few years after her death, he came in after his curfew, expecting to be scolded by his father and found him sitting on his mother's side of the bed holding her nightgown and weeping. It was the only display of emotion he had seen from his father after his mother died.

As he watched his father now, meticulously putting this car together, he knew his father ceased being amongst the living. He was close with Rachel because of their shared interests. Besides Rachel, Chloe, and his fishing buddy, Gus, Thomas really had no one else he interacted with.

Alex shook his head, trying to dislodge the thought that this was what he might become. As hard as his talk at the cemetery was, he knew it was necessary for him to put the past in the past and move forward. Suddenly, he decided to do something he'd never done before and attempt to have a real conversation with his father. Maybe it would do them both some good.

"So ... I met someone ..." He waited for his father's response.

Thomas tightened a screw before looking up and placing his hands on the car.

"Oh yeah?"

He could tell his father was uncomfortable, but he pressed on.

"Yeah, she's really … she's something …" He bit his lip as he toyed with his wedding band for a moment.

"Maybe … I can bring her by for dinner so you can meet her."

His father shuffled from one foot to the other. Using the rag he was holding to wipe off his hands, he came from around the car and stood in front of Alex.

"You want me to meet her?" his father questioned him, disbelievingly.

Alex couldn't read what was in his father's eyes.

"Yeah. Maybe I'll have Rachel and Chloe come, too … we can make it a family dinner?" he said as he gave his father a small smile.

His father ran his hands through his tousled gray hair.

"Umm, sure … that would be nice."

He saw a small hint of a smile on his father's face, but as quickly as it appeared, it disappeared, replaced by the gruff look he always seemed to wear.

"Should I dress up?"

Alex chuckled a bit.

"No, just be comfortable. It's going to be very informal."

He saw his father breathe a sigh of relief.

"Okay, well I better get going. Have to open the restaurant tomorrow."

Before he could step away, his father moved toward him and embraced him in an awkward hug. For a second, Alex was so taken aback by his father's gesture that his arms hung limply at his sides. Finally, he put his arms around his dad. A split second later his father quickly stepped away and looked down at the ground as he walked back to the car.

"Okay … I'll see you for dinner later this week."

Still a little surprised by his father's affection, Alex watched as he picked up the socket wrench and proceeded with his repairs. He couldn't remember the last time his father had hugged him.

The corner of his mouth lifted as he walked back to his car, got in, and drove away.

That night, Alex sat on the edge of the bed examining his wedding band. He slowly pulled the band off and held it between his thumb and forefinger. The weight of what he was about to do was not lost on him. The final link he allowed to tether him to Sam was about to be severed. After taking one last glimpse at the ring, he opened his nightstand and placed it inside. He shut the drawer and stared at it, tempted to yank the ring back out.

Am I really moving on? He rubbed his finger. It felt weird. He was torn between the heaviness and loss of Sam that wearing the ring represented, and the lightness and absence of no longer wearing the ring that represented his future with Gemma. Those conflicted emotions tormented him as he stared at the drawer. There was a part of him that wanted to hold onto the past. After a few minutes, he hastily turned off the lamp and slipped beneath the covers. He wrestled a bit more with his decision before finally falling asleep.

Gemma woke up in the morning with a big smile on her face. Finally kissing Alex was everything she thought it would be. The way he'd listened to her and encouraged her to talk was therapeutic, but also made her feel closer to him. The level of intimacy they shared last night was unlike anything she'd ever experienced before, and it had nothing to do with sex. It was crazy how connected she felt to him already. Smiling to herself, she went about her room tidying up.

She was expecting Shelby any minute. As if on cue, the doorbell rang, but before she could even leave her room, she heard Ms. Ramirez answer the door. The sounds of a muffled conversation floated up to her and then the sounds of footsteps ascending the stairs. Gemma had already opened her bedroom door. Shelby knocked on the open door and waited for Gemma to grant her entrance. They exchanged pleasantries and then Shelby got to work inspecting Gemma's room. Afterward, she instructed Gemma to pee into a cup for the drug test. Shelby was collecting her stuff to leave when she stopped and turned back to Gemma.

"Listen … I'm only saying this because I care about what happens to you. It's just I've seen a lot of women get out and get caught up with some guy, and they end up back inside … I'm not saying that's what's going to happen to you … just, be careful."

Gemma folded her arms across her chest. The expression on her face was a mixture of annoyance and anger. "Alex is a good man."

Shelby nodded her head. "Yes, he is."

The two women stood staring at each other. Gemma knew this woman was only looking out for her best interest, but she couldn't help but be irritated at the same time. It was hard not to feel like Shelby crossed the line.

"I appreciate your concern," Gemma pensively replied as she averted her gaze.

The awkward silence hung between the two women.

"Okay … I'll see you next time."

Gemma didn't respond. Shelby opened her mouth to speak again but thought better of it.

After Shelby left, Gemma felt as if a storm cloud was hanging over her head. Shelby's words were like having a bucket of cold water thrown on her. The feelings she woke up with this morning were now a distant memory.

Things were different with Alex. It wasn't like she instantly went to bed with him; the way she had done with Jason, wanting to prove she was worthy. They were taking things slow, getting to know each other. Gemma knew she didn't have a ton of experience in relationships—Jason being her only serious relationship—but that didn't mean she was incapable of knowing whether she was ready for this or not.

Damn it! Now Shelby had her head a jumbled mess. *Maybe I'm not ready. Maybe this is too soon.* She didn't want to second-guess herself. Gemma sullenly got ready for work, deciding to head in early so she could talk to Alex.

When Gemma arrived at the restaurant, Alex opened the door, happy to have her there so early.

"I was hoping to see you before the madhouse started." He gave her a glorious smile and pulled her into a tight hug. Relaxing into his body, she hugged his waist tightly, his nearness putting her in a bit of a better mood than when she arrived.

"I'm happy to see you, too." She said against his chest as she tried to hide the forlornness she felt.

Suddenly, she felt him pull her away from his body.

"Something's wrong." He said as he scrutinized her face looking for answers.

She shook her head and didn't meet his gaze. *How can he read me so well already?*

He tilted her chin up to look at him.

"Tell me." He kept searching her face.

"It's nothing," Gemma said, lowering her lashes to mask the look in her eyes.

Alex expelled a breath.

"Please talk to me, Gemma."

There was silence as neither spoke. Gemma was hoping he would drop the matter. She lifted her lashes to look back in his eyes and saw the worry written there. As flashes of his playfulness and his kisses flooded her mind, she bit her lip. Not wanting to see the troubled expression on his face, she briefly shut her eyes.

"Shelby warned me to be careful …"

Nodding knowingly, he grimaced at her. "Kind of put a damper on your good mood."

"That woman can be a bit of a buzzkill." He added.

His hand came up and caressed her cheek. "She gave me the same warning the morning after your attack."

She let out a small sigh as he continued rubbing her cheek and his smile reached his eyes this time as he looked at her. She gave him a genuine smile in return.

"Promise me something, Gemma?"

She nodded her head, waiting for what he was about to say.

"Promise me we won't have any secrets from each other. I don't want to build a relationship on lies or mistrust. I want us always to be able to talk to one another. I don't want you to be afraid to come to me about anything."

He tucked her hair behind her ear as he gazed down at her.

"Okay, Alex."

When she smiled up at him, he leaned down and kissed her.

She pulled away first with a question on her lips. "You don't think things are moving too quickly between us?"

This time she didn't bother trying to hide the uncertainty swimming in her eyes. She was furious with Shelby.

"Does it feel right between us, Gemma? Only you can know that. I can't answer that for you." He peered at her anxiously.

He was right. It was stupid of her to let Shelby get in her head. Nothing felt wrong when she was with Alex. She wasn't going to let anyone get in the way of her happiness again.

Decision made, she abruptly rose on her toes and put her arms around Alex and kissed him intensely. She felt his smile against her mouth as he wrapped his arms around her, kissing her back.

"Since you're here early do you want to help me make some pasta?" he asked, smiling down at her as they pulled apart.

"I don't know how," she giggled, running her tongue across her lip, savoring their kiss.

His eyes dropped to her lips once more before he put on the silly Italian accent he used the other night when he brought dinner over to her.

"Well, you are in luck, mia cara, because I am an excellent teacher."

Gemma laughed harder as they walked hand-in-hand toward the kitchen.

When they arrived in the kitchen, Alex left her side to gather the flour and other ingredients they needed to make the pasta dough. She observed him as he was in his element, talking her through the process. She could see his love for cooking while he gently kneaded the dough. He placed a pile of the gooey mass in front of her. After a few minutes, he saw her struggling and came to help her. Stepping behind her, he placed his hands over her hands.

"You have to be gentle when kneading the dough. You don't want to overwork it."

She could feel his chest against her back as his hands helped her correctly form the dough. Her face flushed, and she grew warm. She wanted to lean back into him but found herself rigidly standing as far away from him as she could. She knew she was a little afraid of how strong her feelings were for him. When she looked down at their conjoined hands, she noticed for the first time he no longer wore his wedding band. *What does that mean?* She smiled a little to herself but felt nervous at the implication of his bare finger. *Should I let him mention it first? How do I broach something like that?* 'I see you stopped wearing your wedding band' just didn't seem like the proper etiquette. Yeah, she'd let him bring it up first.

Alex was unaware of what the effect of being this close to her would do to his body. While he'd held her closely as they kissed, this was different. The minute his hands made contact with hers and he pressed himself against her body he became aroused. He was sure she could feel him growing against her. He looked down at her profile and saw the splotch of her blushes on the apple of her cheek. He smirked a little, enjoying her response to him despite her obvious discomfort.

Leaning down, Alex kissed her cheek. He felt her body relax into his and took that as a sign that he was okay to go further.

He began to place slow, soft kisses down her cheek, then her jaw, until he reached her neck. He could feel the pulse of her heartbeat in her throat, and he smiled to himself, knowing her heart was racing. Alex nuzzled her playfully before lapping at the skin on her neck. Gemma pressed back into him even more, and he completely forgot about the dough; wrapping his hands around her waist, he gave her open-mouthed kisses on the silky skin of her neck. He heard her moan and delighted in the pleasure he knew he was bringing her.

Suddenly, Alex spun her around to face him, no longer content to just kiss her neck. His hands grasped her face as he crashed into her mouth. He sucked her tongue and nipped at her lips before kissing her with abandon. Gemma grabbed at his waist, pulling his pelvis into her body, and Alex groaned into her mouth as they rubbed against each other.

He loved that she was so responsive. Gone was the timidity and shyness; she wanted him as much as he wanted her. Alex desired to be closer still. He cupped her buttocks and lifted her onto the countertop. Nudging her thighs apart, he stepped between her legs and rubbed himself against her. Even fully clothed he could feel the heat emanating from her center. It had been a long time since he'd been with a woman.

They were kissing each other feverishly, and Gemma had her legs wrapped around his waist. Neither had come up for air when someone knocking on the door interrupted their make-out session. It took a minute for recognition to blanket them. Reluctantly, they pulled apart, both breathing heavily as they adjusted their clothing. Alex was in a daze as he looked at Gemma's swollen lips. They were bee-stung from all their kissing. *Damn!* She looked sexy sitting there breathless and aroused. He moved toward her, ready to resume their kiss fest.

Gemma's laugh was sultry as she pushed against his chest, murmuring, "Alex … the rest of the staff is here."

He blinked and shook his head to clear it of the lust filled haze. *Oh yeah, right, that's who was knocking.* He gave her a sly grin as he peered into her eyes, placing his hands on either side of her on the counter.

"I got a little carried away."

Biting her lip, she nodded. "We both did," she said huskily.

Neither said a word for a minute as they stared at each other, the knocking resuming in its intensity.

With a half-smile, Alex hung his head. "I guess I better let everyone in."

Gemma nodded and gave him a wistful smile. He helped her down off the counter but pulled her in for another quick kiss before relinquishing her. As he let her go, he saw her touch her lips and smile before heading into the dinging room. He exhaled as he followed her.

That night they could barely keep their eyes off one another. Alex watched her from the kitchen while he cooked and joked around with the staff. As Gemma weaved her way in and out of the diners, taking orders and refilling drinks, she made eyes with Alex regularly. All either could think about was when the dinner service would end.

9

The night didn't pass quickly enough. Once all the customers left for the evening, everyone started cleaning as usual. While Alex was cleaning, he saw Brandon approach Gemma, and he felt a sudden prick of jealousy. He went back to the task he was doing, but kept a watchful eye on them.

Gemma was wiping down a table when someone tapped her on the shoulder. She turned around to find Brandon.

"Hey, Gemma."

Gemma fiddled with the rag in her hand as she responded, "Hi, Brandon."

She saw the concern on his face.

"I just wanted to say I'm happy that you're okay …"

As Brandon's eyes regarded her, Gemma was reminded her face still showed hints of her ordeal, and touched her cheek self-consciously. When everyone arrived earlier they were happy to see her and see she was okay.

"When I heard what happened to you, I was angry."

Gemma glanced over his shoulder and saw Alex discreetly watching them. She turned her attention back to Brandon as he continued speaking.

"I know Alex said he doesn't want the women heading home unescorted, so I wanted to offer you a ride home."

She saw the hopeful expression on Brandon's face and felt bad about having to let him down. She bit her lip.

"I'm sorry, Brandon, I already have a ride home ..." The hurt look on his face didn't go unnoticed.

"Maybe another night?" Placing her hand on his, she gave him a small smile. When she saw his face light up she was concerned she may have given him false hope. She was trying to assuage her own guilt at turning him down, not make him believe there was a chance. Brandon was a sweet guy, but he was delusional if he thought anything would ever transpire between the two of them. Quickly, she drew back her hand.

Brandon smiled warmly at her.

"Great ... I need to get back to the kitchen before chef has my ass."

They shared a brief laugh before he headed back to the kitchen.

As they got to work cleaning the kitchen, Alex overheard Brandon talking to some of their co-workers. "Imma be in there, dude. I know she's feeling me."

Alex could only roll his eyes and shake his head. He'd let Brandon have his little fantasy.

Wiping down the same countertop that he and Gemma used earlier for their make out session, he smirked to himself remembering the feel of her in his arms, her legs wrapped around his waist. He began to wonder what it would feel like to hold her naked. His member stiffened at the thought, and he readjusted himself. No more of those thoughts right now or he'd be in trouble.

Out in the dining room, Gemma wasn't faring much better. Now that she was no longer dealing with memorizing orders or having to listen to the idle chatter of patrons her mind was remembering this afternoon. She felt her face and body heat up at the memory of Alex's onslaught of kisses. Not wanting to explain herself, she ducked her head to avoid any of her co-workers seeing how hot and bothered she was becoming.

At the end of the night, everyone headed to their cars. Thankfully, everyone was laughing and talking so loudly as they all exited, no one noticed her quickly get into Alex's car.

While they drove toward his house, they both were aware of the sexual tension between them. Gemma began to laugh.

"What's so funny?" Alex asked as he turned his attention to her as they sat at the light.

"Your face when Brandon started talking to me earlier tonight."

Things lightened up as they both laughed.

"Well, I'm not jealous of Brandon if that's what you're saying." He tried to hide the smile that appeared after he said the words. It wasn't jealousy so much as it was the way that Brandon thought of her as just another conquest, another notch on his belt. She was so much more than that to him.

Gemma giggled. "Right," she said sarcastically, arching a brow. "Brandon's harmless … you know that, right?"

He smirked as he kept his attention on the road. "Yeah, I know."

Without needing to say it, they ended up at his house. They both knew they wanted to finish what they started earlier in the kitchen at the restaurant.

As soon as they hit the door to his house they were all over each other. Gemma hurriedly pushed his jacket down his shoulders. After yanking his jacket off, he resumed groping her. They both fumbled with her coat as they headed toward the living room; limbs entangled and lips locked together. After they discarded her coat, he picked her up. She wrapped her legs around him, and they stood in the middle of the room kissing passionately. Alex's hand rubbed up and down her back, while his other hand cradled her backside in his palm. Gemma moaned softly into his mouth as they kissed.

Changing position, he cupped her ass in his hands as he maneuvered them toward the sofa so he could lay her down. They finally came up for air when he laid her against the throw pillows. He followed her body, resting between her legs, which still clung to his waist. It was his turn to groan as he felt the heat emanating from the juncture of her thighs where his dick was seeking refuge. He was straining against his pants. He rubbed himself against her, wanting her badly.

His voice dripped with sexual frustration when he finally spoke. "I know we said we were going to take things slow …" He licked his lips as his eyes devoured her face. "But I'm having a hard time with that."

Gemma quivered beneath him. He was definitely having a hard time; she could feel it. She saw the raw lust in his eyes and felt his body vibrating with it. If she was honest with herself, she felt the same way. Her hungry eyes searched his face, and she licked at dry lips, not realizing the torture she was putting him through.

"Don't do that," he breathed out raggedly as his eyes stared transfixed at her mouth.

Gemma was confused. "Do what?"

Alex softly chuckled as he rested his forehead against hers. He loved that she was so unaware of how sexy she was. "Nothing."

He slid off of Gemma to lay behind her, pulled her into his body, spooning her. For some reason, he wasn't ready to ravish her. He wanted her, boy did he want her, but he wanted their first time together to be unforgettable. The way he was feeling right now, he would end up fucking her. There would be time for that when they were familiar with each other's bodies, but he wanted to cherish Gemma the first time they had sex. He didn't want to treat her the way the men in her past treated her. Truth be told, he wanted to obliterate the thought of anyone else before him. He wanted to savor her body all night long.

He pulled her tighter and mumbled, "I have to learn how to control myself around you."

She giggled and couldn't help sighing contentedly. She liked that she had that effect on him. His still throbbing manhood pressed against her, and she wondered what made him stop. Rolling onto her back, she peered up at him. Alex's arm was draped across her waist. He used her new position to reach his hand underneath her shirt. His fingers rubbed drugging circles into the flesh on her side and stomach. She could feel the heat of his gaze as he watched the effect his fingers had on her bare skin. Her lashes fell to her cheeks to mask her desire. When she opened them again, she found him staring at her with such unchecked, raw sexuality it frightened her, and she blurted out the first thing that came to mind.

"I noticed earlier you weren't wearing your wedding band anymore."

Did I really just say that? She felt herself panic inside. She was supposed to let him bring it up. If it wouldn't make her faux pas even more noticeable, she would slap her forehead right about now. Well, she most certainly killed the mood now. She swallowed hard as she stared up at him, waiting to hear his response. Alex didn't seem fazed by her question as he continued rubbing his fingers lightly over her skin as he pondered her statement.

He gave her the full weight of his gaze when he replied, "What kind of man would I be if I brought another woman into the relationship we're trying to start? It wouldn't be fair to you, Gemma ... and you deserve better than that."

For a moment, she couldn't speak. She didn't know what to say to that. *How does he always say the perfect thing?* Sometimes it sounded too good to be true. He seemed too good to be true. She didn't want her negative thinking to ruin their time together.

Leaning down, Alex kissed her lightly on the lips.

"I should get you home," he murmured as he studied her while brushing strands of her hair away from her face.

Gemma searched for a clock and saw how late it was. "Yes, I should get home."

Alex laughed, "Gee, thanks a lot. You're so eager to get away."

She giggled softly. "It's not that ..." She turned to face him, curling her body into his. Feeling his fingers trail from her side to her back, stroking the bare flesh at the base of her spine, she shivered. "I just don't want Shelby to think you're a bad influence on me if I don't turn up at the boarding house."

They both laughed heartily at that. As their laughter subsided Alex spoke,

"You're right. Who knows what Shelby would say if I didn't get you home tonight. Although, I don't mind being a bad influence on you." His voice grew husky with his last statement.

Gemma softly chuckled as she leaned into his body, loving the feel of his hand caressing her. She wished she could stay here, stay the night. As her ear rested against his chest, she felt the rumble of his voice when he gently spoke to her. She loved the timbre and pitch of his voice, the richness of it. She enjoyed resting against him like this so she could feel the sound of his voice as it exited his body.

"I think I'm going to have to kidnap you ..."

"Oh," she said in an amused tone.

His fingers grazed her skin. She liked that he couldn't seem to stop touching her.

"I know you can't stay tonight, but I want you to." He sighed as he kissed her forehead, snuggling her closer to him.

She wanted to stay with him, too.

"Maybe we can have a slumber party tomorrow night."

Gemma felt his body shake with laughter, and she smiled to herself.

"A slumber party?" Alex asked as he continued to chuckle.

"Yes," she said sheepishly. "I always heard about them as a kid, but I never got invited to one. I thought it might be kind of nice to ... have one with you." She looked down to avoid eye contact as she fidgeted with the buttons on his shirt. Her cheeks burned with embarrassment. *I'm such a dope. Why did I say that?*

"I'd like that," he said as he lifted her chin, so he was staring into her eyes. Alex sported a goofy grin as he caressed her cheek.

They stayed like that a while longer before she felt him let go of her and get up from the couch. He straddled her, placing a foot on the ground to stand up.

"We don't have to be in such a hurry, Alex."

She missed the warmth of his arms.

"Oh really? Now look who's not so eager to go home," he jested.

Gemma laughed and smacked his arm playfully.

"The quicker I get you home, the quicker tomorrow will get here and then we can have our slumber party." He gave her an easy smile as he offered his hand for her to take so he could pull her up.

She let him haul her up from the couch. He didn't let her go right away, holding her in his embrace. They lingered in the embrace a moment longer.

"Let's get you home." He planted a kiss on her hair and took her hand, picking up her coat and purse on their path to the door.

In the car, Alex played the radio softly. He rested his hand on her knee as he drove her home. Gemma placed her hand over his as they rode in silence. As her hand lightly traced the veins on Alex's hand, she couldn't help but feel trepidation at how close she felt to this man. In her life, she'd never felt what she felt for him. The way he made her feel was incredible.

It was in the quiet moments like now when she had time to think, that her feelings overwhelmed her, frightened her even. A small part of her cried out for her to slow down, but a bigger part of her longed to plunge headfirst into whatever this was, to drown in this feeling. But wasn't this why Shelby kept issuing her warnings? *Damn Shelby for getting into my head!*

If she was honest with herself, though, it wasn't just Shelby that was warning her against the accelerated pace this relationship was taking. Deep down, the inner voice that protected her for so long and kept everyone out was pleading with her to pump the brakes. She subtly looked at their hands, then back out the window. Her life had consisted of nothing but one ugly situation after another, so maybe life was finally handing her some happy. She didn't want to waste her happy being doubtful and fearful that everything, every person was going to hurt her. She squeezed Alex's hand.

Once they pulled up in front of the house, they sat in silence for a moment.

Alex grinned. "By the way, I almost forgot to mention that I told my dad I wanted you to meet him."

Gemma was shocked. "You do?"

Alex snickered. "Your eyes got so big when I said that."

Gemma wasn't laughing with him.

Unbuckling his seatbelt, he slid closer to her, then unbuckled her seatbelt and removed the strap from her body. Alex pulled her onto his lap; happy she wasn't putting up a fight despite the hesitant expression on her face. He stared at her intently before speaking.

"Remember what we discussed earlier? We said we were going to be honest with each other."

Biting her lip, Gemma nodded her head. Alex watched her and couldn't help but smile a little at the gesture. He rubbed her leg.

"Hey, c'mon. Talk to me. You can't be nervous about meeting my dad. He may be a cantankerous old man, but I promise he's not scary." He chuckled again as he took her hand, rubbing his thumb in circles over the back of it.

She turned her face up, toward him. "It's just wow, I can't believe you want me to meet your dad … already. Isn't that usually when things are serious?"

"Aren't we serious?" Alex stared into her eyes wearing a serious expression.

She fidgeted a bit as she responded, "I just meant that ... are you sure we're not moving too quickly?" She leaned into him as she looked up at him questioningly, her lips pursed.

Even in her uncertainty, she was still gorgeous to him. He pushed her hair behind her ear as he watched her. With all she'd been through in her life he could understand her wanting to be sure about this. He could understand her needing reassurance that the good thing they had going wasn't going to fizzle out into just another bad event in her life that she would have to overcome.

"I know you're scared. I'll tell you a secret ..." He leaned into her and whispered, "I'm scared, too."

There was silence between them as he let what he said sink in.

"I haven't cared about anyone since Sam died and I certainly never expected to feel as strongly as I do ..." Alex looked at her full on as he continued, "Before you came along I wasn't living, Gemma. I was just here. What we've been given is a gift, and as scary as these feelings are, I'm not going to waste this second chance ..." He held her gaze.

"Don't you want to be happy, Gemma?"

Tears sprung up in her eyes.

"Yes," she said tremulously.

Alex caressed her cheeks as he held her face in his hands. "You deserve happiness, Gemma. I know these feelings are intense and scary, and I know you want to question it and doubt it … hell, normally I would do the same, but this just feels so right … I'm falling for you, Gemma."

The tears fell down her cheeks in quick succession, but she gave him a big smile.

"So I'm asking you to fall with me. Let's fall together and see where we land?"

After a small pause she spoke.

"Okay."

His thumbs rubbed away her tears. Cupping his face in her hands, she pulled him in for a kiss.

After a few moments, Alex pulled back and smiled at her.

"So … dinner tomorrow. With my dad, he's a bit of a crotchety old man, but he's harmless … and also Rachel and Chloe …" He smirked at her, reading her mind.

"I know, I know. I hadn't mentioned them earlier, but you know Rachel and my niece is dying to meet you. It'll be fun, I promise." He kissed her quickly to silence her before she could speak.

"Then we can have our slumber party."

The blush that crept across her cheeks didn't go unnoticed when he mentioned the slumber party.

He smiled warmly at her. "I'm very much looking forward to our slumber party."

Gemma giggled. "I bet you are."

When she rubbed his cheek, he leaned into her hand and closed his eyes for a second, enjoying being touched by her. Turning his head, he kissed her palm.

"You should probably head inside. I don't want Ms. Ramirez narcing on you to Shelby."

They shared a laugh, and he kissed her once more. They got a little carried away, but finally, pulled apart. Gemma finally made it out of the car. Before heading into the house he saw her look back and smile. He placed his hand over his heart and smiled back.

Once she got inside to her room, she thought about what he said in the car. She was falling for him, too. The physical part was always the easiest part, but she was entering into new territory with the level of intimacy she was sharing with Alex. They had yet to sleep together, but he knew her so well. He knew her thoughts, and seemed to be in tune with her emotions. It was scary. She'd never had that connection with someone before. She smiled to herself, remembering his words: *"So I'm asking you to fall with me. Let's fall together and see where we land?"* She'd fall with him, but she hoped he would be waiting below to catch her.

God, please don't let this be a long, hard fall that could eventually break me.

10

She was nervous about meeting Alex's father and even his niece. The experience of meeting the family was new to her. Jason never had any family for her to meet and his constant barrage of no-good friends weren't worth her making a good impression. She fidgeted in front of the mirror yet again. It was an expense, but she wanted to look nice, so she purchased a dress. It was a casual dress, but at least she now had a sense of putting her best foot forward to meet Alex's people. Alex never had to worry about feeling the way she was feeling right now because she had no people for him to meet. Smoothing down the front of the dress, she turned left then right, giving herself another once over. Finally satisfied, she grabbed her coat and headed downstairs, encountering Ms. Ramirez on the way.

"Ah, Gemma, you look lovely."

Gemma lowered her eyes but smiled warmly at the older woman even though she was embarrassed by the compliment. She did enjoy the compliments she'd been receiving lately, but the attention made her uncomfortable.

"Thank you."

Gemma decided to wait out on the porch to avoid any more questions, comments, or glances from Ms. Ramirez. She found the woman sweet, yet nosy.

It was a bit chilly, but she fought the urge to put on her coat, wanting Alex to get the full effect of the dress before she covered it. Up the road, she finally saw his car approach. She came down the walk as he pulled up to the curb. Alex quickly hopped out and came around the car to her. His eyes trailed up and down her body, taking in her beauty.

"You look …" He finally met her eyes and smiled warmly at her. "You captivate me, Gemma."

Without warning, he grabbed her face and stepped in close as he kissed her with abandon. It took her a second to catch up and then she put her hands around his waist, pulling him in closer. They stayed locked in their passionate embrace for a minute before he released her.

They were both breathless as they remembered they still had dinner to get through before they could begin their "slumber party."

"We should go." He said.

They both got in the car and tried to calm the sexual heat that was leaping between them before they got to his father's house.

As they stepped out of the car, Gemma was engulfed in nervousness, her sexual tension long forgotten. Alex grabbed the bag of groceries for the dinner from the car before taking her hand. He started walking toward the house when she pulled him back.

"Wait."

When he looked back at her she knew she probably resembled a baby deer staring down a loaded gun, but she couldn't help the fear she felt. She blurted the first thing that popped into her head.

"What if your father has a problem with me being black?" She bit her lip as her anxiousness got the better of her.

Setting the bag on the ground, Alex cupped her face in his hands and tried to reassure her.

"Hey, hey, it's gonna be okay. My father isn't going to care that you're black. I promise. He's gonna love you. Rachel already loves you and Chloe loves everybody ..."

"How do you know? You said he was a crotchety, old man." Hopefully, her voice didn't sound whiny.

He chuckled, and Gemma felt a little of the tension leave her body.

"I know because Rachel dated a couple of black guys when she was dating. My father didn't run them off or seem to have a problem. The biggest reason why he wouldn't care is because, Gus, his best friend is black. I don't think Gus would take to kindly to him having an issue with the race of the dates his children brought home." He said with a smile as he rubbed her cheek.

"There's nothing to fear." He kissed her nose lightly. "C'mon ... the walk of death awaits," Alex said in a sinister voice before erupting into laughter.

Gemma punched him in the arm, unable to suppress her giggles. "That's not funny, Alex." She punched him again.

Alex kept laughing. "Hey, it got you to relax, didn't it?"

Smiling at him, she took his hand again. "Yes ..."

"Okay, let's go inside before I lose my nerve."

They walked inside, and Chloe hurled herself at Alex.

"Uncle Alex!"

"Whoa, kiddo!"

Alex dropped the bag of groceries and started tickling his niece. They finally stopped their playfulness, and he introduced his niece to Gemma.

"Gemma, I would like to introduce you to my niece." Alex tickled her again, and Chloe tried to slap his hand away as she giggled.

"Stop, Uncle Alex!"

She held out her hand to Gemma. "I'm so happy to meet Uncle Alex's girlfriend. I'm Chloe."

Gemma took her hand and felt the heat rise in her cheeks at Chloe calling her Alex's girlfriend. *Is he okay with that? With labels being put on whatever this is?* Alex caught her eye and winked at her.

She looked down at his niece. "Pleased to meet you, Chloe."

"You're really pretty."

Gemma rubbed the back of her neck and bit her lip before politely stammering, "Th-thank you."

Grabbing Gemma's hand, Alex smiled at her as he led her into the kitchen with Chloe close on their heels.

They found his father and Rachel sitting in the kitchen sipping Michelob beers. Upon seeing Gemma, his father stood up from his chair. He smoothed down his hair as he waited for his introduction.

Alex sat the bag of groceries on the counter and then gave Rachel a hug and his father a nod before pulling Gemma forward to present her.

"Dad, this is Gemma, the young woman I was telling you about."

Taking her hand in between both of his, he greeted her, "Very nice to meet you." He nodded his head as he appraised her. "What's your last name, hon? You look familiar."

Her smile faltered a bit before she put it back into place. "It's Gemma … Gemma Peyton, but … I'm fairly new to town. I haven't lived here very long."

Over his father's shoulder she saw Alex cut his eye over to Rachel, and she shrugged and mouthed to him that she said nothing about Gemma being an ex-con. Mr. Chambers nodded his head, continuing to shake her hand.

He chuckled before responding, "Forgive an old man, you look like someone I've seen before. Maybe you remind me of someone from TV … you're very beautiful, Gemma."

She smiled, trying not to look uncomfortable. She wasn't use to so many compliments.

Alex cleared his throat and said good-naturedly, "Okay Dad, why don't you give Gemma back her hand."

They all shared a laugh as Mr. Chambers released her hand. Rachel came over and hugged Gemma and led her to the refrigerator to see what she wanted to drink.

Although he was trying to be discreet, she overheard Alex approach his father and say in a low tone, "What was that all about?"

Mr. Chambers shook his head, a little puzzled. "Nothing, son. I just thought she looked familiar is all ... she's a stunning young woman."

Alex patted his dad on the back before turning to the counter and rolling up his sleeves.

"So who is going to be my sous chef tonight?"

"Me, Uncle Alex!"

Chloe attached herself to his side, seeming eager as she checked out his ingredients. "What are we making?"

Rachel and Gemma sat at the kitchen table with Mr. Chambers after retrieving their drinks and laughed as Alex started using his bad Italian accent to tell Chloe what they were cooking.

Dinner preparation had Alex and Chloe making everyone laugh at their silly antics in the kitchen. Gemma was fully relaxed and enjoying herself. She wiped tears of mirth out of her eyes as she heard the end of a tale about Alex as a young boy from his father. Blushes suffused Alex's cheeks as he chopped up vegetables for the salad.

"Okay, okay, enough stories. I think we're just about ready to eat." He winked at Gemma good-naturedly and asked Rachel to set the table.

The conversation and wine flowed at the dinner table as Mr. Chambers continued to regale her with embarrassing stories of Alex's teen years ... much to his chagrin. Alex was a good sport about it all, even when his father and sister dragged out the childhood photos. She noticed that some of the pictures containing his mother made the family grow quiet. They all still mourned her she could tell. It hurt her heart to see how much this woman was loved even in death. No one had ever loved her like that. She hoped to break the family out of the sorrow that had descended upon them by picking up a naked baby picture of Alex.

"So, what's the story behind this one?"

They all began to laugh again as that prompted Rachel to tell another story about her brother.

At the end of the night, Rachel wouldn't let her come near the sink to help wash dishes, insisting that she and Chloe would clean up.

As they said their good-byes, Rachel hugged her tightly and whispered in her ear, "You brought my brother back to life ... I see it in his eyes. Thank you."

As they pulled apart, she saw Rachel wipe away a tear, and she swallowed back her reply past the lump in her throat. She settled for nodding her head to Rachel and turned away to hug Chloe before she started to cry. If Rachel only knew it was the other way around. Alex was helping her to live again.

The car ride to his house was quiet at first. After a few minutes, she felt his hand on her leg, his thumb rubbing the skin over her knee. She turned to him. "I enjoyed dinner so much, Alex. You have a wonderful family."

He lazily smiled as he watched the road. "I told you they would love you."

As they approached the light, he turned to her. "It's been a long time since I've seen my old man say more than a few words. He was trying hard to impress you. I think you have a new admirer."

"I liked him a lot, too … and Chloe was very sweet. She worships you." She ran her hand through her hair, giving him a shy smile.

"I'm her favorite uncle," he said, pulling through the light with a smirk.

"You're her only uncle," she giggled as she rested her hand on his hand that covered her leg.

Once they arrived at his house, the nervous, sexual energy returned. As they made their way into his home, Gemma realized that it had been years since she had sex. Another thought occurred to her: she couldn't remember doing it with someone she cared about. Very quickly the nervous, sexual energy fizzled out. The first time with Jason hadn't been entirely horrible, but she almost had no recollection of it being good with him. After being brutalized by him so many times, she couldn't remember the act of sex ever being pleasant for her. A shiver ran up her spine, and she clutched her arms over her chest as she stepped over the threshold into Alex's house. Unaware, that he noticed the shift as he flipped on the light.

"Are you cold?"

"No, I'm okay." She said in a small voice.

She walked on shaky legs toward the sofa and sat down. Alex wasn't like that. He wasn't Jason. She had to banish these thoughts or she'd ruin tonight.

Why am I scared now?

He had been so gentle with her. They kissed. He'd held her. She knew he wasn't capable of the things that Jason had done … *Right?* All men seemed nice and kind, gentle even, at the beginning, but could just as quickly morph into monsters. She'd seen it and been on the receiving end of a sheep revealing himself to be a wolf. She peeked at him from underneath her lashes as he moved about the room, closing curtains and flipping on lights, then he walked into the kitchen. It was just nerves talking. She looked down at her shaking hands.

What if after everything she suffered at the hands of her ex-husband, she didn't even like sex? Where would that leave the two of them? It wasn't just the fear that he would hurt her or that it would be unpleasant, but she feared not being good in bed. *What if I'm horrible? He won't want to keep dating me.* She hated that a small part of her had this need to please. After the little bit of time they'd shared together, she'd come to care for him and would be devastated if he cast her away for being inadequate. Her ex-husband's voice echoed in her head telling her she was no good. *Alex's not like that, he's a good man.* Her hands trembled as all the different thoughts swirled around in her head.

Something was wrong. Alex unloaded the dishwasher as he thought. He was giving Gemma some space. She got spooked by something, but he didn't know what. Glancing over his shoulder, he saw her huddled in a corner on the sofa. *Did I do something wrong? Did Rachel or my father say something before we left?* No, that couldn't be it because she was fine in the car. *What has her scared and apprehensive?* He put some plates in the cabinet and went to reach for a glass when the light bulb went off. *How could I be so stupid?* He sighed. *How could I be such an idiot?*

What a fool he'd been to think they would come to his house and just fall into the sack after all the trauma she'd endured at the hands of her ex-husband. No wonder she was shaking like a leaf. She was terrified. He felt like an ass. He didn't want her to think that's all he wanted from her or that he expected her to put out.

As Alex approached, Gemma looked up. He knelt in front of her and gently took her hands in his.

"I don't want you to feel rushed. I know that your ex-husband hurt you … and if you're not ready, if you need more time … it's okay." He peered into her eyes, trying to communicate that he wouldn't force her to do anything she didn't want to do.

She gazed at him with questions in her eyes, as she pressed her fingers to his lips to stop him from speaking. A small half smile formed on her lips.

"What are you some kind of mind reader?"

Underneath her fingers, his lips curled into a smile. Gemma removed her hand.

"I just noticed that you became withdrawn once we got to my house … I would never hurt you …" He could see the tears gathering in her beautiful eyes.

"I'm sorry, Alex ..."

"Gemma, please don't apologize. Listen, I desire you ..."

They both chuckled nervously, but then Alex turned serious.

"But I need you to feel comfortable. If you have any misgivings about us moving forward, tell me ... I understand if you want to change your mind."

His declaration hung in the air. She searched his face as they stared at one another. In his eyes, she saw compassion and understanding.

"I don't want to go home." She bit her lip as she saw his face break into a grin. He leaned in and kissed her softly on the lips before standing up.

"Well, this is supposed to be a slumber party. There should be snacks and movies and silly games ... I can make popcorn and we can watch a movie?"

She could only nod her head; too stunned to believe this man was so good to her. Most men would have considered the night over and taken her home.

Alex went into the kitchen and began making stovetop popcorn. As he was doing that, he called to her from the kitchen, "What kind of movies do you like?"

Gemma finally started to get comfortable and took off her jacket as she curled her feet underneath her.

"Umm, I like scary movies."

He popped his head out from behind the cabinet door. "You do?"

Smirking, she shook her head. "What because I'm a woman, I only want to watch rom-coms? They're a bunch of fairy-tales."

He laughed, "Okay. Scary it is."

He finished the popcorn and they settled in for a horror flick.

Alex half expected her to cling to him in fright at some point, but she sat riveted to the screen, munching her popcorn. He studied her profile as she watched the film. After the atrocities she'd seen and experienced he could understand how she would be unfazed by ghosts, zombies, or crazed murderers that kept coming back from the dead. All that was make-believe, while she'd lived through actual horror.

After the film ended and he'd cleaned the kitchen, he came back to her.

"Lets keep the slumber party going!" He said with a huge grin.

"I could put on another movie or we could play a game. I think Chloe left some of her board games here." He was ready to head down the hall and search for them in the closet when Gemma grabbed his hand.

"I think I'm ready for bed."

"Oh. Okay. " He was a little disappointed. He was hoping for more time with her.

"I think there are clean sheets on the bed in the guest bedroom. I can dou …" Before he could finish, Gemma placed her hand over his mouth. He looked at her intently as her eyes skittered across the room, avoiding his gaze. She licked her bottom lip.

"I wanted us to sleep together … sleep in the same bed." She stammered and removed her hand from his mouth.

He couldn't stop the smile that broke out across his face. The thought of getting to hold her all night made him happy.

"Okay, will you wait here for a second?"

Gemma nodded her head.

Alex went down the hall to his bedroom. Some things were a bit untidy before he left this evening. He quickly threw things into the hamper, shoved things in drawers, and checked the bathroom. He shrugged. It would have to do. Before he left his bedroom, he remembered something. Entering his bathroom, he grabbed the recollected item and placed it on his dresser.

He returned to the living room to get Gemma. As he took her hand and pulled her from the sofa, he could feel the tremor run through her body. He knew how she felt because he was equally as nervous. He hadn't been with anyone since Sam died. He wanted to put her at ease, so after motioning for her to sit on the bed, he grabbed the lighter off his nightstand and walked toward the candle he'd pulled from his bathroom moments ago.

"You know I had this whole seduction planned. I'd wanted to do it how they do it in the movies and have like a million candles, rose petals leading to the bed … unfortunately, I only have this one sad candle that Rachel bought me ages ago."

Alex lit the lone candle. Gemma tried to stifle a nervous giggle, but she quickly erupted into laughter.

"Hey, don't laugh! I'm trying to set the mood here."

Gemma laughed even harder.

"Are you laughing at my attempt to seduce you?"

Gemma tried to speak through her laughter. "Is that what you call it?"

Alex pounced on her and began tickling her mercilessly.

"Alex, no!" Gemma was laughing hysterically now as she tried to fend him off.

Alex straddled her as he tickled her sides. Chuckling, he watched her squirm beneath him. Tears were spilling from her eyes; she was laughing so hard. Finally, he let up and ceased tickling her. They both breathed heavily from their exertions. Gemma wiped at her eyes as she still nursed her case of the giggles. He couldn't help staring at her, as she lay supine beneath him.

"God, you're beautiful."

Gemma immediately sobered at his declaration. He'd said she was beautiful before, but there was a tenderness in his voice and a look in his eyes that was arresting.

Alex traced his finger down the bridge of her nose; then rubbed his thumb softly across her top lip before slowly caressing her cheek with the backs of his fingers. Gemma felt her skin flush, and her body go hot at his delicate touch. He smoothed her hair away from her face, before slowly leaning down and kissing her mouth sensuously. His kiss was unhurried; he took his time savoring each nibble, each lick, before finally sliding his tongue inside her mouth to explore even further. Even then the kiss was drawn out. Gemma matched his pacing. Unlike the duel their tongues were having last night, it was more like a slow dance tonight.

He finally left her mouth to trail kisses from her jawline to her neck. The breathy moans hitched in her throat as she anticipated his mouth moving further down her body. His tongue lapped at her neck, hitting a sensitive spot, and she moaned low in her throat. Whatever trepidation she felt earlier was melting away with every kiss, every caress. No one had ever made her feel so cherished before. Her skin was turning to molten fire at the exploration his hands and tongue made of her body.

He wasn't too gone yet in his sensual haze. Memories from earlier that evening, of her fear, penetrated his brain. He stopped kissing her neck.

"Gemma, is this what you want? Are you positive?" He searched her face, needing to know for sure that she wanted to go through with where this was headed. When he brought her to his bedroom, his intention was for them to just sleep. He would stop the foreplay right now if she didn't want to go down this road.

In response, Gemma stared into his eyes, nodding her head.

"Yes." Her sultry tone wrapped around him.

They smiled deeply at each other before resuming foreplay.

Gemma was hot to the touch as his tongue skimmed over her collarbone savoring the taste of her skin. He could hear the soft little purrs that were issuing forth from deep in her throat. His dick quivered at the primal sound of her body responding to his. That sound touched the most primitive part of his brain, and he was gripped with the need to feel her nakedness upon his.

His hands began to push the dress up her body, and then Gemma helped him by sitting up and pulling the rest of the fabric over her head and tossing it to the floor. His gaze didn't have too long to travel the length of her body before she moved forward to rid him of his shirt. He stood up from the bed then as Gemma followed his movements by rising to her knees as she pulled his shirt over his head.

She bit her lip and went to work on his belt. All he could do was drink her in and sigh at the feel of her feather-light touch on the skin of his abdomen. He leaned into her, breathing in her intoxicating scent, and his hands slid over the curves and contours of the small of her back until he had her pressed tightly against his body. He began to suck at the juncture of her neck and shoulders as she finally got his belt loosened and undid his pants.

Little whimpering noises emitted from her, and she inched even closer trying to meld their bodies into one. He didn't take his mouth from her but used one hand to help her relieve him of his pants, taking his boxer briefs with them. He gave a swift intake of breath as he felt his hard cock brush against her belly after being freed from the confines of his underwear. Gemma wound her arms around his neck as her swollen lips claimed his once more.

He kissed her back with a ferociousness that startled her and made her panties grow damp with her excitement. His fingers went to work at the clasp on her bra and then she felt cold air meeting her nipples before she was crushed once more against the hard planes of his chest. An inaudible groan resonated in her throat as he continued to plunder her mouth.

Once he'd divested her of the garment he cupped one of her pert breasts in his hand, enjoying the heaviness of the round globe in his palm. Releasing her swollen lips, he bent to suckle her left nipple in his mouth. Her nails dug into his shoulders, leaving tiny crescent marks as she felt his warm mouth teasing and licking her nipple. His arms tightened around her as he pulled her closer for his ravishment. Her moans of pleasure were like music to his ears. Wanting to pay tribute to each breast equally, he switched to the other one.

Finally, his hands trailed down her sides, making her shiver as he slid her panties down her thighs, which caused them to break apart. He pressed her back onto the bed as he finished removing the last shred of clothing that stood between them. He stood above her looking down at her naked loveliness. Her body became flushed at his open perusal. The raw lust in his eyes, made her cover her breasts. Alex leapt into action, kneeling between her parted thighs on the bed as he grabbed her wrists and pinned them on either side of her head.

"Don't cover up. I haven't finished looking at you."

His eyes roamed down her body. She watched him with downcast eyes, finally looking her fill at the parts of his body she could see. The muscles in his arms twitched and flexed in the moonlight. His torso tapered off into a V at his waistline that caused her to gulp. When her eyes went back to his face, that's when she noticed the look of awe in his eyes. She glanced down and saw that he was openly appraising her nether region. He whispered something, which she was sure was meant to be a thought in his mind, but as enthralled as he was, had come out of his mouth.

"I knew you'd be beautiful everywhere."

Releasing one of her wrists, he trailed his index finger over the lips of her glistening opening. She arched up from the bed with a loud moan as if his touch scalded her. Her yelp broke him from his trance, and his eyes flew back up to her face. Then a toothy grin broke out on his face as he circled her lips with two fingers, rubbing her. He continued to watch her face while he then used those two fingers to push into her hot, wet opening. He bit his lip when he felt her tightness suck his fingers inside. *She's so tight!* His balls tightened at the thought of what it would feel like sheathed inside her walls. He didn't want to penetrate her just yet. His dick throbbed and pulsated with his want, but he planned to savor her all night long. His fingers continued to move in and out of her, eliciting little cries of pleasure from her. She gripped the bed sheets tightly as her body convulsed with an impending orgasm.

"Mmmm, does that feel good baby?" He hadn't called her that before, but right now it seemed fitting. Her moans answered his question. He pulled his fingers from her and heard her soft whimper of protest.

"It's okay, baby ..." He patted her thigh, as he licked his sticky fingers. "I'm gonna make you feel good."

His eyes closed in pleasure over the sweet taste of her wetness. He needed more. He moved down her body, placing soft open-mouthed kisses as he went. Her spicy, sweet scent hit him as he lowered his face in between her parted thighs and swiped his tongue along her seam. He licked his lips before pushing his tongue into her sopping wet core, and felt her hands fist themselves in his hair.

"Ah, ah, ah ..."

He alternated between sliding his tongue in and out of her and sucking and kissing her sweet nether lips. He broke away from her wet lips to utter words against her thigh as he placed kisses.

"Mmmm, so good ... you taste so sweet, Gemma ..."

Gemma felt his stubble rub against the softness of her skin and the effect almost made her come out of her skin as his tongue dove back into her dewiness. She knew some women didn't like that and preferred their men clean shaven, but it was something about the five o'clock shadow roughing up her skin that reminded her of his maleness, which was what she craved.

While using his mouth to build her toward another climax, he brought his thumb up to rub the small nub of her clitoris. Her generous response to his ministrations egged him on even more, and he quickened the pace of his probing tongue. She ground her pelvis into his face as she neared her release. He removed his thumb to wrap his mouth around her clit and suck. He began to hum as he sucked her, knowing the vibrations would drive her over the edge. Gemma screamed her release as her head thrashed about on the pillows. After a few moments, he finally released her swollen clit and kissed the inside of her thigh.

Finally coming down off her high, Gemma wiped her hand across her forehead where she perspired. She breathed heavily as she saw Alex making his ascent up her body. No one had ever gone down on her before. Jason always said he was disgusted by it and refused at the beginning of their relationship when things were good, and once things deteriorated there was no way she wanted him down there.

Blushing, she bit her lip as Alex smiled down at her, before kissing her deeply, allowing her to taste herself on his tongue. It turned her on even further. She felt the tip of his dick brushing against her thighs, and parted her legs in invitation.

Alex braced his palms on either side of her head as they stared into each other's eyes. Although she'd shared so much of herself with him already, he wanted to make sure she was sure before they went to the next step.

Vulnerability showed in her eyes, along with her want. Her eyes silently gave him the permission he sought before he began the slow slide into her weeping core, never taking his eyes from hers. He could feel her being stretched deliciously to accommodate him. He took shallow breaths as he held onto his control, not to take her swiftly. She felt good, and she fit wonderfully tight around him. He still rested on his palms so he wouldn't give her all of his weight at once. Her chest was heaving with her shallow breaths as she gripped his wrists, trying to allow her body to relax and become accustomed to his girth and size.

"Are you okay, Gemma?" Alex whispered, breathing out through his nose as he fought to remain still inside of her.

She nodded her head. He wanted so badly to begin thrusting, but he didn't want to hurt her. She relinquished her hold on his wrists and placed her hands on his chest. Her breaths were coming slower now. She wrapped her legs around his waist to let him know it was okay to move. Lowering himself to his elbows, he distributed more of his weight onto her as he kissed her lips and began to move within her. She clutched his shoulders.

"I want to make you feel good, Gemma," he breathed into her ear as he thrust slowly into her. He gasped as her walls seemed to suction him in deeper. She bit her lip, holding back her pleasure.

"Moan for me."

He thrust in slow and deep, grinding his hips in a circle after he was inside of her each time. His eyes never left her face.

"Come on, baby, let me hear how my dick is making you feel."

After a moment, Gemma started to moan and pant loudly.

He smiled at hearing his name fall from her lips in ecstasy and his thrusts became faster. Overwhelmed with pleasure, she dug her nails into his back. Gemma began grinding her hips as he moved within her. Making guttural noises deep in his throat, Alex leaned up on his palms to look down where their bodies were joined, and it sent him over the edge. There was something about seeing them connected that made him more frenzied in his pace and expletives spewed from his mouth as he thrust harder and faster.

"Fuck … Gemma." He could feel her tighten around his cock as she was on the verge of her orgasm.

"Come for me. Come hard for me, baby."

At his words, she lost it as she screamed his name.

"Oh yes! Alex, Alex …"

He thrust into her in a furious pace and in a few seconds he was coming. Groaning loudly, he emptied his load deep within her.

He collapsed on her with all of his weight. After a moment, he slid off of her body onto his side. He saw her shiver from their parting and turned her onto her side, pulling her into his body. He exhaled a breath as he pulled her in closer, spooning her from behind. Even though it'd been years since he'd been with a woman, he knew that the experience they just shared was incredible. With all that had happened to her, this woman was incredibly giving with her body. He felt grateful and happy that their joining had been so amazing. He leaned down and nuzzled her neck before kissing her shoulder.

Gemma snuggled her bottom into him, and he contentedly smiled as he softly said into her ear, "I didn't hurt you, did I? Did I get too carried away? You felt so … damn good."

She looked over her shoulder at him and smirked.

"No, Alex …" She bit her lip. "I really enjoyed it too."

Leaning down, he kissed her on the lips as he tightened his hold on her.

She rubbed his arm that now lay draped across her waist. He pulled the covers up over their bodies as he tucked her head beneath his chin. They lay replete in each other's arms as they drifted off to sleep.

11

Gemma awoke first. Her limbs felt sore, and she had a delicious ache between her legs. She wanted to stretch, but she was held securely against Alex's chest, and she didn't want to wake him. Plus, she loved lying in his arms. Softly, she kissed the arm that held her and felt him stir. Once he settled again, and she knew he was asleep, she had the sudden urge to explore his body in the light. If he was awake, she might be too timid to do so. She slowly and carefully slid from his embrace and turned on her side, resting on her elbow to look at his face. His eyelashes rested on his cheeks and the light from the window caught the red, gold flecks of color. Being able to see him this closely in the light she saw that his hair also had reddish, golden undertones in the brown silkiness. She wanted to run her hands through his hair but refrained. Her eyes skimmed down his body and admired his chest, covered by a smattering of the same red-gold, brown hairs.

She pulled the covers back to expose the rest of his body. His muscles made slight twitches as he slumbered and she remembered last night the graceful way they undulated under his skin and rippled with his movements. She smiled in appreciation at his very well put together body. The deep V she noticed the night before made moisture pool in her center, and she licked dry lips. Lastly, her eyes rested on his member, which lay nestled between his thighs. Tiny blue veins stood out along the length of it, and the bulbous head was a soft pink. Even in its flaccid state, she was impressed by his size. His penis twitched, and then began to harden.

Suddenly, she heard the deep rumble of his voice heavy with sleep, and she looked up to find him watching her intently. *How long has he been awake?*

"Did you enjoy the slumber party?"

He saw the deep flush stain her cheeks underneath the soft brown of her skin before she covered her face with her hands.

"How long have you been awake?" she asked, trying to hide her embarrassment.

He held back his amusement. "Long enough to see you lick your lips over me."

He erupted into laughter when she picked up a pillow and swung it at him. She was trying not to giggle as she swung the pillow at him again, catching him on the side of his head, which only made him laugh harder. When he was finally able to sit up, he wrestled the pillow away from her and tossed it to the other end of the bed, then pulled her squealing onto his lap. His penis brushed her bottom as she went laughingly onto his lap.

He was going to continue their bed play by tickling her but wrapped his arms around her instead. The action seemed to catch her off-guard, sobering her immediately. It took her a second, but she slowly and nervously wrapped her arms around him. They sat there locked in their embrace, neither speaking. When he felt her body relax against him, he held her closer and laid his cheek on the top of her head, enjoying the feel of her body snug against him. There was something so vulnerable about holding her naked, skin-to-skin, without kissing or needing to be inside of her.

After minutes of sitting silently and contentedly entwined, he leaned back slightly to kiss her forehead. He thought he heard her sigh.

Even despite what they shared last night, he knew how things could change in the cold light of day and wanted her to know that his feelings hadn't changed, that he didn't plan to use her and toss her aside, that he cared for her.

"So … did you enjoy your slumber party?" He kissed her hair.

She smiled against his chest as she nodded her head. Her fingers played amongst his chest hair as he held her. The underlying meaning of his question was had she enjoyed his performance? After three years of living as a monk, he didn't want to disappoint her by being a bad lover. He stroked her back as he held her, content to just be in her presence.

Gemma felt him tighten his hold on her, and she burrowed deeper into him. Last night was like a dream, and waking up in his arms was like nothing she had ever experienced. It felt like she belonged there—not just in his bed, in his arms, in his heart. Even her first time with Jason never felt like this, like love. *Did I just think that?* Her body tensed. *It's too soon.* She couldn't possibly love Alex … *Could I?* It was just sex; they had sex for the first time. *Don't confuse sex with love; you've done that before.* Plus, there was no way he felt the same or maybe ever would. She didn't want her doubt to spoil their morning, but she was having a hard time shaking this talk of love going on in her head.

Alex must have felt her body go rigid.

"What's wrong, Gemma?"

She heard the concern in his voice.

"What?" She didn't look at him as she tried to relax. She cursed herself silently for giving him any indication of the bedlam going on in her head.

He pulled her away from his body to search her face before asking, "I … I felt you tense up."

His brows creased with concern as he stared at her, waiting for an explanation.

She expelled a breath. "I'm sorry, Alex. I didn't mean to ruin our time together … it's just I couldn't help but think of Shelby pounding on your door looking for me." She bit her lip at the small white lie.

A small smile broke out on his face.

"I hadn't given her a thought, but you're probably right … although I'm not ready to let you go just yet."

A half-truth, he needn't know the turmoil her inner voice was creating inside her head. The racket and white noise were growing louder at his nearness. Fighting the battle to stay in his arms or flee, flight won out.

Gemma began to pull away, searching for any piece of clothing to cover her nakedness and vulnerability. "I should … umm, get dressed. Ms. Ramirez may have already discovered I didn't spend the night at the halfway house last night …"

She scrambled into his shirt as she continued searching the floor for her panties or any other articles of her clothing.

"I just don't want Shelby on the warpath. She already disapproves of us."

From behind she was suddenly hoisted up into strong arms and thrown over Alex's shoulder. His body shook with his laughter when Gemma let out a yelp of surprise.

"Stop worrying. I'll deal with her when the time comes …
I told you I wasn't ready to let you go yet."

She felt him pat her on her naked rear end while he carried
her into his bathroom. As she hung upside down over his
shoulder, she had a great view of his hot, bare ass before he
finally set her back on her feet.

"I'm gonna make you forget about anyone else …" The
huskiness in his voice sent shivers down her spine. He reached
into the shower and cut it on, allowing the water to run and
get hot, before turning his attention back to her. Alex kissed
the corner of her mouth sensuously, then pulled his shirt over
her head and crushed her to his body with one arm. Knuckles
grazed her jaw before his mouth possessed hers in a fierce
kiss.

By the time they finally made it under the hot spray of
water, her body was primed and ready for him. He was like
a starving man as he devoured her. This Alex was different
from the Alex of last night that had been all soft kisses and
caresses. He demanded her body yield to him as he took her
against the shower wall, obliterating all thought. He pounded
into her with an intensity that left her breathless and clawing
the skin of his back as he punished her with his thrusts. Boy,
did he make her forget!

Once they finally left the cocoon of the shower, Alex made them a quick breakfast and took her back to the halfway house. They lingered in the front seat exchanging kisses before Gemma reluctantly broke away to head inside. She turned back a few times, glancing over her shoulder at him and sending him lusty looks until she disappeared inside.

She heard his car pull away as she leaned against the door, lost in her memories of last night. She hadn't noticed Shelby sitting in the living room. On her way to the stairs she heard a throat clear and turned in the direction of the sound. As her eyes landed on Shelby, it was like someone dumped a bucket of cold water on her. She looked down sheepishly, feeling like a teenager caught coming home late by a parent. Better just to admit fault and hope that Shelby would have mercy. She met Shelby's eyes and began to launch into an explanation, hoping to mollify her, but Shelby put her hand up to stop her.

"You do know what a phone is right, Gemma?"

Gemma nodded her head, contrite. Despite the condescending tone of Shelby's voice, Gemma knew she had no right to be angry. She was out on parole and should have returned to the boarding house last night.

"Ms. Ramirez contacted me this morning when she realized you hadn't come home last night. She's an old woman, Gemma. If you couldn't have called her, you at least could have called me instead of worrying her to death …"

Gemma remained with her eyes downcast. For the first time that day she felt horrible about the fact that everyone had been worried. She had been so wrapped up in her time with Alex she never truly took the time to think about anyone being worried.

Shelby let out a sigh. "I don't want the details. I don't wish to know anything … just in the future, you have to let me know where you're going to be."

Shelby stood up, ready to leave. As she went to brush past Gemma, she said over her shoulder, "Don't make me regret breaking the rules for you."

Before Gemma could say anything, Shelby left. She stood staring at the door minutes later. That should have gone so differently. Shelby just gave her special treatment, broke the rules for her. She shook her head, not quite understanding why. *Why is Shelby constantly looking out for me?* It was like having a mother or a big sister who offered advice that you didn't want to take at the time they offered it, but you knew it was good advice, and they gave it because they cared about you. She headed upstairs, trying not to think any longer about Shelby's actions.

Alex was filled with thoughts of this morning's shower as he maneuvered the car into his parking space at the restaurant. His back still tingled from the scratches Gemma gave him when she clawed her way into her second orgasm. As he got out of the car smiling to himself, he was completely oblivious to Brandon and some of the other cooks waiting by the door.

"Boss man got some last night!" Brandon's exclamation broke him out of his daydream.

"You see that big, goofy grin dude's sportin'? He got some!" Brandon guffawed as he high-fived some of the other cooks.

Am I that transparent? Alex tried not to blush. *Am I that late?* He glanced at his watch as he approached everyone.

"It's about time, dude!"

Brandon slapped him on the back while he continued with his comments. "Who was she, dude? Who popped your abstinence cherry?"

"I don't kiss and tell." Alex laughed good-naturedly as he unlocked the door.

Everyone piled into the restaurant, trying to get Alex to divulge his secrets, but he brushed them off and made an escape to his office.

He let out a breath as he sat down slowly in his chair. Brandon and his cronies bombarding him with their questions was unexpected. He wanted the solitude that opening the restaurant gave him so he could be alone with his thoughts.

Kicking the door closed with his foot, he turned his attention to the ledgers lying open on his desk. The numbers all seemed jumbled and scrambled. Concentration eluded him as his mind continued conjuring up images of Gemma's beautiful smile ... and naked body.

He smiled to himself as he thought of her.

Last night and this morning were everything he thought it would be. It exceeded his expectations. He knew it wasn't just how long he'd refrained from sex. There was a generous way in which Gemma gave of herself when they were together. He wanted to be careful that he didn't just take, but gave back to her as well. Waking up to find her exploring his body was very nice, although he wished it was the opposite so he could look his fill at her body without making her self-conscious.

He pulled the schedule from the wall. *Is she working tonight?* The grin spread across his face as his finger scanned her name. He couldn't wait to see her. There was a lightness he felt being in her presence that he hadn't felt in a long time. *How could I be falling for her so quickly?* A knock on the door broke him out of his thoughts.

"Come in."

Brandon poked his head inside. "Hey, the delivery truck is here."

He nodded, and Brandon stepped away. With one more look at Gemma's name on the schedule, he got up to meet the delivery truck.

By the time Alex finished unloading the truck he was a sweaty mess. He was headed to his office to shower, but was stopped in his tracks when he saw her. He looked at his watch. It was later than he thought if Gemma's shift started already. Gemma was in the dining room talking to the hostess, Amanda, as she worked.

Is it possible she's even more beautiful today than she was yesterday? She hadn't noticed him yet, and he enjoyed getting to watch her without her knowing. When she wasn't aware of him, she lost a bit of her shyness. As she laughed with Amanda, he observed that she didn't always cover her mouth as she often did in his presence. He enjoyed seeing her in the moment and not self-conscious. He smiled to himself. Given time, he hoped to break down all of her walls and have her feel as free as possible and not be so inhibited.

She turned around with a tray in her hand and saw him watching her. Almost instantly the demureness returned. He saw the instant change. Although, this time, he thought that maybe the return of her bashfulness may be from seeing her lover fully clothed in the cold light of day after their lusty night together and the amazing shower this morning. It was a strangeness that overtook him, as if they were the only two people in the room, the way she gazed at him with yearning.

He was broken from his reverie as he felt a hand touch his arm. He turned to see Amanda standing right next to him, eyeing him with a knowing look. *When did Amanda come to be standing next to me?*

She leaned in and whispered, "Don't worry, boss, your secret is safe with me. But umm ... you might want to try and mask how enamored you are with her if you're trying to keep it a secret. Otherwise, you're going to let the cat out of the bag ... Gemma's sweet. It's nice to see you getting back out there."

She gave him a pat on the arm and walked away. Alex was astonished that his feelings were that transparent. He didn't care if anyone knew—if he were honest, he would love for everyone to know that he and Gemma were seeing each other. It might stop some of the lecherous looks the male staff gave her. He smirked at this thought, but in the interest of Gemma's privacy, he wanted to know that she felt okay with the whole world knowing that they were together.

Did it just get ten degrees hotter in here? The hungry look she received when she peered into his eyes from across the room was making her body temperature ratchet up a few notches. She tore her gaze away with a small, timid smile on her face. It was slightly awkward to be in the same room, now fully clothed with the man who had just been making your body sing, especially when that man was also your boss. She tried to go back to work, yet she was painfully aware of Alex standing across the room. There were moments when she could feel his eyes upon her, and she was afraid she would melt into a puddle on the floor if she came in contact with him. She just needed to make it through the dinner service.

12

Thankfully, they were slammed during dinner service tonight, and he had no time to be distracted by thoughts
of Gemma. Now it was the end of the night, and his train of
thought couldn't stop running to her. He looked out into the
dining room and saw her making small talk with the other
waitresses as they cleaned up. He wanted her to stay the night
again. Maybe he could talk her into it. He smiled to himself
as he thought of how he would talk her into staying the night.

"Look at boss man over there smilin' to himself and shit."

The line cooks cracked up at Brandon's joke.

"Whoever she is, she must have laid it on you good."

The kitchen erupted into louder gales of laughter.

The color rose in Alex's face, but he refused to be goaded
into reacting to Brandon's wisecracks. Giving them a sheepish
grin, he turned his back to the group and kept cleaning. He
heard their jeers and catcalls for him to respond, but he only
shook his head. "Get back to work so we can get out of here,"
he said with mock authority as he threw a towel at Brandon,
the ringleader.

Everyone reluctantly went back to work as Brandon got in one last pot shot.

"We understand, Alex … the quicker we finish here, the sooner you can make it to your booty call."

The kitchen staff snickered as they resumed their clean up.

"Enough, Brandon," Alex good-naturedly laughed as he shook his head.

Small chit-chat permeated the air as they worked to finish up.

Amanda, Gemma, and some of the wait staff glanced up at the kitchen area when they heard whoops of laughter yet again.

"What do you suppose is going on in there? They sure are having fun."

Amanda curiously watched the kitchen while she tidied up the hosting station.

Gemma shrugged as she glanced at the kitchen. She continued refilling salt and pepper shakers, lost in her thoughts.

Gemma's faraway look didn't go unnoticed by Amanda. She moved closer to Gemma, letting the rest of the wait staff talk amongst themselves. "You both got it bad." She giggled as she saw Gemma startled from her daydream.

Alarmed, Gemma stared at her.

"Wha …?" Gemma could barely form the question.

Seeing the wide-eyed look of fear on Gemma's face, Amanda leaned in closer to reassure her. "I caught him watching you before the shift started earlier today and put two and two together …" She smiled warmly at her. "You don't have to worry. I told Alex it stays in the vault until you two are ready to go public."

Gemma only nodded. Amanda patted her arm and moved off to join the other conversation her co-workers were engaged in, leaving Gemma alone once again with her thoughts.

Go public? She and Alex? She looked toward the kitchen for a brief second as she thought about them being front and center, on display for everyone to see them as a couple. The thought both frightened and excited her. Although, she wasn't sure she was ready to be on display. At least Amanda was going to keep their relationship a secret. She decided to keep to herself the rest of the night; her head was too muddled to be any good in a conversation right now.

Thinking about their relationship made her wonder what was going to happen tonight once the shift was over. Was he going to want her to stay the night again? Shelby said she would turn a blind eye to her missing curfew, which she still didn't understand. It would be nice to stay with Alex again. She caught herself smiling and instantly looked around to see if anyone had noticed her euphoric look. She had to start being careful in case anyone else figured out what was going on between her and Alex. If anything was made known about their relationship she wanted it to be because they were ready and made the decision, not because someone blurted it out and the news spread like wildfire. No, she would steer the direction of this and not have gossip dictating what happened between the two of them.

At the end of the night, somehow they managed to be the only two left in the parking lot with no one being the wiser. Gemma leaned against Alex's car, giving him a coy smile as he approached her. When he reached her, he braced his hand against the car next to her. They stood smiling shyly at one another. She lowered her gaze to the ground as she bit her lip and Alex stuffed his free hand deep in his pocket.

He couldn't wipe the smile off his face as he watched her chew her bottom lip in the way he found so adorable.

"So …"

Her gaze flicked up to meet his for a second, then lowered to the ground again.

"So …"

They shared a nervous laugh.

Alex tucked his other hand in his pocket as he continued to stare at her bowed head. "You want to come back to my place?"

She gave another nervous giggle.

"Okay."

She finally looked up and gave him a soft, natural smile. Grabbing her hand, he pulled her close to his body. Despite working a long shift he could still smell the sweetness of the fragrant soap she used clinging to her skin. He had to fight the urge to lick her neck, and settled for lightly nipping her. He caught the shiver that ran through her body as she sweetly clung to him. Reluctantly, he released her to open the car door so she could get in.

As they drove to his house, Alex reached over and took her hand, entwining his fingers with hers. Gemma glanced down at their joined hands and smiled at him. She leaned back against the seat, content in this moment. She knew she had been telling herself to be cautious and take it slow, but she was ready to chuck all that out the window and just enjoy today and let tomorrow take care of itself. Before she knew it she found herself tracing circles on the back of his hand with her thumb.

He had to school himself to patience once they got inside his house. The primitive man in him yearned to bend her over the sofa and have his way with her until they were both sated, but he wanted more than just to claim her body. He did desire Gemma but he'd never been a 'hit it and quit it' kind of guy. He hoped to know her on a more intimate level. Not only did he want to know how and where to touch her body to make her come undone, but he wanted to know how to touch her heart and mind. Yeah, maybe that sounded cliché, and some other men would probably give him a hard time for saying that, but it was truly how he felt.

Gemma removed her jacket as they came into the living room. He wondered if she was feeling as awkward and unsure as him about how to proceed.

"How about I make us some banana splits?"

Alex saw Gemma's face light up with delight and couldn't keep the grin off his face. Seeing her happy over even the smallest thing brought him so much pleasure. She followed him into the kitchen and sat on one of the barstools at the counter. Alex gathered up the contents for the desserts.

Gemma's eyes followed him as he moved around the kitchen.

There was a gracefulness to Alex when he was in the kitchen. It was something to watch. Yes, it was just a banana split, but he made it look like art. With a flourish, he added the

Maraschino cherry and slid the dish in front of her. He sat on the stool next to her, and they ate in a companionable silence.

After a few spoonfuls of ice cream, Alex spoke, "What about you, Gemma? You know about how I got to the restaurant, but what about you? Before you got married, what did you want out of life?"

Gemma's spoon hovered over the bowl as she contemplated Alex's question. No one ever asked her that before. She thought they were just going to come back to his house and screw, and here they were sitting in his kitchen eating sundaes, and he was asking her what she wanted in life. While yes, she wanted him sexually as well; she was pleasantly surprised when he curbed his lust to get to know her better. More so than the sex, this was what she fantasized about, as she got older, someone caring about her thoughts, feelings, and aspirations. And now it was happening. Life was surreal. She played with the soupy contents of her bowl before answering.

"I always got pretty decent grades in school. I wanted to go to college. Well, as you know that did not happen." She gave a snort as she looked down at the ice cream she continued to mix around the bowl.

"When I was younger and thought of college, I wanted to go and learn how to be a photographer. I never had a real camera of my own, but I would buy the disposable kind and snap pictures of everything." She peeked out from under her lashes at Alex, expecting a laugh or incredulous look, but he watched her with this hopeful enthusiasm.

He stuck a big spoonful of the sweet confection in his mouth before saying, "What's stopping you? You should go. I think you'd be great. Plus, I could be the first subject you shoot."

Smirking, he wiggled his eyebrows at her, the sexual innuendo evident in his tone.

He put his spoon down and wiped his mouth and his grin along with it.

"In all seriousness, Gemma, you should go. Nothing is standing in the way of you going after what you want. You're young."

She snorted again. "Alex, be real. How would I ever get into college now? It's too late."

Alex spun her around to face him and took her chin in his hand, forcing her to meet his gaze.

"You listen to me, Gemma Peyton. So long as you're around me I do not want to hear that defeatist attitude from you again. Got it?"

She stared at him at first, too scared to answer, too afraid to hope.

"Answer me," Alex said softly. He peered into her eyes before continuing, "You're smart, Gemma. It's never too late. If you want to go to school, you can. There are all sorts of grants and scholarships … we can do this."

Gemma bit her lip, yet couldn't help but feel a rush of nervous excitement.

"We?"

He was unaware that he'd made his statement plural, but he meant what he said. He would help her if she wanted him to. He gave her a lopsided grin.

"Yes. I can help you … if you want me to."

He removed his hand from her face and sat with his hands splayed on his thighs as he waited for her response.

"Why? Why do you want to help me?" Her tone was suspicious.

His heart went out to her as he watched her squirm, twisting the napkin in her fingers until it began to come apart.

She looked down as she said the next words.

"You already slept with me, you know. You don't have to help me. You don't have—"

This aggressive, standoffishness that he was unaccustomed to seeing in her took over her face and body language. It took him a second, but he finally saw the behavior for what it was. She was trying to push him away and reject him before he could do it to her, before he could get close enough to hurt her. He was seeing her defense mechanism.

Roughly, he pulled her from her seat and crushed her against his chest as he kissed her deeply and hungrily. His greedy mouth devoured her tongue and lips, and she could taste the chocolate ice cream he was just eating moments ago. Before she could return the kiss fully, his lips left her, but his mouth was still only centimeters away from her own as he said in a deep, aggressive whisper, "Don't do that! I intend to show you that you are priceless." He leaned his forehead against hers.

"Gemma, I don't want to help you because you shared your body with me or because you owe me something, but merely because I care about you."

She couldn't stop the tears that spilled from her eyes. He leaned back to cup her face and used the pads of his thumbs to wipe the tears away.

"Hey now … none of that," he murmured.

She nodded her head, trying to staunch the flow of tears. Continuing to wipe at her face, he consoled her. He peered into her eyes briefly, then leaned forward and kissed her on the forehead. His lips lingered on her skin, and before he could pull away she slipped her arms around him. Her weight sagged against him, and he put his arms around her, pulling her in close. They sat like that for a while.

After minutes of sitting in his comforting embrace, she felt the soothing effects of his nearness making her sleepy. In her drowsy state, she realized he lifted her in his arms. Her eyes fluttered open, and she put her arms around his neck as he carried her to his bed. His hands were on her body, undressing her. Lethargy was claiming her, and she could no longer fight to stay awake. The last thing she remembered before succumbing to sleep was his warm breath as he kissed her good night.

The sunlight streaming through the window awakened her the next morning. She yawned and turned over, expecting to find Alex next to her, but she was alone. She was a bit disappointed to find the bed empty. Looking beneath the sheet, she saw she was still wearing her bra and panties, and smiled. *Ever the gentleman.* That was one of the things she liked about Alex. Most guys she knew would have taken advantage of the situation, but Alex wasn't like any other guy she'd ever met.

He was very chivalrous. And he believed in her. This thought widened the grin on her face even more. She was deep in her thoughts and hadn't heard him walk into the bedroom.

"Damn! I was hoping to wake you up."

She looked up, startled at being pulled from her daydream, but then her face broke into a smile as she saw him balancing a tray in one hand and carrying a laptop computer in another. He had a way of making her feel special.

He almost forgot himself for a moment as he took in the brightness of her eyes as she stared up at him from the bed. Sleep still marked her body and her face, and it made her look even more beautiful. He loved seeing her natural and untouched. Sitting on the edge of the bed in front of her, he placed the tray between them. Her eyes finally left his face to gaze at the plate of food; then she looked back into his eyes with a smile.

"You made me breakfast in bed."

He couldn't tell if she was asking the question or merely making a statement, but he beamed at her. Taking the cover off the dish, he revealed eggs, bacon, toast, yogurt parfait, coffee, and orange juice.

"I was hoping to surprise you, but … this was better." He smoothed her hair away from her face. Unexpectedly, she leaned across the tray and kissed him softly on the lips, taking her time pulling away.

"Thank you, Alex … for everything."

He nodded his head as he took the linen napkin and laid it across her lap. When he heard her giggle, he looked up curiously to find out what was so funny, raising his eyebrow at her in question.

She picked up the tip of the napkin. "What is a single man doing with linen napkins?"

He chuckled softly. "We're not all Neanderthals you know. Men do like the finer things in life, too. Sorry, you didn't manage to nab yourself a knuckle dragger who only eats with his hands."

They both burst into laughter after his comment.

"Okay, okay. No need to get touchy." She smirked at him.

"I am a chef after all. What self-respecting chef doesn't own cloth napkins?"

"Point taken." She stuck her tongue out at him with an impish grin and then started to peruse the food. He watched her bowed head for a moment. He liked this spunky side of her. She was about to pick up the fork, and he playfully smacked her hand away.

"Uh, uh … My house, my rules. I get to feed you." Smiling at her triumphantly, he picked up the fork and speared some eggs on the end before brandishing it in front of her closed mouth. She shook her head at first, toying with him.

"Open up."

Simpering, she finally opened her mouth to receive the food. She licked her lip after chewing. Alex feeding her should be awkward, but it wasn't. She was enjoying being pampered by him. He continued feeding her until she couldn't eat anymore.

"Alex, I'm stuffed."

Placing the fork on the tray, he picked up the tray and sat it on the dresser. He grabbed his laptop as he came back to the bed and sat beside her.

"Do you have work you need to do?"

Grinning, he shook his head. "Nope," he said, and opened the lid of the laptop. "It's for you."

Puzzled, she looked at him. "I don't understand."

He opened up the page and typed in something before responding. "Last night you mentioned that you wanted to go to school. I thought we could check out some schools online and find some grants or scholarships or something ..." He started playing with the keyboard. "I was kind of researching this morning while I made you breakfast."

Gemma was speechless. A few seconds later, he glanced up at her face. She blinked away her shock and finally regained her ability to speak.

"Alex, I don't know what to say. It just never seemed like a possibility … you think I can?" She peered at him with such hopefulness.

"Yes, Gemma, I do. You can go to school and be whatever you want to be."

When he pushed the laptop toward her, she hesitantly pulled the computer a little closer and started researching. Alex scooted over to her as they began talking about the schools and programs she was looking up.

After a half hour, Alex leaned back against the headboard watching Gemma intently as she sat huddled over the keyboard, clicking away at the keys, engrossed in her research. He loved these moments when he got the chance to watch her without her knowing.

Her legs were splayed out in front of her surrounding the laptop; the sunlight played on the smooth brown of her skin, enhancing the richness of her coloring. She flexed her foot, and he noticed she had slender feet. Her toenails were unpainted. His eyes ran back up her body to see her breasts perfectly nestled in her push-up bra, which he hadn't removed last night. He felt his dick stir at the thought of holding the two mounds in his hands and sucking her nipple into his mouth.

Quickly, he averted his eyes and continued his journey upward as he looked his fill. This in no way diminished the awakening his dick was having. The sight of all her unruly curls made him want to put his hands in her hair. The cloud of loose, curly tendrils framed her face beautifully.

The aching in his balls was getting worse; he couldn't stand not touching her anymore. Moving across the bed to sit behind her, he wrapped his arms around her waist as he positioned his thighs around her. He nuzzled her neck, luxuriating in the feel of her skin and the smell of her body. He heard her let out a small sigh and the sound of fingers on keys stopped as he felt her hands cover him—one settled on his hand, and the other rested on his naked thigh.

Suddenly, his boxer briefs felt constricting, but he wanted to stay with her like this for a moment longer. His tongue lapped at the flesh of her neck. She began wiggling her backside up against him, which made him growl deep in his throat. He nipped her neck, causing her to yelp. He would have stopped what he was doing had he not heard the satisfying moan that followed it. It made him even harder hearing how responsive she was.

Ever since the first night with Gemma, it was like the beast had been let out of its cage. His lust was riding him. It was almost blinding in its intensity. His hands cupped her breasts as she began to grind against him. He couldn't take it anymore. Lifting her from the sitting position, he pushed her onto her knees. He came up on his knees behind her as he tore her panties from her waist, and shoved his boxers down his legs, freeing his member from its confines. He had to check his lust before he just thrust straight into her. Leaning over her body, he whispered sweet words as his questing fingers checked to make sure she was ready to receive him.

"Mmmm … baby, you're so wet."

Once he felt the moisture pooling between her thighs he slowly slid home. A grunt escaped his lips as he halted any movement, letting her get accustomed to the fullness of him. Her hands clutched the sheets, and he could feel her labored breathing, as she grew used to his invasion of her body. He placed kisses along her back, hoping to soothe her.

Alex was so big. He seemed even bigger than last night. Her grip on the sheets eased a bit as the tension left her body. She pushed back into him, letting him know it was okay to move. His thrusts were slow at first. She could hear him groan with pleasure as he took her.

Even though she knew his raw lust was driving the train right now, he was still tender with her, kissing her back and neck and even waiting for her to be ready for him. He had a tight grip on her hips while he plunged deep inside of her. She gasped and began to moan even louder as he thrust faster and deeper.

Only the sounds of their mating could be heard, along with skin slapping against skin as he pushed her over the edge. Gemma screamed her release. Her legs shook as Alex pumped into her one final time before climaxing with a loud groan. He collapsed on top of her back. It was a moment before he removed his body from her. They were both still heavily breathing as Alex moved to lie on his side, then pulled Gemma into his body. Her legs still trembled from the force of her orgasm. With his arm wrapped tightly around her, he kissed her ear. Gemma reached back behind her to rub his thigh and his warm breath tickled her skin, making it tingle.

They lay there just enjoying the warmth of the other's body. After a few minutes, Gemma spoke, "You know you owe me new underwear, right?"

Alex's chuckle resonated deep in his throat. She smiled to herself as his laugh enveloped her in its warmth.

Smoothing her hair back away from her neck, he kissed her before responding, "What? You don't like going commando?"

She laughed this time and turned in his arms to face him. "It's not always the most comfortable thing."

She leaned in and kissed him, but when she went to pull away, he captured her lips. Bringing his hands up, he cupped her face as he deepened the kiss. Finally, he released her mouth, his eyes twinkling.

"Mmmm, you taste good."

His statement made her self-conscious and she buried her head in his chest. Before she could raise her head again, his deep baritone rippled down her spine with the next statement.

"Of course there is another part of you that tastes even sweeter."

Her cheeks became inflamed at his words. She squirmed a bit, and he held her tighter to still her as he whispered in her ear, apparently enjoying her discomfort.

"It's okay. I'll taste you later."

She slowly looked up to find him grinning at her lecherously. Shrieking, she grabbed a pillow and hit him with it. Alex was laughing hysterically as she raised herself onto her knees to pummel him with the pillow once again. He tried to shield himself while still cracking up. Collapsing next to him in a fit of laughter, she rolled onto her back.

He loomed over her, resting on his elbow. "You're gorgeous when you laugh."

She began to sober. The look in his eyes told her he was about to start round two when they heard the front door slam.

"Alex, are you here?"

Recognizing Rachel's voice, he let out a groan and fell on his back. *Damn! Why didn't I remember to get her key back the other night at dinner?*

He looked at Gemma apologetically. "Let me get rid of her."

Foregoing his boxer briefs, which were somewhere tangled up in the sheets, he grabbed some sweats and slid into them. Gemma whistled as she received a generous view of his ass as he clambered into his pants. He threw her a grin over his shoulder.

Alex shut the bedroom door behind him before heading down the hall. Rachel was flipping through his mail as he came into the living room. She looked up, not embarrassed to be caught rummaging through his stuff.

"There you are …" She took in his appearance and glanced at her watch. "Are you just now getting up? That's rather late, little brother. You're usually such an early riser. Are you getting sick?"

She approached him, ready to check his temperature, but Alex took a step back.

"I'm not sick, and while we're at it, give me your key."

Suddenly, Rachel slapped her forehead. "I'm such an idiot! You have someone in the bedroom, don't you?"

Alex's face flushed for a moment but he didn't confirm her question.

"The key, Rachel."

Her eyes got even bigger, and her mouth fell open. "It's Gemma, isn't it? You finally got her in the sack. I knew you two would hook up." She slapped him on the arm. This time, he blushed even deeper.

"Stop it, Rachel! Have you been hanging out with Brandon?"

Rachel guffawed. "Are you blushing?"

He ignored her question.

"Can't you respect that I have company and stop being an evil big sister for a second and leave. You know you're cockblocking me right now."

She snorted. "I bet you've had plenty already. I'm sure Gemma could use a break."

She made like she was going to head back to his bedroom and Alex barred her way. Laughing, Rachel held up her hands in surrender. "Okay, okay. I know when I'm not wanted."

Rachel was about to leave when Gemma came down the hall.

"Oh no, Rachel, you're not leaving yet, are you?"

Rachel whirled around.

"Now why would I go when you so clearly want me to stay?" She smiled up at Alex sweetly, only too happy to have thwarted his plans to get rid of her.

He shook his head. "I still want my key back before you leave here."

Rachel turned her back on him, ignoring his remark as she spoke with Gemma.

Over Rachel's shoulder, Gemma watched Alex gesture to her and make faces. She tried to pay attention to what Rachel was saying while attempting not to laugh at Alex's silliness. She had been too uncomfortable to come out wearing any of Alex's clothes in front of Rachel, so she'd opted for putting on her own clothes even though she had to go commando since her ripped panties lay on the floor in his bedroom.

Alex finally stopped making faces at her and walked into the kitchen. "So I guess I'm making you ladies brunch?"

Linking her arm through Gemma's, Rachel smiled mischievously. Gemma smiled back knowingly; she realized this was why Rachel showed up this morning: hoping to be fed. It had only been an hour or so since she ate breakfast, but she hadn't seen Alex eat anything. Any time she'd eaten Alex's cooking it tasted like heaven. She didn't mind eating again; she would just eat something light.

As they entered the kitchen, Alex was already removing pots and pans, while also scavenging for ingredients. Her belly rumbled and she looked away, embarrassed. Thinking about their earlier activities, she knew they probably were contributing to her hunger.

They sat at the counter and engaged Alex in conversation as he cooked brunch for them. It was easy with Alex and Rachel. They included her, but also, just let her be. She enjoyed listening to them joke and talk. She never had this. It would have been nice to have a sibling to share private jokes and good-natured ribbing, but know they always had your back, no matter what. The trust, the bond they shared was something she envied.

Alex finished whipping up an incredible meal effortlessly. As they ate, Gemma had trouble concentrating on her food and trying not to drool over Alex, who still only sported the sweats he put on when he left the bedroom to talk to his sister. She glanced up briefly at his bare chest; her eyes traveled downward to the 'V' that was noticeable at the top of his waistband and disappeared into the confines of his pants.

Quickly, she grabbed her glass of water to help the food go down her suddenly dry throat. Out of the corner of her eye, she saw Rachel giving her a snarky grin as she shoveled food into her mouth. Quickly, she glanced down at the half-eaten contents of her plate. She nearly choked on her water at being caught ogling Alex in front of Rachel. He was completely oblivious to her state as he went about tidying the kitchen; having devoured his meal almost the minute he put food on his plate.

Rachel wiped her mouth with her napkin and laid it on the counter.

"So, Gemma, what are you up to on your day off? How about some girl time?"

Rachel appeared hopeful, and Gemma didn't want to disappoint her.

"Okay … that sounds like fun."

Alex looked a bit disappointed, which he quickly masked, but not before Gemma caught it. Her heart skipped a beat at the thought of him missing her presence and the corner of her mouth turned upward into a smile.

Alex wiped at a smudge on the counter as he said,

"Yeah, I have something I need to take care of … Gemma and I can hang out later today." He glanced at her.

"Pick you up later tonight at about six?"

Gemma nodded her head, trying to suppress the giddiness she felt.

13

No sooner had they gotten in the car and Rachel launched into a million questions about what was going on with her and Alex.

"So are you guys exclusive now? What's going on? I mean … you both looked so cute this morning. I haven't seen my brother this happy in a long time …"

Gemma seemed a bit overwhelmed.

"Please take a breath, Rachel. I can't answer all those questions at once."

She wrung her hands, which rested in her lap.

"Oh my goodness, forgive me for having diarrhea of the mouth. I'm just really excited. I've been hoping you two would hook up."

Gemma saw Rachel's unbridled enthusiasm and gave her a warm smile. Her excitement was catching, and Gemma couldn't help but feel a bigger smile break out across her face. She'd never had a girlfriend to confide in, and it felt nice. Hesitantly, she began to speak.

"I like your brother ... he makes me feel special ... he believes in me ..."

She looked down and fidgeted with her hands, trying to keep the emotion from her voice. She bit her lip before continuing, "I've never had that before ... and I'm terrified it's going to just go away, go up in a puff of smoke and disappear."

Rachel sat in silence after Gemma's admission. After a moment, she leaned over and put her hand on Gemma's.

"Listen, my brother has been alone for over three years, not just because of grief, but by choice as well. It's not like there haven't been other girls to try and catch his eye. But, I know him, and I know that when he falls, he falls hard ... and I can see it, Gemma, he's falling for you."

Tears tumble down Gemma's face.

"Oh please don't cry ... I know it's scary." She rubbed Gemma's arm. "See! I knew you needed some girl time."

They both burst into giggles. Gemma was grateful to have Rachel lighten the mood, but she was also grateful for her words and what she said about Alex.

"Do you think before we go to the mall you could stop by my place? There is something I need to pick up."

As much as he wanted to spend the whole day with Gemma it was good that he got to slip away. It would give him time to pick up a gift he'd been thinking of for her since last night.

Upon entering the camera shop, he was automatically overwhelmed by all the different brands, camera bodies, and accessories. He looked around for a sales person and instantly cornered them and launched a barrage of questions at them.

Leaving the camera shop an hour later—after having to hear the many debates about Sony versus Canon versus Nikon—Alex had a Sony Alpha 7R II, a set of lenses, tripod, and various other accessories. He felt giddy like a child on Christmas morning at the thought of giving her this gift that would start her down a new career path.

As he packed everything in the car, he decided to go by and see his old man.

His father was dependable. He almost laughed at seeing him in the garage, like clockwork, his old man's schedule rarely faltered. Most of the day he tinkered with a car in the garage, taking a break to have lunch and watch *Judge Judy*. Every Sunday he had a standing fishing date out on the lake, often with his old buddy Gus. Alex turned off his car and got out to greet his father who worked on the engine of the car he was repairing.

"Hey, just thought I'd stop by."

His father didn't look up. "Can you hand me that Allen wrench over there?"

Most people would have been annoyed by his father's lack of greeting or even acknowledgment, but he came to accept that it was just who his father was. He turned toward the table behind him where various tools lay. It took him a second before he found the right one and handed it to his father's outstretched hand. They both stood in silence while his father used the wrench to tighten a screw. After a few moments, his father looked up from his handiwork.

"So, what brings you here? This many visits in less than two weeks … I feel like it's my birthday."

Alex chuckled. "Yeah, I deserve that."

His father motioned for him to follow him inside the house. Once inside he grabbed two beers from the fridge and offered one to Alex before sitting at the kitchen table. Alex opened his and took a swig. More silence ensued as they both nursed their beers for a few minutes. Out of nowhere his father spoke.

"Gemma seems like a sweet girl."

Alex couldn't stop the grin that lit up his face at her name. He swallowed another sip of beer before replying, "She is … she really is."

Thoughts of this morning swirled through his brain, before being interrupted by his father.

"I can't put my finger on it, but I've seen her somewhere … I just can't place it." He toyed with the beer bottle in his hands, as he looked perplexed.

"Dad, there is no way that you've met Gemma before, trust me." Alex looked carefully at his father. He hoped this wasn't the early stages of dementia or something. He knew his father said something similar the other night at dinner, but there was no way he could know Gemma, and he wasn't about to tell his dad the reason for that. In time, when Gemma was ready she could divulge that information if she chose to do so. Alex finished up his beer and sat the bottle on the countertop.

"I should be going ... I have some more things to do before I meet up with Gemma later on tonight."

His father stood up with his unfinished beer in his hands. "Okay ..."

He looked uncomfortable as he fumbled around with what to say next.

"Umm ... I enjoyed dinner the other night ... I think it was something your mother would have liked ..." He cast his gaze down at the floor.

Alex was amazed at his father's confession about enjoying last night and for him to mention his mother was even more astonishing.

His father looked back up. "I hope maybe we can do it again ... Gemma was very sweet."

Alex nodded, trying to hide the smile that touched the corner of his mouth. "I think we can do that ... I better go."

He patted his father on the shoulder and headed out. His father wasn't the only one that had been uncomfortable with his father sharing his feelings. Ever since his mother passed, his father's emotions ceased to exist, almost as if someone flipped a switch. After so many years both he and Rachel came to accept it was just who he had become. Now, Chloe was the only one that seemed to turn on a light inside the old man, but maybe Gemma was bringing something out in him. He got into his car and drove away.

His father stood at the window and watched him back out of the driveway. All parents wanted to see their children happy. Alex's pain after Sam's death was unbearable to watch, mirroring his own of many years ago. Often, his own heartache still seemed fresh, festering like an open wound that refused to scab over and heal. Emotionally, he wasn't equipped to help his son, and as a parent that was a crippling feeling. His son nearly became a variation of him. Almost that is until she came along.

Alex had been a jovial child, and while he didn't show it much, it was one of the things he loved about his son. It was hard to watch the grief almost snuff out that light. He did like Gemma, and he didn't want anyone to mistake his trepidation at their pairing for dislike. It's just he couldn't shake this niggling feeling in the back of his mind that he'd seen her before. It wasn't dementia; he wasn't going senile, he would figure out where he knew her from before accepting her as his son's savior.

He sipped at the remnants of his beer. Alex's car had long vanished from sight, but he still lingered at the window. Yes, he wanted to get to know Gemma, so he could finally put this uneasy feeling to rest.

Alex opted for a tie tonight. He was a man that preferred casual dress most days, but sometimes you just had to class it up a bit. He wore an apron to protect his attire as he put the finishing touches on the romantic meal he'd been preparing for the last hour. After his visit with his father, he called Gemma and told her to dress up for their date tonight. She insisted on meeting him at his house, despite all of his resistance to the idea. He knew she needed to feel independent again after her attack, so he finally relented.

Tonight, he was intent on setting the perfect mood. Before he came home, he stopped to pick up more candles and some oysters, which were considered a natural aphrodisiac. He wanted to woo and seduce Gemma. He'd even purchased a set of thousand thread count Egyptian cotton sheets. For a minute in the store he'd contemplated the silk sheets, but knew

Gemma would find that cheesy. He chuckled to himself in the store thinking about her response and getting a warm feeling envisioning her smile and sexy laugh. The one cheesy thing he did, was scatter the bed with rose petals. The reason was because he couldn't wait to smell the flower's fragrance on her skin. Just as he finished setting the table, the doorbell rang. He smiled knowing it was her. As he headed for the door, he discarded the apron on a stool.

He was stunned into silence when he opened the door to reveal her standing on the threshold clothed in a sexy, yet whimsical throwback dress. It reminded him of the dress Natalie Wood wore in *West Side Story* when she did that number alone on the rooftop, but with a modern twist. He only knew what Natalie's dress looked like from the movie because as a kid his mother and sister watched the film almost religiously, which meant he was often stuck watching it. He quickly developed a thing for Natalie Wood.

He opened and closed his mouth like a fish for a few seconds, taking in her perfectly coiffed hair, the exquisite, but natural appliqué of her make-up, and once again her flirty dress. He finished taking her in from head to toe and then glanced back up into her face, speechless. Gemma looked at him demurely.

"I hope you like it … Rachel insisted on playing makeover with me before our date." She lifted the fabric of the skirt in her hand, the periwinkle blue fabric complementing her skin beautifully. Neither said anything for a moment.

Then Gemma said in a breathless whisper, "Please say something."

Alex finally shook himself from his stupor.

"I know I've said it before, but words can't describe how beautiful and ethereal you look tonight. Like you stepped out of some old time movie."

The smile that transfused her face completed the lovely image she made. He wanted to capture this moment; remember how she always looked at this exact second. He opened the door wider to admit her. As she swept past him, he caught a whiff of her scent, and he thought of the rose petals waiting on his bed. He secretly hoped dinner passed quickly. He followed her into the kitchen. It was then he noticed she had a gift-wrapped box in her hands.

"What's this?" he asked, pointing at the box.

She shyly glanced down at the box and back up to him. "Just something that I want you to have." She bit her lip as she smiled at him, giving him the full weight of her gaze.

Slowly he approached her. "I guess I'm not the only one that came bearing gifts." He stood in front of her smirking.

"Let's hold the gifts until after dinner." He stated as he gently removed his gift from her hands and sat it on the counter as he ushered her to her seat so he could serve her.

"Mmmm ... Alex, it smells delicious. I'm starving."

He lay the linen napkin in her lap.

"Good. I hope you brought your appetite." He gifted her with a smile before going to retrieve the oysters from the refrigerator along with some lemons. As he sat them on the table, he saw her wrinkle her nose.

"Uh oh, I see you're not a fan." He chuckled. "Have you ever tried them, or is it just the way they look that you find repugnant?"

"They're slimy looking, like snot."

He threw his head back in laughter. "I can understand … most people eat with their eyes."

His eyes devoured her as he continued making her blood race. She swallowed audibly.

"But do me a favor and try at least one. If you don't like it, you don't have to eat anymore." He squeezed a little lemon over one oyster, the juice mingling with that of the oyster before he sprinkled it with the salt sitting on the table. Holding it near her mouth, he murmured, "Trust me."

She stared at him for a moment, both understanding that his statement held more meaning than just her trying the oyster. Once she agreed there would be no turning back. She was telling him she was in this. Gemma opened her mouth and let Alex tip the mollusk from its half shell down her throat, never removing her eyes from his. The salty tartness that accompanied the briny, metallic taste of the oyster was refreshing on her tongue. She expected revulsion, but she found she quite liked oysters. They both knew she took a bigger leap of faith than just trusting his knowledge that she'd enjoy the oyster. He kept gazing into her eyes seconds after she swallowed the oyster. Putting the shell back on the plate, he then rubbed her cheek before leaning in and kissing her softly on the lips.

"Thank you," he whispered into her lips as he lingered. She touched her forehead to his in response as her hand brushed his. Reluctantly, he pulled away. "The rest of dinner awaits."

He tantalized her taste buds through four scrumptious courses. She patted her stomach after consuming his molten chocolate cake.

"You know how to satisfy a woman." She licked her lips, still tasting the chocolate as she peered at her empty dessert plate. Alex quirked his eyebrows at her bold statement cloaked in sexual innuendo as he removed the empty plate and took the dishes to the sink.

"I'm glad you enjoyed everything," he said in a pleased tone while he rinsed the dishes.

They stayed in silence as he finished dish duty. When he was done, he turned around to face her, wiping his hands on a dishtowel.

"Gift giving time." Smiling widely, he rubbed his hands together and came to sit at the table again. "Ladies first."

She shook her head as she got up from the counter to retrieve the box. Setting it in front of him, she reclaimed her seat. He immediately started tearing at the wrapping paper like an excited child on Christmas morning.

"It's nothing special. It's just something I had, and it made me think of you …"

He stopped and placed his hand over hers. "Hey, it came from you so that automatically makes it special to me." After squeezing her hand, he resumed ripping open the package. When he finally got the box open, it revealed a scuffed pocket watch that was buffed and shined.

He sat looking at it for moments before finally taking it from the box. He could only imagine how important this object was to Gemma.

"Umm, remember the young boy, Ryan, I told you about that taught me how to fight when I was a kid? Once they moved me, I never saw him again … I guess he never forgot me because some years later my caseworker paid me a visit and gave that to me." She pointed to the pocket watch.

"He insisted that I get this ... right before he died in the hospital from a knife wound inflicted by his drunken foster father. I'm not sure who gave it to him. Obviously, someone that cared for him ..."

As she cleared her throat before continuing, he knew she was trying hard to suppress the emotion she felt.

"It's not much, in fact, it's pretty worthless ... but it holds a lot of sentimental value to me and is priceless ... to me." She looked him squarely in the eyes, as hers brimmed with tears.

"He was the only person that truly cared for me ... until I met you."

A single tear slipped down her cheek as she reached across the table to flip the watch over so he saw the back, which was engraved with an inscription. As Alex read it, he realized the inscription was recent and meant for him.

'To Alex, a man that gives me hope.'

Alex looked up at Gemma, humbled he had affected her on such a level. *Does she not know what she's done for me?* Reaching up, he wiped the tear from her face. Words didn't seem to be enough to express his gratitude. This woman just gifted him with her only valuable possession in the world. Part of him wanted to hand it back. He didn't feel worthy enough to take this from her.

"Gemma, I truly don't know what to say ..." He cleared his throat as he was overcome with emotion.

She placed her hand over his, curling her fingers around his. "It's okay, Alex. You don't have to say anything."

He nodded his head and looked down at the watch. "Thank you, Gemma, thank you." Laying the watch back into the box, he stood up.

"Where are you going?" She asked puzzled.

"To get your gift," he called over his shoulder as he headed to the other room.

He had to take a minute before coming back. He let out a breath. *I can't fail her.* She was putting her trust and faith in him, which he was sure didn't come easy for her, after all she had been through and how many people let her down. *Please let me be worthy of her.*

He'd only wrapped the camera itself, deciding instead to leave the accessories to give her later after she saw the camera. The receipts were in a drawer, just in case she wanted to return any items for something different. Gathering himself, he grabbed the box and went back to the kitchen.

Gemma sat waiting for him. He smiled warmly at her as he sat the box in front of her. The excitement was bubbling up inside him; he couldn't wait to see her response to his gift. Alex remained standing as Gemma started to open the gift.

"Aren't you going to sit?" she asked, looking up at him.

"No, I'm okay ... open it, open it." She sensed his urgency and elation and opened the present a bit more quickly. Removing the tissue paper covering the top, she exposed a camera. There was a swift intake of breath as she stared at it with wide eyes. It was several beats before she exhaled and reached out trembling hands to pick up the camera. She turned it about before meeting his gaze.

"Now I'm the one that's speechless …" She glanced back down at the camera again.

Seeming pleased and excited by her response, he began talking rapidly. "I hope I got the right kind. I wasn't sure which was the best. The guy at the store said it's top of the line. I figured once you got into your program you'd need one. I have a bunch of other stuff I picked up along with it. I saved the receipt in case you want to exchange anything … You like it?"

She lovingly stroked her fingers across the features of the camera.

"Oh, Alex … I love it! I've never gotten a gift like this before … and there's more?" she asked incredulously. "This must have cost a fortune."

She sat the camera carefully back in the box.

"I … I can't take this." She stepped back from the table.

"What?" Moving toward the table, Alex picked up the camera and held it out to her. "Of course you can. I bought it for you."

She shook her head. "I can't."

"Gemma." He stepped toward her. "Listen, I know what you're thinking, but please don't. I want you to have this…"

He cradled the camera in his hands. "What you wrote on the back of that watch … I want to live up to that. I want to be that man. Don't you think I feel undeserving?"

She still said nothing as she stared at her shoes. He could see the tears that spiked her lashes.

"I won't take it back, Gemma and I won't let you give it back. I want to see you be the best photographer in the world. I know that whatever you have inside of you will come spilling out in your work and … and everyone will get to see who you are and not what they think you are, and that includes you."

She dabbed at her eyes.

"So please, take the gift."

It took her a second, but she reached out her hands and reluctantly accepted the camera from him. "Thank you, Alex."

"You're welcome," he said as he gently tugged her into his chest and planted a kiss on top of her head.

Pulling away, he took the camera from her, putting it back in its box. "We'll play with that later."

Alex took her by the hand.

"There is something else I wanted to give you … more so a do-over." He glanced back at her as they walked toward his bedroom.

She looked at him questioningly once they arrived at his closed bedroom door. He took a beat and then pushed the door open to reveal the room aglow in candles; rose petals led a path to the bed and then lay scattered among the sheets. He could feel the heat leap between he and Gemma where their hands touched. She let go of him to walk into the room.

Although she had her back to him, he could hear her soft declaration. "I feel like I'm in a dream, and I'm afraid I'm going to wake up."

"You're not dreaming." Coming to stand in front of her, he took her hands in his. "That first night I wanted to make things so special for you and to take my time ..." He chuckled a bit, as his face flushed at remembering his boyish eagerness the first night they were together. "I was so out of practice that I couldn't slow down. Plus, you were incredible."

At his confession, he heard Gemma giggle and look anywhere but at him.

"I just wanted the chance to give you what I wanted to that first night."

She looked up at him, confused. "What's that?"

"A romantic, sensual night of pleasure focused solely on you." He could feel her pulse quicken where he held her hand, and he smiled seductively. "Are you going to let me seduce you, Gemma?"

It took a moment, but she finally nodded her head, unable to form words.

At that, he pulled her into his arms and slowly and deeply kissed her. He wanted her intoxicated from his kisses. After kissing her thoroughly, he began to undress her, unzipping the back of her dress and letting it pool at her feet. Unclasping the strapless bra, he quickly disposed of it as his mouth slowly nipped and sucked at her neck. His hands came up and begin kneading her breasts and toying with her nipples. Moaning, she trembled under his touch.

Picking her up in his arms, he placed her gently on the bed. As he gazed down upon her, he saw the ripples of gooseflesh rise up on her skin. She looked delectable lying amongst the rose petals. He knelt on the bed to remove her panties; then stood back to stare at her while he removed his clothing. She glided her hands down her chest and over her breasts, lingering a moment to fondle her nipples as he crawled naked on the bed toward her. He never took his eyes from her as he parted her thighs and rested between them.

"What a pretty pussy."

Gemma's breathing became shallow as she watched him breathe in her scent. The look he gave her was primal and hungry right before he gave her a good swipe with his tongue. Her back arched off the bed as his mouth made contact with her skin. She was clutching the sheets in a death grip as he positioned her legs over his shoulders and started to nibble, suck, and lick her into oblivion. Alex wanted to see her drunk with passion.

"I love the way you taste." He whispered into her flesh.

After a half hour of toying with her, taking her to the brink and pulling her back, he finally let her come. Gemma's orgasm shook her body as she screamed her release. While she still trembled from her release, Alex kissed his way up to her mouth; her lips were swollen from his earlier kisses. He smiled into her mouth, before nuzzling her neck.

Gemma wound her arms around his neck, enjoying the feel of his tongue lapping at the hollow of her throat. She could feel him nudging her thighs farther apart, and she smiled, welcoming him inside of her. He slid into her; she could feel every inch of him as he slowly rocked his hips. His drag was painfully slow. She wrapped her legs around his waist. Gemma whimpered and moaned, thrusting her hips upward and willing him to go faster.

"Shhh …" He pressed her down into the mattress to still her movements. "I told you I was going to take my time."

Unhurried, he thrust into her until he was seated to the hilt and then he ground his hips. He pulled out gradually until the tip was the only part of him inside of her. She began clawing his back as he repeated the process, never letting his pace get any faster. Her body was singing with every stroke, and she could feel herself about to fly apart with the force of the orgasm that was coming. Alex must have felt it too because he pulled out for a few seconds to keep her from climaxing. He kissed the tops of her breasts before whispering huskily in her ear, "Not yet, baby."

He nipped at her lips as he rubbed the tip of his cock against her slick opening before entering her once more and returning to his super slow assault on her body. Gemma was crazy with the need to come as Alex continued to prolong her orgasm, at least three more times. Both of their bodies were dripping with sweat by the time Alex allowed her body the release it craved.

"Come for me, Gemma! Come now!"

Hearing those words sent Gemma over the edge.

"Ahhhh! Alex! Alex!" Gemma screamed as she climaxed hard. Her walls contracted tightly on his cock and it was all he could do to not come immediately.

She gripped him tighter as he began to piston in and out of her at a quicker pace. Alex's release was powerful as he kept pumping into her until he was spent. He gave a final grunt before collapsing onto her body. They lay there breathing heavily, their bodies slick with sweat. Gemma was still trying to catch her breath as Alex slid to his side. Kissing her collarbone, he pulled her against him, and she snuggled into his body.

He breathed in the scent created by the joining of their bodies. This woman did things to him. Gemma lay replete against him. The warmness of her body made him tighten his hold on her. He didn't want to let her go. There was something about the afterglow of sex that Alex enjoyed. Lying together afterward with their naked bodies touching, redolent with the rose petals was intoxicating. He felt drugged by Gemma's nearness. His nose trailed the hollow of her neck to inhale more of the rose fragrance that lingered there. His eyes closed as he continued nuzzling her. After settling against her, he promptly fell asleep with her secure in his arms.

Once she heard his deep, even breaths of sleepy contentment she lay awake, restless. Gemma's fingers traced the muscle in his thigh as he spooned her from behind. She was still coming down off the high he'd given her. His body was solid against her. It felt so right. She pulled his arm tighter around herself, trying to banish the fear that kept trying to creep inside of her—the fear and doubt that she didn't belong here, didn't belong with him. He kept telling her she was deserving of everything that was happening to her. *Why can't I accept that? Accept that my life is changing for the better?* She shut her eyes against the dark thoughts plaguing her mind and silently chastised herself. *Live in the moment! No more of this kind of talk!* She was determined to take hold of this new life that kept emerging. *Grab it with both hands and don't keep looking back at the past.* Snuggling closer against his warm body, she closed her eyes. She felt him press her closer and smiled before succumbing to a deep, gratifying slumber.

14

The next morning she woke up to an empty bed again. Her eyes landed on the note lying on his pillow. Grabbing it, she read:

Hey Sleeping Beauty,

I couldn't bear to wake you before I had to leave to open the restaurant. Please make yourself at home. I made coffee and a light breakfast before I left.

Alex
P.S. I left the rest of your camera goodies in the dining room for you to check out. Have fun! I'll call you soon.

She smiled and read the note a few more times before climbing from the bed and reaching for his discarded shirt from last night. Padding to the kitchen in bare feet, she found toast, coffee, and eggs waiting. She breathed deeply, inhaling the appealing aroma of the simple breakfast. *How does he*

manage to make something as basic as eggs seem gourmet?
She wolfed down the breakfast and cleaned her dishes
immediately afterward.

Wandering into the dining room, she found all of the
camera accessories he mentioned in his note placed carefully
on the table awaiting her perusal. Over the next half hour,
she rummaged through the different packages and boxes,
unearthing some pieces of equipment that were unfamiliar. She
set those items to the side, making a mental note to ask Alex
their purpose. A shrill telephone ring interrupted her treasure
hunt. By the second ring, she remembered Alex's note said he
would call her, and she jumped up to grab the phone.

"Hello?"

"Hey. For a minute I thought you might still be asleep."

She could hear the smile in his voice.

"I hope breakfast wasn't too cold by the time you ate?"

"No, it was perfect, Alex. Thank you so much. You didn't
have to."

"I wanted to ... I figured you'd be hungry after last night."

Gemma felt the tips of her ears burn at the reference to
the marathon orgasm session he gave her. She was glad he
couldn't see her right now.

"I was rather famished this morning," she said with a
knowing smile.

Both were silent for a moment before he boldly said, "I'm
happy I could satisfy your hunger ... again."

She leaned against the counter, enjoying the deep timbre his voice took on when he was trying to be sexy. It definitely worked. The change in his voice made her body heat rise by about ten degrees.

She didn't know what to say to that, and she heard him laugh.

"I'll stop making you blush now."

She giggled this time. "How did you know—"

He cut her off, "I know you, Gemma." Before silence could descend, Alex continued, "By the way, yesterday I picked up an extra toothbrush and some panties so you would have something in the morning when you took a shower. I still forgot soap that's more suitable for a lady. Sorry, I'll remember next time."

Shocked he had been so thoughtful, she could only mumble, "Thank you."

She heard noises and then other voices in the background.

"Sorry, I have to run, the shipment just arrived ... Feel free to stick around, okay? I know you don't work today, so relax and figure out your camera. I'll bring dinner home ..."

More noises interrupted him again.

"Gotta go."

She heard a dial tone before she could respond. As she clicked the phone off, she got a funny feeling in her gut. *Did he just say he'll bring dinner home? Home? Bring dinner home to me?* It was all so domestic. She turned this over in her mind as she walked back into the dining room. If this were yesterday, she would be asking again if they were moving too fast, but since she promised herself she wasn't going to keep questioning everything she let the thought go and went back to learning about her new camera.

Dinner service was going especially well tonight. He'd even allowed Brandon to take the reins a bit in calling out the orders and running the kitchen. He figured he needed to start grooming him to run the kitchen nights he wasn't here. The thought wasn't lost that he was considering letting someone else run his kitchen so he could take off occasionally to spend time with Gemma. The idea of not being at the restaurant 24/7 seemed like a foreign concept—that he might have a life outside of this place, he hadn't considered … since Sam. He hadn't thought about her in the past couple days. This made him pause mid-chop. He couldn't remember a time since her death when she hadn't come unbidden to his thoughts. He didn't notice Brandon look at him with concern.

"Hey, Alex. You okay?"

He heard the worry laced in Brandon's voice and the absence of his usual moniker.

"Sorry, Brandon, I'm okay." He gave him a reassuring smile and went back to his chopping. A little guilt nibbled at him at not having thought of Sam. He didn't want to forget her, but surely she wouldn't want him eating guilt cookies the rest of his days. She'd want him to move on; not thinking of her for a few days didn't make him a terrible person. Scooping up the chopped vegetables, he deposited them in a pan on the stove. He needed to go by and leave some flowers at her grave.

Halfway through the night, Rachel put in an appearance. Earlier, she phoned in a dinner order for her and Chloe. She came into the kitchen and managed to stay out of the way of the line cooks and bus boys running to and fro in the kitchen.

"Hey," she called out to him as she stole some garnish off a plate and stuffed it in her mouth.

"Hey," Alex said, removing the plate out of Rachel's reach as he continued firing orders.

"What's up?" Brandon asked as he walked by on the way to the refrigerator.

"Nothing much."

Rachel was able to grab another scrap of food off another passing plate and received a death glare from the waiter who had to stop and redress the plate.

"Stop it!" Alex walked over and thrust her to-go bag at her.

She gave him a saccharine-sweet smile.

"Where's Gemma? I didn't see her out in the dining room."

Alex continued working, trying to remain uninterested in what Rachel was asking.

"I'm not sure."

Rachel gave him a crazy look. "What do you mean you're not sure? I thought you saw her last night."

This comment caught the attention of some of the kitchen staff, in particular, Brandon, who started exchanging glances with some of the line cooks.

Grabbing his sister's arm, he ushered her out of the kitchen. Apparently, she hadn't received the memo that he didn't want to discuss him and Gemma, least of all here at work. They went through the swinging door exiting the kitchen to rumblings from the cook staff, much to Alex's chagrin. He released Rachel's arm once they were safely out of earshot.

"What are you doing? No one here knows about Gemma and me, and I would've liked to have kept it that way until you opened your big mouth."

He ran his hand through his hair in exasperation.

"You do know that Brandon expressed interest in her, and now you've just outed me, right?" He paced the hall.

"Listen, little brother, I didn't realize that you and Gemma weren't public. As for Brandon, I don't think he'll be that put out by not getting to date Gemma. There are plenty of women in this city that haven't blown him off yet. He'll live." She grabbed his arm to stop his pacing. "Hey."

He looked down at his sister, and his face softened a bit.

"It's not me I'm concerned about. It's Gemma ..." He gave her a boyish grin. "Truth be told, I could shout the way

I feel about her from the rooftops." Folding his arms across his chest, he looked at her in earnest. "I didn't expect these feelings to come so fast, Rachel … if I'm honest I didn't expect to have them again."

She placed her hand on his shoulder as she beamed at him. "Alex, this is great. I'm happy to see you moving on. You know how much we all loved Sam, but I want to see you happy. No one expected you to be a monk the rest of your life, and you shouldn't feel guilty for moving on. Sam would approve."

If Alex was as good at detecting things with his sister as he was with Gemma, he would have heard the false note in her voice. Frankly, she couldn't give a shit how Sam would feel.

Some of the tension eased from his shoulders at her last statement.

"Gemma's right for you, and I think you're good for her … I would never betray her confidence, but I think I can safely say that she's into you as well."

A huge grin transfixed Alex's face causing his sister's jaw to drop slightly.

"Alex, I haven't seen you look this happy in a long time. This is serious. You're truly happy, and could it be …" He watched his sister stare at him with this goofy look on her face and was just about to ask her what she was going to say when she resumed speaking.

"Anyways, I should run. Chloe's waiting for me to bring dinner home … and I'm sure you have a kitchen full of rumors that you need to put to rest." Rachel giggled as she started to walk away.

"You pest!" Alex snapped the dishtowel in his hand at his sister as she walked away.

"You start tongues wagging about shit and then you just take off." Alex laughed as Rachel kept chuckling and walking away. Shaking his head, he headed back to the kitchen.

Everyone pretended to be engrossed in their work.

"Whatever, guys. You don't have to pretend you're working hard."

The kitchen erupted in laughter and conversation. Some of the staff started peppering him with questions about what his sister said before she left. Putting up his hands, he tried to suppress the grin that was creeping across his face.

"I'm not answering any questions."

"Aww, c'mon, man," one of the line cooks said.

"Let's just get back to work, dinner isn't going to cook itself," Alex replied good-naturedly as he put pans on the stovetop.

Later that night, Alex turned his key in the lock and found Gemma sprawled on the floor with the camera next to her as she peered at his laptop. She looked up, giving him a lopsided grin.

"Hey, c'mere." She beckoned him to join her on the floor by patting the space next to her. After setting the bag of food on the ground, he sat Indian-style next to her. She clicked back to a previous screen, and it was filled with pictures of people and nature.

"Whaddaya think?" Gemma asked him with an eager expression as she bit her lower lip.

He stared at the pictures in awe as he picked up the laptop and sat it in his lap. He started going through her photos. Gemma scooted closer to him, looking over his shoulder as he perused her work.

"Gemma, these are stunning …" He turned to her. "You have such a good eye, and you're already such a natural at capturing the light."

She leaned back, looking at him delightfully puzzled. "What do you know about photography?"

He shrugged, trying to hide his smile. "An old high-school girlfriend dabbled. We spent a lot of time in the dark room, a couple of things stuck."

They both giggled knowing Alex and his high school girlfriend did more than develop pictures in the dark room. Gemma glanced at the computer screen, which held images of her photos, and then turned back to him.

"You think they're good?"

He nodded his head.   "I do … I think school will only enhance your skills. You're a natural, kid." He smiled broadly at her, then continued going through her work.

"When I left here to collect some things from the boarding house I took the camera with me, and on the way back I decided to stop by the park … I just wanted to start taking pictures. Some of the programs I found online expect you to have a portfolio for them to review before they consider accepting you."

Placing the laptop on the floor, he pulled her onto his lap. "Then I guess we better get started on creating a portfolio for you."

He sucked on her bottom lip, savoring it before finally kissing her skillfully. She kissed him back and then pulled away for a second. She could feel him palming her ass.

"Is this your idea of working on my portfolio?"

He waggled his eyebrows at her and said in a sexy voice, "Is it working?"

"Mmmhmm."

They smiled into each other's eyes. She broke their intense gaze by glancing toward the bag he dropped earlier when he came in; then flicked her eyes back to his.

"What's in the bag?"

"Dinner …" He leaned up and kissed her nose. "We could have dinner first or," he kissed her neck, "afterwards." He looked at her knowingly, waiting for her response. She gave the food a cursory glance before giving him a slow, sweet kiss in answer.

A couple of hours later they sat in his bed wrapped in sheets, eating reheated take-out from the restaurant. He kept trying to feed her while she laughed at his corny accent.

He enjoyed making her laugh. She wiped a tear from her eye as she tried to contain her laughter. At first, she insisted on going back to the boarding house tonight, but he managed to coax her to stay the night again. He noticed her yawning.

"I think Sleeping Beauty is tired." Alex's mouth quirked up into a grin. He removed the cartons of food from the bed and patted the open spot next to him. "Come to papa."

Gemma giggled as she rolled to her side to face him. "Are you always this goofy?"

She ruffled his hair as she tried to stifle another yawn.

He smirked at her. "Only for you."

Her sleepy smile was adorable as he leaned over to kiss her softly on the lips before turning out the light.

Within minutes, they were both asleep, nestled in each other's arms.

Gemma awakened first and found Alex still sleeping peacefully on his stomach. His hair was mussed, and she could just barely hear his deep, even breathing. An idea suddenly hit her, and she slipped out of bed and put on Alex's shirt before going to get her camera.

She came around to his side of the bed. Alex was resting on his stomach with his face turned away from her now. Despite this, Gemma didn't feel she had missed getting some good shots of him. Alex had such a strong back. Thankfully, he'd kicked the covers off a bit, and the top of his buttocks was exposed. The image he presented was sexy, but there was something serene about it as well. She snapped a few shots and then checked the frame. The way the light was hitting him and the bed was almost magical, like he was being bathed in the sunlight. She kept snapping pictures, varying her angle a little each time.

Suddenly, Alex rolled onto his back. Gemma froze, hoping she hadn't woken him up. She waited with bated breath. His deep, even breathing resumed as she saw him rub his hand down his chest. His face was angled toward the camera. For a second, her camera was forgotten as she watched him in slumber. He looked peaceful. She slowly put her camera back in place and took a few long shots, but then pushed in for close-up shots of his face, and then extreme close-ups of his closed eyelids so that she saw the tiny blue veins and the golden brown of his eyelashes. Then she changed to taking close-up shots of his hand resting on his chest.

After finishing her impromptu photo session, she crawled back into bed next to him. She sat up watching him for a moment, and then she quietly lie down beside him. Inching closer to his body, she turned the camera around and clicked a selfie. She was about to click another when she heard his groggy, sleep addled voice.

"Good morning."

Gemma almost dropped her camera after being startled by him.

Alex chuckled when he saw her fumble with the camera. He rubbed his hand over his face.

"How long have you been awake?"

"Not long."

She held her camera against her chest. She didn't want him to know about the pictures she took of him while he was asleep. She'd show them to him eventually, just not today. He looked over at her, finally noticing the camera, and ran his hands through his hair still trying to wake up.

Yawning he asked, "Were you up taking pictures?"

She nodded her head.

"Take a picture of us."

"What?" she asked.

He pulled her closer. "Take a picture of us. It will be our first picture together."

Gemma looked at him warmly, fighting the big grin that wanted to break across her face. "Okay."

She smiled at him before turning back to hoist her camera above them. As she was about to click the photo, Alex turned, leaned in, and kissed her on the cheek as the flash went off, leaving a happy but surprised expression on her face. When she was hitting the button again to take another picture, Alex turned her face toward him and kissed her full on the lips as the flash went off once more. Then Gemma felt his hand taking the camera out of her hands while he kept kissing her. She obligingly leaned into his body, hungry for his kisses, and he wrapped her in his arms as they continued their good morning kiss.

After a few more minutes she pulled away sufficiently satisfied. She licked her bottom lip as she grinned at him. "I should get home … and get ready for work later."

Alex deflated at her proclamation and held her a little tighter.

"Why don't you stay a while longer?" He looked at her with a pouty face, and she giggled. He nuzzled her neck before she could resume speaking.

"Both you and Rachel use that puppy dog look when you're trying to get your way, and I can tell you that she is more effective."

Alex guffawed at this statement, pulling away from assaulting her neck. The storm clouds that recently marred his brow at her talk of going home departed.

"My pouty face doesn't work on you? Seriously?"

She relented a bit, "Okay, maybe just a little …" She dropped her gaze to his chest. "It's just I haven't been home in like two days and ..." She was not sure how to finish her thought. Looking back into his eyes, she decided to confess, "I don't want to feel like I'm ... crowding you, Alex."

"It's not crowding if I want you to stay," he softly said.

He pressed her closer as his warm blue eyes searched her face. When he saw her about to protest further, he leaned in, placing a tender, soft kiss on her lips before giving her the full intent of his gaze.

"I want you here, Gemma." He touched his forehead to hers. "I want you here ..." He exhaled a breath and said in a whisper, "It scares me how much I want you here."

Her breath caught on a sigh as she leaned closer to him, breathing in his breath, taking him into her lungs. No one had ever wanted her to stay. She could only ever remember being shushed or shooed, driven from rooms with withering looks or often with the threat of abuse. And here this man was afraid that she'd leave. He turned her into a pool of emotions; the happy tears welled in her eyes, blurring her vision. She kissed him deeply.

After a few minutes of blissful kisses, he pulled back and licked his bottom lip.

"By the way, I should probably tell you ... I meant to tell you last night, but we got sidetracked. The cat's out of the bag ... about us that is." He appeared a bit sheepish as he peered at her face.

She looked astonished. "How? When?"

"Rachel."

He quickly started talking again, feeling like an ass for throwing Rachel under the bus. "But listen, it isn't her fault. I never told her it was a secret, so don't be mad at her, okay?"

Smiling at Alex, she touched his face. "It's okay. I'm not mad. It's not like I'm embarrassed to be with you or something. It's not like you have a hunchback, or you're some hideous beast." She giggled as he began tickling her and joining in the laughter. After a few minutes, he let up.

"Good. Now I can tell everyone you're my girlfriend, and Brandon can stop drooling all over you."

Her heart skipped a beat at Alex calling her his girlfriend. It was nice to see he wasn't afraid to put a label on their relationship. She wasn't going to make a big deal out of it.

"Well, your girlfriend is hungry. If you're going to make me stay then you need to feed me."

"Oh really, Miss Bossy Pants?" He started tickling her again and making her squeal. After a bit more tickling and stolen kisses, they finally exited the bed to make breakfast together.

Later that day he took enjoyment in driving them to work, and even more pleasure in taking her hand in his as they walked into the restaurant. Some of the staff had already arrived and did double takes as they saw their boss holding hands with her.

Alex felt Gemma trying to pull her hand away and tightened his grip, and then sent her hand a reassuring squeeze. She glanced up at him as she bit her lip. Despite her bravado this morning, he knew she was feeling nervous about them being out in the open now. The murmurs and whispers of the staff had not gone unnoticed. He knew most of the staff had a fondness for Gemma and hoped they would still treat her kindly. She was finally letting her guard down a bit more, and the doubt had crept away. He didn't want all of that returning because of the behavior of his staff. He would nip it in the bud if he had to. But before he could say anything, Brandon appeared in the doorway of the kitchen.

"Boss man's finally got himself a girl ..."

Brandon approached Alex and Gemma and looked between the two of them with a blank expression. Alex was unsure how this would go; he knew Brandon had a thing for Gemma.

Suddenly, Brandon clapped Alex on the back as his face broke into a broad grin.

"It's good to see you happy again, Alex." He turned to Gemma. "I'm sorry things didn't work out for you and me, but it seems like you're doing the world a service by going out with this guy," Brandon said jokingly.

He dropped his voice a bit so only Gemma could hear. "Take care of him, okay?"

She smiled up at Brandon, grateful for his kindness; then kissed him on the cheek in gratitude.

"Hey!" Alex exclaimed in jest. "Are you trying to steal my woman right out from under my nose?" He put his arm around Gemma's waist, pulling her close as everyone erupted in laughter.

Alex and Brandon began to play fight and then walked off toward the kitchen together. Once Alex left her side, Gemma became surrounded by some of the female wait staff wanting to find out details about how she bagged the boss. Amanda must have sensed her unease over all the fussing and attention because she quickly came to her rescue.

"Let the girl breathe! She doesn't want to answer a bunch of questions from some sex-starved, crazy women."

Gemma sent her a look of thanks, as the women bickered with Amanda. Making a quick escape to the break room, she stored her items and got herself ready for her shift. Alex snuck up behind her and wrapped his arms around her before planting a kiss on her neck.

"Alex," she groaned with pleasure. "We shouldn't do this at work with everyone here."

He nuzzled her neck some more. "So, you're saying it's okay when no one is here? Well, let me go clear the building." He made as if to walk away.

Laughing, Gemma playfully punched him in the arm. "Not funny."

Alex pulled her into his arms and spoke softly, "I know you were nervous about everyone's reaction to us, but see, everything is fine."

The grin he gave her calmed her nerves. She nodded her head and returned his smile.

"Well let me get to work. I don't want anyone to think I'm going to get special treatment now just because we're dating." She quickly stood on tiptoes and planted a kiss on his lips and walked out of the break room with him trailing her.

15

Thomas sat at his older model computer, which Alex and Rachel talked him into getting years ago, even though he told them he was an analog man and would stay that way. It took him over half an hour to finally get the computer started and then make his way onto the Internet. Now he knew what Chloe meant when she was always telling him to Google everything.

He typed in Gemma Peyton to see if he would find anything and came up empty handed. He just knew there was something, but had found nothing so far. While deep in thought his glance roamed the room and landed on a picture of his now adult kids as children. They were both pulling silly faces at the camera. He remembered his wife took that photo. It still pierced his heart when he thought of her, not just the loss of her, but the struggle she endured right until her final day.

If there was anything about Gemma, he knew he had to find it—not only to put to rest this suspicion he had of her but to protect his son from any more heartache.

"I got in! Oh, Alex, I got in!"

Gemma threw her arms around his neck, and Alex smiled into the crook of her neck as he held her. He was so incredibly happy for her. Once he pulled back, he saw her eyes sparkled with her good news. He finally set her back on her feet.

"I knew you would." He smiled down into her face. "Everyone has been rooting for you. How about we celebrate with my family who I know can't wait to hear the news? Then you and I can celebrate privately later." His smile turned mischievous at his last statement.

Giggling, she wrapped her arms around his waist. "I like that idea." Rising up on her tiptoes, Gemma kissed his lips.

Over the past two months between shifts at the restaurant and spending time with Alex, Gemma managed to put her portfolio together. She submitted it a week ago in time for the new session at the community college to begin. Getting the acceptance letter meant the world to her, but Alex's belief in her meant even more. The past four weeks had been pure bliss. She stayed at his home more than the boarding house, much to Shelby's dismay. For some reason, her parole officer had a soft spot for her and tended to look the other way as long as they met once a week, and she passed her drug tests, which was never an issue. She also found a family in Alex's sister, niece, and father. His dad was still a bit rough around the edges, but he was pleasant enough. She adored Chloe, and Rachel was the sister she never had.

Alex patted her butt as he walked into the kitchen to figure out what to make for her celebratory dinner.

"Hey, babe, what do you want? I can put something on the grill or make whatever you want. I want to make a list so I can figure out if I need to go to the store."

Gemma came up behind him as he stood at the counter and put her arms around his waist. "Mmmm, let's put something on the grill. It's such a beautiful day. I bet it will be warm tonight with it being the beginning of summer."

Alex rubbed her arm and smiled at her nearness. "Good choice. You want anything in particular?"

"No, surprise me."

Gemma went to walk off and leave him to it, but he grabbed her hand and pulled her back against his body. He fingered the weathered fabric of one of his old navy colored T-shirts she'd made her own. It had become her favorite. Truth be told, it looked better on her than it ever did on him.

"Did I tell you again how proud I am of you?" His face beamed at her with such adoration. In return, she gave him a brilliant smile.

"Yes, you did …" She leaned up and kissed him. "Because you're the best boyfriend ever."

"And don't you forget it."

That sent them both off into peals of laughter. She slapped his arm as she stepped away.

"Okay, baby, let me know if you want me to go with you to the store. Otherwise, I'll be going through my latest batch of photos."

Alex kissed her hand before releasing her. "Okay."

He headed off to the store alone, wanting to let Gemma work and get things prepared for classes starting. Pushing the cart down the aisles of the supermarket, he picked up the items he needed for the celebratory cookout.

Alex loaded the groceries into the trunk. As he was about to get into the car, he noticed the jewelry store on the corner. Maybe he'd find a nice congratulatory gift for Gemma.

That's not a bad idea.

Pulling the pocket watch that Gemma gave him out of his pocket, he checked the time. More than enough time to check and see if he would find anything. He locked his car and headed over to the jewelry store.

Upon entering the shop, a salesperson greeted him. He smiled and nodded.

"Just looking for now. Thank you."

The woman gave him a mega-watt smile. "Please let me know if you find anything you'd like to take a closer look at and I can display it for you." She moved away as another customer entered.

Alex jammed his hands into his pockets as he began to wander around the store looking at the necklaces, earrings, and bracelets. Before long he found himself in the ring section. Alex removed his hands from his pockets as he seriously began to peruse the cases filled with gold, platinum, and silver engagement and wedding rings.

Gemma. His mind caressed her name as he thought about slipping one of these rings onto her finger and making her his wife. Flashes of a life not yet lived together went through his head: the wedding, the honeymoon, fighting and making up, doing chores together, taking care of her when she was sick, hearing the news that she was carrying his child. That thought nearly knocked him on his ass. The idea of Gemma far gone in pregnancy made him smile broadly. He thought of them playfully arguing over baby names, and he knew … he knew beyond a shadow of a doubt that he wanted her forever. At that revelation, his eyes suddenly alighted on an art deco style ring that he couldn't imagine being anywhere other than on her finger.

He looked up and got the attention of Ms. Mega-Watt Smile.

"Miss, I'd like to see that ring." He pointed to the ring and waited for the saleswoman to remove it from the case and display it on the velvet mat.

"That's the ring," he muttered to himself as the diamonds sparkled back at him.

"Are congratulations in order, sir? Would you like me to have it sized for you?" She flashed the dazzling white smile at him.

He'd been totally unaware that he would need that, not that Alex had known he would be picking out an engagement ring today. For a moment, he felt disappointment.

"I don't know her size."

"Well, I can always hold the ring for you until you find out."

There was that blinding smile again, but he didn't mind.

"Yes, yes ... please hold it. I'll come back with the size and purchase the ring. Thank you so much for your help."

"No problem, sir. I'll just need to get your credit card to hold a deposit, and if you could just fill out this form."

Alex gave her his credit card and signed the form. He took one last wistful look at the ring before she took it away for safe keeping in the back of the store. He left with his heart singing.

Once they arrived at his father's house, everyone hugged and congratulated Gemma. Excitement filled the air as they celebrated her news. Alex's mind kept wandering back to the ring. He couldn't wait to be here amongst his family celebrating their engagement. He could just hear Chloe and Rachel squealing over Gemma's hand as she showed off the ring and it made him smile inwardly. After spending some time catching up with everyone, he excused himself to go man the grill.

The smoke funneled into the sky, as the smell of sizzling meat permeated the air. Alex immensely enjoyed being outdoors cooking over an open flame. He took a sip of his beer as he flipped the burgers over on the grill and looked up. The scene that met him caused him to pause. Gemma sat curled up on the lounger with Chloe, their heads bent together over some magazine while Chloe painted Gemma's nails. He could hear the snippets of conversation as Chloe discussed the boy she was interested in and who she was feuding with on her soccer team. Gemma was listening intently and offering advice. He loved seeing her ensconced in this domestic scene, comfortably counseling his niece. It felt natural, so right. She fit so perfectly into his life. His family loved her … he loved her.

At that moment, she lifted her face and caught his gaze. She gifted him with a radiant smile before returning to her girl talk with Chloe. Some people might say he was rushing or hadn't thought it through, or even that they hadn't known each other long, but he didn't think he needed any more time to know what he felt in his heart. He wanted to make Gemma his wife. He swigged his beer as he continued to watch her. A few seconds later, Rachel interrupted his daydream.

"Aren't the burgers ready yet, Alex? I'm starving." She walked up beside him and peered at the food on the grill. Alex chuckled to himself. Leave it to Rachel to ruin a moment.

"Only a few more minutes." Alex said distractedly as he continued to watch Gemma.

"Enjoying the scenery?" she asked jokingly as she nudged him in the side.

Alex shook his head with a laugh and set his now empty beer bottle down as he turned to address his sister. "Do you have something you want to say or are you just going to be a pest?"

Rachel laughed. "You've been standing there staring at Gemma and drooling all over her ..." She glanced down at the burgers. "I hope you didn't drool on the burgers."

Alex couldn't help but laugh as he playfully smacked his sister with the spatula. "So what! I care about her. Plus, she's my girlfriend. I can watch her if I want, Rachel."

Alex began taking the burgers from the grill, as Rachel watched him closely before speaking.

"Have you told her yet, that you love her?" she asked softly.

He stopped in the middle of what he was doing. It was a minute before he looked at Rachel, and then over at Gemma and Chloe.

"Am I that transparent?" He finally returned his attention to Rachel.

"Anyone looking at you could tell you have it bad."

They both shared a laugh. He gave Gemma and Chloe another glance before pulling Rachel away from hearing distance.

"I'm going to propose." Alex began to babble, "I don't have a ring yet. I mean, I was in the jewelry store today, and the ring is on hold, but I didn't know her size. I didn't even go in there to look at engagement rings. The plan was to get a gift, but then I saw the rings, and it just felt right … It feels right. I can't imagine her not being in my life every day …"

Before he could continue Rachel's excitement got the better of her.

"What? Oh my, goodness Alex!" Her enthusiastic words broke him from his musings. His head spun around to check and see if Gemma and Chloe overheard. He was glad that Rachel's outburst didn't send either of them investigating.

"Can't you ever keep your voice down," he hissed at her, and ran his hand through his hair in exasperation. "Why do I ever tell you anything?"

Rachel appeared contrite, but only a little. Her excitement couldn't be contained. She said in a whisper, "Sorry, sorry …

I'm just ecstatic. I think you two are MFEO. I'd love to have Gemma as a sister-in-law."

Puzzled, he stared at his sister. "What the hell is MFEO?"

She shook her head, before saying like he was the dumbest person on the planet, "Made for each other."

Alex's face quirked into a slight grin at hearing the meaning of MFEO. Then his smile faded and was replaced by sadness. Alex tried to push his guilt over Sam to the side. Rachel placed her hand on her brother's arm.

"Alex, you don't have to feel guilty. Sam would want you to move on. She'd want you to be happy … marry her."

Giving her a smile of gratitude, he patted his sister's hand. "I guess you're not always a pest."

They both laughed softly, and Rachel smacked him on the arm.

"Get the food off the grill so we can eat, little brother," she smirked at him and stuck out her tongue, then ran inside before he could retaliate.

Alex took the rest of the food off the grill.

"Gemma, Chloe, we're ready to eat," he called to them.

Thomas hated that every day he'd spent in Gemma's presence he'd grown to like her more and more, and she seemed good for Alex. Unfortunately, he couldn't just let things go. When he'd been unable to produce anything in his feeble search a month ago, he'd hired a private investigator. Maybe some thought he was crazy, but he'd rather the professional turn up nothing than to not have gone through with the search that would finally put his mind to rest. He didn't understand what was taking so long. He smiled as Gemma passed him the platter of burgers. Everyone talked and laughed around him, and he did his best to keep on top of the ongoing conversation. The phone rang, and Thomas immediately got up to answer it.

"Dad, let the machine get it." Alex waved him back to his seat.

"It could be my doctor …" He saw everyone's concerned expressions, and knew he'd better say something quick. "It's nothing, just a refill on my medication. Nothing to be alarmed about." He quickly excused himself and went to the phone, hoping it was the investigator. He hated to tell the lie, but he didn't want anyone knowing he had Gemma investigated, especially if there was nothing hidden.

"Hello," he said upon picking up.

"Mr. Chambers, we're calling on behalf of the Local Law Enforcement Foundation wondering if you'd like to make a donation?"

Thomas deflated at hearing the solicitor.

"No, not at this time." He didn't give the woman a chance to respond before he hung up the phone. Sighing heavily, he made his way back into the dining room and attempted to enjoy the rest of dinner.

That night back at his house he couldn't take his eyes off of her. He watched her move around the bedroom, shrugging off her sundress, removing her jewelry, grabbing a hair tie to put her hair up in a messy bun. Over time, he'd watched her become more comfortable with being naked when they weren't intimate. It was very sexy to watch her walk around the bedroom in just her panties as she gathered some stray magazines. She turned down the covers and sat on the bed flipping through one of the magazines. He was drawn to her as she sat reading, unaware that he watched her. Sitting on the edge of the bed, he lifted her legs and put them on his lap.

Gemma glanced up as she felt the bed dip and Alex pick up her feet. Warmth spread through her at his touch. Even though they had been intimate more times than she could count, her body still eagerly responded to him. He didn't say anything, just began to massage her calf muscles. He appeared deep in thought as he rubbed her legs. His hands finally reached her feet. His fingers kneaded her arches. Closing her eyes, she enjoyed his touch on her skin. When she reopened them, he stared deeply into her eyes, and she squirmed under his gaze.

"I love you, Gemma." He said it softly, but with such conviction, it made her heart skip a beat. She had hoped, wished, wanted to hear him say those words to her because it was how she had felt about him for some time.

"I love you, too, Alex," she said on a tremulous sigh.

Happy tears gathered in the corners of her eyes. The grin that spread across his face made her smile in return. They both reached for each other at the same time. She pulled him down on top of her, and he absently pushed her magazine to the floor as they kissed passionately, lost in each other.

Later that night, after a marathon of making love both in the bed and in the shower, they lay in bed together. Her head rested on his chest. He absently ran his fingers up and down her back while they talked about her being nervous about starting college.

"You're going to do just fine," he reassured her.

She smiled into his chest, always grateful for his faith in her. "Can I ask you something?"

He glanced down at the top of her head. "You can ask me anything."

Resting her arm across his chest, she peered up at him. "When did you know?" She saw his look of puzzlement. "When did you know you loved me?"

Alex smiled warmly at her as he rubbed the backs of his fingers along her cheek.

"I think I loved you long before I acknowledged it to myself ... but I think the moment I knew was when you gave me the pocket watch. It was so selfless of you to give me something that must mean the world to you."

She rubbed her chin slowly across the skin of his stomach and reveled in the nearness their bodies shared in this intimate moment.

"When did you know?" he asked her as he continued to rub his fingers along her cheek.

She gazed up at him. "The morning after our first night together. You held me so tenderly in your lap ... and I just felt cherished."

"You are cherished Gemma and don't ever forget that I love you." Sitting up, he pulled her into his lap and began to place gentle kisses softly and slowly all over her face before the descent down her body. Pushing her back on the bed, he lavished her body with the attention it deserved to show her just how much he cherished her.

That night after Gemma fell asleep, Alex carefully measured her ring finger so he could have the ring sized to fit her slender finger. He looked forward to slipping it on her and seeing her face light up.

16

School was kicking her butt. She started off at a disadvantage to some of her peers because she hadn't been in school in ages. At first, she felt intimidated by the youth and intelligence that surrounded her, but she soon learned she had nothing to fear. It took her a little while to get acclimated to the course load, but soon she found her rhythm. Of course, her photography classes were her favorite. Work and school kept her busy lately; she and Alex were barely able to spend time together. They tried to make sure to see each other at least two nights out of the week, but this wasn't enough for either of them. Tonight, she wanted to do something special for him because he'd been incredibly supportive. So, she was making him dinner. He was always cooking for her, and she wanted to give him a break for once. Plus, it was fun to be here in his kitchen cooking for him, it felt very … domestic. She moved around the kitchen prepping ingredients and cooking on the stovetop. She wanted everything to be perfect for the love of her life. A small smile lifted the corners of her mouth as she remembered him declaring his love for her. It was a dream come true to know his feelings mirrored her own.

Gemma Johnson. That's what held up the investigation. Alex nor Gemma ever disclosed that Gemma was married before. This whole time he had the investigator looking for Gemma Peyton. When the investigator called today with the news he'd been waiting for all this time, he was ecstatic to know that his gut hadn't been wrong, but distraught at the thought of ruining Alex's happiness. Unfortunately, his sense of duty wouldn't let him dismiss this, especially not when he saw what the investigator's report had to say.

Looking over at the clock, Gemma realized she only had two hours before he would be home. Suddenly, the doorbell rang. *Who would be coming to Alex's house right now?* She grabbed a dishtowel on her way to answer the door. Upon answering, she was greeted by the severe figure of Thomas Chambers. Gemma smiled uneasily at Alex's father as she welcomed him, unsure why he seemed so hostile.

"Hi, Mr. Chambers. Alex isn't home yet. Did you want to come in and wait for him?"

Mr. Chambers swept in without a smile or a hello. Gemma stepped back, opening the door wider to permit him.

"Is everything okay?" Gemma asked, perplexed. *Why is he acting so weird?* She wiped her hands on the dishtowel.

He moved farther into the living room without speaking, so she followed. Finally, he turned to face her.

"I knew there was something about you when I first met you ..."

His allegation hung in the air between them. Gemma stood speechless, still uncertain what had brought on this change in Mr. Chambers.

"Were you ever going to say anything about what you did, who you are, or was it all some sick joke to you?"

Her face flushed at the words he spat at her. She could understand how he might feel like she was a fraud. It had been plaguing her a bit lately that she still hadn't been forthcoming about her past to Mr. Chambers; that she was an ex-con. She wanted to tell Alex's family, but she was embarrassed, and now his father had found out on his own. It sounded like he believed she may have kept it from Alex, which would explain his anger. She could only hope he would be as understanding as Alex. He told her she could wait and reveal to his family when she was ready, and he never asked what misdeed landed her in prison. As close as they had grown, she was poised to tell him soon. Well no need to let Mr. Chambers stew in front of her. She might as well say what he already knew. She looked down at the floor, twisting the dishtowel into knots as she spoke.

"Mr. Chambers … I'm sorry I didn't just tell you before …" She finally looked up. "I'm an ex-con. I was just too embarrassed to tell you. I didn't want you to think I wasn't good enough for your son."

He still continued to stare at her strangely, so she continued explaining.

"Alex does know. He kept my secret because I wasn't ready to tell you yet … I just wanted you guys to like me." She bit her lip pensively.

"What kind of game are you playing at? Why would you do this to him? I refuse to believe he knows what you've done."

She looked at him, confused and hurt.

"I would never hurt Alex … I love him. No, I haven't shared the specifics, but it never mattered to him because he said it was the past."

He stared at her for what seemed like an eternity, until she saw his expression change from anger to disbelief.

Gemma saw the hostility leave Mr. Chambers features, but he suddenly appeared weary and old.

He sighed heavily.

"Gemma, I think you better sit."

She reluctantly took a seat on the sofa. Fear gripped her heart. What was he about to tell her?

He took the seat across from her before breaking the earth-shattering news. "Gemma, the reason you seemed familiar the night we met is because I'd seen you before … at your sentencing hearing."

Gemma looked at him incredulously. "Why were you there? I … I don't understand. I didn't know you then."

In his mind, he couldn't help but think, *How did this happen?*

Suddenly, he wasn't just concerned about the fallout and aftermath that would affect his son, but also what this news was going to do to Gemma. But, he knew he couldn't keep it a secret because eventually it would come out. Better for it to come out now versus later.

"I was there Gemma because the woman you killed that night was Alex's wife. I … I just didn't put two and two together the night Alex introduced you because you were going by your married name at the hearing and I only got a glimpse of you."

Gemma felt like all the air had been sucked out of the room. The feeling that she just received a punch to the gut was overwhelming.

What did he just say?

"What?" she stated in a hoarse whisper. She couldn't hold back the tears that came unbidden to her eyes. Although she heard what he said, it clearly wasn't registering.

"That can't be … that can't be." Her breathing was getting erratic. She was trying to keep the hysteria at bay. "The woman … the woman I kill—" She couldn't get the word past her lips. It lodged itself in her throat. She could no longer control the tears.

"Her name was Abigail Woodson," she said in a shaky, trembling voice.

He nodded his head gravely. "Yes, that was her name. She never liked the name Abigail, thought it was too old-fashioned, so she went by her middle name, which was Samantha. Alex always called her Sam …"

Gemma continued to wind the towel in knots. He placed his hand over hers to still her movement.

She bit her lip again before speaking. "But her last name …" she said in almost a whisper, willing what Mr. Chambers just revealed to her not to be true.

Thomas looked down at his lap, unable to see the devastation and despair in her eyes. "She kept her last name when they married because she was the last of her family. She'd lost both her parents before she and Alex were married and was an only child … she didn't have any other living family."

Gemma had never come across as manipulative or calculating. It wasn't like she plowed her car into Sam's and then bided her time in jail waiting to claim Alex as her own. It was evident she truly didn't know she was connected to Alex, long before they met.

They both sat in silence. The longer Gemma sat with this new information, the more she felt the bile rising in her throat and knew she was going to be sick. She rushed to the bathroom and relieved the contents of her stomach into the toilet, continuing to retch long after there was nothing. After some minutes, Gemma was finally able to extricate herself from the toilet. As she cleaned her face, it took her a moment before she could look at her reflection in the mirror. She stared at herself. A shiver ran through her body and then she visibly began to tremble. She hugged her arms across her body trying to stop it, but she couldn't.

What am I going to do?

Finally, she left the sanctuary of the bathroom to face Mr. Chambers. She found him in the kitchen.

"Your dinner was burning so I ... I moved it from the stove," Mr. Chambers said, eyes downcast, looking at the floor. He felt so ill-equipped to handle this situation. He thought he would be uncovering fraud and instead he was about to make two lives miserable. They stood in opposite corners of the kitchen, both in deep thought. He hated to say it, but he knew he must.

"Gemma, you have to tell him."

She looked up at him sharply, tears spiked her lashes, but whatever Gemma was about to say died on her lips, and she only nodded her head in despair.

"I'm sorry that this happened—"

Gemma put her hand up to stop whatever else he was about to say and shook her head. The tears slipped silently down her face.

"Maybe I'll just show myself out."

Gemma gave no response as he walked back through the house and let himself out.

It had been a while since they were able to spend time with each other and not just see each other in passing. He couldn't wait to get home. Tonight was the night. He was going to propose. He'd gone back to get the ring weeks ago, but there never seemed to be the right time. So when Gemma mentioned making him dinner, he knew tonight would be the perfect opportunity. He hoped she liked the ring. For the millionth time today he touched the black velvet box that had been in his pocket all day.

Just one more stop before he headed to the house. He glanced at the flowers lying on the passenger seat. He wouldn't be empty-handed this time. This trip to the cemetery was no less difficult than the previous one, but he had to let Sam know of his plans.

He walked to Sam's grave. The groundskeeper must have been doing their job because her grave was tidier than he'd found it last time. He stooped and sat the colorful array of flowers on the ground.

"I come bearing gifts." He stood back up and chuckled uneasily.

"I didn't forget this time, Sam." He ran his hand through his hair, unsure how to deliver his news. Although, he was sure she already knew the reason for his visit.

"Remember the woman I was telling you about? Gemma?" He stuffed his hands in his pockets and paced a few steps before he looked back at her gravestone. "I love her, Sam. I'm planning to propose ... tonight."

"Yeah, I know you think I could have eased into that more, but I figured it was just better to rip the Band-Aid off ..." He sighed heavily.

"I just want you to tell me this is okay. I guess ... I feel guilty that the life you wanted us to have ... I'm going to have with her." He stood staring at her headstone as a single tear trickled down his cheek. He swiped at it.

"I'm always gonna love you, Sam ... that'll never change ... just know that." He swiped at his face once more before turning and leaving the cemetery.

It was some time after Alex's father finally left before she found herself sitting in the living room. Her knees were drawn up to her chest. As the light fell from the sky, the shadows casting themselves across the room were ominous. The smells of the food, which were once inviting and delicious, now curdled her stomach. It tore at her heart that she was responsible for Alex's heartache and grief. His wife died by her hands.

What a cruel joke that they would fall in love with each other to have it ripped away by the ugly truth. She was a murderer, but not just any murderer, his wife's killer. She didn't want to imagine how often after that awful night he went to bed in anguish, missing her.

She sobbed loudly—not only at what she caused, but also for her despair in this very moment. After so many years, she'd finally found happiness, and now it was about to be ripped away. A wretched scream tore itself from her throat. She held no hope he would ever forgive her. Her wailing was so distressed no one would deny the agony and torment her heart was in at this moment.

After the tears turned to a trickle, she sat gasping for breath. Her throat was parched, but she couldn't muster the strength to go to the kitchen for water. Alex was going to be home soon.

How am I going to face him? How am I going to get the words to come out?

Alex touched the lump in his pocket for the millionth and one time and grabbed the second set of flowers from his car before heading into the house. Things were eerily quiet. He'd expected to hear the rattle of pots and pans and possibly a radio or the TV, but he was met with silence.

"Gemma?" he asked apprehensively, as his nose led him toward the kitchen.

Whatever Gemma had been cooking sat congealing in the pan. He looked around nervously as he sat the flowers on the counter. *Why isn't she answering? Is she not here? Did something happen?* He walked into the darkened living room, and that's where he found her.

"Gemma? Why are you sitting here in the dark?" He clicked on the light. Gemma winced as her eyes adjusted to the light.

Once the light illuminated the room and he got a good look at her, he knew something was wrong. She refused to meet his eyes. *What happened?* Going over to the sofa, he sat down near her and reached out his hand to touch her, but she quickly scooted off the couch and stood. Her reactions made Alex pull back as if he'd been slapped. It was hard to hide the hurt that sprung up in his eyes when she avoided his touch and his unease increased.

"Alex, I need to tell you something," she said in a small voice.

He abruptly stood up. Her tone and demeanor were making him uneasy. This wasn't how tonight was supposed to go. They were supposed to be enjoying dinner while he figured out when exactly he would slip to one knee and ask her to spend the rest of her life with him. He licked dry lips as he went to approach her. Sticking her hand up to ward him off, she backed up. He heard her voice tremble.

"Please, Alex, please don't come any closer. If you do, I won't be able to say what needs to be said."

He could tell she had been crying. Her throat was hoarse, her voice scratchy. *What happened?* He ceased his movements toward her.

"Okay ... okay. What do you need to tell me?" He said trying to soothe her.

Gemma paced as she bit her lip. The tears cascaded down her face and she quickly wiped them away. "I think you should sit," she said shakily.

Alex unwillingly sat on the sofa, giving her his undivided attention, but the nervousness that sat in his stomach like a weight now turned into full-blown fear. Something was greatly disturbing and upsetting Gemma, and she refused to let him comfort her. His finger unconsciously grazed the lump in his pocket where the little black box sat.

She finally looked into his eyes. Her eyes were filled with terror and he could tell she was trying to be brave, despite the fact that her body was shaking like a leaf.

"Gemma, please ... whatever it is just tell me. Whatever it is we'll get through it." He looked at her pleadingly.

She bit her lip again as more tears fell before she started to speak.

"You and I ... we never discussed why I was in prison ..."

Alex shook his head. "It's your past, Gemma. You paid for your crimes."

She shook her head vigorously.

"Stop! Stop! It does matter!" Her raised voice bordered on hysterical.

He'd never seen her like this. Nothing would keep him in his seat right now. He rushed toward her and grabbed her shoulders, trying to pull her into his body for consolation, but she fought him, pushing with all her might against his chest.

"Gemma! Gemma! Please stop! I can't sit there and watch you in so much anguish and not try and do something about it. Please let me." He implored despite her struggling against him.

His pleas pierced her heart. She could no longer keep the words bottled up while he made overtures of love and soothing gestures. Her emotions got the better of her, and she began yelling.

"I'm a murderer! A murderer, Alex! I'm the reason your wife is dead!"

She felt the quick release of his hold as he recoiled from her as if he'd been burned. The loss of his nearness caused a pain so deep she wasn't sure if she would ever recover. She knew a deep chasm had just opened up between them that would probably never heal. He stared at her, his mouth agape for what seemed an eternity before he finally spoke.

"What? What did you say?" His voice was filled with shock and bewilderment.

Her tears nearly blinded her vision as she struggled to answer him.

"I ... I was the driver of the car that night ... I'm responsible for your wife's death." She said on a strangled sob.

Alex staggered backward, retreating farther across the room, away from Gemma. He clutched the arm of the chair for support. His breathing was labored as he tried to wrap his head around the words she just uttered.

This isn't happening! How could this be happening?

He looked at her and then at the floor. There was a pounding in his ears and his heartbeat felt erratic. His heart was being broken all over again as his mind went back to the night of his wife's death. Tears gathered in his eyes as he remembered the police trying to console him after delivering the news.

He recalled the rage he felt at knowing the other person yet lived while Sam was now lying in a grave. That rage gripped him now, but it also dueled with his deep grief over the rift that cut him off from Gemma. He loved this woman. Tonight had been the night he was going to propose, make her his wife.

But how can I replace Sam with her killer?

The revulsion and torment he felt gripped his heart and sent a shudder through his body. Tears fell hot down his cheeks.

How can I say that I love her?

She was the reason his wife no longer breathed.

Did she know before she started seeing me who I was?! Was this her sick, twisted plan?

His eyes found her, and he quickly advanced on her.

"Did you know? Did you know before we started seeing each other?" he asked menacingly, barely holding his rage in check.

Gemma's back hit the shelf. There was nowhere for her to run. If he struck her right now, she wouldn't be able to blame him, but she was also scared. She'd never seen this side of Alex, let alone this terrible anger directed at her.

"No. I promise, Alex. Your father told me today. I would never hurt you like that … I love you."

She saw him visibly flinch, and his action caused her to stuff her fist in her mouth to keep from crying out. She'd given up trying to stop the flow of tears. She was dying a thousand deaths as she watched him physically and mentally distance himself from her.

Alex's head and heart were warring mightily within him as he moved across the room away from her. He clutched his head suddenly as if the pain became physical. When the grief and despair of Sam's death was raw at the beginning, he could remember lying in bed some nights and plotting his vengeance on the person that stole her from him, and now that person stood in front of him, and he was in love with her.

What have I done to deserve this torture?

He glared at her as tears glistened in his eyes; fists clenched at his sides, he advanced on her again. She was shaking, but she stood her ground. He came within an inch of her, his chest rising and falling with his agitation. He stared at her for minutes. He wanted to both rip her apart and take her in his arms and console her. These conflicting emotions were tearing him apart. He fought the urge to caress her cheek versus wrapping his hand around her delicate throat.

She stared back, willing her hands to stay by her side when all she wanted to do was comfort him, say something that would bind them together again, fix this mess. She noticed the tic in his jaw; saw the internal fight that raged like an inferno. The fierce anger that marred the rigid lines of his face were in direct contrast to the regret and heartache which filled his eyes. She swallowed as she continued to weep.

His body wanted to commit violence, but he couldn't hurt her … yet he also couldn't stand to be in her presence. She was the author of his misery and the captor of his heart all at the same time. His vision became obscured as the tears streamed down his cheeks. His body relaxed when the fight left him. In that instant, as they held each other's tortured gaze, something between them broke.

"Get out." He shut his eyes as he spoke the words so softly Gemma didn't hear what he said.

"What?" she asked breathlessly.

"Get out!" he bellowed, his eyes flying open. This time, there was no misinterpretation of what he said. The enraged look in his eyes helped confirm it.

The explosiveness of his anger pushed her farther into the shelf for a moment and a sob tore from her throat. She quickly clapped her hand over her mouth, unable to look at him anymore, and she fled, ran toward the door, never stopping to search for her purse or any item that belonged to her. She left and never glanced back, knowing that any look back would be pure misery because she knew exactly what she just lost.

Despite it being late summer and the night being a bit balmy, she felt a chill in her bones. Wrapping her arms tightly around her body, she continued to walk the streets. The tears wouldn't stop. She planned to walk all the way back to the boarding house, but it was too far. At the corner, she noticed a payphone, which seemed like a Godsend considering in this day and age of cell phones that any pay phones still existed. She dug in her pocket for change as she approached. Slipping the coins into the slot, it was a second before she recalled the number and dialed.

She stood trembling as she willed the line to be picked up. Three rings later, a female voice came through on the other line.

"Hello?"

Gemma let out a grateful sigh of relief before the floodgates opened yet again. "Shelby … could you please come and get me?"

17

He stood staring at the spot she'd just vacated for long minutes. His emotions were still a roiling mass inside of him. No longer able to contain his rage and overwhelming sadness, he sunk to his knees and howled and cried and cursed. He wanted to destroy anything, hurt something until it felt the agonizing pain he was feeling. But right now he would settle for feeling absolutely nothing. He wanted to be wrapped in a blanket of numbness.

Picking his body up from the floor, he dragged himself to the kitchen in search of whatever booze he had in the house. He wanted to get trashed, wasted, shit-faced, stinking drunk, whatever you wished to call it. Fumbling around in the freezer produced a half full bottle of vodka. He quickly unscrewed the cap and downed the contents of the bottle. Some of the fiery liquid poured from his lips in his haste to swallow every drop.

After he finished, he discarded it on the counter and went in pursuit of any other alcohol he could find. Over the next thirty minutes, he unearthed a full bottle of chilled white wine and three cans of imported beer in the fridge, a partially empty bottle of tequila and some cooking sherry in the cabinets and he consumed every ounce. When he didn't locate anymore, he staggered to the couch and sat down heavily. His brain was now coated in a thick fog, a beautiful haze that kept him from feeling the sharpness, the sting of his emotions.

He was comfortably numb. He chuckled to himself.

Isn't that a song? Comfortably numb?

He began to laugh louder, almost like a maniac, until suddenly his laughter slowly died away to be replaced by tears. The liquor hadn't helped anything; it only made him feel more depressed. He started crying in earnest. Leaning forward with his elbows on his knees, he held his head in his hands and wept. At some point, he finally passed out from exhaustion and the effects of the alcohol.

Rachel pulled her car into Alex's driveway giddy with excitement. She knew he'd planned to propose last night. Although, the lovebirds would likely still be in bed celebrating she just couldn't wait to congratulate them. Upon entering the house, she was met with the reek of stale food.

Had they been so excited over their engagement they left their dinner out overnight?

First, she walked toward the kitchen to see what the stench was. That's when she saw the counter littered with the remnants of the preparation for dinner, the empty liquor bottles, and the uncooked dinner congealing on the stovetop. It would have been one thing to find dinner sitting half eaten on plates, but it looked like they never even made it to that point. The other thing that struck her as odd was all the empty alcohol containers. She picked one up and looked at it in confusion. Neither Alex nor Gemma were big drinkers. While they may have had something to celebrate they would have never emptied the contents of all this alcohol in one night. Something did not seem right about the situation. Instead of going for the element of surprise, she decided to announce herself.

"Alex? Gemma?" she called out as she moved through the house. She stopped dead in her tracks when she came into the living room. Alex lay sprawled on the sofa fully clothed. Her calling his name hadn't roused him at all. As she slowly moved closer to his sleeping figure, she caught the alcohol fumes coming off of him and wrinkled her nose. Confused, she looked around.

Why is Alex sleeping on the sofa, alone, the night after his engagement? And where is Gemma?

She nudged Alex's shoulder.

"Alex, wake up."

After a few more seconds of trying to wake him and only getting unconscious grunts, she went back to the kitchen and filled a glass with water. Marching back into the living room, she proceeded to dump it in his face. Alex instantly sat up with a bark after being doused with the cold water. He smoothed his hair back and wiped the water from his eyes as he caught his breath. Then he turned a baleful look on her. She saw his expression and took a step back as he rose unsteadily from the couch.

Rachel stumbled over her words as she tried to explain, "I-I'm sorry … I tried t-to wake you and you wouldn't wake up …"

Alex strode past her into the kitchen, as she followed on his heels.

"Umm, where's Gemma?"

He retrieved a glass from the cabinet and filled it from the faucet, all the while ignoring her flustered behavior.

"I came by because I wanted to congratulate you both." She looked around once more; searching for Gemma while Alex drank down the contents of his glass.

"Alex, what's going on?" she asked, concerned. Alex continued to stare at her as he leaned against the counter with his arms now folded across his chest. There was a charged silence in the room as they both stood staring at each other.

Normally, Rachel would win a staring contest, but not today. She eventually averted her gaze to take in the mess decorating the kitchen. Finally, Alex pushed himself up off the counter to plant his hands on the island, which stood between him and his sister.

"Where is my key? I want you to return it right now. No more coming in here when you please." His tone brooked no refusal, and Rachel pouted as she pulled it from her purse and laid it on the counter between them. After several more minutes of awkward silence, Rachel was about to ask again where Gemma was when Alex spoke.

"I don't know where Gem … she is." He scratched at something on the surface of the counter as he looked down.

"But I don't understand … didn't you propose last night?"

Alex resumed his silence.

"Alex …"

His head snapped up in anger as he heard her whining. His dark look made her swallow the rest of her words.

"No more questions, Rachel."

Rachel relented and tried another tactic. She went to move around the counter toward him and saw him take steps backward to avoid contact. She halted her step.

"Hey, why don't you get a shower and I'll start cleaning up here? I'll make some coffee."

Alex backed out of the kitchen to head to his room, but not before taking her spare key with him.

After his departure, Rachel looked around the kitchen trying to figure out where to start, but also gravely concerned that Gemma was missing, and Alex was being tight-lipped.

What happened last night?

Alex and Gemma were happy and in love. She'd spoken to and hung out with them both as a couple and individually over the last few weeks and nothing seemed to be amiss. Alex was going to propose for crying out loud. She decided to put some coffee on first before tackling the dishes. Maybe once he'd showered and cleared his head a bit, he would be more amenable to talking. She was worried about them both and needed some answers.

Alex let his clothes fall to the floor before he stepped into the stinging hot spray of the shower. The water battered his body. He braced his hand against the wall and hung his head. He couldn't take Rachel pummeling him with more questions, or he was going to crack. Before he knew what he was doing, the hand that rested on the shower wall unconsciously balled into a fist. His body was rigid with anger. He could feel his fury rolling off of his body in waves. In the kitchen, he hadn't been able to bring himself to say her name.

Not only was he angry with her, he was angry with the world, with his father. How did he come by the information and why …

Why did he feel the need to destroy our happiness?

But it wasn't just his doing.

In a sudden burst of anger, he struck the wall with his closed fist. He felt the pain radiate down his arm, and he welcomed it. As he pulled his hand back from his assault on the wall, he saw the blood dripping from his bruised knuckles and watched it disappear down the drain in a swirl of water.

Once he stepped from the shower and wrapped the lower half of his body in a towel, he found the first aid kit in his medicine cabinet and wrapped a bandage around his injured hand.

Hair still damp from his shower, Alex came into the kitchen in a T-shirt and jeans. The smell of the fresh coffee beans drew him to the coffee pot. He filled one of the mugs that Rachel sat out.

She sat quietly on one of the barstools at the counter, hands clasped in front of her. As he raised the mug to his lips, she noticed the bandage wrapped around his hand.

So he isn't just taking out his anger verbally, he's also lashing out at anything in his path.

He sipped at the warm brew. Rachel looked at him, incredulous that he wasn't just going to volunteer information. She angrily tore herself from the barstool and lambasted him for his lack of caring.

"Alex, I can't just sit here and act as if nothing is wrong. I come here expecting to walk into a love nest, and instead, I find you passed out on the sofa surrounded by alcohol fumes, alone ... then you come back from your shower looking like your hand lost a fight with the wall. Why won't you tell me what's going on? And where the hell is Gemma?" She folded her arms across her chest, waiting for a response.

He stared at her as he sipped at his coffee a bit more before sitting the cup on the counter forcefully.

"Fine, you want to know what happened? Yesterday, I came home ready to propose to my girlfriend, and found her crying and distraught because our father came here and told her that she was my wife's killer ..."

Rachel stared at Alex aghast. "Oh my God! Alex ..." She saw the angry tears he was trying to hold back.

"So excuse me if I didn't feel in a sharing mood this morning when you let yourself into my house and threw water on me, then proceeded to demand I tell you what's wrong." He turned away from her sorrowful expression and chucked his coffee mug into the sink, causing it to break into shards.

Rachel tried to comfort her brother.

"Just fucking stop it, okay! I don't need you to fix anything or trying to coddle me! Just get out of here!"

Although she was hurt at her brother's angry outburst, she knew how much he was hurting. She was reeling with the shock of his news. He stood glowering at her, struggling to hold his emotions in check. She only nodded her head as she turned and left.

Once Rachel was back in her car, she couldn't hold back the tears. Sobbing, she hung her head over the steering wheel. She hated to see her brother like that again. It seemed even worse this time, because not only was he reliving Sam's death, but now he'd just lost the woman he loved. It was heart wrenching to watch him try and hold it together, devastating to see him allow the beast of anger to consume him and swallow him whole. Not only that, but what of Gemma?

As Alex's sister, she knew her loyalty should lay with her brother, but she had come to care for and love Gemma like a sister, and she knew whatever happened out on the road that night over three years ago, Gemma wasn't a cold blooded killer. She had to find out the details of that night and make sure she was okay. Rachel knew Gemma had no one.

One thing she was sure of, Alex wouldn't be hurting as much as he was if he didn't still love her. Although many people told her she butted into other people's business too often or they called her a busybody, this was one time when she would not be deterred from meddling and trying to put the two of them back together. First things first, she needed to see her father and find out how he came by this information and what exactly he knew.

Pouring a second cup of coffee, Shelby glanced over at the sofa where Gemma slept. Throughout the night she heard the young woman wake up in fits of grief, uncontrollably sobbing until she would cry herself back to sleep. When she'd picked her up last night, Gemma refused to talk about what happened. She became borderline hysterical when Shelby attempted to take her to the boarding house, so against professional protocol and ethics she bought Gemma back to her apartment.

Shelby knew whatever had Gemma so distraught had to do with Alex. Today she was determined to make Gemma unburden herself with the story. Usually, when she gave the young women parolees advice about not getting involved with a guy she turned out to be right, she never thought she'd be right about Gemma and Alex. She didn't want to be right. She genuinely hoped Gemma would find some happiness. As Shelby sipped the hot beverage and contemplated what the situation could be, Gemma began to stir. Shelby sat her mug on the counter and approached the sofa.

Gemma turned over, and the light from the window hurt her eyes. It took her a minute before she realized Shelby was standing next to her. She knew she was going to have to give her some answers, but she just didn't know if she was up to recounting the events of last night.

Slowly, she sat up. She didn't want to make eye contact with her. She could see Shelby's shoe tapping the floor. Sighing, she looked up at her. There was a mix of puzzlement and sympathy that sat on her face. Gemma bit her lip to stop the tremble that began, before looking back down at the floor. She couldn't control her hands; they moved of their own accord as they balled themselves into fists and kept moving in her lap. She knew her eyes were swollen and puffy without having to look in the mirror. Her throat was dry. She licked at her chapped lips before speaking.

"May I have some water?" she asked in a croak.

Shelby moved into the kitchen and came back with a bottle of water.

"Thank you," Gemma mumbled as she removed the cap and gulped down the water.

Shelby watched her. Even once Gemma finished off the water they sat not speaking. Finally, Shelby broke the silence.

"Gemma, I gave you last night, because clearly you were in no state to talk, but today I need answers. What happened?"

Gemma rubbed her hands on her jeans as she tried to fight back tears.

"Ale—" She faltered at saying his name. A single tear fell. "He ... I told him ... his dad came by and told me that I killed Alex's wife," she said in a jumbled rush.

Gemma then broke down wailing. Having to say those words all over again and thinking about what she was responsible for were too much for her.

Shelby stood in shock.

How could this have happened?

She hesitated at going to Gemma and offering her comfort. She had never been an emotional woman. Gemma's tears and distraught state made her uncomfortable.

Finally, she made the decision to go to her. She sat next to Gemma and awkwardly pulled her into her arms and let the other woman sob her heart out. Gemma's cries were so broken.

Once Gemma quieted down and it seemed like the flow of tears were staunched, she fell into a fitful sleep.

Shelby used that time to comb through Gemma's file again.

What did I miss?

She read over the report of what happened the night of the accident and when she saw the name of the victim she looked puzzled. Abigail Woodson. She'd only ever heard Alex's late wife referred to by the name Sam, and that was only in passing. She never bothered to find out what happened to her, somehow assuming she died from an illness. She looked up when she heard Gemma waking up. Walking back into the room, Gemma looked up at her as she sat up.

"I'm sorry ... thank you," she hiccupped as she composed herself.

"It's okay," Shelby replied, coming closer to stand in front of her. "Umm, I'm still just trying to wrap my head around what you told me. How it could have happened ... I mean how you could have ended up in the same place as ... I don't understand ..." Shelby said mystified.

Gemma turned hurt, accusing eyes on Shelby. "I was going to ask you the same question. How could this have happened? You had my file; you didn't know it was Ale—" Gemma stopped herself again before saying his name.

"You didn't know that was his wife?" The accusation in her tone wasn't lost on Shelby.

Shelby looked a bit affronted, but could understand Gemma's anger. She was supposed to be looking out for her, and she failed.

"Listen, you have every right to be upset. I'm not sure how the system didn't catch the connection ..." Shelby shook her head, still baffled over the situation. "The thing is, I don't know Alex very well like you might think. Besides him taking on some of the parolees I bring to him, we've never said more than just a few pleasantries to each other. Every now and again I ask him how someone is working out. So, I didn't know his story and … the couple times I heard someone mention his wife it was in passing and they didn't say much. I knew her name to be Sam … that's about all." She looked at Gemma apologetically.

Gemma nodded her head in understanding and mumbled under her breath, "Sometimes life just deals us a cruel hand … repeatedly."

Shelby stared at Gemma's bowed head. She was never one to mince words, so she just decided to ask the other question that now needed to be asked.

"You may feel it's too soon for me to ask, but … please tell me you at least protected yourself, that you guys used protection?"

Gemma looked down in shame and sniffled. She was so head over heels in a love bubble with Alex she hadn't been thinking like a rational, adult woman. Shelby's judgmental gaze bored into her until she finally looked away.

"I know it was foolish … but we didn't use condoms all the time." She bit her lip to keep from letting out a sob. Her gaze returned to her lap. The last thing she wanted was Shelby's disappointment heaped on top of everything else.

"I thought you were one of the smart ones, Gemma …" Shelby stated. Gemma's head whipped up sharply to glare daggers at Shelby. Her words felt like a slap, but how could she be angry with Shelby? The person she was upset with was herself. Gemma's anger deflated as she hung her head.

She told herself she wouldn't put herself into the same situation as she had with Jason, by rushing headlong into a relationship or situation and that's exactly what she'd done. She only had herself to thank for her predicament. As Shelby's question sunk in, she now became terrified she could be pregnant, and her hand absentmindedly swept over her stomach.

Rachel leapt from the car and slammed the door as she exited. She stormed into her father's house and found him in the kitchen. Without preamble, she launched into her tirade.

"Why, Dad? Why did you do it? Alex was happier than we'd seen him in a long time."

Even once he turned around to face her, she still continued her heated ranting.

"I don't know why we're acting like Alex and Sam had the happiest marriage. Her death made him forget how miserable the two of them had become the last six months before she died."

Her father gave her a horrified look.

"Don't look at me like that. You know it's true. I'm not doubting Alex loved her, but come on. Do we still believe that if Sam were alive today they would still be married?"

Her father said nothing but remained tight-lipped.

"Exactly!"

They both stood in silence, each lost in their thoughts. Rachel resumed her censure, although her father had yet to speak.

"Aren't you even concerned about Gemma? She's out there somewhere grief-stricken and alone. I know how much she loved Alex." Rachel got a little emotional thinking about Gemma being by herself after what happened. Her father averted his gaze guiltily. Rachel remembered what Alex mentioned to her.

"Speaking of Gemma, Alex told me you delivered the news to her. How? How did you find out?"

Her father stood there looking like a kid caught getting into mischief.

"What did you do? Tell me how you found out?" Rachel demanded.

Thomas sighed. "When I couldn't find anything online on my own, I ... I hired a private investigator." He looked sheepish after his admission.

"I want to see the report the investigator sent you." Rachel's look let her father know she wasn't taking no for an answer. Entering his office, with Rachel close on his heels, he opened his desk drawer and retrieved the file. He reluctantly held it out to her. She snatched it from his grasp and plopped down in one of the chairs. He slowly sat down in the chair behind his desk as he waited for Rachel to finish her examination of the contents of the report.

Her eyebrows went up in surprise, and her facial expressions frequently changed as she read the file's contents. The details covered Gemma's youth spent in and out of foster homes, her medical records that chronicled her numerous hospital visits and abuse at the hands of her husband, and of course the circumstances and events of the night of the accident. After nearly an hour of taking everything in, she looked up at her father with accusatory eyes.

"Have you read this report all the way through?"

Her father looked down at his lap, suddenly finding a piece of lint on his pants.

"That's what I thought …" She returned her attention to the documents and her eyes scanned the pages again. "If you had finished reading this then you would know that Gemma wasn't just some irresponsible, drunk twenty-year-old out for a joyride that night. She was fleeing her abusive husband, who'd just raped her earlier that night. The doctor who cared for her at the hospital testified in her defense." She shook her head with disgust as she glared at her father.

"How does it feel to know you've ruined two lives because you just had to be right?" She stalked from his office with the report clutched in her hand.

That night, as Alex was trying to fall asleep, he rolled over facing her side of the bed and was greeted by her scent. His gut knotted at the assault on his olfactory senses. He quickly sat up and moved away, running his hands through his hair. He chanced a glance at her pillow then quickly turned his gaze back to the foot of the bed. Before he could stop himself, he dragged her pillow into his arms and crushed it to his body as he took in a lungful of her sweet, intoxicating scent. He knew it was wrong; his body was traitorous when it came to her. He couldn't admit out loud that he missed her.

Unfortunately, every chance his body got, it reminded him. Hurriedly, he cast her pillow to the side and rose from the bed disgusted with himself. He began aggressively stripping the sheets off the bed, trying to rid himself of her scent, which was haunting him. Chest heaving after his exertions, he stood staring at the bare mattress and realized it would be a while before he could sleep alone in this bed. He left the sheets laying on the floor as he went down the hall. Removing a blanket from the hall closet, he then stretched out on the sofa.

Sleep eluded him for a long while before Morpheus finally snatched him away to a hellish dreamland.

18

It had been two weeks, four days, eleven hours, twenty-eight minutes, and thirty-seven seconds since she'd last seen the angry tortured look in his eyes. Time seemed to take on a new meaning. The period of her life with him and now the hell she was living in post him.

Gemma couldn't afford to miss too many of her classes or she would have fallen behind. She returned only two days after the incident. Shelby mentioned to her about taking a leave of absence, but she couldn't. She worked too hard to get here. Yes, this was painful to deal with, there were no words to describe it, but she wouldn't allow herself to stop her life because she had a broken heart. That was something the old Gemma might do, but she had to keep moving forward.

Despite how she felt about Shelby's lack of tact or a filter, the woman was someone to lean on. She went and retrieved her purse and other belongings from Alex's house. Even acquiesced when Gemma begged her not to stay at the boarding house and quickly helped her find a tiny studio apartment that classified for government subsidies. The rent was cheap, and the place was a dump, but at least she didn't have to be under Ms. Ramirez's watchful gaze. That place held too many memories. If she had to move forward without … him, then she wanted no reminders. She had enough of them as it was. She still hadn't stopped crying herself to sleep.

Of course, that meant her time working at his restaurant also came to an end. She could only imagine the gossip swirling around at her swift and sudden departure. She said no good-byes or farewells. She just never went into work. The one thing she could count on was that Ale— he would be silent as a tomb on the subject. It hurt not to be amongst the team at the restaurant, but she couldn't bear to face anyone there and have them find out the horrible secret that was the reason for her absence. She would just have to forget everyone.

Another area Shelby had yet been helpful on was getting her a new job. The diner was pretty crummy, and the clientele left something to be desired, but it put money in her pocket and allowed her to work evenings and weekends so she could go to school.

Which is where she now sat, in class. The latest portfolio she'd turned into her photography professor was a definite departure from her previous work in its theme and tone. His worried looks in her direction hadn't gone unnoticed. He was clearly concerned. She was afraid he would try and nab her after class and get her to talk. She knew her work was darker than it usually was and she obviously knew why, but she wasn't ready for him to prod her until she cracked.

Most days she could barely hold it together when the mere thought of him crossed her mind. Trying not to be distracted, she looked up at the professor and attempted to focus, but he sounded like the Peanuts teacher to her. Her brain was a jumbled mess. Even though she knew it was destructive behavior, all she wanted to do was go home and sleep so she wouldn't have to think.

Finally, the class was dismissed, and she was able to duck out before the professor could ask to see her. Thankfully, the class ass kisser was in there trying to suck up while she made her getaway.

As she walked in the door of her sparse studio, she immediately went to the bathroom. Lying on the counter was the pregnancy test that had stared her in the face for the past week. After her conversation with Shelby she bought it, but she was too chicken to take it. Picking it up, she turned it over and over in her hands. She eyed it with trepidation as she placed it back on the counter. Exiting the bathroom, she thought yet again that she hadn't felt sick, and her body didn't feel weird. There was no way she was pregnant. She only half-heartedly believed that. She sat on the threadbare sofa she managed to pilfer from the curbside with the help of a classmate. It had a few stains and wasn't the most comfortable, but at least it didn't smell. She had lived in worst.

What am I going to do if I'm pregnant?

The tears stung her eyes as she tried not to cry. The last thing she wanted was to end up a welfare mother, but she had no money. Getting herself into this place had taken what money she had saved at that point. When she wasn't in class, she tried to grab every shift at the diner she could. Her mind couldn't stop thinking about how she would care for a baby.

Damn it! Why was I so careless? Why didn't I think about condoms or birth control? I knew better!

She ran her hand across her belly. Abortion was not an option; even if she were pregnant, she would figure something out.

One of the waitresses was in the bathroom crying, and it was his fault. On his first day back to the restaurant right after everything happened he was bombarded with questions about Gem … her whereabouts since she missed her shift. When he continually refused to answer or said he didn't know, he knew he was only stoking the fires of the rumor mill, but he didn't care. It wasn't anyone's business.

These days it seemed like he couldn't manage to have a polite word or conversation with anyone, which is why one of his most valuable waitresses was now licking her wounds in the bathroom. She endured his verbal attack with tears in her eyes then ran off to the restroom once he finished. Amanda was in there trying to coax her out. He knew he should feel like an ass, but there was a part of him that was happy to finally feed the beast of his anger and tear into someone. Most of the staff gave him a wide berth this last week once they realized something clearly changed about the Alex they knew. She just got in his path at the wrong time.

The kitchen door swung open and slammed into the wall. He didn't bother to look up; he knew he was about to be reprimanded.

"What the fuck, Alex?" Amanda, his hostess, crossed her arms over her chest and glowered at him.

He continued chopping up the prep ingredients for tonight's dinner service and didn't look up at her.

"You know Cindy is the best waitress we have, and you have her ready to quit ..."

Even as she eyeballed him, Alex offered no apology.

"I was able to talk her off the ledge, but ..." She watched him as he still continued to work. "Are you even listening to me?"

He put his knife down, but still didn't look in her direction. Amanda's demeanor changed.

"Listen, Alex, we've known each other for a long time ... I don't know what happened with Gemma ..."

This got his attention, and he gave her a warning look to tread carefully. She put up her hands in peace.

"I'm not saying it's any of my business; I'm just saying that clearly you're hurting … I'm just telling you that whatever you're dealing with, taking it out on the staff isn't healthy for anyone. Pretty soon you could start losing people."

Alex looked back down at the cutting board.

"I'm not expecting you to be Mr. Happy, but maybe refrain from talking to the staff right now." She sighed, defeated by his silence. "I'm going to go finish getting the front of the house ready for tonight."

He heard the door swinging back and forth on its hinges after Amanda left the kitchen. Even though he knew she was right, he was afraid if he said anything then she would think it was an open invitation to discuss his situation further. He stood gripping the knife in his hand for several minutes before he slowly resumed his chopping and cutting. His chopping became erratic as his thoughts trailed to the source of his anger. He finally flung the knife away and stood seething. It just seemed like it would never let up. He ran his hands through his hair in frustration. If it wasn't his staff walking around giving him pitying glances, he had to avoid Rachel who wanted to "talk". Didn't anyone understand that all he wanted to do was just lash out and hurt or destroy something until it made him feel better?

The problem was that deep down he knew no amount of hurting someone else or destroying something would make him feel better and he didn't know what to do about that. Leaning his forehead against the shelf, he closed his eyes for a second. Once he opened them again, he found another knife and tried to calm himself down and get ready for the dinner rush.

Dinner service managed to go by without incident; no one suffered a bout of crying and Alex kept any unkind words or angry retorts to himself. He sent the staff home early and put the kitchen in order on his own. Working the long hours alone helped him work off some of his aggression.

Arriving home well after midnight, he showered and grabbed a beer from the fridge. He plopped down on the sofa, clad in only a towel. The sofa had become his bed. His blanket and pillow lay disheveled beneath him. He took a long sip of the beer and sat staring into the darkness.

In another time, he would have turned on the TV or the radio … in another time she would be here, they would have come home together, or she would already be here with her head bent over a textbook or cleaning her camera. He took another pull from his beer.

Don't go down that road.

That line of thinking only brought misery and sleepless nights. Who was he kidding, he had sleepless nights regardless most of the time. Thankfully, between the grueling cleaning of the kitchen and the beer he was starting to feel drowsy. Maybe he would get a good night's sleep. He didn't remember putting the bottle on the coffee table before he fell into a deep sleep.

"Have you taken the test yet?" Shelby's voice asked quizzically through the other end of the phone.

"No."

She heard the other woman's exasperated sigh.

"Gemma, I thought we talked about this. Don't you want to know so that you can make a decision or at least not have it hanging over your head?"

The last thing she needed was Shelby trying to force her hand. She had to do this in her own time.

"It's not that easy … I wish I could understand it myself. Obviously, I'm terrified of having a baby and being a single mother … but there is a part of me that's secretly excited that a life Ale— he and I created might be growing inside of me. I may not get to be with him, but at least I'll get to have a piece of him …"

when Gemma was met with only Shelby's silence she continued to speak.

"Maybe he or she will be the best parts of both of us … either answer terrifies me in different ways. In one instance I lose him forever if I'm not pregnant and in another I'm left with a daily reminder of him if I am. I'm not sure what's worse."

The infinite sadness that pervaded Gemma's voice was palpable. Although Shelby knew Gemma needed a friend, that wasn't her role. She was her parole officer. Yes, Gemma was heartbroken, but right now she needed some tough love. Usually, she didn't get this involved in the parolees' lives this deeply. She didn't know why she kept allowing herself to get sucked into Gemma's issues, but right now she was deeply entrenched, and there wasn't too much she could do but try her best to help Gemma make good decisions.

"Listen, you can't keep waiting. The longer you wait, if you are pregnant, particular options are off the table …"

Gemma blanched at Shelby's statement even though the other woman couldn't see her.

"That will never be an option!" she said tightly.

There was a charged silence before Gemma continued, "If I'm pregnant, I'm going to keep the baby. I'm not sure how I'm going to raise it on my own, but I'll figure it out."

A little more gently, this time, Shelby addressed her, "Okay, Gemma. Just let me know when you know something, okay?"

"Yeah ... I gotta go."

Before Shelby could say good-bye Gemma disconnected the phone.

He felt her run her tongue up his inner thigh, and he smiled to himself. The wet trail came to the juncture of his thigh and his groin. Her breath tickled his balls. He felt his length grow as she took him in her hand. Her sweet, delicate mouth covered the tip and sucked and licked at him. Gripping her hair, he gently applied pressure, wanting her to take more of him. It was a silent plea to feel her hot mouth swallowing him whole. He quickly sucked in a breath as he felt her comply and take him fully into her mouth. She bobbed up and down over him. It was pure ecstasy. He lifted her hair out of the way so he could watch as he disappeared up her throat and suddenly the desire came over him to see it disappearing inside of her other lips.

Roughly pulling her mouth from him, he dragged her up the length of his body and crushed her lips in a ravenous kiss. He felt her legs straddle his waist as her small hand gripped him, and he placed his hands on her hips, helping guide her. She was sliding down his length too slowly. Gripping her hips, he quickly tugged her down onto his upthrust member.

A groan of pleasure escaped him, as she gave a yelp of bliss at being completely impaled on him. She began to ride him with abandon. He enjoyed the view as he repeatedly disappeared inside of her. Her head was thrown back, as she moaned. The lushness of her breasts beckoned to him, and he sat up and pulled her close. His tongue encircled her nipple before sucking it whole into his mouth. She pulled his head to her chest as she began to grind on him, her breath ragged from moaning. He switched to her other nipple. Cupping the round globes of her ass, he started to aid her efforts as she rode him. He couldn't get enough of her. Moving her up and down on his dick even faster, he could feel her climax building. Her walls squeezed him. He was going to come.

With a jolt, he came awake.

Shit!

He'd almost spent, the dream felt so real. He hadn't had a wet dream since he was thirteen years old. He'd been so close to disgracing himself. The dream was vivid. He was sweating profusely and had the hardest morning wood he'd ever had in his life. It was almost excruciating.

As much as he didn't want to, he found himself taking his dick in his hand to give himself some relief. He used the remnants of his fantasy to get himself off. Afterward, he used the towel he'd been wearing last night to clean himself up.

When am I going to stop dreaming of her?

He lay there chastising himself before finally getting up and walking naked into the kitchen. Standing in the coolness of the refrigerator, he drank from a carton of orange juice. Suddenly, he heard a key turning in his lock and before he could react, Rachel walked into the kitchen.

"Oh gross! Alex, put some clothes on! I think you've burned my eyes out of the sockets!" She averted her eyes from her brother's nakedness.

Alex looked annoyingly at his sister. He took one last swig from the carton and put it back into the fridge before responding,

"This is my house, Rachel, I can walk around naked whenever I want! What the hell are you doing here? I thought I took your key."

Rachel stayed turned away from him as she replied, "Of course, I had another copy … I figured I'd given you sufficient time to stew …" No longer caring about his lack of clothing, she turned to address him eye to eye—at least the kitchen island separated them, shielding her eyes from his lower half.

"We need to talk."

She saw his face go red with anger.

"If this is about—"

"Gemma?" she interrupted him, knowing he wasn't going to say her name. "Yes! Of course, it's about Gemma. You need to read something."

Marching around the counter, he grabbed her by the arm and proceeded to drag her to the front door. "I don't need to read anything! I need you to stop meddling!"

"Alex, please wait! Just hear me out!" She dug in her heels, trying to stop him from putting her out, but he was stronger. She almost dropped the file as he unceremoniously shoved her out the door. "Alex, please!"

He slammed the door in her face, and before she could knock it swung open. Alex ripped her key out of her hand and shut it again. She heard the locks click.

"You asshole! The least you could do is listen! I know you still care about her!" Rachel screamed at the door, then kicked it.

She turned away, walking back to her car. How was she going to get him to read this when he wouldn't answer his phone half the time and then she was always being thrown out of his house? He was a stubborn ass. It didn't help that Gemma vanished into thin air. No one had seen her. How was she going to get them back together if she couldn't find her? She sat in her car pondering the matter and pouting when a light bulb went off.

The school.

She knew where Gemma was enrolled in school. She could go on a stakeout and hopefully, find her on the campus. Brilliant! She started her car and drove off.

Gemma hated to admit Shelby was even the teeniest bit right. She needed to shit or get off the pot so to speak. So, here she sat on the top of the toilet biting her lip, waiting for the plus or minus sign that would determine her fate. She fidgeted, unable to keep still. Looking at her watch, she knew the test should have an answer for her. She slowly picked up the stick with a trembling hand.

Alex sat in his car a little ways down the street from his father's house. Many times he'd driven past with the intention of stopping, but then he would keep going. They had yet to speak since he … ruined everything. Unlike Rachel, he'd only called once and left a two-word message: 'I'm sorry.' He decided it was time to pay the old man a visit. Starting the car, he drove down the street and pulled into his father's driveway. The garage door wasn't open. Shocking that the old man wasn't tinkering with a car. He opened the front door and walked in.

Sounds from the TV in the kitchen floated down the hall to him. As he walked into the kitchen, his father looked up from making his sandwich. If he was surprised to see him, he didn't show it. Alex took a seat at the table. For minutes, neither man said a word. Eventually, his father joined him at the table. His sandwich sat untouched on the counter. It took his father a second to make eye contact.

There was a smoldering anger in his son's eyes he understood. It pained him he was the one that put it there. Before his thought could go any further, Alex spoke.

"Why, Dad? Why? Why'd you do it? Just couldn't leave it alone, could you? You want me to become a miserable old man just like you? Huh?! Is that what you want?"

The pain and anger laced in his words tore at Thomas' heart. He tried to protest.

"Alex, I was just trying to protect you. You're my son. It would have come out eventually, even if it wasn't me who unearthed it. Something like that always has a way of coming out. Better if it's now than years down the road and the two of you are married."

At the mention of the word married, Alex's face took on a sour expression, and Thomas knew he hit a sore spot. Suddenly, recognition bit him in the ass. Alex saw the realization pass across his face.

"Oh no … Alex, I'm sorry …"

Alex looked away before responding, the hint of tears in his eyes.

"Yeah, what do you care? It's not happening now. You should be happy. You saved me, Dad. Congratulations!" he said sarcastically before getting up and slamming out the door.

Back in his car, he knew there was more he planned to ask, to say, but all he could manage was to be angry. He was always angry. He pounded the door furiously with his fist. After one more glance back to the house, he started the car and pulled out of the driveway.

19

The big minus sign stared back at her. She could feel her fingers gripping the stick so tightly. Tears welled up in her eyes and streamed down her face. Dropping the stick, she began to sob. For a minute, she was unsure if she was crying out of relief or sadness. As she continued to cry, she knew it was more out of sorrow. She sunk to the cold linoleum and wept for a child that never was and never would be. But more than that, for him, for the life she had hoped to have. Although she had no idea how she would have supported them both, part of her wanted his baby, their baby, so she could always have a part of him. Now she truly had nothing left. She cried so pitifully at the loss.

Hours later when she was able to pull herself together, she called Shelby. On the second ring, she answered.

"Gemma?"

"Yes, it's me … I just wanted to tell you I'm not pregnant."

She knew the forlornness was evident in her voice.

"I'm not sure whether to offer my condolences or congratulate you, Gemma. I know you were conflicted about what you wanted the outcome to be, and it may not be my place to say, but eventually I think you'll see this as a blessing in disguise."

Gemma knew Shelby was well meaning, but she could slap her at this moment. Sometimes she could be so callous. Unfortunately, she was the only person Gemma had.

Shelby continued, "I appreciate you letting me know."

Gemma remained silent.

"Okay, well I will see you at our next appointment. Just think, in a few months, you'll no longer be on parole. You'll be a free woman."

When she was still with him, Gemma thought of it often—the moment her life would be completely her own again, no one to answer to. Now it almost seemed empty. She would have no one to celebrate with.

"Great … I'll see you next week," Gemma replied in a deadpan voice, and then hung up.

Two months later

Rachel was hanging out at the community college whenever she had free time, which unfortunately wasn't often. When she tried to get a copy of Gemma's schedule from the registrar's office she was denied because she wasn't family.

Between running the auto body shop and being a single mother, it didn't exactly leave her a lot of time to be an amateur sleuth. At one point, she started stopping some of the students and showing them Gemma's photo to see if anyone knew her. She must have creeped someone out because it wasn't too long before campus security shut her down. She was relegated to sitting in her car or just walking the campus looking around to avoid any further actions from the rent-a-cops.

She sipped at the soda that was nearly finished as she looked around at the passing students. Since the weather had grown even colder, Rachel opted to sit in her heated car today.

How could one person be so hard to track down?

She was starting to think Gemma didn't want to be found. She cranked up the heat a bit more. It had been nearly three hours; she needed to get Chloe picked up soon. Just as she was about to call it a day, she saw her. She blinked her eyes, trying to be sure she was seeing her. It was Gemma; there she was carrying a camera bag and some books. Rachel leapt from the car and ran over to her.

"Gemma! Gemma!"

Gemma turned around, startled at hearing her name called so vehemently. As she spun around, she found herself being crushed in a tight hug. She had not gotten a look at the woman's face before being wrapped in a bear hug.

"Oh my goodness, I'm so glad I finally found you," the muffled voice said.

She pushed against her, still not certain who was so excited to be in her company.

When Rachel released her and stepped back, Gemma gasped with shock and surprise at seeing her standing there.

"Wh-what are you doing here?"

Not exactly the reception Rachel was expecting.

"Are you kidding me? I've been looking for you for over two months." Rachel smiled at her.

Gemma couldn't help but throw hopeful glances over Rachel's shoulders, wondering if he was here with her.

Is he looking for me, too?

Rachel was crestfallen when she realized Gemma was searching for Alex.

"I'm sorry, Gemma ..." She shook her head. "He's not with me."

Gemma gave her a weak smile and nodded her head. She bit her lip, avoiding eye contact with Rachel by staring at the ground.

"I guess you know the story?" She looked back up at Rachel with a pained expression.

Rachel nodded.

"Then why are you here? You must hate me." A tear escaped before she could stop it.

"Gemma, I know it wasn't intentional. It was a mistake …
I know everything that happened that night. Everything."

More tears fell. Gemma became embarrassed. She tried to
stop crying.

"I don't want your pity," she blubbered.

"Gemma, I'm not here because I pity you. I was worried
about you … we'd become friends. In case, you didn't notice,
I don't have a lot of girlfriends …" Rachel seemed sheepish.
"I thought we were friends, so when you just left without a
word, it hurt my feelings."

Gemma hiccupped through her tears as she tried to speak.
"B-but you're Ale— his s-sister … I just assumed you'd hate
me for what I did and never want to see me again."

Rachel pulled her into another quick hug. "We all make
mistakes, and you've more than paid for yours. My brother's
being a jerk."

Gemma quickly pulled away and wiped at her eyes before
reprimanding Rachel for her comment. "Rachel, he has every
right to feel the way he does, it was his wife! I … I—"

"Stop, Gemma! Stop beating yourself up! I know what
you did, and I know that if you could you'd take it all back …"
Tears fell from Rachel's eyes.

"I know you're sorry, Gemma … and I'm sorry because I
know how much you love Alex."

Gemma turned away as the tears continued streaming down her cheeks. She wiped at them before looking back at Rachel.

"Well, I guess that's not enough." She sniffled.

"I understand, though. I did a horrible thing. I don't know if I'd talk to me either." Her lip quivered as she said in a small voice, "Although, I wish he would." She cried even harder, and Rachel pulled her into another hug, trying to console her.

"Hey, let's go somewhere and sit and talk, okay? It's cold out here." Rachel said as she rubbed her back.

Gemma nodded her head and Rachel took some of her books as they headed to her car. Seeing Rachel again was unexpected and surprising. She assumed after hearing the news of her being responsible for Sam's death that the woman would never want to see her again. For once, she was so happy to be wrong. She was beyond thankful to have Rachel back in her life. The relationship she had with her was always one of camaraderie and fun. It was nice to have a friend again.

They ended up talking and catching up for hours after Rachel called to get a friend to pick up Chloe. Of course, there had been more tears shed. A couple of times, Rachel tried to slip Alex into the conversation and tell her how he was doing, but Gemma insisted that she didn't want to know. Her imagination already conjured up enough misery she had inflicted. She didn't need to know that it was much worse. They parted ways at the end of the night with the agreement to see each other soon, and Rachel promised to bring Chloe to the next meet up.

Life had settled into a boring routine. He pretty much kept to himself these days. He worked until he was bone tired and then came home to fall into bed … or more like the couch. That's all he wanted to do tonight was come home; maybe have a nightcap and call it a day. Instead, what did he come home to? His sister camped out in his kitchen. He shook his head as he stood in the doorway. They hadn't seen each other much in the past couple months. He hoped she had finally given up on talking to him, but her presence in his kitchen indicated otherwise.

"I was pretty sure I took your last key, so I'm interested to hear how you got in here this time," he said slightly annoyed.

Rachel sat up straighter on her barstool. "You know how resourceful I can be … I picked the lock."

Chuckling to himself, Alex pulled a beer from the fridge and turned around to assess his sister. She was persistent; he'd give her that. He popped the cap off of his beer and took a long hard swallow. It would have been satisfying if he hadn't been staring at Rachel.

"So, what do you want?"

Rachel was silent for a minute before speaking. "You know what I want, Alex. If you would just listen—"

Before she could finish her sentence, he slammed his beer down, came around the island, and yanked her from the stool.

"Wait," she said breathlessly.

His plan was to throw her out again. He was gripping her arm as he dragged her to the door and she was trying her best to twist out of his grasp. Finally, she stuck her foot in front of his and tripped them both. They went sprawling across the floor. Rachel scrambled to stand up. As she stood up, she backed farther into the living room away from the door.

"Now you're going to listen to me, do you hear me, Alex Chambers?"

He'd never quite heard his sister so livid. A bit amused and a little nervous, he was about to stand back up, but thought better of it and remained sitting on the floor. He nodded his head at her. Rachel pulled the file from her tote and placed it forcefully on the table.

"I'm leaving this file, and you are going to read it. For two months you have refused to hear me out. I don't ask much from you …"

He cocked an eyebrow at her in incredulity. She had the decency to blush.

"Okay … we'll skip the last part of that. Anyways, what I'm saying is that you'll regret it if you don't read this file …" Rachel knelt in front of him and took his hand.

"Alex, ever since we were kids, then when Mom got sick … and when she died … I always felt like your protector. Why do you think I always tried to make you laugh or take you on crazy adventures? I just wanted you to be happy. I'm your big sister and when I see you hurting all I want to do is fix it."

He looked at her sadly.

"I know, Rachel." He patted her hand.

"I don't want another three years or longer to go by and see you lonely and miserable. You were happy with her … even happier than when you were with Sam."

Alex gave an exasperated sigh and went to stand up.

"Don't, Rachel!"

"No! You're going to listen to what I have to say." Rachel shoved him back down.

"When Sam died it's like a light went out inside of you and I understood it. You'd just lost your wife. Of course, you're going to grieve. The thing is, even when Sam was alive, you guys never seemed that happy with each other. She was always trying to change you. When she died, you forgot all of that, forgot all the bad. I never said anything because it was your wife, your marriage and I wasn't going to interfere. Then Gemma …"

He looked away at the mention of her name.

"That's right, I said her name. Gemma. Gemma turned a light on inside of you that I hadn't seen in a very long time … and not just since Sam's death, but before it. I've never seen you so happy, and the fact that you were training Brandon so you could have more time with her should tell you that. You wouldn't do that for Sam."

She stared at him angrily.

"If I found the kind of love that the two of you share, you'd have to pry it from my cold, dead fingers … and you, you'd just so easily throw it away." His sister scolded him.

Glaring at his sister, he yelled, "Do you think this is a cakewalk for me? Every day is a chore to keep getting up. I'm in pain, Rachel. I feel like I'm being torn in two. Except it's not a physical pain that someone can fix. Do you know what it is to want to do someone physical harm, and at the same time wrap them in your arms? It's torment!" He cleared his throat.

"Would you be so easy to forgive if it had been your husband? It's easy to stand there and have such contempt for me." Alex looked at his hands, trying his best to avoid his sister's hard gaze.

She spoke softly, "I know learning that Gemma was responsible for Sam's death was hard. I can't even imagine … but I know she paid for that, and now you're making her pay some more, but it's not just her who's suffering. Alex, look at you. I've never seen you like this … this isn't my brother." Rachel slowly stood up.

"I know you still love her, or you wouldn't be hurting the way you are. So I'm asking you … no, I'm begging you to read that file."

Alex couldn't fight the tears that trickled down his face.

"I've said what I needed to say. I'm not going to take up any more of your time." She walked toward the door straightening her jacket.

"I love you, Alex."

He heard the door shut and stayed on the floor, lost in his thoughts and emotions.

Why is Rachel always being so meddlesome?

He just wanted to forget everything, forget why he was so angry, but she couldn't leave well enough alone. He cradled his head in his hands. It was agonizing to think of Gemma. He looked at the file lying on the table. Part of him wanted to be petty and not give Rachel the satisfaction of reading the file, at least not right away. The other part of him was curious.

What in there is so important that I need to know?

Glancing down at his arm, he noticed he had somehow cut himself during their fall. He got up and went into the kitchen and ran water over the cut. As he was fishing through the drawer for a Band-Aid, his finger hit something metal. He pulled it out to see what it was. The clock face of the scuffed pocket watch stared up at him. He remembered the night she gave it to him. Turning it over, he read the inscription. *'To Alex, a man that gives me hope.'* He cringed. What an ass he was. He had given her hope and then yanked it away from her.

But how can I forgive what she did?

He found himself glancing again at the file Rachel left. She was so adamant he read this thing. Picking it up, he held it in front of him, unsure if he was ready to know what lay inside. The pocket watch grew hot in his hand. He, at least, owed it to her to read it. Slowly, he opened the folder and started to read.

After a few minutes of starting his perusal of the file, he collapsed onto a barstool. The first document of the file showed the police report of the night of the murder. There weren't too many of those details he didn't already know, but reading about what the cops found when they arrived on the scene made him experience everything first hand.

Sam was pronounced dead at the scene, but Gemma suffered many injuries, some of which were life threatening and she narrowly escaped death herself. He swallowed at the thought. After the police report, there was a detailed history of Gemma's time spent in foster care. To say there were many homes was an understatement. During their first date, when Gemma talked about her life, he realized how much she hadn't shared with him.

Many times Gemma hadn't stayed more than a few months before being shuffled off to another home. Mixed in amongst the foster home reports were numerous medical records detailing broken bones or other injuries that were more than likely at the hands of an abusive foster parent or sibling. Then he noticed that as she got older, the hospital visits increased, and the injuries she sustained were more severe, some resulting in days spent recovering.

Gemma never went into detail about her ex-husband, but the documents and numerous medical records painted the picture of what her life was like living with that monster. His anger found a new home when he thought about the man who verbally, physically, and mentally kept Gemma in a prison. The last documents in the file were Gemma's account of the details leading up to the car accident, and then a doctor's report and testimony to Gemma's condition pre-car accident and what transpired at the hospital. That bastard forced her to drink all night, and then beat and raped her! Alex smashed his fist onto the counter.

Gemma.

With all she had been through and all he put her through, he was the bastard.

He looked over at the pocket watch again. Despite all the crap people in her life subjected her to, she still managed to give him all of her and not once had she held back. The inner turmoil he'd been feeling since this all happened dissipated a bit. He still wasn't sure if he could forgive her right now, but he was beginning to see through the red mist of his anger. He was about to shut the file when his eye caught something written in his sister's hand; it was an address with a note. Underneath the address it simply said, *'Go to her.'*

Looking at the address again, he quickly grabbed his keys and the pocket watch, and left the house before he could talk himself out of it. It took him about thirty minutes to reach the destination his sister wrote on a scrap of paper. He expected to arrive at an apartment or a house, but instead he pulled up outside a hole-in-the-wall diner. Then he saw her.

He had yet to get out of the car, but through the big picture window, he saw her move amongst the patrons. The diner was a greasy spoon, and she wore a dated waitress uniform, the type that almost resembled a hotel maid's uniform. She was still as beautiful as he remembered, but something had changed about her. He stared for long minutes, watching her refill coffee, take orders, and make light conversation with the customers. Then he knew. It was her eyes. No longer did they have a sparkle that made them so expressive. As she smiled at her current customer, he saw it didn't reach her eyes.

Once she finished dealing with the customer, she walked toward the kitchen where he could still see her. She thought no one was watching. He saw the façade fall. She looked sad. The pain he'd seen in her eyes upon first meeting her was multiplied. Someone must have called out to her because he instantly saw the façade come back into place as she went back to serving the clientele.

He wasn't sure how long he watched her from his car, but he couldn't bring himself to go inside. Yes, Gemma was guilty, but she'd paid for her crimes, and that night when she'd confided in him he condemned her. She put so much trust and faith in him and how had he repaid her? By shunning her and abandoning her. He couldn't walk in there right now.

Why would she want to see me again after the way I left things?

He couldn't just go in unprepared. He needed to think this through.

The pocket watch lay in the seat next to him, and the inscription came to his mind. He wanted to be the man that gave her hope again, see the sparkle return to her eyes, but he needed to work through some things first. Before driving away, he took another look through the window at her and then drove back home.

20

It was a terrible thing not to have your children speaking to you. Thomas worked on his car as he thought about his two grown children. Rachel dropped Chloe off for occasional visits, but barely stepped foot in his house over the last two months, and when she did it was awkward and tense.

Out of his two children, he had always had a strong relationship with Rachel, so it hurt to have her be angry with him. Right after their mother's death it was almost painful to look at his daughter, she so favored his wife. As time went on, that likeness was a balm to his broken soul. His wife still lived through their children. While physically Rachel had his wife's looks, Alex had her spirit and heart. He needed his kids back. He knew he had failed as a father once his wife passed. The love and affection a child should be sure of from a parent, he had been incapable of giving. Intuitively, Alex and Rachel must have known that because he saw their mother's death bond them even closer.

He set aside the tool in his hand. Usually working on a car was soothing, but lately, it wasn't working as a distraction to the loneliness he was feeling. He went inside and poured himself a cup of the coffee left over from this morning. Taking it, he went to his office and sat at his desk where the second copy of Gemma's file lay. He was finally going to take Rachel's advice and read the whole thing. He had to make amends for the destruction he caused.

Classes were winding down in preparations for the holidays. Gemma turned in her latest portfolio earlier and Professor MacGregor, her photography professor, summoned her to a meeting in his office after class. She was feeling a bit nervous.

Does he think my portfolio is horrible? Is that why he wants this private meeting with me?

She knew she was distracted over a month ago, but she buckled down and started working harder. She was focused and dedicated to doing the best work she could. She couldn't keep her hands still as she waited in a seat outside the professor's office while he finished with another student.

Fifteen minutes later, the office door opened, and Professor MacGregor walked out with a student. They shook hands, and the student walked away down the hall. The professor's attention turned to Gemma.

"Come in, Gemma."

She entered the office nervously, and they each took their respective seats.

"Thank you for being so patient." Professor MacGregor opened her portfolio and perused it as he began to speak. "Miss Peyton, I'm very impressed with your latest batch of photos, the composition and lighting are nothing short of stunning. If you don't mind me speaking candidly?"

She shook her head, a bit surprised.

"You're a bit older than most of the students in this class, and with that brings more life experience … I'm not sure what you were going through over a month ago, and it's none of my business, but it transformed your work ... I admit I was a bit concerned at first, but I can see I had no reason to be. Normally, I would only recommend my second or third year photography students, but I would love to recommend you for a spot in the yearly photo exhibition. Only five students get the honor and I think you deserve one of those spots."

Gemma's mouth opened and closed like a fish as she took in what he said.

"I'm … I'm shocked, and I'm flattered professor …" She paused, averting her gaze for a moment in contemplation. "I was expecting to be reprimanded or something," she said with a nervous chuckle.

Professor MacGregor smiled at her.

"Not this … I don't know what to say."

This time, Professor MacGregor laughed.

"Just say thank you, Gemma. Your work speaks for itself. You're gifted; you've got talent, and you deserve this." He stood up from his desk, and Gemma quickly followed suit, jumping to her feet and stretching out her hand.

"Of course, thank you. Thank you so much for everything." Blushing, she shook his hand.

As Gemma left his office, it felt like ages since she'd felt anything close to happiness. She couldn't believe what just happened. Her work would be featured in the yearly photo exhibition. For a moment, she had the quick thought of wanting to call Alex and tell him about her good news. She felt a pang of sorrow but quickly quelled it. She wouldn't let today be marred by unhappy thoughts.

Rachel. She'd call Rachel. They could go out and celebrate this weekend and then she could see Chloe. She smiled as she left the campus for the diner.

The meeting with her professor left her very excited. She couldn't wait to share the news with Rachel. There was so much she had to do to prepare. Her mind had been turning ever since their conversation on what theme her photos would cover. *Nothing can sour my mood today*, she thought as she worked her shift. Even when a patron stiffed her on a tip and later when another one gave her straight attitude, she still was on cloud nine.

A new customer sat in one of the vacant booths while she was on her fifteen- minute break. She walked over to offer the customer coffee.

"Hi, what can I—" The words died on her lips as she laid eyes on the patron, Thomas Chambers. Her hand holding the coffee pot shook slightly.

"Why are you here?" The anger and hurt shone in her eyes as she addressed him.

"Please, Gemma, I know I don't have a right to be here … or to ask your forgiveness …"

Gemma could feel the tears stinging her eyes. As much as she wanted to lay all of her misery at his door, she knew he couldn't hold all the blame. Her actions had put her in this position. Plus, she knew what it was to want and need forgiveness. How could she be seeking that for herself and not offer it to this man who'd just been trying to protect his son? The tension left her body. She could, at least, hear him out.

Thomas motioned to the empty seat across from him. "Do you have a minute? Would you like to sit?"

Gemma looked around the diner and noticed that it was virtually empty. Nodding her head, she slid into the seat opposite him. She sat the coffee pot on the far side of the table.

Her eyes finally came to rest on his face, and she noticed he looked exhausted and sad.

"What do you want?" Despite her agreement to speak with him she was still guarded.

"I came to apologize for being a meddlesome old man." He gave her a small smile; Gemma's response was a blank expression. He swallowed, realizing that maybe it was too soon for humor. He didn't want to screw this up. He just wanted to make things right.

"Gemma, I'm sorry … I know those words must seem hollow." He looked her earnestly in the eyes.

"The last thing I wanted was to … to …" He couldn't find the words, because he had wanted to break them up, but only because he thought she was lying.

He folded his hands on the table in front of him. "I can't apologize, Gemma."

The hurt sprung back into her eyes, before being replaced by a righteous anger. She grabbed the coffee pot and was rising from the seat when he hurriedly rose from the booth.

"Wait, please!" Sighing, he glanced around the restaurant. The one other patron shifted in his seat to peer at them, and the cook stuck his head out of the window from the kitchen.

"Please, sit back down, let me explain."

The air around them was charged.

"Hey, Gem, everything okay out there?" The gruff looking cook had now come to stand in the doorway leading into the kitchen. He was a big, burly man that glared menacingly at Thomas. He knew one word from Gemma and this man would more than escort him to the door and see him out.

Turning his attention back to Gemma, he saw her reluctance and said a bit more pleadingly, "Please. Just hear me out and I promise if you don't like what I have to say, I won't bother you again."

After a few seconds, Gemma relented. She called over her shoulder, "I'm fine, Jake."

Out of the corner of his eye, Thomas saw the cook return to his domain as the door swung back and forth after his departure. He sighed with relief inwardly as they both took their seats again.

"Thank you." Thomas fidgeted with his hands as he tried to find the right words to fix his earlier blunder.

"Just hear me out completely, all right? I'm not very eloquent."

He licked dry lips before continuing, "That previous comment didn't exactly come out right. What I was trying to say is that I can't take back something I meant at the time … you see when I came there that day I thought I was uncovering some lie. I thought you were pulling the wool over Alex's eyes. It wasn't until I'd already opened my big mouth and saw your reaction that I realized that wasn't the case at all … You weren't a liar at all, you just weren't aware that you were connected to him already …" He stared intently at her and noticed the unshed tears there.

"Gemma, please don't hate me for saying this, but I wouldn't take it back … he's my only son and I was merely trying to protect him."

Tears slipped down her cheeks, and she quickly dashed them away.

Thomas turned his head away, as tears formed in his own eyes. He swallowed before he continued.

"What I feel a deep sadness over is what the truth did to you and Alex … I know how much you two love each other. If there is anyone that knows what the loss of love feels like … I do." A single tear fell once he finished.

Gemma sat regarding Thomas for a minute. His last statement quenched some of the anger she was feeling. She was not a parent, so she could not begin to fathom what kind of feelings and emotions prompted Thomas to act in the best interest of his son, even if the fallout that followed was utter devastation. Would she have done the same thing if she was in his position? She felt conflicted.

Her mind drifted back to that painful day when he confronted her. She knew he felt like she had been deceiving and manipulating Alex. He was stunned when he realized she was ignorant of the situation. There was a tiny piece of her that wanted to hang onto her anger, to clutch at it like a lifeline. But, if there was one thing she'd seen in the many homes she'd grown up in through foster care, were people that held onto anger. Anger over a failed or bad relationship, a wayward child that was a constant disappointment, the injustices that life seemed to heap on them or just feeling like life dealt them a shitty hand. They let the anger fester and grow until it ate them up inside, consumed them until they just had to lash out at anyone and anything to not be swallowed whole by it. She remembered many times bearing the brunt of that anger. No, she wouldn't choose anger. Even though Alex was no longer in her life, things were looking up.

"I ... forgive you."

It was as if she could visibly see the weight lift from his shoulders as he sagged back into the booth. The relief that was etched into his face made him appear younger, and she realized just what he was carrying around this whole time. She knew she was doing the right thing.

She placed her hand over his. "Mr. Chambers, I'm not a parent ... and I can't begin to know what you felt when ... when you thought, I was deceiving Alex ..." She bit her lip to control her emotion before continuing.

"Yes, I was angry with you," her lip trembled a moment, "but I was angry with myself, too ... I also played a hand in destroying our happiness. It's so easy to point the finger, but I know it's important to take responsibility for my actions. If I hadn't been on the road that night, in the condition I was in—"

Thomas quickly placed his other hand on top of her hand, which was lying on his, causing her to look up.

"Don't!" He shook his head at her.

"It was a mistake ... you made a mistake. You can't spend the rest of your life apologizing for it. You did your time. You weren't out on that road because you wanted to be. You were out there because you had to be. I don't blame you ... and I think in time, Alex will know that, too."

Gemma wiped at her eyes, and for a while they just sat together in silence.

After long minutes, she took her hand back and got up, grabbing the coffee pot.

"I'm sorry, I have to get back to work ..."

He nodded his head as he got up to leave. She turned around to head to the kitchen, but then he called out to her, "Gemma?"

She turned around. "Yes?"

"Umm, I was just wondering if it would be okay if I stopped by for a cup of coffee from time to time ... see how you're doing?" He shuffled around on his feet, unable to look at her as he made his request.

When she didn't speak right away, he peered at her from under his bushy eyebrows, holding his breath.

Finally, she gave him a small smile. "That would be fine."

His mouth twitched into a smile, and he nodded at her before leaving.

Ever since she'd stormed out of his house that night, he hadn't seen her, which was odd. As annoying as he found her to be at times, he'd missed her. Plus, he hadn't seen the kid in a while, too, which wasn't right. He got out of the car and walked up to the door. Normally, he would have walked right in, but the way things had been between them lately, he didn't feel he had the right. He rang the bell and then jammed his hands into his pockets as he waited for the door to be answered.

The door was flung open, and he looked down into Chloe's face. Her face lit up like a Christmas tree.

"Uncle Alex!" She flung herself into his arms, and he caught her.

"Hey, kiddo!"

He grinned as he hugged his niece. Over the top of her head, he saw his sister. She wore a neutral expression as she took in the scene before her. He let his niece down, so her feet touched the ground again.

"Look, Mom, Uncle Alex is here."

Rachel only nodded her head. "Finish your pizza, and then brush your teeth."

Chloe's shoulders slumped. "But—"

"No buts. I'm the mom, and I said to finish your dinner and get ready for bed. Now go."

As Chloe walked past her into the house, Rachel swatted her softly on the butt.

Once they were alone, she stared at Alex. He looked back at her, waiting for her to say something ... for her to let him in.

"Okay, I deserve that," he muttered.

Rachel only nodded her head.

"Fine! What do you want me to say? I've been an ass!"

"It's a start," she said, opening the door wider to permit him. He walked inside and followed her back toward the kitchen. Neither said a word for minutes as Rachel went about the kitchen throwing away paper plates and discarding the pizza box. She started wiping down counters.

He didn't look at his sister as he began to speak.

"I read the file." He noticed the brief pause in her polishing the countertops before she resumed without a word or a look.

"I read it that night ... after I threw you out ..." He scrubbed a finger over a spot on the granite. "I've been doing a lot of thinking, about what you said ... about me and Sam."

This time, she did stop and look at him, but she still said nothing.

"It's funny because in my thinking I remembered all of these little things I hadn't thought about in a long time. She never seemed happy that last year. I remember she didn't want me to open the restaurant. She kept wanting me to take a job with a company that sold restaurant supplies." He grimaced at the thought as he continued to rub at the spot on the counter.

"It was a good, stable job in her eyes." He swallowed as he stared at the countertop.

"I don't think she believed in me. I don't think it was just nervous fear about starting a business … it was me. She didn't believe that I could be successful, and that's why she wanted me to take that job. The more I kept thinking I remembered all these little digs she used to make. I always thought that it was just her being playful and funny, but … but now I think it was her passive aggressive way of showing her disapproval when I didn't give her what she wanted or when she realized I wasn't what she thought I was going to be …" He looked up at his sister then, with tears brimming in his eyes.

"How could I forget that? How could I forget all the times we fought because she wanted me to change myself and be someone else? How could I forget that my wife thought I was a big disappointment?"

He started getting worked up and agitated as he continued, "How could I forget how it made me feel when she chipped away at every little thing I did?" He slammed his fist into the counter.

"It's why after a while I started staying away, claiming the restaurant needed me ..." The tears spilled down his face.

"I know it wasn't always bad, but at the end, it was nearly intolerable ... I think me mourning her made me forget that. I only wanted the good memories ... she'd already died so horribly, how could I hold a grudge or be upset?" He wiped at the tears still cascading down his face.

Rushing over, Rachel held her brother in a tight hug. He hugged her back.

"Alex ..."

He pulled away from her for a second, not aware she planned to say anything further.

"I couldn't help but think of her ..."

Rachel looked at him puzzled.

"Gemma. It was never like that with her ... she always saw me, not someone she wanted me to be, but me."

"I know. I'm glad you finally realized that." She gave him a half smile, and his mouth quirked upwards in a faint smile. Leave it to her to always lighten the mood.

He wiped the remainder of his tears away. "Now that we're talking again ... don't eat any more of that crap, okay? I can't believe what you've been feeding my niece."

Rachel gave a full out belly laugh this time and punched her brother in the shoulder.

"Oh thank God! I can't eat anymore crappy take out, Alex. I've missed your cooking. Plus, I think I gained ten pounds."

He laughed as he pulled his sister into another hug.

Later that night, Alex sat in his car outside the diner. The last light was just shut off inside the restaurant. She exited the building with one other waitress and the line cook. They said their good-byes to her and went in the opposite direction. As he watched her walk down the street, he noticed she seemed to be in quiet contemplation.

Over the past couple weeks of following her, tonight she seemed happy. She pulled up the collar of her coat to ward off the wind that was whipping around. He had to stop himself from pulling over and offering to drive her home. The second night he'd shown up at the diner he was dismayed at the end of the night to see she either walked home or rode the bus. So he'd taken to coming by here at night to follow her and make sure she got home safely. He couldn't get the image of her lying beaten and broken in that alley—where he'd found her being assaulted—out of his head. He still blamed himself. There was no way he would let her be a victim again. Unfortunately, he knew he wasn't ready to approach her yet, so he kept his distance.

She pushed her hair off her face where the wind kept blowing it. A small smile broke out on her face, and he wondered what she was thinking.

Has she already met someone else? Has she moved on?

His heart twisted at the thought. She reached her place and let herself inside. Minutes after she went inside he sat in his car thinking. He desperately wanted the smile on her face to be because of him. That thought stopped him. No, that was selfish. He wanted her to be happy, whether it was with him or not, because she deserved it. But he would be lying if he didn't admit he wanted to be part of her happiness once again.

21

Gemma wasn't sure what she was doing here, but she wasn't going to chicken out now. Somehow she felt she owed it to her. The flowers felt like dead weight in her hand, which was now sweating and sticking to the cellophane wrapper that held the bouquet. She hadn't wanted to show up empty handed.

Even though it was cold outside, underneath her jacket she felt the trickle of perspiration run down her back as she trudged up the hill. Finally, she arrived at the grave of Abigail Samantha Woodson. It's wasn't that she'd never been to a cemetery before, it was just odd to stand there and look at someone's gravestone and see their life summed up so trivially in just a beginning and end date.

Was this all that was left once you ceased to exist?

The thought sent a shiver down her spine. She placed the flowers on the grave and stood staring at it for long minutes before she finally spoke aloud.

"I'm not sure what to say … I just knew I had to come."

The wind whipped her hair across her face, and she smoothed it back behind her ear.

"I'm sorry that you're there … and I'm here." She bit her trembling lip.

"You must hate me. I think if I were you I'd hate me …" she said on a sob.

The overwhelming emotion took her by surprise. She fumbled for a tissue in her pocket. Of course, she would be feeling emotional standing at the grave of the woman she was responsible for killing. Not only that, but she dated the woman's husband. Somehow it just seemed wrong, although she could never deny she still loved Alex.

Am I here to apologize for that? She sank to her knees.

"Abigail … wait, Thomas said you didn't like that name. I can't call you Sam … that's too personal. I guess Samantha it is." She wiped a stray tear.

"Samantha, I don't know what to say. I wish I understood why God chose to take your life and spare mine … and then in another comic twist your husband and I fall in love …" She looked at her lap, trying to understand how odd life could sometimes be.

"Somehow it seems cruel. Not just to us, but to you, too …" Contemplating this, she sat in silence with only the wind for company.

"Or, maybe he just saw two broken people who needed each other …" She shook her head and gazed out across the rows and rows of gravestones.

Is this a mistake? Biting her lip, she looked back at the tombstone.

"I should go … I just thought I owed it to you to come." She pulled her jacket tighter around her as she left. Where she was hot and perspiring on arrival, she now was chilled to the bone and felt her teeth chatter.

Alex stared at the sparkling ring sitting in the black velvet box. He'd tucked it away in his bedside drawer. He planned to return it when things ended, but he could never bring himself to take it back. Even now the only place he could ever see it was on her finger. Although he was uncertain if that would ever happen—after seeing her look so happy the other night. Pulling the ring out, he thought about the evening he planned to propose.

What if things had gone according to plan that night? What if I'd walked in to find her setting the table and singing along to the radio?

She would have greeted him with a kiss. They would have talked, laughed, kissed, and touched throughout dinner and then maybe before dessert he would have sunk to one knee and asked her to be his wife. Or no, what if he'd waited until they were being silly while washing the dishes together? She would have had suds on her hand when she went to wipe the happy tears away after saying yes and then they both would have laughed. Maybe they would have ended up making love on the kitchen floor before moving to the bedroom to further celebrate.

It had been three months, and if that night had resulted in their engagement, the biggest problem they would have right now was over the wedding cake or where to go on their honeymoon. Closing the box with a snap, he slid the ring back into the drawer. No use thinking about what ifs. He had to think about how to approach her.

What should I say? He knew that sorry wasn't enough.

How am I ever going to earn her trust again?

He abandoned her after telling her repeatedly that her past was just that, her past … that it didn't matter. And at the first mention of her past he left her alone. Yes, he could make the argument about the accident and whose fault it was, but it was just that: a horrible accident. She'd paid dearly, and he had mourned enough. It was truly time to move on. He would do all he could to convince her he would never run out on her again and that he loved her.

After putting on his jacket, he headed to the restaurant. Things were a bit better since he removed his head from his ass. He still had a long way to go to making amends for his behavior. Everything was almost back to normal. Brandon really stepped up and took over some nights as head chef. Which was helpful to him, because he started to look forward to leaving earlier on certain nights to make sure Gemma made it home safely.

It was raining out, and unlike most days the diner was a bit empty.

Guess it's going to be a slow day for tips.

Gemma was still pondering her trip to the cemetery when Thomas walked in shaking droplets of water from his jacket. He came and sat at the counter. She was a bit surprised to see him, but retrieved a coffee mug and sat it in front of him, then poured him some coffee. He gave her a shy smile.

"Thanks." He sipped the hot liquid, thankful for the warmth.

"Why did you come out in this weather?" She shook her head, perplexed.

"I heard the coffee ain't half bad here. Plus, the company was pretty good last time."

A small smile appeared as she leaned on the counter.

"You know I did forgive you last time you were here, right? You don't have to flatter me or show up here as some sort of penance. You don't owe me anything," she said half joking.

He looked slightly taken aback and possibly a bit hurt, and she suddenly felt bad for the offhanded remark.

"Maybe I should go." He got up from the stool and made to leave.

"Wait, Mr. Chambers, I'm sorry ..." She came from around the counter.

"When you asked to come back, somehow I didn't think you meant it, so I was a little shocked to see you walk through the door." She looked at him apologetically as she chewed her lip.

"It's all right. I'm sure I deserved that a little. While we're being honest ... I was lonely. So I came here." He dropped his gaze to the ground.

"Neither Rachel or Alex are speaking to me. I'm not telling you that because I'm looking for sympathy." He said quickly as he continued to eye the ground.

"I hope it's okay." When he looked back up at her nervously she was watching him.

Over her shoulder, he saw Jake peering out the pass through window at him. The look wasn't exactly friendly.

"Of course it's okay. Please sit down. Do you want anything besides the coffee?"

He took a seat, still sneaking glances at Jake. "Umm, sure … what kind of pie do you have?"

She began to rattle them off. "Peach, apple, lemon meringue, cherry …"

"How about lemon meringue?"

Gemma imperceptibly shook her head. He looked at her questioningly.

She leaned in and whispered, "You don't want that one; it's not fresh." She stood back up.

"You'll have the apple." She smiled at him.

"Okay …" He caught Jake's less than friendly look again.

"By the way, do you mind telling your co-worker that you're okay? I don't think I'm his favorite person."

Gemma chuckled as she turned to see the scowl that Jake had leveled at Thomas.

"Jake, he's good people. No more trying to intimidate him, okay?"

With a grunt, Jake finally returned his full attention to the stovetop. Gemma walked back into the kitchen to get the slice of apple pie.

As Thomas sat and ate, Gemma refilled customer's drinks, cleared dishes, and took orders before returning to him. She watched him for a minute as he quietly ate his pie and drank his coffee. She could understand his loneliness; she pretty much felt it her whole life. Never feeling like she had anyone to belong to … until Alex. Her heart hitched at the thought, and she wondered if she would ever be able to think of him again without feeling a deep sense of loss.

Despite the reason for their separation, here his family was opening their arms to her. She could feel her eyes get a bit misty, and she shook it off.

"Can I ask you a question?"

He nodded his head since his mouth was full of pie.

"What was she like, your wife?"

Sitting back, Thomas took his napkin and wiped his mouth. He got a faraway expression on his face. Everyone he knew had known his wife, so he wasn't asked this question often. Chloe didn't ask about her grandmother, and that could be because Rachel told her not to ask. As he thought about sharing her, talking about her, it gave him a warm feeling.

His voice was filled with awe, nostalgia, and reverence as he began to speak of his late wife, which made Gemma smile.

"Catherine, that was her name ... she was beautiful. We met in the mid 70's when she was in college. The moment I saw her, I knew I wanted to make her my wife. She just had this warmth about her. She lit up a room the moment she walked into it. I was a different man then ..."

She noticed the wistful look on his face.

"You couldn't be around her and not feel giddy. I always tried to do things to keep that smile on her face. When she got diagnosed, we were sure she would beat it ..." His eyes dimmed a bit as she could see him recalling those days of her illness.

"Through it all, she always retained a positive attitude. Even when the doctor gave her a death sentence ... she merely said we would make the most of the little bit of time she had left. And we did ..."

She moved closer to the counter. "You don't have to continue."

He shook his head, like he was shaking off something before continuing.

"Those last few months she made magical for the kids. She took them on so many adventures ... I didn't always go because I couldn't see the upside of only having so little time left with her. Rachel was a trooper. She kept it together. She always took her job as big sister very seriously. Alex … well, you know Alex," he said, casting her a sideways glance, before dropping his eyes back to the empty pie plate.

"He's kind of like his old man. He internalizes a lot of his emotion. If he was bothered, he didn't show it. He cried, but he didn't talk about it." He swiped a stray tear.

Now that Gemma thought about it, Alex never really did speak about his mother … or Samantha for that matter. She'd never thought about Alex as closed off or internalizing his feelings or thoughts, but Mr. Chambers' comments and observations gave her pause. She offered him a weak smile.

"Thank you for telling me a bit about her. I'm sorry if it was upsetting."

He leaned forward on the counter.

"Please don't apologize, Gemma. It was nice to speak of her. You know, sometimes I still talk to her. I miss her every day." Tears glistened in his eyes as he looked at her.

She felt herself tearing up. Before she could stop herself, she came around the counter and gave him a hug. For a minute, he didn't reciprocate. After a couple more seconds ticked by, he squashed her in a bear hug. She smiled before pulling away.

"Thank you for listening to the ramblings of an old man." He started to put on his jacket. "I better head out."

She nodded her head. Thomas reached into his jacket to pay for the pie, but Gemma shook her head. "My treat."

He nodded his head in gratitude and she watched him leave before resuming her rounds of checking on the customers.

It had been a very interesting day. Between her visit to the cemetery and Mr. Chambers showing up to keep her company at the diner, it was strange. Strange, but nice. She smiled at Jake after he locked the door and headed off to his car. Buttoning up her coat, she made the short walk to her apartment.

If it's this cold right before Thanksgiving, what will the weather be like by Christmas?

She didn't mind the cold really—the crisp chilliness gave the air a sweet, clean smell she loved. She inhaled deeply. The air felt good in her lungs. The rain had cleared out the sky, and she looked up and saw the stars shining brightly. She couldn't help but think about the twists and turns her life had taken over the last year. It was bittersweet.

She sighed as she reached her door. She went to retrieve her keys from her coat pocket and didn't find them there. Maybe she stuffed them in her purse in her haste to leave this morning. She opened her bag and began rummaging through the contents. She grew anxious as she realized they weren't there. It was late. Unfortunately, the building didn't have a twenty-four hour super.

What am I going to do?

She remembered the pre-paid cell phone was tucked in the side-pocket of her purse and pulled it out only to find the battery dead. She could have called Rachel or Shelby if the phone wasn't dead. She threw up her hands in frustration.

Now what?

As she looked up and down the street, that's when she noticed a figure approaching her. *Damn!* Her mace was on her key ring. She gripped the Chapstick tube in her bag. From that distance, the person would never make out that it wasn't pepper spray.

"Don't come any closer! I have mace! I'll use it! Plus, I know karate! I'm deadly!"

The figure put up their hands in surrender.

"Gemma, it's just me."

She stood up ramrod straight as the familiar voice wormed its way around her insides. She never thought in a million years she would hear that voice again. Her arms dropped limply to her sides. Her voice seemed far away in her ears as she responded.

"Alex?"

For a moment, they just stood staring at one another, neither saying a word. Finally, she shook her head, clearing the fog that had fallen over her at hearing his voice.

"What are you doing here?"

Alex was flustered for a moment as he realized he had to explain what he was doing there.

"Umm, I happened to be passing by on my way home, and I saw you, and you looked like you needed help."

She looked around and then at him a bit baffled.

"You were passing by here? This is clear across town from the restaurant and where you live?"

He appeared sheepish. How could he tell her he'd been following her and making sure she was safe each night? He stepped closer and looked down at the sidewalk before responding.

"Can we save that question for another day? I just ... I saw you needed help ..."

He turned toward her building.

"Did you lock yourself out?" he asked changing the conversation around and walking toward her door. He tried pulling on it.

She stared at his back, knowing he was embarrassed and also hiding something. She wouldn't press him.

"Yes. I must have left my keys when I walked out this morning, and I was going to call someone, but my cell phone is dead."

He still had his back turned to her as he was trying to get in the door. It was freezing outside, but seeing him again, hearing his voice and having him so close had a warmth radiating within her. She didn't care what had him on her street at this late hour, but she was glad he was here.

He turned back to her. "I couldn't get in."

They both looked down at the ground.

"I could call a locksmith if you want? I'm pretty sure there is at least one twenty-four hour one around." He started scrolling through his cell phone.

She bit her lip. "I can't afford that," she muttered, too ashamed to meet his eyes.

He hated that she felt embarrassed, but he knew better than to offer to pay. An awkward silence settled over them.

Finally, he suggested, "You could just spend the night at my place, and I could bring you back in the morning to deal with your landlord." He tried not to look too hopeful that she would say yes.

Gemma seemed unsure as she chewed her bottom lip.

"You're welcome to take my bed, and I'll sleep on the sofa." He would have offered her the guest bedroom, but he didn't want to tell her he had demolished it one night in a fit of rage, and was still putting it back together.

"Okay, I'll go, but I'm fine to sleep on the couch."

He nodded his head.

There was no way she would sleep alone in the bed she once shared with him. It would be too hard. This was already surreal, only adding to the strangeness of her day. They headed to his car, and he held the door open for her.

They drove in silence toward his house, both deep in their thoughts. Alex had not expected tonight to be the night he would resume contact with her, but when he saw her outside of her apartment unable to get in, it was like God was giving him an opportunity and he couldn't squander it. Plus, there was no way he was going to have her out on the street if she couldn't get into her apartment.

While things seemed easy between them out on the street, the tension in the car was clearly palpable with all the unsaid things that lay between them. However, you don't just jump into that kind of conversation.

Gemma was uncomfortable in the car with him. She kept her gaze focused out the passenger side window. How do you act normal in the car with an ex-lover that you had a horrible falling out with? The last time she'd seen him he was yelling at her to leave, and now here they were in his car, like none of that had ever happened. Like she never killed his wife. Well, it all happened … and sooner or later there would have to be a hard conversation.

He'd come to her rescue again. She was still puzzled as to what he was doing in that neighborhood that late at night. Eventually, she would get him to come clean about that.

Did Rachel tell him?

She snuck a sideways glance at him. He still looked amazing. His hair had grown out a bit, but she liked it. The thought of running her fingers through his hair had her hands restless in her lap.

Old habits die hard, right?

Gemma looked back out the window, remembering all the times she curled up closer to him in the front seat of this car, and now she sat as far away from him as she could, like a virtual stranger. She was scared of his closeness if she was honest. To be this close and not have him touch her, hold her, was torture.

Alex was thankful to be driving. Driving required he stay focused on the road. Unfortunately, that only occupied one of his senses. His other senses were in overdrive. He could smell the scent that was uniquely her. In the quietness of the car, he could even pick up on her breathing occasionally. Even though their bodies weren't touching in any way, the air crackled with intensity. His body was on high alert. His mind was buzzing with all the thoughts and things he wanted to say to her, to apologize for, but he didn't want them to come out rushed. He hated that things felt awkward between them. It hurt. He had to fix this.

At the stoplight, he let his gaze drift over to her. She was still beautiful. Her hair sat atop her head in a messy bun, and he could tell she was tired. He fought the urge to reach out and caress her cheek. His eyes returned to the road, and they finally made it to his house minutes later.

He unlocked the door and walked inside, flipping on the lights.

She halted at the door, filled with thoughts of her running from the house. As she finally stepped across the threshold, a shiver ran up her body. She stood in the living room, not venturing farther into the house.

"Are you thirsty?" Alex called from the kitchen.

"No, I'm fine."

He walked back into the room. They stood in front of each other; their eyes averted, looking at anything but each other.

"Are you sure you don't want the bed?"

She shook her head. "Thanks, but the couch is fine." She turned toward it as she took off her coat.

On instinct, he came up behind her to help her take it off and instantly realized his mistake as electricity leapt between them. They both jumped apart as if they had been burned. Rubbing the back of his neck, he stared at the ground.

Did she feel that, too?

Gemma still had her back to him and was trying to catch her breath. The electric current that passed between them when he came up to help her off with her jacket was surprising. She laid her coat across the seat and composed herself before turning around to face him.

"I'm really tired."

He shook himself from his thoughts. "Of course, you are, let me just go get blankets and pillows …" His voice trailed off as he left to retrieve the items.

She paced around the living room, once again unable to believe she was back in his house. A house she was very familiar with.

Minutes later, he returned carrying everything along with a shirt and a toothbrush. He sat the items on the sofa.

"I brought you a shirt to change into. Umm that was your tooth … I figured you might want to brush your teeth before bed," he said, gesturing at the items.

She knew he stopped himself from making a reference to their previous life together.

She fingered the shirt. It was one of his. It had been her favorite one to lounge around in when she stayed over.

Did he remember that?

It couldn't have been a coincidence he brought her this shirt. Her finger traced over the worn navy fabric. She was lost in old memories for a moment.

"Did you need anything else?" His voice disrupted her trip down memory lane.

She didn't turn around to answer. She choked back the emotion that was lodged in her throat. "No, I'm good."

He stood watching her, unable to move. He wanted to go to her so badly. Turning, he walked off down the hall, but then found himself coming back. He found her still standing in the same place.

"Gemma?"

It was a second before she glanced over her shoulder in acknowledgment, but didn't look at him. He just stood staring at her profile, unable to get the words out.

"I just wanted to say good night," he lied.

"Good night," she murmured.

Slowly, he walked back down the hallway to his room. After showering, he sat on the edge of his bed. Pulling the ring from his drawer, he looked at it as he thought about the woman who rested just down the hall from him. He let his head fall back as he pinched the bridge of his nose.

How am I supposed to make this right?

He shut the ring box and shoved it back in the drawer. Turning off the lamp, he lay back on the bed. Sleep was a million miles away.

Both of them managed to avoid talking about the big elephant in the room the whole time they were in each other's presence tonight. Maybe the reason he was having trouble starting this hard conversation was because he was afraid. He could finally admit to himself he was afraid she had either moved on, or worse … she stopped loving him. His fist pounded the mattress out of frustration. She was right down the hall, and he was terrified to approach her. It was easier to lay here and keep himself warm with the memories of what once was, than it was to embrace a future where she no longer wanted him. Turning on his side, he attempted to put his fear to rest. Maybe things would be different in the morning after some sleep, if he could fall asleep.

After changing in the bathroom, she couldn't stop sniffing the shirt as she lay down for bed. She'd forgotten how much she loved his scent. Shutting her eyes, she reveled in the familiarity. Her fingers trailed over the frayed and well-worn edges. Down the hall, the man she loved slept.

This day had gone from strange to weird. She never expected to step foot in this house again and now she was sleeping on the sofa, in his shirt, that had been her favorite a lifetime ago.

When he came back down the hall after she thought he left, she held out hope somehow he was going to take her in his arms and tell her he'd missed her and couldn't live without her. Unfortunately, this wasn't the movies, and it wasn't a fairytale. She would more than likely never get a happily ever after with Alex. Even though he was speaking to her, he probably hadn't forgiven her and he was just being polite. That would be the worst. The last person's pity or obligation she wanted was Alex. She didn't want him feeling sorry for her and only talking to her because he felt bad for her. The tears pricked her eyes at the thought. In the morning she would take the bus back to her apartment and have the landlord let her in. She brushed the back of her hand across her eyelids to wipe away the errant tears.

I don't want to keep crying, but why does this hurt so bad?

Her mouth opened in a silent sob and she buried her face in the pillow, unable to hold the pain at bay. It was torture to be near him, but not with him. After she'd drenched her pillow thoroughly, her river of tears finally carried her off to sleep.

Now that things were back to normal, Rachel was only too happy to show up on Alex's doorstep for breakfast. The other night he even returned a copy of the key to his house.

Hopefully, his guilt over how he'd treated her over the past few months would earn them a vast breakfast spread. As she and Chloe bounded into the house, thoughts of waffles dripping with syrup and crispy bacon made her salivate.

Rachel bellowed, "Alex, we're here."

Alex heard his sister's loud voice behind his closed bedroom door, and his eyes got as big as saucers when he realized Gemma was still asleep out on the sofa. He quickly pulled on jeans and a shirt, hoping to catch her before she found Gemma.

Gemma's eyes fluttered open and she squinted as her eyes adjusted to the sunlight. For a minute, she was unsure where she was, but then last night came back to her. Alex came to her rescue like old times. That's where she was, at his house on the couch. And that was Rachel's voice. Her eyes grew wide with anxiety at what Rachel was going to think when she saw her here. Before she had time to process anything further, she heard her name spoken in disbelief.

"Gemma?"

She slowly rolled over to see Rachel and Chloe standing in the doorway with their mouths on the ground, and then in the next second Alex was standing in the opposite doorway half-dressed and barefoot. Well, this sure looked questionable.

"Uncle Alex, does this mean you and Gemma are back together?"

22

Both Alex and Gemma began to babble at the same time, trying to explain why Gemma was there.

"She locked herself out …" Alex said.

"He was just helping me," Gemma stated.

Silence descended on the room once more, and Rachel eyed them both dubiously.

"Not sure what we just walked into the middle of, but we'll be in the kitchen moving some pots and pans around." As she spoke, she pushed Chloe toward the kitchen.

Chloe broke away from her mother and ran over to Gemma.

"Gemma, please don't leave like that again. I missed you … we all missed you …" She dropped her voice to a low though still audible whisper for the last part.

"Plus, I've had no one to tell all my latest gossip. You'll never believe who likes me."

She raised her voice to normal speaking level again. "You're staying for breakfast right?"

Gemma looked helplessly from Rachel to Alex. They both just shrugged their shoulders at her equally as helpless. *Chloe's just a child*, Gemma told herself. She didn't exactly understand why she stayed away so long. Gemma could tell Chloe obviously missed her. If she were truthful, she missed her, too. Hanging with Chloe was like having a little sister. She gave her a small smile.

"Yeah, sounds good."

Chloe gave her a big smile before throwing her arms around her. The hug took Gemma by surprise, but she wrapped her arms around Chloe before the young girl released her and headed into the kitchen.

After Rachel and Chloe excused themselves to the kitchen, Alex and Gemma awkwardly shared space. Gemma folded her arms across her chest to keep from fidgeting. Her eyes stared at the pattern of the blanket that still covered her lower half. She hadn't expected to be ambushed by Rachel and Chloe. Of course, it wasn't their fault. They didn't know she was here. She could see Alex's restless presence from the corner of her eye hovering in the doorway. It was difficult to make small talk when there were more important things that needed to be discussed.

Why did I ever give Rachel back that key?

He shook his head as he paced in the doorway. How was he supposed to have a conversation with her now, when his sister and niece were in the next room? He didn't know how the talk between the two of them would go, and he didn't want an audience. Unfortunately, he'd have to put it off a little while longer. He approached the sofa.

"I'm sorry … I forgot they were coming by."

"It's okay," Gemma responded as she picked at lint on the blanket. Alex noticed she still hadn't met his eyes. He squatted down next to her, eyeing her face intently. Things between them used to be easy. He reached his hand out hesitantly to touch her but thought better of it. If it were just Rachel here by herself, he would kick her out so he could talk to Gemma, but he couldn't do that to Chloe. She was excited to see Gemma.

He sighed. "If you don't want to stay for breakfast, I can always make an excuse."

"I don't want to disappoint Chloe." She turned away from him, but not before he saw the hurt in her eyes.

That came out all wrong. The last thing he wanted was for her to leave.

"Gemma?"

She didn't look at him. He lightly touched her arm, hoping not to cause the same sparks that occurred last night. She turned to him, but her eyes were still downcast.

"I didn't mean it that way. I want you to stay … for breakfast." He shut his eyes tightly for a second, angry with himself for punking out. Why couldn't he just let that stand on its own? He had to add 'for breakfast'.

What is wrong with me?

He wanted her to stay indefinitely, and he kept fucking it up. "I want you here … I just didn't want you to feel like you had to stay if it makes you uncomfortable."

Gemma looked at him then. "Does it make you uncomfortable, me being here?" She bit her bottom lip as she waited for his response.

Staring into her eyes, he shook his head. "No."

It was the first time since they reconnected last night that they had looked at each other. Her lips parted in a question as her eyes searched his. Alex opened his mouth to say something.

"Uncle Alex! Mom is about to burn the kitchen down!"

The spell between them was broken by Chloe's sudden outburst. Whatever was about to be said, the moment was now gone. Cursing, Alex broke eye contact first. He had a mind to put them both out. When he looked back at Gemma, she was getting up from the sofa, no longer giving him her attention. As he was standing up from his squatting position, he caught a glimpse of the silken expanse of her thigh before seeing her lovely legs and recalled what they once felt like when they were wrapped around him in ecstasy. Clearing his throat when he felt the tightening in his balls, he turned away to readjust himself.

Over his shoulder, he told her, "I guess I better check on Rachel before she destroys the kitchen."

Once he entered the kitchen, Gemma let out the breath she was holding. She was unsure whether she was grateful for whatever mischief Rachel was getting into in the kitchen or upset they were interrupted.

What was the look I saw in his eyes? She wondered as she folded up the blanket.

Thankfully, Rachel hadn't messed anything up too badly, but she had scorched the bottom of his favorite pan. He still sported a scowl as he continued salvaging breakfast.

What possessed her to try and cook?

She could barely boil water. Chloe was setting the table.

"Did you need help with anything?"

Alex looked up from the pan he was manning at hearing Gemma's voice.

When she entered the kitchen, he saw her hair was damp and piled on top of her head. She donned her uniform again since she lacked extra clothing.

Before he could respond, Rachel answered, "No, Alex has things covered, and Chloe is just about finished setting the table. Sit with me."

Even though she took a seat at one of the barstools, Gemma still threw him a glance to check with him. He offered her a small smile as he shook his head at her to let her know it was fine. Rachel and Gemma made small talk for a few minutes, or rather Gemma listened to Rachel, but once Alex started to serve up the food they moved to the table. Rachel dug in before anyone else and moaned with pleasure at the first bite of food.

"I've missed this so much. Alex, you outdid yourself." She continued digging in. Between bites of her food Rachel started to talk. "I got your message about getting into that photo exhibition. Congrats! Count on me to be there."

Gemma looked down shyly. "Thanks," she muttered before taking a bite of food.

Alex looked between his sister and Gemma with interest and then stared directly at Gemma, who wouldn't meet his gaze.

"Gemma, that's great. Congratulations. I take it classes have been going well. When does the exhibition take place?" He was genuinely happy for her. She deserved the success. He didn't know what her latest portfolio looked like, but he knew she had an excellent eye.

"Right before Christmas break."

He noticed she didn't extend an invitation, so he took it upon himself to broach the subject in an indirect manner.

"I'd love to see how your work has progressed."

Out of the corner of his eye, he could see Rachel silently watching the conversation like a tennis match as she stuffed her face.

Is that how he's going to play this? Trying to say things without being direct? Well, two could play that game. She responded before taking a bite of food, "Well, the exhibition is open to the public. Anyone can come."

She looked at him pointedly as she put some eggs in her mouth. As she looked down into her plate, he saw the corner of her mouth quirk into a grin.

Is she toying with me? He smiled to himself.

She isn't going to make this easy is she ... Nor should she, he thought, swallowing some orange juice. It was up to him to initiate the talk. He sought her out, not the other way around. This was a new side to her. He liked the feistiness she demonstrated. Not that he'd ever felt like Gemma was a pushover, but there did seem to be a new level of confidence, of strength that now manifested itself outwardly and not just inwardly.

After breakfast, they all cleaned up the kitchen together. Afterward, Alex was preparing to take Gemma back to her place and rehearsing how he would start the conversation. As he walked back into the room, he noticed she already wore her jacket. He gave her a shy smile. "Someone's eager to get away."

Thoughts of another night, long ago drifted back to him as he remembered saying those words to her before. She smiled shyly back at him, and he wondered if she recalled that night as well. She shook her head.

"Rachel and Chloe offered to take me home. I just wanted to thank you for last night, Alex."

His smile faltered.

Is she so ready to get away from me?

Rachel came into the living room before he could protest.

"You ready to go, Gemma?" Rachel asked as her curious gaze wandered between the two of them.

Gemma gave him one more look.

"I better go. Thanks again for coming to my rescue." She turned away, but Alex caught her hand. There was a shock that happened when he touched her, but this time, he didn't let go.

He stared directly into her eyes. "I'd like to see you again?" He gave her a pleading look as he held her gaze.

It was a moment before she responded.

"I have a late shift at the diner tomorrow. Come by at ten o'clock."

She gently pulled her hand away and walked out with Rachel.

As Rachel was backing out of the driveway, Gemma anxiously looked back at Alex's house.

"I guess all that bravado in there was just that?"

Gemma pouted. "Was I that obvious?"

Rachel gave her a sympathetic look.

"I can't imagine what it must have been like seeing him again, Gemma, especially with everything that's happened between the two of you. But I don't understand … I thought you wanted to get back together. Why did you tell him I offered you a ride when you practically begged me to take you home? I thought you'd want to hang around so the two of you could talk."

Chloe poked her head between the two front seats. "You never did answer earlier, Gemma. Are you and Uncle Alex getting back together?"

She saw the hopeful expression on Chloe's face, but couldn't give the girl false hope.

"It's complicated," was all she could say.

Gemma couldn't hide her discomfort.

"Sit back and put on your seatbelt, Chloe. No more questions for Gemma, okay?"

Chloe silently slumped onto the backseat and put on her seatbelt before she directed her attention back to her cell phone.

"I don't know what I'm doing, Rachel. I'm scared. I do want him back …" She shook her head. "But I don't want things to be how they were. Not that they weren't good … they were great. But something your father said has me rethinking how things were."

Rachel screeched to a halt on the side of the road.

"My father? What are you talking about? Something he said before he broke the two of you up?" She gave Gemma a look of astonishment.

Biting her lip, Gemma sheepishly replied, "No, he's come to see me at the diner … we've talked."

Rachel put the car in park as she gaped at Gemma.

"What are you guys like besties now? Did you forget how he ruined your life?" Rachel stared at her incredulously.

Gemma was touched that Rachel cared so much about her that she had been angry at her father's actions as well, but now it had just gone too far.

"If there was anyone who was more upset with your father months ago, it was me, but once I had time to think I understood he was only trying to look out for Alex …" She glanced over the backseat to look at Chloe and found her swaying along to whatever music was coming from her headphones as she texted on her phone. She turned back to Rachel.

"Think about it, Rachel, you're a mother. When Chloe starts dating and some guy you're not sure about comes around, don't tell me you wouldn't do everything you could to make sure she doesn't get hurt?"

Rachel huffed.

"He's your father, and he's lonely. All he has is you guys." Gemma tried to get her attention, but Rachel was staring out the window as she gripped the steering wheel tightly.

"I know it's hard for you to understand. Forgiveness isn't always easy, but I also know how unhealthy it is to hold onto all that anger and bitterness. It's toxic …"

As she continued to speak, she noticed Rachel's grip on the steering wheel ease up.

"How could I ever seek Alex's forgiveness if I was unwilling to extend it to your father? Even if Alex never forgave me, I knew I still had to forgive your father for my sake. Plus, your father isn't the only guilty party in this whole mess, Rachel … we all know that."

Rachel's eyes finally came to rest on Gemma's face. Then she looked out the windshield.

"I hate being wrong, and it's not always easy to admit when I am, but what you said … makes sense." She turned and gave Gemma a small smile.

"I'll go by and see him."

Gemma smiled at her. "Thank you."

At the restaurant, Alex was very distracted as he went over inventory with Amanda. A few times she had to correct his count of some of their produce.

She placed her clipboard on the shelf.

"Okay, out with it. What's going on, Alex? You're acting stranger than usual. You're highly distracted. I'm afraid you're going to go into dinner service like this and slice off a finger." She eyed him curiously as she crossed her arms over her chest and waited for him to spill.

Alex sighed knowing Amanda wasn't going to just let this go.

"I saw Gemma last night … and this morning." He saw Amanda's eyebrows go up in a speculative expression, and he shook his head.

"It wasn't like that. She locked herself out and spent the night on my sofa."

"What? You made her sleep on the sofa, Alex? I thought you were more of a gentleman than that! Why didn't you offer her your bed?"

He stood up, agitated.

"I did!" He paced back and forth as Amanda watched him before moving the conversation forward.

"Okay, back to the real story. It's been over three months, how did you end up seeing her? I don't understand. Are you guys back together?"

Putting his hand up to stop her from asking any more questions, he sat back in his chair.

"Slow down. Too many questions." He put his face in his hands.

"No, we're not back together. Last night I was driving by her place—"

"Driving by her place? Alex, I thought you didn't know where she lived? Are you stalking her?"

Alex huffed in annoyance. "Could you please let me finish? Damn, I'm beginning to wonder if you're related to Rachel ... And no, I'm not stalking Gemma. Come on, Amanda."

She leaned back against the shelf. "Okay, I'm shutting up now. Just tell me what's going on that has you so distracted."

He got up, and began pacing the room again. He didn't want to betray Gemma by sharing details of her past with Amanda, but he needed to talk to someone.

"I can't go into detail ... all I can say is that when Gemma needed me and I was supposed to be there for her, I wasn't. That's what caused our break-up. And now that I have a chance to make it right and try and get her back ... I'm scared."

"That was cryptic," she mumbled, then sat quietly assessing him before responding. "It sounds like you just need to man up and apologize and beg her forgiveness. Hopefully, she still feels the same way and takes you back …"

She turned more serious before saying the next part.

"But even if it doesn't happen like that, she deserves to know how sorry you are, especially if you still love her like I think you do."

He shook his head. "But what if she's moved on or … or—"

Amanda cut him off. "Or she's stopped loving you?"

She stared him directly in the eyes as she continued, "Alex, unfortunately, that's just a chance you have to take … love is risky for a reason because it means you have to make yourself vulnerable to someone even when you don't know how they feel."

He saw something akin to regret swimming in Amanda's eyes as she spoke to him.

"I consider you a friend. So listen when I say that you run the risk of having your heart trampled on again if Gemma doesn't respond the way you want her to, but you run an even greater risk if you say nothing … I speak from experience." She squeezed his shoulder as she grabbed her clipboard and exited the room, leaving Alex alone with his thoughts.

Rachel stepped through the door hesitantly. He wasn't out tinkering in the garage when she arrived so she let herself inside. She walked down the hall to the den where she could hear some idiot telling Judge Judy why they took their girlfriend's TV as payment for an unpaid loan.

Was that always the reason people appeared on her show? A domestic squabble over who loaned or owed money to their ex-lover or spouse? Her dad couldn't possibly find that drivel fascinating. Maybe he just had a thing for the judge herself.

When she finally entered the den, she found her father dozing in his La-Z-Boy. She smiled sadly at the picture he painted.

When did he get so old?

Even in adulthood, her father always exuded strength. Maybe it was something all women felt toward their fathers, but right now in sleep, he seemed vulnerable, small. She had always loved her father, and if she was truthful, she'd missed spending time with him. She walked toward him. The little noises her movements made must have woken him because he came to and shook the sleep from his body.

"Rachel?" He stared at her, amazed to find her there.

"Dad."

They both said nothing for moments. She held up a six-pack.

"The game's on tonight. Just thought you could use some company." She sat on the couch. She took a beat before saying more.

"Gemma told me you went to see her."

Their eyes locked, as she continued. "I don't want to go making this a whole big deal or anything. Can we both just agree that we're sorry?"

She could have said nothing, and he would have gladly welcomed her back without an explanation or apology. She was his child. He would always forgive her.

"Toss your old man one of those beers, would ya?"

A grin spread across her face as she tore off one of the beers and offered it to him. They quickly and easily settled into a debate over what players would perform favorably and who needed to retire.

About an hour later, as the halftime show blared from the TV, he cut his eye over and watched Rachel bop along to the song the cheerleaders were dancing to. He had Gemma to thank for having his daughter back. At least one of his kids was back. Hopefully, he could patch things up with Alex. Rachel's bold move to extend the olive branch first made Thomas realize he owed it to Alex to approach him in making things right between them.

After his talk with Amanda yesterday, Alex knew what he needed to do, although he was nervous as hell. He hadn't been able to eat anything all day. What happened tonight could dictate the rest of his life. He wasn't sure what he would do if she said she didn't want him. He swallowed. He couldn't think about that right now. Smoothing his hair back, he pulled the door open to the diner and walked in. So many nights of watching her from his car, it seemed weird now to walk through the door and take a seat at the counter.

He spotted her right away; she was tucking her hair behind her ear and smiling at a customer as she finished taking their order. When she turned to walk toward the counter she noticed him. The smile faltered a bit as she looked at him and he saw her recover. He gave her a small pained smile as he realized that things very well might not go as he hoped.

Is she not glad to see me? He watched her as she approached him.

"You're a little early ... can I get you something? I still have about twenty minutes," she said, glancing down at her watch.

He shook his head. "I'm okay."

Her mouth quirked upwards, but he noticed it wasn't a smile; it was more like a grimace. He touched her arm.

"Hey, if you want me to go ..."

She looked at him then. "No, it's okay." She bit her lip.

"Let me just finish up and then we can go."

His hand dropped back to his side. Despite him touching her, no fireworks had gone off today. There was no spark. He watched her as she walked up to another table. Now, he was frightened. When he turned back around, he caught the eye of the cook in the back who was eyeing him suspiciously.

The last twenty minutes dragged on for Alex as he waited for her to finish her shift.

For Gemma, the last minutes of her shift flew by at lightning speed. If he was only here to clear his conscience and make a clean break of things, he didn't need to bother. The uneasiness about what he had to say sat in her stomach like a stone.

She finished giving directions for her remaining tables to the incoming waitress and then grabbed her jacket.

Alex followed her out the door, and they walked next to each other down the street.

His fingers tingled at the nearness of her, and he wished he could take her hand in his. Trying to break the uneasy silence that descended the moment they stepped out of the diner, he finally spoke.

"I'm sorry again about yesterday. Rachel and Chloe …
I forgot I told them they could come by for breakfast." He
shoved his hand in his pocket.

"It's okay." She put her hands into her coat pockets.

They walked the rest of the way to her apartment in
silence. Going up the stairs to her second-floor studio, Alex
felt trepidation.

Gemma opened the door and clicked on the light and
began to remove her jacket.

"Can I get you something to drink?"

He noticed she wouldn't look at him. He wouldn't do this
all night. He couldn't. They couldn't keep tiptoeing around
each other afraid to address all the unsaid things between
them.

He came up behind her. "Let's not keep talking to each
other like we're strangers, okay?"

She turned, trembling to face him, although she kept her
eyes on the ground.

"Okay."

Alex was about to speak when Gemma rushed headlong
into a nervous speech.

"It was hard after everything happened, really hard … I
didn't know if I'd recover or be whole again. I'd just started
to feel like I would be okay and then you showed up the other
night and … and …" As she paused for a breath to collect
her thoughts, he could only stare at her. She lifted her eyes

briefly to meet his, and he finally glimpsed the uncertainty, the fear, the pain, all the things he was feeling. She feared his rejection as much as he feared hers. He breathed a heavy sigh as he stepped closer and brought his hand up to caress her cheek. Her eyes closed at the feel of his touch, and he leaned his forehead against hers. They breathed in each other for a moment before he felt her push against his chest and back away. She turned from him and hugged her body. He knew he owed her an apology. It was wrong of him to touch her when he hadn't even said what he'd come here to say.

"I'm sorry, I shouldn't have done that." He stepped toward her, but she moved away from his reach.

Damn! Have I already messed things up before I could fix them? He didn't want her to keep retreating. He stood where he was.

"Gemma, would you please look at me?"

It took several moments, but she finally faced him. The tears that trickled down her face gutted him. Her raw pain was no longer concealed. It stared him in the face.

"I, I ..."

Everything he'd rehearsed, everything he thought he was going to say, suddenly seemed inadequate and not enough. The pain he caused her choked him. Months she carried around the pain of his rejection, the loss of what they shared ... the loss of his love. His selfish, unrelenting, righteous indignation nearly decimated her.

Without thinking, he moved quickly and was down on his knees before her, with his arms around her lower body. Her name came out of his mouth on a strangled sob, "Gemma, Gemma ..."

She heard the anguish and pleading in his voice as he tried to get out the words. She held her hands up not knowing what to do. She cried harder. Slowly, she placed her hand on the top of his head. His face was buried in her mid-section. He tilted his head back to look up at her.

"Gemma, how can I ever begin to tell you ... to show you how sorry I am for what happened? For what I did ... It will never be enough ..." He swallowed.

"I love you, and I hurt you so bad, how can I expect you to forgive me?"

Is he really on his knees asking me for forgiveness? She touched his cheek and his eyes closed.

"Please get up ..."

He slowly clambered to his feet as she helped him up. Once he stood facing her, she cleared away his tears with the pads of her thumbs.

"We both have a lot to be sorry for."

Reaching up, he took her hands in his.

"No, no ..." He began to talk over her. "I won't let you apologize anymore for that. I know how sorry you are. I know it wasn't intentional."

She shook her head. "Stop, Alex! Stop!"

He stopped talking as he saw her get upset.

"Can't you see that's what got us into this mess in the first place; not talking about everything, about the past?" She stared intently into his eyes.

"Why didn't we ever talk more deeply about my past or your wife? Or even your mother?"

He looked at her, wondering where this was all coming from.

"Do we know each other as well as we think we do? I mean … those are things that we should have discussed, don't you think?"

"What good would talking about all of that do?" The irritation was evident in his voice.

She pulled her hands from his grasp.

"I did an awful thing, Alex. I killed someone …" Her chest was heaving with the weight of saying those words out loud.

"I killed your wife," she said in a tiny voice.

"Stop saying that!" He shut his eyes, trying to block out what she was saying.

"But it's what I did, Alex. Even if it was an accident … you had every right to be angry with me, to hate me," she said on a hiccup, through her crying.

"I don't hate you; I love you." Taking her by the shoulders, his face took on a pained expression as he gazed at her.

"I didn't want to talk about those things because what good does it do? It doesn't bring the people you love back. It just makes it hurt more …"

Pulling out of his arms, she wiped at her tears.

"The thing is; I've been trying to understand why you didn't want to know my crime to begin with. Were you afraid that you couldn't love me once you knew what I'd done?"

She paused as she held his gaze.

"I shared a lot with you; I told you stuff that was painful and ugly. I shared my hurt with you, but when I think back, you were closed off from me. We always discussed me … you talked, but you didn't tell me things that mattered … you say you love me, but if you do, then you should have shared yourself with me, all of yourself. Not just the good parts, or the funny bits, but the baring your soul, loathsome kind of stuff that's scary to talk about."

He heard her sniffle and went to say something.

"Let me finish. I love you, Alex. I held out hope you would forgive me … come back to me even … I want to be with you, but I want to know that I have all of you, that you'll share every part of yourself with me and let me know who you are." Gemma bit her lip.

All of this caught him by surprise, not that he expected her to fall into his arms, but he was unprepared to answer the questions she asked him.

What good did talking about those things do anyone? The things she asked him about were painful.

Can't she understand I just don't want to hurt anymore?

He knew she shared everything with him and would have more than likely told him in detail about what landed her in prison if he hadn't always insisted it was her past, and it didn't matter. As he stood in front of her, he asked himself why was he so intent on keeping the past locked away. He looked at her with tormented eyes.

"I never meant to hold back from you, Gemma. I never realized that … I guess I just didn't think you needed to know those things …" He bit his tongue as he realized the lie that rolled off his lips. He shook his head.

"No, that's not true." He licked dry lips.

"When I started falling for you, it seemed like all the pain and anger I'd been feeling receded. Why would I have wanted to relive that when you made me forget all the bad, all the hurt I felt?" The tears shone in his eyes as he continued.

"That night when it came out that you were partly responsible for some of that pain, it tore me apart … I wasn't just angry at you for what you'd done, but for making me feel all of that pain again and making me feel it toward you." He shook his head at the memory of it, as the tears splashed down his face.

"But, Alex, life doesn't work that way, you can't separate the good and the bad," she said, giving him a look of sympathy.

"I didn't want to associate you with the misery my life became before I met you. Oh, Alex has a mom that died of cancer, oh Alex's wife got killed … I just wanted you, us to be something that was finally good in my life."

He looked at her as he took a breath before continuing, "You say you can't separate the good and the bad … and you're probably right, but I was trying hard because once I met you and fell in love with you, I knew it was the happiest I'd ever been, and then I fucked it up … that night I was horrible to you …"

Gemma shook her head vehemently.

"No, no, let me finish. You'd done nothing but love me despite probably knowing you should guard your heart, but you loved me unconditionally, openly and without pause … and I threw it back in your face that night. It wasn't until I finally read the file … the stuff my dad gathered on you that I realized I was a complete ass to you … and more than likely messed up the best thing that ever happened to me."

They both stood staring at each other after he was finished speaking. After a moment, he took a tentative step toward her, then another one, until he was standing within a few inches of her. He gazed down into her face. He was scared to reach out and touch her, in case she was still skittish and tried to run.

"Tell me, Gemma … have I messed up the best thing that's ever happen to me?"

23

Gemma stood staring at Alex. How many times had she wished to be back in his arms and here he was standing in front of her asking her to take him back. The desperation was palpable in his eyes.

"I'd be a fool to turn you away when we've both been so miserable." She gave him a small smile.

The biggest grin broke out on Alex's face, and he advanced upon her. She put her hand up to stop him.

"First, there are two things you have to promise me."

He stopped in his tracks and stared at the obstinate stubbornness written on her face. He knew he would do whatever it took to win her back.

"Anything."

Gemma took a deep breath. "I want us to go slow, Alex. I don't want to go rushing into things, and I want you to talk to me about things in your life …"

He nodded his head vigorously as he began approaching her once more.

"I'm not finished." She took a step back, but was unable to conceal the grin lifting up the corner of her mouth.

"But that was two things, Gemma." Alex quirked his eyebrow at her with a mischievous smile and he took one more tentative step toward her.

"Okay, well I meant three things you have to promise."

He nodded his head at her to continue.

"You need to forgive your father."

At that, he halted all movement. Gemma saw him stop and continued speaking, hoping to persuade him.

"Listen, if I of all people could forgive him, then you should be able to as well. He's your father, and he loves you." She could see she was breaking down his defenses.

"Alex, you know I grew up without family. I would give anything to have a parent who cared about me, so if you can't do it for him, do it for me."

Alex looked at her unbelievingly.

How is she able to be so forgiving?

It made him love her even more. Even still, it wasn't so easy for him to just let it go, what his father did, but he had to try if it meant that much to her.

"I'm not going to lie, Gemma, I'm still angry with him. I'm not saying it's going to be easy or that I'm going to go over there tomorrow and start speaking to him … but I will try."

She assessed him, gauging the sincerity of his words. "Okay."

He smiled warmly at her. "Okay?"

She nodded her head as he walked toward her and slowly pulled her into his body. His eyes roamed over her face. He was holding her again.

"Can I kiss you now?" he asked in a husky voice.

She nodded as she gazed into his eyes, too breathless at his nearness to give her verbal consent. Before she knew it, his lips crashed down on hers in a ferociously intense kiss that made her weak in the knees. After minutes, he finally released her mouth, both of them panting. His hands came up and caressed her face. He couldn't tear his eyes away.

"I've missed you," he spoke low, as he began covering her face with soft kisses. When his lips touched her cheek, he could feel the smile on her face.

"I missed you, too," she breathed out, and her eyes fluttered closed at the whisper of his lips kissing her eyelid.

"I love you, Gemma … I never stopped loving you."

Her eyes opened at his declaration and they stared into each other's eyes. He continued caressing her cheek.

"I know how angry I was, but I never stopped loving you even then."

She leaned into him, eager to soak up his loving touch she missed so much. She could remember lying in bed craving him and starving for his mere presence during long, lonely nights. Happy tears glistened in her eyes.

"Alex," his name came out on a sigh.

He smiled, before leaning down and kissing her long and slow. A couple of minutes later he broke the kiss. He breathed deeply as he caught his breath.

"I know you said you want to take things slow, but could I stay the night?"

Uncertainty creased her brow.

"We don't have to do anything … I'd just like to sleep next to you." Embarrassed, Alex averted his gaze as he toyed with a lock of her hair. "I've missed sleeping next to you …" he stated, lifting his head.

"I'll be honest, it was hell sleeping without you." He admitted.

The warm smile she became accustomed to seeing during their time together spread across his face now.

"Okay, you can stay, but we're only sleeping." She chuckled as she went to walk away from him.

"Do you want a shower?" she tossed back over her shoulder.

Before she could take another step, she felt his arms wrap around her waist, right before his breath tickled her ear.

"Are you going to be in there?"

She playfully smacked his hand and pulled away before she could give into the feelings heating up her body.

She continued, ignoring his question, "Do you want towels?"

"Sure."

Gemma walked off to the bathroom fanning herself. She needed to get out of the same room before she ripped off her clothes and begged him to make love to her. Her body was reacting to months of pent-up sexual frustration. She only went into retrieve towels, but she shut the door behind her and leaned against it. He was here. They just made up, and he still wanted her. It felt surreal. She walked over to the mirror and looked at her face. Biting her lip, she stared back at her reflection.

What am I doing? I want to take things slow, so why did I agree to let him stay the night? And in the same bed, no less?

She shook her head as she turned away to rummage in the linen closet. Thankfully, when she moved in Shelby gifted her with a nice towel and linen set, so she didn't have to offer him the threadbare ones she initially found at the Goodwill. She paused to get herself in control of her raging hormones before opening the door and heading back into the room.

Their fingers brushed as she passed him the towels.

"Thanks."

Once he disappeared into the bathroom, and she heard the shower cut on, she finally got a chance to look around the room. Embarrassment assailed her at what he must think of her threadbare, meager furnishings. Not only that, she saw the disarray she left her place in earlier that morning. Her dirty breakfast dishes sat near the sink, some of her portfolio for the showcase lay scattered on the dining table, and her pajamas and some other clothing were haphazardly tossed over the back of the couch.

When did I become such a slob?

She hurriedly began tidying up. Hopefully, he was so focused on the two of them making up and apologizing he didn't see the state of her apartment.

Just as he exited the bathroom, Gemma stuffed the last of her dirty clothes into the hamper. She turned to find him wrapped only in a towel, a very short towel at that. Turning her back to him quickly, she let out a breath as she felt moisture pool between her thighs. His skin was still damp from the steam that lingered from his shower and the towel was doing nothing to cover the outline of his package. She forgot how well endowed he was. She needed to do something to busy herself.

"Do you want some tea?" She was already rummaging for teabags and pulling cups from the cupboard, as she was putting on the kettle. Even though she felt him enter the tiny kitchen space, she nearly jumped out of her skin when his hand touched her hip. Nervously, she turned to face him.

"Want some help?"

She smiled faintly, troubled at his nearness.

"Why don't you let the water boil …" Maneuvering out of the kitchen and toward the bathroom clumsily, Gemma backed away. "I'm just going to take a shower."

Alex stared at the bathroom door he watched Gemma disappear behind. He smirked as he turned toward the kettle. Yeah, he could have put on his jeans after his shower, but he couldn't resist watching her squirm. He could tell she was just as hot for him as he was for her. She wanted to take things slow, but they had both been denied each other's bodies for so long and right now all he could think about was being inside of her. He wandered over to the dining room table to sit while the water boiled and saw all of the pictures she tried to stuff into a folder.

Perusing the photos, he saw her style had developed and matured over the time they were apart. It had a slightly darker quality to it, but not in a morbid way. Her photos were quite breathtaking. His hand paused as he came across a photo that seemed familiar to him, not because he'd seen it before, but because what the picture contained seemed known to him. He brought the image closer to his face and realized it was his bedroom; the picture was of him, lying in his bed. He picked up picture after picture that contained various shots of him lying on his stomach, his side and close up shots of different body parts. They were beautiful, artful shots caught of him in the morning light. Suddenly, he remembered that morning with startling clarity. He'd awakened to find her messing about with her camera, wearing his shirt before he'd gotten her to take pictures with him.

As that memory occurred, and he moved a stack of pictures around, there was the picture of the two of them staring back at him. Gemma was staring straight into the camera with a surprised and happy look on her face as he stole a kiss.

Before he really had the opportunity to look at it, the shower cut off and he scrambled to put the pictures back in the folder. He felt like an ass for disturbing her privacy. Even though the pictures were of him, he had no right to snoop. He quickly got up to check on the kettle.

She exited the bathroom to find Alex pouring steaming water into two mugs.

Damn! The man had an ass.

Biting her bottom lip, she fidgeted her hands as she walked into the kitchen.

"Do you need any help?"

He turned to look at her and thought she was a vision. Her damp hair sat pinned on top of her head, and she wore an oversized nightshirt. He turned back to the tea before answering her.

"No, I got it … sit on the couch, and I'll bring it to you."

Gemma did as she was told. She had no TV, so the silence in the apartment seemed deafening as she waited for Alex to bring her tea.

A couple of minutes later, he pressed the warm mug into her hands. She sipped at the hot liquid as he sat rather closely next to her. He peered over the rim of his cup at her, watching her with hooded eyes, as they both sat drinking the steaming brew without speaking. He could tell she was trying her hardest to avoid eye contact with him. His leg brushed hers, and it gave him a thrill to see how his nearness affected her. She spluttered in her tea when his leg brushed hers a second time and he tried to contain his chuckle. She looked up in time to catch the mischievous grin that crossed his face before he had time to bury it in his coffee mug.

"Alex! You did that on purpose!" She smacked at him, and he began to laugh as he sat his mug on the coffee table and then grabbed her cup and put it on the table next to his. She smacked his arm again, and then he descended on her, tickling her mercilessly. She squealed and laughed while his fingers danced over her sides. As he moved over her, continuing the horseplay, his towel came off.

Suddenly, the humor left Gemma as she struggled to sit up. Averting her eyes, she pulled her nightshirt to a dignified position. Not only were her cheeks burning, the flames that licked at her insides were screaming to be extinguished.

Alex retrieved his towel from the floor and was tying it around his waist. She abruptly turned to him just as he knotted the towel.

"I don't think this is a good idea."

Before she could take her next breath, he was on her. His hands were running up and down her arms to soothe her.

"Hey, hey …"

She was looking down but quickly realized that view only offered trouble in the way of seeing his penis barely concealed by the towel that only moments ago slipped away to reveal his arousal. Looking up into his eyes, she could tell he was trying to keep his passion in check.

"You said you wanted to take things slow, and we can do that."

She looked at him skeptically.

"Scout's honor." He grinned at her. "I just want to sleep next to you ..." he said earnestly as she nodded her head and turned toward the bed.

"Would you get the light?"

He walked over and flicked the switch as she turned down the bed, casting the room in shadows. By the time he reached the bed, Gemma had already slipped under the covers and lay on her side facing away from him. He slid in next to her and lay on his back, hands behind his head. He looked over at her and could almost make out the rigid lines of her back beneath the shirt she wore. His body called out to her. Thankfully, he was only wearing this towel, because his body felt like it was burning up. He was so hot to be inside of her, to feel her slick warmth cover him. He was trying to quell his lust, but it was hard laying this close to her. He turned on his side facing her.

All she could see when she shut her eyes was the size of his cock. Her eyes swung open trying to dispel the image from her brain. She was practically leaning off the bed she was trying so hard not to touch him.

Why did I agree to this?

It's not that she didn't want to be with him, but she was afraid to get lost in the feelings of what being with him meant. She didn't want to abandon all reason, and she knew once they started sleeping together again, she would get swallowed up in those feelings of euphoria that being with him caused. If she was honest, she was still afraid he would wake up in the morning and realize he'd made a mistake in taking her back.

She kept reminding herself that she got what she wanted, they were back together, yet she was laying with two feet of space between them. She couldn't keep the fear at bay. Sometimes it was just easier to put up the wall and protect herself like she had always done. At least that way if Alex changed his mind, decided he didn't want her, this time she would be prepared. As she lay overthinking the situation to the point of drowsiness, she felt his chest press against her back as his arms came around her. For a moment she grew rigid, afraid he would try for more. She felt herself slipping into the beckoning allure of the temptress known as sleep. Before she knew it the black abyss claimed her, she was fast asleep, nestled securely in his embrace.

The moment he took her in his arms he felt her body tense for only a second before she relaxed against him. Not long after, he heard her deep, even breathing as she fell asleep. He smiled into her hair as he simply held her. As much as he wanted her, he knew what she needed at the moment was him and the reassurance his nearness bought, not his raging hard-on. If he was honest with himself, he missed this more than the sex, the intimacy. Yes, his body wanted one thing, but his mind and heart were content. He could quell his carnal appetite tonight and give her exactly what she needed. Their future held plenty of hot-blooded nights filled with passion. He snuggled her closer, sniffing her hair and relishing the scent of her shampoo as he slipped into unconsciousness himself.

24

The sounds of cooking woke Alex from a deep sleep. He rubbed his eyes. The sheet fell to his waist when he sat up in Gemma's bed. She had her back to him as she stood at the stove scrambling eggs. He couldn't help but watch her for a moment. He'd missed catching her in these unguarded moments when she didn't realize he was watching her. She was relaxed and absently humming some tune he couldn't make out.

He ran his fingers through his hair as he contemplated whether to surprise her in the kitchen or to call out to her and let her know he was awake. He settled back against the pillows, content to just watch her for now. Thinking back to last night, he was aware she was scared, and she had every right to be. He needed to make sure she knew he would never leave her again. Also, he wanted her to open up to him again like she used to, share with him. Earning her trust back was his top priority.

They just got back together, so it was too early to propose. He knew their relationship walked a tenuous thread; it was by no means stable. He had a lot to prove and make her believe he was in this for the long haul. Plus, he promised her he would reconcile with his father. It didn't go unnoticed by him that she could so easily forgive him, and here he was having an issue with letting bygones be bygones with the old man. He was so deep in his thoughts he hadn't realized she figured out he was awake.

"Alex?" Her voice brought him out of his thoughts.

"Hey," he said in a husky voice as he sat up straighter, giving her his full attention. Her eyes wandered down to where the sheet settled around his waist. She quickly brought her eyes back up to his face.

"I hope you're hungry. I made breakfast." She bit her lip as she offered him a grin.

Smiling warmly, he made to get out of the bed, and Gemma quickly turned back to the stove. When Alex noticed her turn her back, he looked down and realized he was naked. He smirked as he realized the towel came off in the night and was probably wrapped up somewhere in the sheets. Staring at Gemma's back, he retrieved his jeans and put them on. It would be cruel to make her suffer through breakfast with him naked.

Gemma pretended to have something she needed to deal with on the stove once Alex started getting up from the bed. She already knew he was naked beneath the sheet because when she'd woken up, his naked erection was poking her in all the right places, which prompted her quick exit from the bed.

For a while, she sat watching him from the sofa. He always looked sexy and peaceful as he slept. She was tempted to take some photographs of him but refrained. After a while, she'd eventually wandered into the kitchen and started to make eggs and bacon. She didn't have anything lavish like he would have on hand to make an omelet or something more gourmet.

She was unsure why her meager surroundings and lack of certain things made her feel embarrassed and inadequate around him. Yes, they had not been around each other for months, but it wasn't like he didn't know her, didn't know her background or her history. But, it was true they had always been at his house, since he wasn't allowed into the boarding house.

She tried to shake off the feeling as she turned to make a plate for each of them once she was sure he had at least put on some pants. Before she could sit the plates on the table, he occupied one of the chairs sans shirt. She could be thankful he was at least now wearing pants and not tempting her.

She took the seat opposite him, and they ate in companionable silence for a while. She looked at him with hooded eyes and then she remembered the other night.

"So, are you finally going to tell me what you were doing outside my apartment the other night?" Gemma asked as she put a bite of eggs into her mouth. She toyed with her bacon as she waited for his response.

Alex cut his eyes at her, as a blush crossed his face. He dragged his fork through his food knowing he had to come clean on his late night stakeout sessions. Biting his lip, he dropped his fork onto the plate and leaned his elbows on the table.

"I was following you."

Gemma's jaw dropped open as she stared at him. "You were ... following me?"

He saw the look of confusion on her face and rushed to explain.

"It's not how it sounds. It came out wrong."

She still gaped at him, waiting for his explanation.

"I was worried about you ... after I read the reports about you, Rachel left a note in the back of the file with the address of the diner, so I went there ... but I couldn't bring myself to go inside. I wasn't prepared to face you, so I watched you ... then that night when you closed up, and I realized you walked home, all I could think about was the night you were attacked

…" He looked into her eyes and she swallowed, nodding her head in understanding.

"I wouldn't have been able to rest at night knowing you were walking alone late at night and not knowing if you made it home safely, so I would come and make sure you got home."

They sat in silence for a minute, before Gemma said in a deadpan voice, "For a minute, I thought you'd turned into a creeper."

The mood was lightened as Alex bust out laughing. He lifted his fork to resume eating breakfast, but before he could, she quickly leaned across the table and placed a kiss at the corner of his mouth, catching him off-guard.

She leaned back slightly and looked him in the eyes, as she softly said, "Thank you."

He knew he was trying to give her space, but he couldn't help himself. In a matter of seconds, he was out of his seat. He grabbed her face as his lips crashed into hers. The dishes clattered as he knocked into the table trying to get closer to her. She didn't resist him, but frantically groped for him. He deepened the kiss as they both stood up. Alex moved swiftly around the table to take her in his arms.

She was drowning in his mouth, in this kiss, as he backed her up against the wall. The heat emanating from his bare chest being pressed against her made her moan into his mouth. His hands tugged at the hem of her nightshirt, ready to lift it out of the way of his questing fingers. Suddenly it was like cold water was thrown on her as her brain took over the thinking from her hormones. Pushing against him, she broke their kiss. They stood panting, trying to catch their breath.

"I can't, Alex."

He was still holding onto her waist, unable to stop touching her. He leaned his forehead against hers and let out a sigh. "I know, you have to get to school, right?"

In the cloud of lust she was enveloped in when he kissed her, she forgot she did, in fact, have class in half an hour. However, that wasn't the reason she put the brakes on what was sure to have turned into amazing back together sex. She knew once she crossed that line with him, it was the point of no return. She would once again lose her head and her heart. If later he changed his mind about them, she wasn't sure she would recover. The rational side of her brain said she should just voice her fears, but she wasn't ready to let him in that deep. Not yet. Damn it! That made her a hypocrite. Hadn't she just told him last night she didn't want him keeping things from her? She bit her lip in frustration, lost in the swirl of her thoughts.

"Hey …" The silky timbre of his voice, his nearness, and the backs of his fingers brushing lightly against her cheek almost made her forget herself. She nearly threw him on the table and mounted him. He was staring at her with this intense look. She'd forgotten how much she loved his eyes. He stared at her like he was trying to discern her thoughts. She averted her gaze and gently pushed against him so he would back up. He didn't budge.

"Come to my house tonight for dinner?"

She looked back into his eyes briefly and saw the pleading look there. Her tongue darted out to lick her suddenly dry lips. She was still oblivious to the effect the small action had on him.

The nervous habit didn't go unnoticed by Alex. He felt himself harden, and his jeans were now very constricting.

"What have I told you about doing that?" he said playfully, backing up a little to allow her to move.

If he kept her caged in any longer, he knew he wouldn't let her get away or leave her apartment to go to school. He'd make love to her against this wall, on the countertop, in her bed. He shook his head, trying to stop thinking with the hard-on he now couldn't get rid of. He'd seen the look in her eyes, and he knew she had trepidation about letting him back in the door to her heart. He wasn't upset; he knew he had work to do in earning her trust again. A person with Gemma's background didn't trust or love lightly, and he'd broken her when he sent her away that night. It was just so hard not to touch her, want to be inside of her, when he was within her vicinity. It was as if her body sang a siren song and he couldn't help but to answer her call.

If he could get her to agree to dinner tonight, he could try and reassure her. The way she responded to his kiss told him she was still just as highly attracted to him as he was to her. Desire wasn't the issue. He had to let her know he wasn't going anywhere.

He could see she started to retreat inside her head. "So dinner tonight, my house at seven o'clock."

He made it a statement this time so she wouldn't be able to finagle her way out of it. Slipping his shirt over his head, he glanced at the photos on the table before asking, "So ... are you finally going to officially invite me to your photo exhibition?"

This caused her to smirk at him. He was happy his question pulled her from her thoughts. He finished dressing and walked toward her.

She began toying with him. "Hmmm, am I going to invite you to my photo exhibition?"

He could see the joyful gleam in her eyes as she held him in suspense. He started tickling her sides.

"Oh, Alex, no!" She gasped as she laughed trying to free herself. He loved watching her laugh. He tickled her for a moment longer before stopping and pulling her close for another breath-stopping kiss. Her arms twined about his neck. As he pulled away after a few more seconds, Gemma said breathlessly, "Yes."

Puzzled, he cocked his head to the side. "What?"

"I'd like you to come … I mean to be there." She bit her lip, as her cheeks became inflamed after the sexually charged innuendo the first part of that statement hinted at.

"I would like you to be there at my photo exhibition," she said, straightening up.

He smiled widely at her. "I accept …"

Leaning in, he kissed her quickly on the lips once more.

"Dinner, my house, seven o'clock." He was out the door before she could respond.

The few classes she attended went by in a blur, and she practically sleepwalked through her shift at the diner. They were back together, and all she could think about was that he would leave once more. She felt like a small child again, like how she used to at the beginning when she would get comfortable at a foster home, just to be moved again. Eventually, she stopped thinking life would settle and be stable, that she'd finally find a family who wanted her. She thought those feelings faded, but obviously, they hadn't. Maybe she would never stop feeling fear over being unwanted.

She tried to shake these thoughts as she rode the bus to Alex's house. As much as she wished things could go back to the way they were, she knew they couldn't. The realistic side of her told herself she shouldn't want things to go back to the way they were. Everything was out in the open now, and they could move forward … she just had to get out of her own way. After arriving at her stop, she walked the short distance to his door. She stood on the doorstep for a minute, not yet ready to ring the bell. With a deep breath, she prepared herself.

He'd been excited to see her all day. When he opened the door to her, he immediately wrapped her in a warm embrace and devoured her mouth slowly. He knew he caught her off guard. Once he released her mouth, he looked down into her startled face and smiled.

"Hey … I've missed you." He saw her face relax, as she gave him a small smile.

"You just saw me this morning."

Alex softly chuckled as he let her go and took her hand, leading them to the kitchen. "Can't a guy miss his girl?"

He felt her fingers grip his tightly for a second, and he glanced back at her. He saw the troubled look in her eyes she was trying to mask with the false smile, but he only offered a smile back. The walls she had up at the beginning seemed to pale in comparison to the barrier she currently appeared to erect between them now. He had his work cut out for him. Letting go of her hand, he walked back to the stove and stirred what was in the sauté pan.

"Come here and try this. Tell me if it needs any salt." Yes, he was a chef and didn't need anyone to tell him if the food needed anymore seasoning, but he needed to engage her. Get her out of her head. He held the spoon out for her to taste. He watched with longing as her tongue licked the spoon.

"It's fine."

She turned away from him and sat on one of the barstools, pretending to be preoccupied with the contents of her purse. He remembered a time when she would have lingered over the spoon, teasing him. He would have turned off the burner, and they would have proceeded to make love in the kitchen.

He wasn't going to spend the evening dancing around what was happening. They hadn't just gone through the heart-wrenching forgiveness, we're getting back together session last night to be acting like strangers. He turned the stove off and leaned against it, folding his arms across his chest.

"What's going on, Gemma?"

She stopped rummaging in her bag but didn't look up at him. "What are you talking about?"

He huffed. "Come on, Gemma."

Finally, she leveled her gaze at him, and he could see the unshed tears in her eyes.

"Last night, you told me you didn't want me to keep things from you, and now that's exactly what you're doing." He didn't mean to sound judgmental. His expression softened.

"I know I have a lot to make up for, to prove … I'm not going anywhere, Gemma."

A single tear slipped down her cheek. She shook her head. "Don't say that …"

"It's the truth," he said, coming toward her.

Suddenly, she exploded off the stool.

"Don't you understand I'm terrified? You say that … people say that, but everyone always just ends up walking away. You're back, and everything I know says that this," she gestured between the two of them, "it won't last. I don't want to get hurt again, Alex," she finished on a sob.

He was unnerved as he saw the tears pour down her face. She hugged her body while she wailed, trying to offer herself some solace. He immediately rushed to comfort her. Even as she feebly pushed against his chest, he held her tighter, offering soothing words and trying to reassure her.

"Hey, it's okay. Gemma, I'm here. I promise I'm not going anywhere." He uttered as he tried to calm her down.

After some time, she relented and sobbed uncontrollably into his chest. Picking her up in his arms, he carried her over to the sofa and gathered her onto his lap, just holding her.

As he cradled her in his arms, his brain screamed for him to get the engagement ring and propose. The rational part of him said that now was not the right time. When he asked her to be his wife, he didn't want there to be any other reason besides his love and desire for her. He didn't want there to be any doubt as to why he wanted her as a wife. It wasn't out of pity or obligation. If he proposed right now, that was what her perception would be, and she would reject the proposal and possibly reject him. He just had to be patient.

After a while, her crying turned into sniffles and eventually she fell asleep resting against him. He stroked her hair. She seemed small in his arms. If he held her any tighter, he might break her. He loosened his grip, before standing up and walking her down the hall to his room. After laying her on the bed, he pulled the comforter up to cover her. She was sleeping soundly, and he couldn't help but watch her. Even though she moved restlessly for a moment, she remained asleep. Once she settled again, he gently moved a strand of hair away from her face. He wanted to make her feel safe and secure. The thought that she felt anything but that with him, pained him. He knew he was to blame for the feelings she was having. Knowing she could be asleep for a while, he looked at his watch. Maybe he would step out for a minute. There was something he needed to do.

Thomas finished warming up the Campbell's soup and went back into the living room. He sat the warm bowl on the tray that had permanent residence near his La-Z-Boy. As he was getting himself situated in his chair, he heard the front door open and assumed it was Rachel.

"Hey, you're just in time for the game."

Tucking a napkin into his collar, he prepared to eat his soup. Before he could get the spoon to his lips, he saw Alex plop down onto the sofa. To say he was shocked would be an understatement. He planned to pay Alex a visit tomorrow, not expecting a good outcome, and now here he sat in front of him. He lowered the spoon back to the bowl. They both regarded each other for a moment.

Finally, Alex broke the silence. "Are you going to eat that crap?"

Thomas glanced down at his bowl of lackluster chicken noodle soup and tore the napkin from around his neck.

"Well, when you say it like that ... I think I lost my appetite."

Silence filled the room once again.

"I'm here for her," Alex muttered with an edge to his voice.

Thomas nodded his head in resigned understanding, as they both looked anywhere but at each other.

So, they reconciled.

He wondered how it happened as he thought of his stubborn son, who was so like him, and suppressed his smile at the thought of Gemma being happy.

Alex and he obviously had a long way to go, but it was a start. There was a beat before Thomas slid back on his seat and turned the volume up. He didn't resume eating his soup; only the sounds of the game coming from the TV could be heard.

Alex knew Gemma wouldn't want him talking to his father just because she wanted him to. She wanted him to do this for himself, but it wasn't easy. He looked at his old man out of the corner of his eye. It wasn't that he didn't love his father, he did. If he was honest with himself, it wasn't his father he was angry with. He was angry with himself. Even when hearing the horrible news, it was on him to choose how to react. He'd been blinded by his anger and pain, and the only one there that night to lash out at was Gemma. Once she was gone, it was easy to stoke the flames of his anger by roasting his father over the spit.

How hard must it have been for her to confront him and admit her guilt, the responsibility for the loss of a life? Despite that, she had. He remembered her shaking like a leaf as she stood before him to profess her sins. She was at the most vulnerable he'd ever seen her, and instead of forgiving her and comforting her right then and there and demonstrating his love for her, he let the long simmering—but not forgotten—rage and hurt consume him and destroy her. His chin sunk to his chest with his admission of responsibility for the state of things. He couldn't put the whole burden on the old man's shoulders as much as he wanted to. His father may have lit the match that started the fire, but he's the one who poured gasoline on it and let the house burn down. It was him. He was the real culprit, the reason that everything turned to shit so quickly. He needed to get out of here.

He stood up abruptly from the sofa and walked out.

Thomas watched from his La-Z-Boy, as his son walked to the front door and left without saying another word. He slumped back in his seat, no longer interested in the game. Would Alex be back, or did his hasty departure mean he thought his visit was a mistake? He'd let Alex have tonight, but he would go to him tomorrow so they could hash this out.

Alex pulled up in front of his house and sat in the car for a minute. The whole ride he'd been consumed with his thoughts. He could feel the anger trying to choke him even now. The red-hot rage was creeping over him like a dark mist. It was a mental battle to crush it down. For once he allowed thoughts and feelings he kept at bay to come pouring over him. The anger started around the time his mother got sick. He remembered being mad at everyone and everything. Why was this sweet woman about to be taken away? He was angry, but he'd internalized it until it was a fine simmering stew living just below the surface.

As he grew older, he'd learned to mask and control it with humor, but it was always there. He could have let it explode when he lost Sam, but again he put the rage in his own little Pandora's box and let it fester. When he'd learned that night about Gemma, he could no longer contain it. That iron control he'd spent so long cultivating eroded in an instant, and unfortunately he unleashed it on Gemma and continued to give everyone a taste for the past few months.

It wasn't until he'd read the file that night and realized the destruction he caused that he truly became aware that the price of his anger was high. He alienated his family, and he pushed away the woman he came to love so dearly. Mending things with Rachel was relatively easy. With Gemma and his father, it was proving to be a bumpy road, but he had to try. He had to make things right. He wanted to say especially with her, but he knew he needed to truly make things right with his father as well.

Opening the car door, he trudged up the walkway and went inside. A lamp in the living room was suddenly cut on. He instantly turned around to find Gemma sitting on the sofa. She was looking down at her lap. Her hands were restless. He stood in the doorway unsure whether she wanted him to come any closer.

"I wasn't sure if you were coming back," she said in a small voice.

"If you'd acted the way I had … I'm not sure I'd come back either." She glanced up at him quickly before returning her gaze to her hands.

He slowly left the doorway and knelt before her. He placed his hand over hers, not just to calm her, but to let her know he wasn't going anywhere.

"Don't you know you're stuck with me?"

Gemma finally looked at him then, and he saw the hope and the fear that lived there hand-in-hand.

"I'm not going anywhere. I won't be scared away again … I promise." He cupped her face in his hands and gave her a chaste kiss on the lips. He felt her fingers fumbling to cover his.

"I'm here, and I'm not leaving," he whispered to her as he leaned in and kissed her again with more urgency.

Suddenly he could feel her hot tears on his cheeks as her other hand came up to grip his face. She was kissing him back. The kiss was questing, pleading, wanting more. His lips parted, and her tongue swirled inside to claim his. He kissed her back while pulling her up from the sofa. She pressed her body to him, letting him know she wasn't going to resist him this time.

Picking her up, he felt her limbs snake around his waist to hold him captive. He turned and walked them down the hall to his bedroom … no, their bedroom. It hadn't just been his since he met her. It hadn't felt like just his when she was gone, and now she was back and it felt right. He smiled into her mouth and continued his ravishment as their bodies pushed the door open.

Setting her on her feet in front of the bed they both began to slowly undress, never taking their eyes from each other. He finished undressing before she did and took her in his arms and began worshipping her with his mouth as he peeled the rest of her clothes from her body; kissing, sucking, licking, nipping at her exposed skin before leaving a trail down to her breasts. His tongue curled around her right nipple as his hand gently squeezed and massaged her other breast. She moaned low in her throat as she gripped his shoulders. Breaking away, he picked her up and laid her gently on the bed. He moved her legs so that he was on his knees positioned between her thighs, then rubbed his hands up and down her thighs as he gazed at her naked splendor.

"Do you know how much I love you?"

He heard her breath hitch in her throat at his declaration, and even though he couldn't see it, he knew her face and body was flushed. He leaned down and reverently placed light kisses all over her chest. He could feel her breathing pick up. His fingers made the trek down her body. He felt her legs part wider in open invitation. His fingers rubbed along her silky folds and stroked her softly.

She emitted soft little purrs as he played with her. After a short while, she sat up and pulled him up her body until he lay flush against her. He hardened even further when he felt the pulse of her core against the length of him. He groaned deep in his throat before her hands found their way around his neck and pulled him even closer. Their noses touched as she dragged his bottom lip between her teeth. She rubbed herself against him, making his hips buck.

"Condom." She said against his mouth.

Quickly, he reached into the bedside drawer and retrieved a condom. He came up on his knees as he tore the foil wrapper. Once he rolled it down his shaft he returned to his position.

She licked his bottom lip where her sharp little teeth left an imprint. He forced his tongue into her mouth and kissed her hard. It was as if they both needed to claim each other, to mark one another. He wanted to wear her brand on his skin. He wanted her to sear herself into his flesh. Her hand reached between their bodies and wrapped around his cock.

"Please," he heard her husky whisper.

She lined up the tip with her entrance. He didn't need to be told that she needed it just as badly as he did as he thrust home. Entering her that swiftly made them both gasp. He'd forgotten how tight she was. As if she could read his thoughts, her inner walls squeezed him deliciously.

Their mating was unlike anything they shared before; it was animalistic. He rutted on top of her, thrusting faster and harder, needing his actions to prove how much he needed her, wanted her. She met him thrust for thrust. A cacophony of naked, sweaty bodies slapping together, his feral grunts and her carnal moans were the only sounds that could be heard. Neither wanted their mating to end, but he could feel himself being pushed to the edge with every stroke.

Gemma's body was on fire. Her hair was slicked with sweat. She didn't care. All she cared about was feeling him buried deep inside of her. He pounded into her repeatedly without any rhythm, and it had never felt so good. Raking her nails down his back, she bit his shoulder when the pleasure bordered on sensually painful. She wanted it, the mixture of ecstasy and torment that his body kept giving her. She didn't want it to end, but she could feel her orgasm building. Before she could try and slow it down or stop it, her climax came hard and fast, making her cry out.

Alex continued thrusting into her while her orgasm shook her body. As she was coming down from her high, she felt him flood into the condom as he thrust once, twice, then fell limply over her body. She welcomed his weight.

He breathed heavily into her ear, trying to catch his breath. After a few more seconds he propped himself on his elbows. He smoothed her hair off of her brow as he stared into her eyes. She offered him a warm smile of satisfaction, before tugging his face down for a kiss.

Afterwards, he pulled out of her body, which caused them both to exhale and mourn the loss of no longer being connected. She watched as he removed the condom and got up from the bed to dispose of it. Once he returned to the bed he flopped onto his back but held out his arm out to her. Willingly, she rolled onto her side and lay on his chest, enjoying the warmth from his body. She snuggled deeper into his side feeling drowsy. His fingers came up to tangle in her hair and languidly massage her scalp. She let out a small yawn and fell asleep.

Alex knew the moment she drifted to sleep because her body practically molded itself into his side. He smiled contentedly and held her closer as he fell into some of the best sleep he'd had in a long time.

When she opened her eyes the next morning, he was watching her. She put her hand over her face and let out a small chuckle.

"How long have you been awake, watching me?"

He pulled her hand from her face as he laughed and scooted closer to her, taking her in his arms.

"Don't hide. I think you look beautiful in the morning … I missed this." He kissed her temple.

She shivered at his words. "I missed this, too."

They were engulfed in a comfortable silence for a few minutes before he spoke again.

"About last night … I don't want you to doubt us … doubt me. I know I have to earn your trust again, just know that I want you."

She stroked his chest as he spoke, unable to look at him. She didn't mean to get emotional. Plus, the lump in her throat wouldn't allow her to respond without her voice cracking. She nodded her head vigorously to let him know she would have faith in him, trust in their love for one another. He squeezed her tighter and kissed the top of her head.

At that moment, her stomach gave a loud rumble. Her cheeks flushed with her embarrassment, she buried her head in his chest too mortified to look at him. He laughed as he tried to extricate her from her hiding spot.

"Was that a monster in your stomach?" He guffawed.

"Let me feed you."

Before he could continue teasing her, the doorbell rang. She glanced up at him, and they shared a confused look. If it were Rachel, she would have just come in without knocking, ringing the bell or without invitation.

"Stay here." Alex climbed out of bed and started putting on sweats and a T-shirt. "I'll get rid of whoever it is and then feed my baby."

He quirked his eyebrow at her seductively, before leaving the room. It was not until he was down the hall that his irritation at whoever interrupted their time together showed.

25

Thomas stood on Alex's doorstep, rehearsing in his mind what he was going to say to his son. Things were always distant between him and Alex. It wasn't just with the death of his wife.

Were all fathers and sons like that?

He didn't remember riding Alex too hard about playing sports or making good grades. He disciplined them both, he and Rachel, the same. He never raised his voice or a hand to either of them. Yes, he remembered being a bit disappointed that Alex didn't share his same enthusiasm and affinity for cars, but that never made him love him any less. Maybe they were too much the same man in their manners and bearing.

Why couldn't Alex see what he'd done he'd done for him ... because he loved him? He didn't want anything or anyone to hurt him, and so he protected him. Maybe it was because Alex wasn't a parent yet himself and didn't yet understand what that love could cause you to do. A parent would rip someone apart with their bare hands if that person caused their child harm. He'd heard stories of mothers picking up two-ton cars to save their child.

I would kill for Alex and Rachel. Don't they know that?

One day Alex would understand when he welcomed his child into the world and looked at them for the first time. Yes, then he would understand the lengths to which you would go to protect them.

He would make Alex talk to him, even if that meant they screamed the roof down yelling at each other. But he wouldn't leave until they resolved this thing between them. Before he could ring the bell again, the door was thrown open by a very aggravated Alex.

His jaw tightened as he stared at his father standing uninvited on his doorstep.

Why is he here?

Despite what he thought about last night, he planned to address the situation with his father when he was ready and not before. He kept the old man standing at the door.

"Why are you here?"

Thomas tried not to show hurt feelings at Alex's irritated tone or the fact that he had yet to invite him inside.

"What? You can show up at my house, but I show up here, and you make a fuss?"

Alex huffed. "That was a mistake."

Thomas chose to disregard Alex's remark. "Are you gonna let me in?"

Alex debated for a second before deciding he would be a real bastard for not letting his father inside. If Gemma found out he'd turned him away, there would be hell to pay. Stepping back, he opened the door to admit him. His father moved into the living room. Alex turned to face him with his hands folded across his chest. He watched his father fidget with the hat in his hand. Alex wasn't going to make it easy for his father. The old man better say what he came to say, or he was going to usher him back out the door.

"I came here … I came here because we need to talk."

Alex only continued to glower at him.

Thomas became angry watching his son stand there and not offer the olive branch back in return.

Why can't he meet me halfway? He was trying here.

Why does Alex have to be just like me?

"Damn it, Alex! Why do you have to be so stubborn all the time? I came here to work this out."

Alex took a step forward, dropping his arms, hands clenched at his sides. His father had some nerve coming here and trying to force the conversation.

"No one asked you to!"

Thomas puffed up his chest before bellowing out his response. "Alex, I'm your father, I was only trying to protect you …"

Alex's furious anger kicked into overdrive. He wasn't a child. The time for being over-protective had come and gone.

"Even if that meant ruining my life?"

Thomas inched closer as the fight heated up. "I thought she was lying to you!"

Alex nearly put his finger in his father's chest, emphasizing his next point. "What gave you the right to interfere? I almost lost the woman I love because of you!"

"Oh, so now everything is my fault?" Thomas threw his hands up in the air. "Why don't you take some responsibility for your actions?!"

Now they were nose to nose.

"This all started because you stuck your nose where it didn't belong!"

The anger and frustration Thomas felt at Alex were about to choke him. "Well, I'm trying to make it right!"

Gemma heard the raised voices. She sat up, straining to hear who exactly earned Alex's wrath. It only took a second to realize Alex was having an altercation with Thomas. She needed to stop this before things went too far and they said things to each other that would be unforgivable. She threw on her clothes as quickly as she could, and ended up having to go commando because she couldn't figure out where Alex tossed her panties last night.

She arrived in the living room to find the two men face-to-face yelling at each other at the top of their voices. She did the only thing she could think to do, and ran over and wedged herself in between them.

"Stop this! Stop this right now!"

She pushed against both men, trying to stop them and break them apart. It seemed almost impossible that her slight frame would cause either man to budge. She raised her voice again, attempting to gain their attention as she pushed against each man that stood like a tree with angry roots twisted into the ground. It took a minute for them to step back and then another minute for them to acknowledge her presence. She was unsure if it was her physical presence they finally acknowledged or her shrill screams that penetrated their thick skulls. They both stood panting and glaring daggers at each other after the exertion of their argument.

Gemma glanced back and forth between the two men. "What is going on?"

Both answered simultaneously, identically and like children, "He started it."

She rolled her eyes at the absurdity of the two grown men fighting like they were boys in the schoolyard. She moved from between them to stand in front of them. Folding her arms across her chest, she looked at the pair, seeing the similarities not just in their features but their personalities. They had awoken her anger, but all she could feel was sad when she realized she was the cause of their squabble. As much as she wanted to lay into the two of them she couldn't bring herself to do it. She sighed out of exasperation.

"I'm sorry."

Their heads whipped around to look at her baffled. Alex spoke first.

"What do you have to be sorry for?"

Gemma put her hand up to stop any more questions. It took her a minute to speak.

"I'm sorry ... because if I never came here you wouldn't be arguing and at each other's throats." She sniffed to keep the tears away.

"I wish I'd had a parent who loved me like that, that cared enough to make me despise them even if it meant keeping me safe ..." She exhaled as she peered into Alex's eyes.

"If I can forgive him then why can't you? I don't want to be the cause of any more strife between the two of you." She slowly walked the few steps to stand in front of Alex and took his hands in hers.

"Alex ... I asked you the other night when we got back together to make peace with your father. I didn't just want you to do that for me ... I wanted you to do it for yourself." She looked over at Thomas and smiled warmly.

"He's your dad. He loves you ..." She glanced back at Alex expectantly. "And I know you love him, too."

Alex swallowed as he took in her words, but said nothing, averting his gaze as he mulled things over. Gemma watched him.

"I could stand here and give you an ultimatum, tell you something crazy like unless you talk to your father then I won't see you again or some such nonsense, but then I know you'd only be making amends because of me and it wouldn't be real, it wouldn't be genuine ... I will tell you that I would be disappointed if you let this continue because I know you're a good man ..."

She looked at him as a single tear slid down her cheek and said in a tiny voice, "You forgave me."

She wiped the tear away quickly and stood gazing at him.

Before Alex could say anything, Thomas' voice cracked as he was about to speak. He paused and cleared his throat.

"Alex ... I'll forever be sorry for the effect my actions had, but I can't stand here and tell you I wouldn't do it again ..." He saw the angry expression once again cross Alex's face.

"Let me finish before you get upset." He nodded his head toward Gemma. "She and I have had this conversation ..." Thomas gripped his hat tighter, trying to staunch the flow of emotions that were coursing through him right now.

"If your mother were still alive she would have wanted me to make sure you were protected. It doesn't matter that you're a grown man ..."

Alex saw his father trying not to get choked up after mentioning his mother.

"I was worried, worried about you, worried you were being taken advantage of ... afraid you'd fallen in love with the wrong woman. I was wrong ... I won't regret or be bullied into not doing what I thought was right at the time … I know I shut down once your mother passed away and I wasn't very good at saying it …" A tear slipped from Thomas' eye and he looked down at the floor.

"But I love you, son. I only want what's best for you and I always hoped you and your sister would find a love like I had with your mother. And when I see you and Gemma standing there together, well … I think you have."

Thomas looked back up at them. Gemma was openly crying now, and Alex's face lost the hostility and animosity.

Alex felt like an ass. His shoulders sagged as he felt the knot of anger in his gut unfurl. He couldn't continue to take the anger he felt at himself out on his father. It wasn't right or fair and eventually it would drive a wedge between him and Gemma. There was no way he would mess up their relationship again. He was a jackass for withholding forgiveness from his father. Hell, he was a jackass for withholding forgiveness from Gemma for as long as he had. Why did he choose to torment the people that loved him, and yet here they still were. Fighting for him. He shook his head, lost in his thoughts for a moment.

"You've both given me your apologies many times … please don't apologize anymore." He glanced sorrowfully at

Thomas first and then Gemma. "I owe you both an apology …
I've been a real stubborn ass."

He gave Gemma's hand a gentle squeeze as he continued,
returning his gaze to his father.

"Dad, I was going to make things right between us … I
was. I just needed to work through things in my head before I
did. It wasn't you. It was me." He gave a light chuckle as he
tilted his head to look at the ceiling.

"Damn, I sound like some prick breaking up with his
girlfriend … the old it's not you, it's me routine." He shook
his head before looking at his father again. The smile left his
face and took on a somber expression.

"Joking aside … I'm sorry for what I put you through the
last few months …"

He turned back to Gemma and ran his fingers lightly down
the side of her face.

"Both of you." He released Gemma's hand to address his
father, "I handled things poorly and it wasn't fair to either of
you … I don't want to be angry anymore."

He exhaled loudly, feeling like that action released some
the angry toxicity he kept stored over the years. He half
whispered to himself again as he realized the truth of his
words.

"I don't want to be angry anymore." He shuffled his feet,
trying not to feel overwhelmed by the emotions coursing
through his body.

"Can we just start fresh?"

Seeing Gemma and Thomas' faces he smirked. "I know that sounds hokey."

Gemma put her arms around his waist. "I think that's a good idea."

He let go of Gemma and stepped toward his father. The men stood staring at each other for a moment before hesitantly reaching out to each other for an awkward hug. They patted each other on the back before releasing each other.

Thomas fidgeted with his hat, unsure what to do next.

"Well, I'll get out of your hair for now."

Before Gemma or Alex could say anything, or Thomas could make a move to leave, they heard the front door open.

"Alex! Chloe and I are here for a late breakfast!"

Chloe rounded the corner and stopped in her tracks, causing Rachel to run into the back of her at the entrance to the living room, where they found Alex, Gemma, and Thomas standing.

"Was there a party and someone forgot to invite us?" Rachel put on a fake pouty face for a second as she looked around at everyone. The brief silence was interrupted by Chloe's exclamation.

"Gemma!" Chloe ran over and threw her hands around Gemma, happy to see her again.

"Hey, sweetie." Gemma hugged her back.

"What about your ole grandpa? Do I get a hug, too?"

Chloe released Gemma and smiled at Thomas as she gave her grandfather a hug. He embraced her as he chuckled.

Rachel continued to look between her father, brother, and Gemma.

"Okay, what's going on? This time, I'm not excusing myself to the kitchen like a stepchild so out with it. What did I miss?"

Alex laughed as he shook his head. "You just can't stand to be left out of something can you, pest?"

"Just tell me what I missed." Rachel smirked at him before punching him in the arm.

Alex walked toward the kitchen as he called over his shoulder, "I'll fill you in later, I've got to make breakfast."

He loved his sister, he did, but he had no intention of telling her exactly what happened today. This didn't concern her. It was between the three of them, and it would stay that way. Without saying anything, he knew the other two felt the same way.

Rachel watched her brother walk off toward the kitchen. Typically, she would try her best to force him to tell her what she wanted to know. Usually, he gave in, if only to shut her up. Things seemed different. He seemed different. She'd walked into something, but she could only smile to herself knowing the three of them were in the same room together, and things seemed good … peaceful. Yes, she'd be lying if she didn't say she was dying of curiosity to know how it all went down, but right now she was content just to let things be. She smirked. Alex couldn't think she was going easy on him.

"You better be happy I'm hungry, or I wouldn't let you off so easily."

As he pulled pots and pans out of cupboards and rummaged for ingredients in the fridge, he watched Gemma and his family interact. It was nice to have things back to the way they had been. No, that was wrong. Things were better than they had been. After something like what they went through, things were never going to be the same, and he didn't want them to be. He was happy. He was truly happy. Everyone began making their way into the kitchen and without being told what to do started helping out.

As they all helped out in the kitchen, chopping up ingredients, setting the table or assisting with clean up,

Gemma couldn't help but smile. It was nice to feel truly part of a family. To feel love and acceptance despite the things she'd done in her life. Despite who she thought she was as a person, these people loved and cared for her. Alex loved her.

In that dark part of her, she felt the negative Nancy saying it would never last, but she blocked her pessimistic inner monologue. Nothing was going to ruin the joy she felt at this moment.

Chloe's voice broke her out of her reverie. "Gemma, did you want juice? Mom asked me to set the table, and I just wanted to know if I needed to set a glass for you."

Gemma smiled at her. "Yes, thank you."

Her eyes found Alex. He was flipping over an omelet. He must have sensed her watching because he looked at her then and offered a lazy smile as he continued to cook. She smiled back then turned her attention to whatever sports argument Rachel and Thomas were having. She loved Alex's family, but she couldn't wait to get him alone. She smiled to herself thinking about later.

Done with chopping up the rest of the garnish for the omelets, she helped

Chloe set the table. In doing so, Chloe pulled her into her middle school world of boys, soccer, and gossip. She was happy to listen to the younger girl ramble about her carefree life. It was always nice to listen to Chloe discuss what seemed like the end of the world and she was happy the girl would know nothing of what she knew of at her age.

Once all the food was cooked and placed on the table, they all sat down to enjoy the mouth-watering fare and the great company. Gemma knew it had been ages since they all sat down for a meal together. Everyone laughed and joked, not wanting their time together to end. Eventually, breakfast did come to a close. Rachel and Chloe drove home and Thomas left to tinker on his car. Then it was just the two of them.

After everyone left, they showered together, luxuriating underneath the warm spray of the water as they slowly and tenderly washed each other's bodies. Alex needed to head to the restaurant to take care of some things. While he was gone, Gemma returned to her place to pick up some clothes, books, her camera, and photos for the exhibition.

By the time Alex returned home, Gemma was ensconced in their bed, which was strewn with her photos. She looked beautiful wearing his old shirt she'd always loved, hair done up in a sloppy bun, her gorgeous, naked legs splayed out to allow room for her to study. He wanted to join her right away but resisted long enough to wash the smell of the restaurant from his body. Walking back into the bedroom, he noticed she cleaned up her messy clusters of pictures from the bed. He stood in the doorway taking her in for a moment, loving the feeling of coming home to her, finding her waiting for him. She looked up from the stack of photos in her lap and gifted him with an easy smile. He walked toward the bed and sat down. Taking some of the black and white photos from her hand, he shuffled through them. Even though he was focused on her art, out of the corner of his eye he could see her worrying her bottom lip with her teeth.

"You know, these are really good."

Leaning over, he grasped her chin in his hands and gently pulled down to make her stop biting her lip. She smiled a nervous smile as her lashes made crescents on her cheeks.

"They're good, you hear me?"

She looked up at him. "So then you're not angry the pictures are of you, and I'm going to use them in the show?"

He laughed. "Are you kidding me? What man doesn't want to be on display? I'm in good shape ..." He flexed his arm to show off his muscle, making Gemma laugh.

"Obviously, my woman thinks so." He winked at her.

"I don't mind at all, Gemma. The pictures are fantastic. I'm happy to be your model any day, babe."

Gemma could only smile hugely at him, before pouncing on him with a sloppy kiss. After he threw the pictures onto the floor, he put his arms around her and pulled her down on top of him. The kiss quickly escalated and soon they were both naked. He enjoyed having her seated atop him as he plunged upwards, filling her completely. He heard her gasp and then she began to ride him. He didn't want to take his eyes from her, but she was feeling so good. He shut his eyes in ecstasy as his back arched from the bed involuntarily. They both must have wanted each other so badly because before he knew it he could feel her honeyed walls tighten around him and they were both climaxing. Once their spasms subsided, he pulled her down to him and kissed her deeply. He kept her locked in his embrace as he ravished her mouth for what seemed like hours.

Finally, when he let her escape she disappeared into the bathroom to clean herself up. He watched from the bed with his hands behind his head, as she put back on her bra and panties before joining him again. She straddled him over the sheet, making him laugh.

"Why'd you get dressed?" He fingered the strap of her bra, attempting to pull it off her shoulder.

She laughed throatily as she playfully swatted his hand away. "I don't call this dressed, Alex." She ran her fingers up and down his chest.

He shut his eyes, loving the feel of her stroking his flesh. His eyes opened. Her actions were making him drowsy, but he didn't want to succumb to sleep. He was enjoying this too much. She always made him feel good. He took in her face, and a soft sigh escaped his lips. He wanted this, her always.

"Move in with me."

He wanted more than what he offered her but knew it was too soon for that. He would settle for what he could get ... for now.

He rubbed his hands up her soft, supple thighs as he looked up at her, waiting for her response. He saw the smile that graced her lips, but the gleam of sorrow was in her eyes. Somehow he knew she would reject this idea, but he'd needed to ask. He wanted her here, but only when she was ready.

"Alex ... we just got back together ..."

He lowered his gaze for a moment, finding enjoyment in her luscious breasts that rose and fell in her push up bra. For a minute, he wished once more she hadn't donned the damn thing again.

"Shhhh ..." he soothed in a calming voice.

She quieted for a moment. Once he looked back up into her face, he noticed she seemed ready to launch into her apology on why she couldn't stay with him.

"It's okay, Gemma. I'm not going to pressure you to move in." He sat up then and propped himself against the pillows before pulling her into his body and dropping a kiss on the top of her head. He smiled when he felt her nestle into his chest.

"This is your home, too, okay? I know you may not be ready, or it's too soon ... just know it's not going to stop me from asking ..."

Gemma chuckled at his words and he smiled even wider.

"Hey, a guy can be persistent. Maybe I'll eventually wear down your defenses and get you to say yes."

She pulled away then to look up at him. "And I'll enjoy saying no each time."

The playful look in her eyes and in her tone caused him to start laughing, and he began to tickle her. Enjoyment overcame him at seeing her squirm beneath his fingers, her face crinkled into giggles. Forget make-up, he just wanted to see her wearing a smile for the rest of their lives.

26

Two months later

Gemma stood back and looked at her photographs hanging around the swanky gallery. She was about to have her first show, even if it was just a school exhibition. Her professor told her it could lead to mentorships working with some renowned photographers. She was excited at the prospect, but still equally excited to be a part of the prestigious show. She wiped her hands on her jeans. They finished hanging the last piece in preparation for tonight. She was able to coax Alex into posing for more photos to include into tonight's showing, which led to a few nights of lechery. A smirk crossed her face as she thought about those nights where the photo sessions evolved into some very passionate lovemaking. Pulling herself away from her lurid thoughts, she checked her watch. She needed to get to Alex's house and get ready.

Things were really good. The last month of getting ready for the show was grueling, but exciting. Her relationship with Alex couldn't be better. Shortly after they'd gotten back together, Gemma decided it would be a good idea for her to see a therapist. She was determined that nothing would stand in the way of her happiness, including herself. Once she started going, and Alex saw how much it helped her, he began going as well. Sometimes they shared things from therapy with one another. It bonded them even closer.

Alex kept pushing her to move in, just like he said he would. Even though she still always answered with a no, he would just smile at her and say I'll ask again tomorrow. Gemma loved Alex but wanted to maintain her independence and stand on her own two feet. She couldn't remember a time in her life when she'd had that. It was important to her. Alex understood, but there was just this part of him that always wanted her close. He finally confessed to her that therapy made him realize the loss of his mother and then his wife, made him fearful of losing her, which was the underlying, driving force behind why he wanted her to move in so quickly.

Although there was nothing he could do to prevent something from happening to her, her moving in was like a security blanket. She understood, given her fear of abandonment and not wanting to feel like someone was always going to leave.

Aren't we a pair?

When Alex asked her about moving in, she knew it wasn't him pressuring her, it now turned into their private, shared understanding of one another's neuroses. She rather enjoyed hearing him ask, and he never minded hearing no.

Her professor helped her get a job working at a photography studio. She was just a helper, but at least she wasn't working at the diner anymore; plus, the pay was better. It might take her a while, but she was putting money away to get a used car. Even if the car was a hooptie she didn't care, it would be something she owned, and she'd never owned anything in her life.

While she did maintain her residence, she started spending nights over at Alex's again. She was riding the bus over to his place now to get ready. He was insistent they go together. His whole family was excited. She smiled to herself as she thought about having people that truly cared about her come to her show. She wouldn't be alone. There would be people there to lend support and cheer her on. It meant so much to finally have a family. Okay, they weren't her family per se, but they felt like her family. Shelby was even coming tonight. The woman became a friend to her, again something she never had before.

She got off at the stop near Alex's house and rushed inside. She knew right away he wasn't home yet. There was a note on the counter that said he'd gone to the restaurant to take care of something. As soon as she reached the bedroom she started removing her clothes and turned on the shower. After tying her hair up, she stepped under the warm spray and began to pamper her skin. She wanted to look beautiful for what could be a life-changing night.

He could hear Gemma in the shower once he got home. He showered and shaved before he left earlier. The little white lie he'd told about an issue at the restaurant made him feel slightly guilty, but it was necessary since he couldn't tell her he'd gone to the jewelry store to have her engagement ring cleaned. Opening the little black box, he stared at the ring again.

Tonight's the perfect night. He smiled to himself.

Things only got better over the last two months. He'd never dreamt that was possible. The restaurant was doing better than it ever had, and he started letting Brandon run the kitchen at least two nights a week. No one at the restaurant knew those two nights were his sessions with his therapist. He'd come to truly value that time of finally opening up and figuring out what made him so angry.

It opened up communication between him and Gemma even more, which had done intense things for their sex life. He thought it was good before, but now it was mind-blowing. It was like the more they connected on this deeper level of understanding each other, the deeper and more intense the sex got. Their bodies communicated in this language all its own. It became some next level shit. They hadn't tried tantric sex yet, but he felt what they experienced now was kind of close. He damn near cried the other night after he came and he was holding her.

One of the things they both agreed upon was she should get on birth control after she finally disclosed how she thought she was pregnant after he'd made her leave. He felt like the biggest ass thinking of her out there in the world pregnant and alone. What if he'd never forgiven her and she had been pregnant and too scared to turn to him and struggled to raise the child on her own? His blood ran cold at the thought. He would never again let any harm come to her or be the cause of any more of her suffering.

Yes, she still refused to move in, but he respected her need to be her own woman. After being under that bastard of an ex-husband's thumb, he made sure to give her space when she asked. He was aware that even though she knew he would do anything or give anything to her and for her, she needed her independence. He wouldn't take that away from her. Plus, he enjoyed hearing her tell him no.

What man doesn't enjoy the chase?

He and his father had gone on two fishing trips together. Fishing wasn't his favorite thing in the world, and even though they didn't speak of anything important it was nice to spend some quality time with his father, who seemed to smile more these days. He needed to get the old man laid, or at least get him a lady friend so he could spend time with someone. Maybe some viable option would present itself at the exhibition tonight.

Wait, didn't Gemma say that Ms. Ramirez, the woman who ran the boarding house, would be there this evening?

If he remembered correctly, they seemed to be close in age, and she was a bit of a looker for an older woman. He'd get Gemma to play matchmaker and hook the old man up.

"Babe? Isn't Ms. Ramirez coming tonight?" he called out to her as he heard the shower turn off.

Gemma stuck her head into the bedroom. "Hey, baby. Yeah, she said she would be running a little late, but she'd be there. Why?" She retreated into the bathroom before hearing his response, leaving the door open as she continued getting ready.

Alex stood up from the bed and walked toward the bathroom, pausing in the doorway as his eyes traveled upwards from her shapely calf muscles to the back of her lovely curls that lay piled on her head. He immediately forgot he'd come in here to explain why he was asking about Ms. Ramirez.

"You look good enough to eat." He waggled his eyebrows at her as he came toward her and put his arms around her. They stared at each other in the mirror. She chuckled softly.

"I'm not even dressed yet, baby."

"I know. That's why you look so delectable." He started nibbling and sucking on her neck and shoulder like he was eating her, which made her giggle.

"Stop, Alex, or we'll be late."

He kept nuzzling her, ignoring her comment about being late.

"What's wrong with being fashionably late when you're one of the honorees?" He reached beneath the towel and said into her ear in a husky voice, "C'mon, babe, I'll be quick."

His member grew against her backside. He could feel her skin grow hot with desire at his words. She swallowed a moan as he continued molesting the skin of her throat and shoulder. His fingers were traveling up her inner thigh, and already knew their destination. He could tell she was on the verge of giving in but seemed to quickly rein in her urges as she spun around in his arms.

"Baby, I'll make it up to you tonight. I promise." She rose on her tiptoes and kissed him quickly on the lips before stepping out of his clutches.

Smirking, he adjusted his crotch. "I'm gonna hold you to that." He followed her into the bedroom and sat down on the bed to watch her dress, which didn't help the hard-on he was sporting. Thankfully, he remembered what he'd initially been talking about, and that helped to ease the ache in his pants.

"So, I was asking about Ms. Ramirez, because I need to hook my dad up with someone."

She giggled as she slipped on her dress. "Really? You think he's ready?"

He looked down at the carpet to avoid being distracted by her supple flesh, which kept enticing him to touch her.

"Babe, if I have to go on one more fishing trip I think I'll go crazy."

They both laughed.

Walking over to him, she placed her hand on his shoulder for stability as she slipped on her heels. "That's a bit dramatic. It can't be that bad?"

"Look, he's lonely, and he needs some companionship." He gripped her hips as she put on the second shoe. "Just do me a favor and introduce them tonight ... please?"

She smiled, gazing down at him. "Okay." She kissed him quickly and pulled away.

Alex smirked knowing her hasty retreat was to make sure he didn't try any funny business that would make them late.

"Gemma, you are the star of the show tonight. No one can stop talking about your work." Professor MacGregor hugged her as he congratulated her. "Enjoy tonight. You deserve it."

She watched him walk away to congratulate another student. Everyone showed up tonight. The amount of support she received was overwhelming. She was shocked when she saw the whole crew from Alex's restaurant. Amanda and Brandon flanked Alex when he confessed to shutting down the kitchen for the night so everyone could attend. They all hugged her and presented her with flowers. She dabbed her eyes to keep the tears at bay and made sure her mascara didn't run.

So many people attended the event. She had no idea so many people would turn up for the event.

Professor MacGregor mentioned a few days ago she could be offered the chance at a mentorship tonight, and already she fielded two offers, and they were only two hours into the show. The biggest surprise was a few attendees also asked to purchase some of her work. She couldn't stop grinning, and she hadn't stopped saying thank you all night. Just as she thought she was going to get the opportunity to grab something to drink or some food, a handsome photographer started complimenting her work.

"Thank you so much for the kind words." She grinned like the Cheshire cat as the visiting travel photographer continued to pay homage to her work. She palmed his card as he told her to give him a call if she was interested in seeing the world and capturing landscapes. Somehow, she suspected his offer was for more than just work considering he couldn't stop eyeing her cleavage or salivating over her like he was a starving man and she was his last meal. Glancing around the room, she tried to search for Alex while still acting interested in what this man was saying.

Across the room, he watched her glow from the praise being heaped upon her and her work. He couldn't be prouder of her. She deserved every 'job well done' that was being said to her. Sipping his glass of champagne, he glared at the guy currently chatting her up. He'd lingered a bit too long for Alex's taste.

He sauntered over and put his arm around Gemma's waist, pulling her into his side. Turning grateful eyes up to him, she leaned in and planted a kiss on his lips.

"Hey, hon."

He smiled down at her realizing she needed saving, and he arrived in the nick of time. They both turned to the awaiting photographer who stood with his drink slightly poised at his lips, gaping at them. The man quickly made an excuse and walked away.

Chuckling, they held each other, and he kissed her again. It was a testament to how close they'd grown that she initiated such heated PDA right in front of someone.

"You always rescue me at just the right time … my knight in shining armor."

Her eyes sparkled as she gazed at him.

"And how's my princess enjoying her ball?"

"It's a fairytale, Alex," Gemma breathlessly sighed as she looked around. "I just never thought ..."

Even though she trailed off, she didn't need to continue. He knew what was going through her head. After the life she lived, in her wildest dreams, she never thought things could turn out like this. He smiled to himself thinking of the little black box tucked inside of his suit coat. He couldn't wait to make her night a dream come true.

He excused himself, claiming a need to relieve himself after too much champagne. Leaving her in the care of one of her many admirers, he went in search of Rachel, and found her scavenging at one of the hors d'oeuvres tables.

"Having fun?" He smirked at her as she shoved some pastry thingy into her mouth.

"It's cool ..." She swallowed before speaking again. "Gemma's photos are incredible. By the way, the model in the photos is you, right?"

He nodded his head.

Rachel nibbled on a tea sandwich as she mock shivered. "People are ogling my brother's man bits ... ugh."

Alex laughed heartily. "Nothing is showing. It's all very tasteful ... That's not why I came over here."

Rachel was about to eat more food, but Alex took the plate from her hand and sat it on the table.

MONI BOYCE

"Do me a favor? Make sure Dad and Chloe are around in a minute. I don't want them to miss what happens next, okay?"

Rachel seemed puzzled as she lifted a champagne flute from a passing tray and guzzled down the contents.

"What would they miss?"

He glanced around to make sure no one would see before he quickly pulled the black, velvet ring box from the inside pocket of his suit and flashed it at his sister before returning it.

"Alex, why didn't you tell me you were gonna propose to her tonight?" She had happy tears in her eyes as she asked the question.

"I didn't want your big mouth ruining the surprise," he said with a smirk.

Rachel continued looking all moony-eyed at the thought of the public proposal that Alex was about to perform.

"I didn't want anyone's nervous excitement tipping Gemma off to what I planned for tonight, so just please … make sure they don't miss the proposal, okay, pest?"

She nodded her head as she wiped away a tear. He was a little surprised not to receive a witty rejoinder over being called pest.

Gemma ran her fingers through her curls as she shook hands with yet another patron of the arts that wanted to purchase one of her photos. Her face hurt from all the smiling, but she couldn't help it. Alex seemed to materialize out of nowhere, and her face lit up at the sight of him.

"Babe, I think only another thirty minutes and then I can leave. They have gallerists who will deal with the purchases …" Noticing he had a weird look on his face, she touched his cheek. "Everything okay?"

Alex took her hand in his and he never stopped staring into her eyes.

"Everything is just fine." He kissed the back of her hand before he sank to one knee. Her heart began to beat an erratic pace against her ribcage as she became aware of what was about to take place. Looking up for a second, she saw that his family and their close friends were gathered around.

When did everyone encircle the two of us?

He released her hand. She looked back down into his face as he reached into his jacket pocket and pulled out a little black box. Her hand covered the 'O' shape her mouth formed. It felt like all the breath left her body. This couldn't be happening.

Is this real? Is Alex about to propose?

She bit her lip trying not to cry. Her face was flushed.

He opened the box to display the ring. A reflection bounced off the diamonds and sparkled brightly.

"Gemma, we've been through a lot over the last year. When I finally came to my senses and pulled my head out of my ass …"

People laughed and made snide comments. He smiled, but continued, sobering a bit. "I realized what I almost lost and it scared me …" He swallowed as he thought about what he almost tossed away because of his anger and pride.

"I've been profoundly affected and changed by you. My life will never be the same, and I wouldn't want it to be … you've made me a better man. You are so wonderfully loving and giving. From the moment I met you, despite all that happened to you, you gave me your heart completely."

Gemma's vision was getting blurry as the tears welled up in her eyes at his words, and she took a stuttering breath as she continued to listen to his proposal.

"I love you so much, and I'm asking you to stay by my side so that we can walk hand and hand through life …"

Everyone waited with bated breath for him to continue. A few sniffles could be heard from the audience that watched. Alex licked at his suddenly dry lips.

"So I hope you will make me the happiest man alive and be my wife?"

He looked up at her, his face brimming with love and hopefulness.

Gemma collapsed down on her knees in front of him, covering his face with kisses before finally kissing him on the mouth. He laughed as he held her close, kissing her back.

"So is that a yes?" he mumbled against her lips.

She kissed him again.

"Come on, babe, we've got an audience, don't leave me hanging," he said jokingly.

She giggled. "Yes! Yes!"

Everyone erupted into applause and cheers, as Alex removed the ring from the box and placed it on her finger. He helped her to her feet and kissed her one last time, before she was pulled away by Rachel, Shelby, Ms. Ramirez, Amanda, and the other female members of his crew. They squealed over her ring and congratulated her.

Alex was surrounded by his father, Brandon, and the rest of the male staff from his restaurant. Even as they patted him on the back, they made jokes about him getting ready to have a ball and chain. He and Gemma stared at each other through the throng of people flanking them; they only had eyes for each other.

After all the happy chaos of the night, they were both glad to finally make it back to the house to celebrate their engagement and Gemma's success privately. In the car ride home, he watched her quietly stare at her ring with a blissful expression on her face. He didn't know why he didn't want to interrupt whatever private moment she was having. He was content for the two of them to finally be alone. After a few more minutes of gazing at her engagement ring, she placed her hand on his and snuggled next to him the rest of the ride home.

When they finally reached the house, she kicked off her shoes and turned to him, pulling him into an embrace. Her smile was contagious, and as he looked at her, he couldn't help grinning like a fool. Even though he was sure he knew the answer he asked anyways.

"Are you happy?"

If it was possible, her smile got even wider.

"Yes ..." She nodded her head.

"So happy, in fact, that I almost can't believe it."

He touched her cheek. "I know what you mean. Do you know how long I've wanted to propose?"

Her eyes lit up with merriment. "How long?"

His eyes looked away, as he smirked, wondering if he should tell her the truth. She caught the mischievous glimmer in his eye and punched him in the arm.

"Tell me!"

Chuckling, he rubbed at his shoulder, pretending she hurt him.

"Let's just say it was before the break-up." Alex laughed again when he saw her eyes go wide in shock.

"It's true, but let's not make a big deal out of it, okay?"

She only nodded her head and grinned up at him. He could see her mind working a mile a minute. He didn't want her asking questions or for either of them to rehash that period. He just wanted tonight to remain light and happy.

"Now what shall we do, how to celebrate?"

Gemma was quite aware of him suggestively rubbing himself against her. She needed no reminder of what she promised earlier tonight before they left the house, but she wanted to tease him.

"I want …" Gazing at him seductively, she licked her bottom lip. She saw his eyes take on a hungry look as he watched her tongue.

"Ice cream," she said in a husky tone.

She noticed he was leaning toward her ready to kiss her when his brain finally caught his body up to the fact she said nothing about kisses, sex, or romance. She bit her lip to refrain from laughing at his crestfallen expression; that was quite adorable.

"Ice cream? Ice cream it is." His mouth quirked into a grin, and he touched her chin before giving her a chaste kiss. Walking into the kitchen, he flicked on the light and started pulling down condiments. She hugged herself as she followed him into the kitchen and took a seat at the counter.

Laughter was trying to bubble its way to the surface as she watched him fill the bowl with ice cream, chocolate sauce, and chopped nuts. Ever the chef, he could never just let a meal be simple. She loved that he poured so much thought, care, and love into what he prepared for her, even something as simple as a dish of ice cream. He pushed the bowl toward her, before joining her.

Before she could put a spoon into the dish, he pulled it away from her and shook his head. She looked at him confused for a moment until he picked up a spoon and filled it with ice cream and held it toward her lips. She smiled as she opened her mouth to let him feed her. The only thing she could think as he fed her, then fed himself was how blessed she was to be marrying this kind, loving man that wanted to take care of her. She teased him long enough. Before he could feed her any more ice cream she took the spoon from his hand and sat it on the counter. As she got up, she tugged him from his seat toward the bedroom. He followed without saying a word.

Once they were inside, she turned her back to him and lifted her hair. Without having to be asked, he unzipped her dress, and she stepped out of it. When she turned around, she silently reached for his tie and unknotted it, slowly pulling it from around his neck. Her fingers undid the buttons on his shirt, and he tugged his suit coat off. Then he placed his hands on her hips.

Gemma gazed into his eyes as she pushed his shirt down his shoulders. They hadn't spoken a word since the ice cream, and she found it a turn on that they silently communicated. Now she only wanted their bodies to do the talking. She could feel his breath hitch in his throat as her nails grazed the skin of his abs. They kept their eyes locked on each other as she unbuckled his belt.

He didn't want to break the spell, so he kept his hands on her waist and let her continue to undress him. She smelled nice. He couldn't stop looking at her as she stood before him clad only in her bra and panties. His future wife looked gorgeous in the moonlight. Once she finished disrobing him, she grabbed his hand pulling him with her as she seductively took steps backward until the backs of her legs hit the bed. He was nude while she still was dressed in her underwear. Reaching behind her back he unclasped her bra and slid it down her arms, discarding it on the floor. He pushed her down to sit on the bed, and she took his cue and laid back. His hands skimmed her thighs on the way up to the waistband of her panties. He lingered a moment as they stared at one another before bringing the offending garment down her legs. Finally, nothing separated them.

He was in no rush. Tonight was special. He crawled up her body and wrapped his arms around her, pulling her toward him until they both rested on their sides, facing each other. He could only stare at her, taking in her beautiful face. He was going to get to wake up to her for the rest of his life ... and he couldn't wait.

His hand went to her face as he stroked her cheek. Yes, he was hard for her, but he could bank his desire to just enjoy the intimacy. The feel of skin on skin, their bodies touching without being joined felt fantastic. He could feel the goosebumps on her flesh. Leaning toward her he trailed his tongue down her neck and gently kissed her collarbone. He could feel her heat as she brought her leg up over his hip so that he was flush against her wet core. He rocked his hips into her, rubbing himself against her, giving her the friction she needed. She was scalding. Her soft little moans egged him on.

It was as if she needed to be a part of him. Her fingers wound their way into the hair at the back of his neck and pulled him closer. She began to match his rocking motion. His hand slid down her side until it came to rest on the curve of her ass, and then he pressed her closer.

He couldn't wait any longer to be inside of her, and it didn't feel like she could either. Positioning himself at her entrance, he thrust into her and paused. Her swift intake of breath let him know it felt just as good to her as it did to him. Their bodies moved together in rhythm. No matter how many times he joined his body to hers, it always felt even more amazing than the last time. Each time he felt her walls began to tighten around him he would slow down his pace and prolong their release.

Finally, after the third time of stalling the end of their mating, he thrust deeply into her pulling passionate cries from deep within her. As her body spasmed in his arms she bit his shoulder, and he came hard, pouring his essence inside of her. They both lay limp and sated, breathing heavily. He couldn't bear to pull out of her just yet. He placed tiny kisses all over her shoulder as they luxuriated in still being connected, hoping to keep the little death at bay a few seconds more. When he finally slipped out of her, they didn't release their hold on one another. Then she finally spoke, her head buried in his shoulder.

"I'm going to be Mrs. Gemma Chambers."

It was muffled because she was speaking into his body. He pulled her away from him. "What did you say, babe?"

She looked at him with a brilliant smile painting her face.

"I said, 'I'm going to be Mrs. Gemma Chambers.'"

All he could do was smile. Nothing made him happier than the thought of spending the rest of his life with this incredible woman.

Epilogue

Three years later

"Just one more push, honey. The baby's almost here. You're doing so well."

Alex wiped Gemma's brow. He knew this labor wasn't easy for her. It wasn't easy on him either seeing her in such anguish. She tried to put on a brave face, but he knew she'd been in a lot of pain. He'd attempted to talk her into the epidural, but she was having none of it. It wasn't that she was trying to protect the baby. He hadn't found out until their first check-up that Gemma was deathly afraid of needles. Not wanting to cause her or the baby any further distress, he ceased asking her so she would remain calm ... well, as calm as a pregnant woman enduring sixteen hours of labor could be.

He'd fed her ice chips; rubbed her back and feet. They'd watched copious amounts of TV when she wasn't in agony. He'd see her doze off for a few moments when the contractions let up. As time wore on, nap times grew shorter the closer she became to being fully dilated. She would latch onto him for comfort and reassurance when he came near—clinging to his arm or hand, needing his closeness, his strength. He'd kiss her brow and wipe the perspiration from her forehead … and now here they were. She only had one final push. The baby's head was already crowning.

To have the first three years of their marriage punctuated by the arrival of their first child was unbelievably amazing. As he stood waiting to find out what sex his child would be, he reflected back on them building a life together after getting married. He opened up a second 'Umbria Ristorante', which was a huge undertaking, but extremely satisfying.

Gemma, on the other hand, was the one that shined. The exhibition opened up doors for her, and a couple of renowned photographers offered her an apprenticeship. She chose one that suited her, and after graduation had enough of a portfolio under her belt to start getting work on her own with the backing of her mentor. She photographed mainly weddings these days and became in demand and much sought after.

There were many days at the beginning of their marriage he woke up early to find her on the window seat in their bedroom in contemplative thought. The first time he'd found her like that with tears in her eyes, he'd taken her in his arms, trying to find out what was wrong. Smiling, she'd told him she couldn't believe this was her life; it felt like a dream, but she knew it wasn't. She promised they were happy tears of appreciation, for how sweet her life became after beginning with so much pain.

Occasionally, there were still mornings when he'd wake up and find her this way. Sometimes he'd leave her alone and other times he would bring her back to bed, and he'd make love to her sweetly. Once she became pregnant, some mornings he found her up rubbing her belly and murmuring words of love and encouragement. Sometimes when he found himself awake before her, he pulled the covers back and tentatively reached out his hand, placing it over her stomach, and whispered to the baby. He would kiss her belly reverently.

Finally, their most prized accomplishment was about to make its debut, and he was overwhelmed with emotion. A tiny little combination version of the two of them was coming into the world.

"Come on, baby, I know you can do it." He rubbed her back gently, trying to soothe her.

"Honey, one more push and you're all done." He placed a lingering kiss on her brow and gave her hand a light squeeze. She gripped his hand with a strength he didn't know she possessed and gave a feral noise between a scream and a grunt as she gave the final push that brought their child into the world. He tried to look down between her parted thighs to see their child and still hold her. Gemma was breathing raggedly as she attempted to lean forward and get a glimpse of the baby.

"I wanna see," she muttered tiredly.

"You did good, baby." He kissed her forehead.

Smiling, the doctor looked up. "It's a girl."

She lifted her up so they could take in the sight of their beautiful newborn daughter. Their eyes drunk her in. He was not sure what rushed through Gemma's head at this moment, but for him, it was as if the world stopped turning on its axis. He was sure everyone said their child was the most beautiful thing when they first laid eyes on the tiny, little, struggling body that was angry at being ripped from its mother's womb, but his daughter truly was the most beautiful thing he'd ever seen next to her mother. Sure they still needed to clean her up, but he knew his baby girl was the most precious thing he'd ever seen in his life. At that moment, he knew he would give her the world and lay it at her feet. He would chop off heads and destroy nations to keep her safe. She was the creation of he and Gemma ... and she was perfect.

Turning to Gemma, Alex tenderly took her face in between his hands and kissed her. He could feel her tears cover his fingers.

"I love you," he murmured against her lips repeatedly.

Gemma grasped at one of his hands, which still covered her face, and whispered back to him, "I love you, too."

The doctor broke into their private moment. "Would you like to cut the umbilical cord?"

He could only nod his head as the lump of emotion lodged in his throat prevented him from speaking. Taking the scissors from the doctor's hand, he snipped at the only thing still tethering their baby daughter to Gemma. He heard Gemma give a sharp gasp. The doctor quickly passed their now crying daughter over to a nurse to be cleaned up, while Alex glanced from Gemma to the doctor with a silent, panicked question in his eyes.

"Nothing to worry about, Alex. We just need to deliver the placenta."

He let out a breath of relief.

The doctor addressed Gemma in a soothing tone, "Okay, Gemma, I know you're tired, but I just need one more push, okay?"

She braced herself and reached for Alex. When he gripped her hand, he felt her body tense as she forced one last push.

Everyone was gathered out in the waiting room, hungry for the announcement of the sex of the child. Was it a boy or a girl? Thomas tapped his foot impatiently as they all sat around quietly. They ceased speaking the minute they knew Gemma finally went into labor. Despite all the modern technology, you just never knew if there would be complications with the birth.

Rachel grabbed his hand and gave him a reassuring look. Chloe was asleep on the bench across from them. He still remembered the day she was born. The memories of how much he fretted over Rachel and the then unknown Chloe during the delivery made him smile weakly. That had not been an easy birth.

What if things were going terribly wrong and Alex just hadn't been able to tell them?

Ms. Ramirez entered the room and handed him a cup of coffee as she took the seat next to him. "Any word?"

He patted her knee. "Not yet."

He sipped on the hot liquid. Rachel let go of his hand to get up and go to the vending machine for more junk. Sometimes he wished Alex's cooking skills rubbed off on her. He sat his coffee on the ground and reached for Nancy's hand. While everyone else addressed her as Ms. Ramirez, she became his Nancy.

He was very aware Alex was trying to set him up from the minute he introduced the two of them at Gemma's photo exhibition all those years ago. Rude wouldn't exactly describe how he treated her that night, but he had not been ready to let go of the memory of his wife to embrace the idea of someone else.

It took two more forced family dinners—where Nancy was the surprise guest—for him to finally come around. It was her telling him off after the second dinner that ignited a spark. She had every right to be upset over his behavior. He was contrite, and a couple of days later asked her out for coffee. The rest as they say was history. Neither was looking for marriage. After some time together and many long conversations they both knew the spouses they lost had been the loves of their life, and they weren't looking to replace them. They came to respect and care for one another deeply. It was nice to have someone to share life with again, to snuggle with on rainy days, sit and play long games of Scrabble. She not only enjoyed going fishing with him, but she even showed an interest in learning about cars. It was nice having her warm body next to him the nights she stayed over.

He looked over at Rachel, who was forcefully hitting the vending machine that wouldn't release her snack item. If only his daughter could find someone for herself. That would make him happy. They all knew there was a man who'd been showing his interest by sending flowers and small gifts, and even taking her abuse, but she still had yet to agree to a date.

Thomas had invited him to one of the family dinners unbeknownst to Rachel. She offered only saccharine sweet smiles and responses all throughout the meal, storing her venom until after the poor guy's departure. The moment the door closed on the man she unleashed on all of them. Alex took the brunt of her ire, but only pushed back, and eventually the two left the group to have a talk of their own behind closed doors. When they emerged again Rachel was crying, but she hugged Alex. Alex never shared what happened, but he knew Rachel's trust in men after Chloe's father left took a dive, and she hadn't let anyone close since. The thought of being broken by someone else kept her defenses up, but he was hopeful she might let down the walls a bit to at least let this guy try.

Shelby and some of the staff from the restaurant stopped by and left flowers, stuffed animals, and other trinkets for Gemma and the baby. Everyone wanted to know when the baby was born. The waiting was torturous. While he was just as anxious to know if he had another granddaughter or a grandson, he was more interested to know if mother and baby were doing okay. Gemma became a daughter to him, and she made Alex happy. He couldn't help but tap his foot again. Then suddenly Alex appeared in the doorway with the most joyous expression on his face and tears in his eyes. Thomas stood abruptly from his seat, and Nancy followed suit. Rachel stepped away from the vending machine and shook Chloe awake.

"It's a girl," he said in a cheerful, tremulous voice.

They rushed toward him as the tears spilled down Alex's cheeks and he embraced them all. Congratulations and questions were lobbed at Alex, and he continued to grin as he answered them. He also took the time to send out texts and make a few calls to Shelby and some of the staff. Even though Chloe was now an aloof teenager, even her eyes were alight with the news of the new addition to the family.

"When can we see them, Uncle Alex?"

He smiled down at her. "Soon. Why don't you all grab some lunch? They have to clean both Gemma and the baby up, and do some other paperwork and things. I'll come and grab you the minute you can see them."

They all nodded their heads.

"I gotta get back ..."

As everyone else backed away, Thomas grabbed Alex's shoulder and pulled him in close.

"I'm happy for you, son. I wish your mom were here to see what a fine man and father you turned out to be," he said low enough, only for his ears.

Alex pulled him into a tighter hug, and Thomas could feel Alex's tears against his cheek. It seemed like ages since they shared a genuine hug and not the usual pat on the back style hug that most men delivered. He almost choked on the emotion of getting to see his son become a father. He also couldn't help but feel some sadness that his wife wasn't there to witness it.

Finally, Alex pulled away and gifted him with a brilliant smile, before turning and jogging back down the hall.

While Alex was down in the waiting room talking to the family, the nurses helped Gemma get out of bed. After they changed the sheets and cleaned her up, they tucked her back into bed. She was drowsy and fighting the sleep that wasn't only pulling at her mind, but all of her extremities. It was like a narcotic trying to desperately claim her, but she wanted to see her daughter. She would be lying if she didn't admit she was hoping to get a few moments alone with their daughter before Alex came back.

She felt a bit selfish, but she was greedy to have a few more minutes alone with her. It was the two of them for nine months, and now she was going to have to share her. A small chuckle left her lips at that thought. She didn't want anyone to get the wrong idea. The fact that the three of them were going to be a family excited her. She was going to have a family.

Before she could continue with her musing, she was interrupted by the nurse wheeling in her baby. Gemma couldn't stop the tear that slid down her cheek. The nurse smiled at her as she lifted the small bundle from the mobile crib and placed her in her arms. She was so speechless—as she gazed at the tiny little face staring back at her with wonder—that she couldn't even say thank you.

"I'll give you some time alone with her … then I'll come back and show you how to breastfeed."

She nodded her head as the nurse retreated and left the room. She cradled the little girl in her arms and stroked her finger over the soft down of her little cheek. Opening the blanket that swaddled her, she counted ten fingers and ten adorable tiny toes.

Thank you, God. Her daughter was healthy and perfect.

"You are beautiful," she whispered down to her baby girl, then placed a kiss on her forehead.

Her little forehead crinkled, and Gemma saw she had Alex's eyes and nose, her lips and cheekbones. Suddenly, she was ready for Alex to come to them, come to his family. She'd had enough alone time with their daughter. She wanted for the two of them to ooh and ahh over her together, wrap themselves in a cocoon that was just the three of them and enjoy the newness of being a threesome.

The door pushed open, and Alex walked in beaming at her. She graced him with a radiant smile and patted the side of the bed, beckoning him over.

Alex quietly walked over and slid into bed next to her. He leaned into her, smiling down at their daughter. His eyes raked over her face.

"She has your lips." He said with a huge smile before he cooed at the baby.

"You want to hold her?"

He nodded his head, and she delicately placed the baby in his arms. She watched as the father and daughter shared a moment, joy blossoming in her chest. To be able to have the gift of a healthy relationship, with a loving husband, and now a beautiful baby, was overwhelming. She felt so blessed.

"Have you thought about a name?" Alex asked as he rocked their baby girl.

"I have," she replied, her voice breaking.

"Catherine Hope Chambers." She looked at him expectantly.

His eyes got misty as he looked at her with profound gratitude.

"Thank you. It's perfect ... she's perfect," he said a bit choked up. He stared down at Catherine's now sleeping form, before continuing, "I guess it makes this rather fitting." Reaching into his pocket, he pulled out the pocket watch she'd given him years ago and handed it to her.

She looked at it with fondness, but confusion, before she lifted her gaze and peered back into Alex's face.

"Turn it over."

Her fingers flipped the watch to reveal something added to the inscription. Underneath, 'To Alex, a man that gives me hope,' another engraving now read:

'*Never forget, no matter what kind of hand life deals you, there is always hope.*'

Gemma swiped at the errant tear, as she smiled beautifully at Alex. He smiled back at her before explaining, "I want to pass it to her when she's older."

She leaned in and kissed him deeply. As she went to pull away, Catherine gurgled. They both smiled down at her, lost in the world of their new family.

Acknowledgments

First and foremost, I have to thank God, because without him none of this would be possible. I wrote this book a chapter at a time usually writing in the wee hours after coming home from working 12-16 hour days on a film shoot, producing an event or working an event for Getty Images. The idea showed up one day and poured out of me and for that I'm grateful and thankful.

I'm thankful to my two sisters, Tanya and Desi, for always being super supportive. Your belief in me sometimes exceeds my own. I'm grateful to have you guys in my corner. Also, thank you to my two biggest fans, my parents, who have always encouraged and supported by dreams.

I want to take the time to thank all the people that helped get this book ready for publication. Thank you to Vid Buggs of 4-U-Nique Publishing, LLC for all the copious amounts of writing and self-publishing advice, suggestions, recommendations and know-how you shared over many hours. It was invaluable. You have my deepest gratitude.

Thank you to Angel Pointer of OneNine2Five Fotography for photographing the cover and for the graphic design work you did on the cover as well. You toiled with me and never seemed to get frustrated no matter how many times I changed my mind or even when I sat on things for long periods of time and did nothing.

Thanks to Melissa Ringsted of There For You Editing Services for doing a professional edit of the book and teaching me about using unnecessary words like then and just. You've helped improve my writing.

I must give a special thank you to some of my Scandal ladies and fellow Gladiators on Twitter that encouraged me to get back into writing when I was healing after my divorce. It started out with poetry and graduated to fan fiction and then this book was born. You planted the seed and it grew and bore fruit.

Also, I want to thank all the ladies on Valent Chamber that read this story and critiqued it. I'm very appreciative of all the feedback I received. There is plenty more where this came from and I hope you'll stick around for more stories.

A very big shout out to my family and close friends for always being loving, encouraging, supportive and just plain awesome. You guys mean the world to me.

And last, but certainly not least, thank you to the many readers that purchased this book, shared this book and read it. I know how much you have going on in your day and it means a lot that you used some of your free time to read my book. Please sign up for my newsletter at moniboyce.com to get updates on new books, events, giveaways and more. Thank you. I hope you'll continue to be a loyal reader.

What Did You Think of Redemption of the Heart?

First of all, thank you for purchasing this book **Redemption of the Heart**. *I know you could have picked any number of books to read, but you picked this book and for that I am extremely grateful.*

I hope that it added value and quality to your everyday life. If so, it would be really nice if you could share this book with your friends and family by posting to Facebook and Twitter.

If you enjoyed this book and found some benefit in reading this, I'd like to hear from you and hope that you could take some time to post a review. Your feedback and support will help me as an author to greatly improve my writing craft for future projects and make this book even better.

ABOUT THE AUTHOR

MONI BOYCE is a writer, filmmaker, poet and author of the new romance novel Redemption of the Heart. She spent the last fifteen years working in the film industry and now creates characters of her own and brings them to life on the page. Moni has ghostwritten romance novellas and novels for over a year now and decided to put some of her own creations out in the world. She considers herself a bookworm, film buff, foodie, music lover and an avid world traveler having visited 32 countries and counting. She lives a bit of a nomadic life, but considers Los Angeles home. Which is the subject of her first travel book: Greater Than A Tourist – Los Angeles, California: 50 Travel Tips From A Local.

You can follow me or contact me via:
https://moniboyce.com
Twitter: @moniboyce
Instagram: @moniboyce
Facebook: fb.me/MoniBoyceWrites